The Experiment

Landry Love Series
BOOK ONE

AMY ALVES

ISBN: 978-1-7774301-5-3 (ebook)

ISBN: 978-1-7774301-0-8 (paperback)

https://amyalvesbooks.com

Cover Design: Braden Power

Editing & Proofreading: My Brother's Editor

❀ Created with Vellum

DEDICATION

My 'buff beta reader' husband—you and the kids really are my everything.
XOXO

PROLOGUE

SIX YEARS AGO...

Jess

I'm a schmuck. An attractive, successful, sexually resplendent schmuck.

My big foray into the world of love, loyalty, and devotion came to a jarring crash last week. My soon-to-be ex-fiancée, Ashleigh, is a beautiful and carefully orchestrated lie. Cruelly, artificially beautiful. Seemingly sculpted by a higher power for temptation and manipulation.

I fell in love with a lie.

My love life, family, and career were all on the path to success. I had some side projects in productivity software that had already been quite lucrative for me.

Yes, I was the smartest type of idiot.

It should have been obvious. She conformed to whatever I liked, whatever I wanted. I was in love with compliance, a pretty face, and a temptress's body, which makes me feel like a complete asshole. Thinking with my dick, just like I'm sure she planned.

Upside? At least she was a good fuck…

See? Schmuck.

What plagues me though, is how I didn't recognize that she didn't love me, that she was just biding her time.

Last week, I found detailed evidence of her betrayal. So much fucking betrayal. Not a damn thing I could do about the damage already done. I secured what I could, created safeguards, and set a plan to evict her from my life.

So here I sit, awaiting her scheduled return. I told her I'd be in Landry visiting my parents but would be back in a few days. This way she wouldn't think twice about coming for her things.

I stare at her as she walks in the door, holding a couple of duffel bags. She does a cute little jump when she sees me, feigning a happy surprise. Lies.

"Baby! What are you doing home? I thought you were visiting your family?" she asks, eyes shifting around the room, noticing the disarray.

"I wanted to be here when you returned from your work trip." I put down my wine glass, deciding I want to be clearheaded to have this conversation. "We have a few things we need to discuss, Ashleigh."

She walks over to me, cradles my face, concern darkening her bright blue irises. "What's wrong? Is your family okay?"

That hint of doubt worms its way into my heart. She is always so thoughtful and remembers everything. What was once endearing and admirable, now comes across as intentionally manipulative.

"Who is Alex?" I manage to ask.

Shock transforms her face from innocent concern to sheer panic.

"No one. He's in my past. An ex, nothing more." She brushes it off, caressing my jaw. "Jess, why are you asking? We've been together for two years and you're just now getting curious about exes?"

I ignore that. "What was the money for, Ash?"

She backs up, making her way to the bags she left by the door. "Oh, is that what this is about? I used some money from your account to pay for wedding expenses. Deposits. That kind of thing." She shrugs, but it's anything except nonchalant. "Was that not okay?"

"One hundred and fifty grand?" I fire at her.

She blanches, caught.

I've practiced deep breathing techniques for my anger, but I can feel the rage bubbling beneath the surface. Why does it hurt so badly? Why did I allow the tiny glimmer of hope in? Idiot.

I need her to confess, and so far, she's not cracking much.

"No response?" I question as she continues to gape at me. "You brought empty bags, I see. Going somewhere?"

"Um… what?" The chance to explain, to correct my assumptions has passed, so catch up, sweetheart.

"Going somewhere?" I repeat, pointing at the bags.

"Oh. Well, I was just going to spend the weekend with a friend while you were gone." She pauses. "Since you said you'd be with your brother for a few days. Uh, Sydney invited me for the weekend. Didn't I tell you about that?"

Mmm, yes, fake details. That'll convince me.

"I packed your shit, so you can go see 'Sydney' whenever you want. In fact, stay there. I insist."

"What? Baby, what are you talking about?" she asks, her face full of innocence, but there's a noticeable tremble in her question.

I lean forward. "The bank account transfers, the delinquent you're fucking, the wedding deposits. I know." I wait and wave a hand out, giving her the floor. "Go ahead, explain. I'm sure it'll be good. Or do you need to call Alex first to get your stories straight?" I cross my arms, waiting.

"Jess, hon, I just told you that was for wedding expenses. I must have added a zero by accident." She laughs, a tinkling sound I used to crave, not knowing it was the sound of deception. "And I'm not 'fucking' anyone but you, baby. I haven't seen Alex in years. Has he been harassing you or something? I don't understand, please explain what's going on." She's good, I'll give her that. I can hardly tell she's lying. Except her face has gone pale and shiny.

Doubt creeps back in for a moment. What are the chances Alex orchestrated this and was working alone? Or is maybe blackmailing her?

No. You fucking moron. You saw the emails and texts. She met with him, multiple times while she was supposedly 'away for work'. He helped her play me.

"I called the venue and caterer, Ashleigh. You canceled everything and kept the refunds." Her jaw clenches. "I've done a lot of research in the last week. I'm a tech guy, and your sweet manipulations don't work on computers. There isn't an electronic communication I can't acquire."

Her face blanks, her eyes shift to the left as she considers what I may have uncovered.

"Jess, I can explain." Her face goes hard, her eyes darting back to the door. "I'm in a bad spot and didn't want to drag you into it. I needed to move around some funds just for a few weeks. So, I used the wedding money and some of our savings."

Our savings? Ha!

"We can get married anywhere and I can rebook everything." She moves closer to me. Bold move. She places a hand hesitantly on my chest. "Jess, you're everything, babe," she purrs, repeating the same line she always uses to wrap me around her little finger. The line that used to appease the romantic in me. Now it just makes my stomach churn. "You've got this all wrong. All I want is you."

I shake my head. She doesn't seem to get that I already know everything. That it's already over.

I grab her hand and remove it from my chest. "Bull. Shit. What the fuck aren't you understanding here, Ash?" I grind out between clenched teeth. Flicking off her wayward hand, I continue. "I know you and Alex planned all of this. There's proof of collusion, a paper trail of embezzlement—you know, since you stole the money from my company accounts." She likely doesn't know what any of that shit means.

"Why, Ash? Why the hell did you do this to us. We were

building a life together. You and I were in this. Forever. How could you turn out to be such a fucking mistake? I loved you. Fuck, I loved you. And you—" I lock my teeth together and fist my hands in my hair. I didn't intend to show her any of this. I didn't want to give her the satisfaction of seeing my turmoil or pain.

Her sad, innocent pout has dropped from her face. Replaced instead with indignation.

Her spine straightens, and she cocks her head. "Oh, please. I was the pretty little trophy you could shower with affection and check off your life 'to-do' boxes with. I cared for you. For a time. But we never had the relationship you're insinuating. Or we didn't until you decided you wanted more. Until *you* changed." She points a white-tipped nail in my direction.

"Well, fuck me for falling in love with you! Sorry that change inconvenienced you so much!"

"But *I* was never in love with *you*," she shouts back.

That's no longer news to me, but it's still a fucking blow.

She looks regretful for a moment as she takes in my reaction. "That's not what this was. You're the one who got carried away, proposing, making this into something it never was."

"You didn't have to say yes. You could have told me the truth, talked to me. Instead, you said fuck all and just went along with it, let me love you."

She rolls her eyes at me. "Whether you admit it or not, you never truly loved me. You loved the idea of me. We fit together, sure. Our lives, at one point, meshed quite well. The sex was amazing. But that all started to fade, and you wanted more. When we first got together we talked about travel, career goals, having fun. But then our relationship changed." She looks away, frowning.

"At first, I thought I could be your wife. I tried to be what you wanted because we made sense together. Until we didn't anymore. You want a family, holidays at your folks' place, romantic getaways, being in each other's pockets. I don't. It's why

I've been on so many work trips, why I clam up when you bring up kids or our future. I put in my time and when I saw an opportunity, I took it."

Has she always been this selfish?

Her face changes with her next thought. It's her 'going in for the kill' look.

"Regardless of what you think happened, I get half of everything, anyway. So what if I took it early? It doesn't matter that we aren't married yet."

How could she go from telling me how right we were for each other to justifying her lies, manipulations, and theft?

"Jesus, you are a piece of work. I can't even list how many things are wrong with that statement." There were a half dozen words I'd like to call her, but I reined it in.

"The state of California allows you half of our personal assets. *Unfortunately*. But you took company funds, which need to be returned, or I will sue you and you may even go to jail. I'm sure your boyfriend could give you some good tips on how to stay safe in there," I suggest.

She doesn't know I already reversed the transaction. I want to see what she'll say, who she is now that all the chips are down.

"Fuck you, Jess," she spits back at me.

"No, thanks. I'm all done with you."

She gives me a high-pitched growl. "You owe me half!"

"Half of our assets. Not half of a line of credit owned by my company. Consider your half the money you got from our wedding deposits and the two years of rent you're past due."

She comes toward me, violence in her eyes, but I hold out a hand to stop her.

"Not to worry, I've taken care of reversing the transfer, since I'm sure we can agree that was a big fucking mistake on your part and you don't want to go to jail. Right?" I hand her the printout of the bank balances and she gapes.

Her left eye twitches at me and she rips the sheets from my hand. "I've let you keep the wedding deposits, the rest of our finances have always been separate. Don't even fucking think of asking for more."

She still doesn't say a word as she tosses the paper, flips me off, and then tries to leave.

"Your choice, Ashleigh. Tell me you understand and that I'll never hear from you again. If not, I can always call the authorities and have you arrested. However, I'd like to put you so fucking far in my rearview mirror that I can't tell if you were ever really there. What's your decision?"

The rage on her face soothes my jaded heart.

She nods.

"Good. After this, I never want to see or hear from you again."

Once she collects all her shit that I packed, I open the door for her, using the good manners my mom taught me, and tell her to get the fuck out.

My future just blew up, heart and mind shattered, yet my mind is on my next work project. Perhaps that's safest for right now. My heart can't be trusted.

CHAPTER 1

PRESENT

Emma

What they don't tell you about small-town life is the inability to pick up tampons at any time of the night, or for example, when necessary. And why is Lauren away for the weekend? Best friends bring tampons, no questions asked.

Oh, right, she went camping. In March. If it wasn't for her job, she would never have considered something like that. Then she would have helped me with this menstrual issue. Or at least let me know if any pharmacies are open past nine p.m. because I've had no luck so far. I've only been here for about a week and she is the only person I know in this town. She is the reason I chose Landry as my new home.

I find a couple random tampons in an old gym bag. They are even the plastic-wrapped ones, not the paper ones. Thank you, Jesus! Must have been a man who created that paper product wrap that disintegrates the moment it hits the inside of a handbag.

Note to self: look into menstrual cups.

Next, I need to finish unpacking my last few (dozen) boxes. Perhaps a glass of wine first. Mmm, yes, a nice glass of Shiraz on my new porch, which has the perfect view of the moon, stars, and those beautiful Sonoma County hills.

The wine is mouthwatering, finishes smooth and goes down a little too fast. My love of wine and the simple delight of trying something new, or pairing it with food, has brought me a little happiness in the last few bleak years. Without Lauren, I've been living a fairly boring, lonely, workaholic lifestyle. And while I don't tend to over imbibe, I do enjoy being a wine dork. I've been asked if I prefer red or white. My answer is that I do not discriminate.

Bringing the bottle out to the back porch, I enjoy my new surroundings and take in the peaceful life of small-town Landry. There's a trail directly behind my house that leads to a beautiful park near the center of town. I see my neighbors making use of it regularly and even spot running and biking groups that meet up several times a week. Opposite my house are a few neighbors with larger lots and spectacular views of the riverbed and slow-flowing water just beyond their back yards. I'm in the southern part of town, which is farther from the town center where most of the businesses are locally owned, and closer to the larger, sprawling California ranch-style houses built along the river.

Having a high stress, high-paying job in the finance division of an oil and gas company back in Seattle had a few advantages. One being that I made a nice living. Not a nice life, but an impressive wage and a sense of professional accomplishment.

The other advantage is that I now appreciate the little, quiet things life has to offer. I had climbed the corporate ladder quickly, which left little room for friends, sleep, or any kind of social life. I was a hard-working and driven woman in finance.

My father had been the driving force behind my decision to enter the oil and gas world. He set a strict example of how to succeed in the corporate world while also painting a realistic picture of what it meant to climb the ladder. He was the CFO of an oil company for many years, and I felt compelled to follow in his footsteps. Perhaps out of a need to have that common ground to fall back on after experiencing the disconnect during the infrequent occasions he was home for dinner. His executive lifestyle was everything to him, and while he attempted to portray a good role model and father figure, he fell short in ways I didn't fully understand until after I moved away.

I haven't told my father yet about resigning from my position. Or that I moved. Or that I may be experiencing a midlife crisis at thirty-one years old. He will express his disappointment or even be critical, but I can't find it in me to tell him the reason. Not yet.

He isn't one to discuss feelings or hardships. He believes feelings have no place in business and you get what you work for. Unfortunately, this idiom also found its way into our home. His generation got married, had kids, moved up the corporate ladder. Some men, even today, sacrifice home and family life for their careers.

As for the woman of our household, my mother, she abandoned us, and that left Father to fill roles he never envisioned. So, he hired it out. Nannies, tutors, and housekeepers were all a regular part of my childhood. It was not a terrible life, but it was an empty one. Once I was permitted to attend a private high school, the drastic differences rocked my world. The sliding spectrum of family dynamics was nearly a physical, identifiable factor among my peers. Of course, the one girl I was most drawn to also had family dysfunction in spades. While our problems differed, Lauren and I gave to each other what was lacking in our lives and we formed a beautiful friendship.

So, I've decided to wait to tell my father. Maybe once I make some headway on my fresh start, I'll reassess. I'll just keep sipping my wine and listening to that peaceful hum of country life.

A shriek interrupts my peaceful moment.

Oh god, is someone getting murdered on my property?!

"Shhh! It's just a spider web, go around it," a rough voice whisper-yells.

"Is it on me?! Why did we have to go for a walk?" I hear her nasally, high-maintenance voice complain. Now, I don't tend to be this judgmental, especially without seeing or experiencing the owner of said voice first. Yet, I can't imagine many heterosexual females who would complain about spending time with the tall, broad-shouldered, deep-voiced man next door.

"Stop whining! At least you have someone!" The words leave my mouth before I can stop them. Wine gives me loose lips.

I need to stop eavesdropping on my neighbor. I haven't even seen him in the light of day, but his shadowy silhouette is enough to make the dormant parts of my libido perk up.

I scurry back inside, closing the door.

"Who the hell was that?" his new companion asks.

"I think that's my new neighbor," he says.

Yes, I'm listening from the living room window. This entire side of my house consists of many windows and a wraparound porch, so my view into the neighbor's yard is unobstructed. Our lots may be enormous compared to what I'm used to in the city, but there still is little room for privacy in this quiet neighborhood.

So, this is my life now. I spy on my neighbor while drinking wine solo like I'm taking in a theater production. If Lauren were here, she would have dragged us out somewhere and attempted to introduce me to the whole town.

She called earlier to see if I'd gone to Taps & Tapas yet, explaining that it was the best local pub with great drinks, decent food, and the hot spot for gaining new companions. That is something I definitely need to work on.

Neighbor Guy, on the other hand, does not seem to lack companions. Tonight's seems to be a perfect fit for the personality profile I've been imagining. I preferred the giggler he brought home last week. The weekend produced a few drunken ladies, but given the number of people at the gathering he held, I can't be sure which one was his.

It's not that I'm a creep—I'm merely curious, intrigued.

For almost a year, sexual contact has been uncomfortable. I am a strong and smart woman, but some days that's harder to believe. Is there a personality type that draws in sexual predators?

The cold 'Em-bot', as they called me at work, was not an alluring target, or so I thought. See, here's the thing about this form of predation. It isn't about your personality or intelligence. It's not even about your physical appearance. No, it's about power. Being vulnerable in this way had never occurred to me. I hadn't allowed myself to be emotionally vulnerable since I was a child, other than a few instances with my best friend. I felt ill-prepared for the fallout.

Telling someone close to me about what happened last year is the right thing to do. I know this. My therapist encouraged me to start by telling one friend or family member, but I was raised to disregard my feelings.

My family does one of two things: ignores feelings or runs from them. Since I never knew how to process emotions, I couldn't comprehend how to deal with what happened to me. Or I didn't until I started therapy for sexual assault victims. It's been a long journey of healing and self-discovery. I'm still working on how to access and connect with my inner emotions, and I now have the tools.

I knew that I had to leave my work situation. Since work was my entire life for the last eight years, I left everything I knew behind for a small-town named Landry. It felt good.

It was the end of a loathsome era.

As of now, I am ignoring and running from my feelings for the last time.

This is my new life, and this time, I plan to do things differently.

CHAPTER 2

Emma

It has been a few days since I've seen or heard from my closest neighbor. I should introduce myself to maintain good neighborly relations, find out his name and give some kind of perception that I am a normal, functioning member of society.

I'm not sure if I will achieve that last part as I have done some damage there.

It's already quite dark, and I see Neighbor Guy come out on his back deck. I gather the materials to start the fire pit in my new yard, excited for a little burning. I hear his sliding door open again, but ignore him and get to work with the gasoline and a few logs I collected for my fire-making task.

I don't have a clue how to build a fire, but I do know gasoline is flammable.

I toss each piece of my tainted work clothes into the flames while shouting nonsense. I watch the skirt Dale put his filthy hands on catch flame, and I feel just a little bit lighter.

There's movement next door and I see Neighbor Guy come back outside and plunk down the item he'd gone to retrieve. He sits on the steps to watch the show, tipping his ball cap in my direction.

The item he has with him looks suspiciously like a large fire extinguisher. Alarmist. I roll my eyes in his direction and continue with my fire dance.

Yes, fine, I must look insane. Although, it's best he knows this now so he can prepare for future disturbances. Guaranteed I'm going to make a mess of this new way of life.

I send an awkward wave to the safety-conscious man.

He doesn't wave back.

I open my mouth to start a conversation, but don't know what to say to him. Social queues and small talk are all areas where I need some serious practice. These are not topics you study, memorize, and implement. Otherwise, I would have caught on better in school. Lauren and I have talked about this many times. I will always be awkward, feel awkward, and because of my sympathetic nervous system's hair-trigger response to stress, look awkward. I sweat and become very pale. It's not attractive.

Thankfully, Neighbor Guy is too far away to notice as he is fixated on the fire and his mistrust in my ability to keep it in check.

Friends, social life, sleep, fulfillment, and happiness. Those are the things I will be focusing on now. My life in Seattle had very little of this. You can't give your entire life to work and expect to have any actual life left.

At least I always had Lauren.

Lauren and I are like Jimmy Fallon and Justin Timberlake. You don't know how the friendship came to be, but it works, you can't stop laughing, and you gush about how great the other person is.

She has always been the outgoing one. The one who draws attention and couldn't care less about what others think of her. Being gorgeous and having that charming, ball-buster thing going for her, men trip over themselves to talk to her.

She also started her life over when she moved to Landry. I am so proud of her. And just a smidge envious of all she offers. She draws people in. Like the delicious smell of freshly baked cookies.

My 'scent' is probably the human equivalent of mosquito

repellent. The good stuff with forty percent DEET. Now it sounds like I have a body odor problem. I don't. I don't think anyway. I make a note to ask Lauren.

She must be back in a cell service area given the dramatic text I just received.

LAUR: I know what you did, Em.
ME: What are you talking about?
LAUR: You embezzled money from those upper management shitheads. Good for you! Hope you got enough to keep us in expensive wine for a while!
ME: You are still guessing why I left my job? I told you, the stress wore on me and I wanted a life. It's not the job I want. It's not the life I want. You've been trying to tell me this for years.

Well, at least that part is true. I want a different life. That life-style is not for me. Not anymore.

LAUR: Did you set the top floor on fire? I've heard how much you like fire.

What? Who ratted me out about my solo firepit party? Does Lauren know my neighbors? Or is this just how small towns work? I mean, I've heard everyone knows everyone's business, but seeing it in action is another thing altogether.

LAUR: Did you have an affair?
LAUR: Did you lose billions from an insider tip? You can tell me! I can help you go 'off the grid'. We will need to research this because I don't know what it means.
ME: Laur, we've gone over this. I am not a stock trader or investor.
ME: How's camping?
I know it's futile to try to distract her, but it's worth an attempt.

LAUR: Camping has been… interesting and confusing. We'll talk about that later. Stop trying to distract me!
LAUR: I know something is wrong. You wouldn't just quit your job so suddenly, Em. We've avoided this topic for long enough. Maybe you realized what you were putting into work wasn't worth it anymore, but something big happened. You've been acting strange since before I moved here. Tell me when you are ready. I love you.
ME: I will. Promise.
LAUR: Pinky promise!
ME: Pinky promise!
LAUR: Fine, but I am checking in on you tomorrow. And we are going out.
ME: Acceptable. No bars. Somewhere quiet.
ME: Quick unbiased opinion needed. Do I have body odor?
LAUR: What? No.
LAUR: I'll sniff test you next time I see you, just to be sure.

This is why we are best friends.

Jess

My brother owes me. Big. He may not have known that a quirky pyro lady would buy the house next door to him, but he left for a year and asked me to house-sit for him. I thought I'd have this peaceful, cushy year, gulping Guinness on Garrett's deck.

In reality, I am doing minor home repairs and maintenance, lawn care (who needs this much yard space?), installing a new smart home system, on top of monitoring the crazy lady next door who may just burn down this entire riverside neighborhood.

It puts a sly smile on my face, thinking about what Garrett will do when he comes back home to a smart home system. He won't even know how to get into his house, let alone change the thermostat. I laugh knowing I'll be showing him everything, but the panic in the brainiac's eyes when he sees what I've done to his house will more than make up for it.

Now, what to do with his computer? I have just over six months left before he gets back. There are so many delightful surprises I could leave him when he opens his laptop next.

Although, he's helping families in a third world country and living without most amenities right now. Garrett and his noble shit make it almost impossible to give him a hard time.

Fine, I won't touch his computer. Who knows what manner of depraved stuff I'd find on the computer of a repressed, book-smart doctor. Ha. He's very private, but at least he has had a few longer relationships. From what our sister, Chloe, has told me, they usually end amicably and with little drama.

In contrast, I only casually date. I'm the guy who will tell you straight up that I won't love you, won't do romantic gestures, relationships, or anything resembling commitment. My big, soft, tainted heart needs protecting because, as my brother Garrett would tell you, I'm a pussy. I disagree, but I'm not even sure he has feelings, so he wouldn't care. When he gets laid, I'm guessing he grunts twice, pulls out, shakes her hand, and escorts her to the door.

Landry is a smaller town with a smaller pool of companions from which to choose. Here, your neighbors are practically family, with very little in terms of boundaries, and everyone knows you. There is literally a group of residents who call themselves the Landry Life League who act as an information network for the town. Want to know if Jimmy skipped baseball practice? Text Mrs. Henderson, a retired daycare owner, or Mr. Dwyer, owner of Martin's Market grocery store, and they'll have an answer for you within ten minutes.

When I lived here, I never got away with shit. Garrett and his best friend Taylor were smarter and used this network to their advantage. I still can't get away with anything here. I typically have to take my dates out of town just so my mom doesn't find out. Because yes, my mom is still a part of the League, even though she doesn't live here anymore.

Which is why even though tourists that come through are aplenty, I often go into Napa, Santa Rosa or even some smaller surrounding towns to expand the pool, and it's been working well for me.

Do I still get judgmental looks? Sure. Even from new residents like pyro neighbor lady.

I've only ever seen her in the dark from afar. We both spend most late evenings on our decks, enjoying the scenery, the quiet. She sometimes likes to fill that quiet with commentary on my occasional late-night visitors. I believe I heard, "Oh! A new one…" just last week.

Thanks, *Mom*, I get enough of that from my actual family.

Despite my grumbling, this gig has been working well for me so far. I work from home, designing software, building custom platforms and even contracting for big tech companies in southern California.

At thirty-two, I haven't 'settled down', as my mother likes to point out. I tell her I've had a successful business for the better part of a decade. That's all the permanency I need. Settling down means picking a place, a person, a life—forever. Why would I try that again? I make good money doing what I love from wherever I want, meet anyone, do anything.

I love my mom, but I have no issues with her resuming her disappointment. Perhaps it's the Italian in her, but she has this burning need to take care of everyone, especially her youngest son.

Since my parents moved to a retirement community near here, I've had to endure the babying slightly less than Garrett since I tend not to be in this area as much. But not today. Not now that I'm back in Landry.

I answer my phone before the fourth ring, knowing she'll take offense if I let it go any longer.

"Hi sweetheart, just calling to talk about Labor Day festivities." No pause for me to respond. "Oh, and I've been meaning to stop by and fill the pantry. Your brother doesn't eat processed foods, so you'll have none of the good snacks."

"No, Mamma." Camilla, or Millie as she prefers, is originally from Italy, so naturally, she's passed down a bit of the language and culture on to the rest of us. Usually by force. A loving, meddlesome, motherly force. "If you can believe it, I was driving around just the other day, and wound up at a large store named Martin's Market. I went right in and found an assortment of groceries."

"Mhmm. I wasn't sure you'd remember, what with your infrequent visits back home over the last few years."

Ah, so a guilt trip is on the agenda of today's call.

"You don't even live here anymore, Mamma."

"Close enough."

"Well, now that I've had a refresher, I'll come around here more often after I move back to San Francisco," I placate.

"Good. Now tell me about the new girl!"

I haven't seen Tasha in a while, and not usually around Landry, so it can't be her. Who would have been chatting my mom up about a lady friend of mine?

Fuck. Taylor Shaw.

"Have you been talking to Taylor?"

"You didn't answer my question, sweetheart."

I sigh, and she hears me. She tsks me and waits.

Some people feel the need to fill the silence? Not my mom. She's patient like that.

"I don't know what you're talking about."

"Taylor says you have a female friend. She's shy and you are taking things slow…"

What in the ever-loving…? Why my brother's best friend insists on sticking his nose into my personal life—and then sharing it with my mom—is anyone's guess. He probably thinks I'm a suitable substitute while Garrett is away.

"Mom, if there was something to tell you or a woman I was

serious about, I'd call you. No, I'd text you. I wouldn't want to hear the squealing firsthand."

There's silence.

Except for one snort of smothered laughter from the porch about twenty feet from mine.

Ah, Pyro Neighbor Lady. Eavesdropping again.

The silence continues on the other end of the phone.

"Mom?" Nothing. "Mamma."

"I'm here. Sorry, I'm just a teensy bit disappointed. This sounded so promising." She sighs. "Are you happy? You're busy, successful, healthy, yes. But I worry that you are not happy. What does the rest matter without joy?"

"Mamma, I'm doing just fine. I don't need someone else to make me happy. I have you, right? That's all I need right now." I grin, knowing that will throw her off my scent for a little while.

Truth is, I'm not sure if I'm happy or not. I wouldn't say I'm filled with joy, but I'm content enough. Though, I have been wondering if I'm lonely. Even with a smattering of friends in each of my home base cities and plenty of overnight company when needed, it still feels monotonous and empty.

Bottom line though, it works and I've avoided excessive drama and heartbreak. Hard to beat that.

"For now, I will let that go." That sounds ominous. "Did Chloe tell you she's good with having our Labor Day weekend celebration in Landry?"

"News to me, but she might have emailed me. Why are we planning this so early? Labor Day is almost five months away still."

"Dad and I are heading to Italy for a few months, remember? So, I talked with Chloe and convinced her to come to the barbecue. We will have it at Garrett's if you're okay with hosting?"

"Or..." I scramble. "Since you are the ultimate host and this isn't my home, that position could fall—I mean, be awarded to you." Or my sister, Chloe. As long as it's not me.

She hums at me again. "Better I make the decisions, anyway." I hear muffled chatter. "Sorry Jess, Dad needs me to help him with the garden. Visit soon!" She kisses twice into the phone.

Whether that was a 'come for a visit soon!' or 'I'm going to visit you soon!', only time will tell.

"Oh, and maybe try to find a nice woman to bring to the barbecue! A real date. Not one of your 'usual women'."

"Mom. I'm not bringing a random person to our family barbecue." I try to reason with her, but I can hear by the excitement in her tone that this idea isn't going away.

"Well it's a good thing we are planning this early, giving you lots of time to find a lady friend." She whispers something to Dad. "Okay honey, I have to go. I'll call you later in the week. Love you." I get two more air kisses before she disconnects.

Every year, my mom pushes settling down a little harder. She worries about me, can sense something isn't quite right, I'm sure. In the past, I have brought dates to family events to appease them.

Problem is, I attract a wild assortment of women. I've dated crazy girls, conniving ladies, and violent hotheads. Lesson learned.

Finding the type of woman my mom is referring to, would not be an easy task. Those wholesome, sweet, strong, future-ready women tend not to want the same type of relationship I prefer. And while I may experience some deep-seated feelings of seclusion and restlessness occasionally, the risks aren't worth the unguaranteed rewards.

Not going to happen, sorry, Mom.

I hear the shuffling sound of a sliding patio door and look up to find my neighbor's deck empty once again. Show's over, I guess.

My curious neighbor can sit out on that porch, watching me, judging me, or appreciating me all she wants. It won't change who I am.

She's likely in the crazy lady group, anyway.

CHAPTER 3

Emma

"Oh! You're the new gal who moved into the gorgeous ranch house next to us! Welcome! I'm Stella."

I jump as a middle-aged woman with curly hair colored a bright auburn leers down at me from under an enormous sun hat. Nope. Visor. An enormous visor. Visor lady. I hope I didn't say that out loud. I'll never make friends if that keeps happening.

Surprised, I stare at her for a few moments longer than normal.

Snapping out of it, I reply, "Um, yes! I just moved in a few weeks ago. I'm Emma Mahoney." I smile, trying for charming, but there might be panic in my eyes. My social anxiety is kicking up a notch with this impromptu greeting.

"Once you're settled, come over for a visit, dear! We can get acquainted, and Greg and I would love to add another member to our book club. Greg is my husband. Twenty-nine years this past January." She smiles fondly. "Anyway, dear, we'd love to have you over and our patio is always open!" She chuckles as if she has a secret, pats my arm, and then power walks away, arms pumping.

Once Stella sped off in a whirlwind of motion, I could breathe again.

Well, that went better than expected. Wait, was she laughing at me? I wonder if she saw my fire the other night? Although, only Neighbor Guy's back deck is close enough to see what's happening in my yard… I'm overthinking this. Wiping the sheen of sweat from my upper lip, I curse my inability to control my body.

I'm nothing if not a great avoider of emotions. I'm sure I get that from my mother. She didn't love being a mom, living in San Francisco, or the expectations that family life and having a husband who worked away half the year entailed. She left when I was seven, and I developed a new coping skill: avoidance.

A while after she left, I pretended as though I never had a mom. When my dog died a year after Mom left, I'd think 'what dog? Time for a puppy'. Powerful CEO makes unwanted and escalating aggressive sexual advances, threatening to frame or fire me once the sting of rejection and threats of criminal charges settles in… I press charges, but then run on autopilot, telling no one else and obsessively working for months before quitting.

Yes, I have a finely-honed coping mechanism in place.

Therapy and starting fresh in a new town helped bring me out of my stupor and attack the parts of my life I've been avoiding for years. It's time to tell Lauren. Then I can begin making progress on my new life goals.

~

Lauren and I chose to meet at Taps & Tapas, her favorite local bar and grill in town. I am two glasses deep when she walks in, assessing me with her ever-watchful gaze. Her face saddens. She knows I'm going to tell her everything, and she knows it's bad.

She's quiet and waits until I begin. I begin the story of why I left a top position at one of the biggest companies on the west coast.

"He was harassing you? That dick! Did you stab him in the eye?"

"Yes. At first, it was shameless flirting, which I avoided and had HR send out a memo about unprofessional workplace conversation and behavior." I wince as Lauren gives me a disapproving look, "I realize now that I should have confronted him and told him to stop his unprofessional behavior right then. I just wasn't sure if he was truly flirting.... Not many people flirt with 'Em-bot', so I was surprised." My work nickname may be unflattering, but at least it provided a nice buffer to ward off unwanted advances. Dale was unbothered by my cold, apathetic, but ambitious work demeanor and was fine with the robotic personality I portray at work. In fact, I now believe he considered it a challenge he wanted to best.

"Oh, hon. Did he keep making comments?" she asked, thinking that was the end of the disgusting tale.

"Yes. But there's more. Things... escalated." I peeked at her through my lashes, assessing her level of concern. My therapist said telling loved ones about what I went through is an important step in healing. I continued, "He would show up at my condo, leave creepy anonymous notes on my desk, include me in meetings I didn't need to be in, book appointments with me just to be around me. He wasn't used to people saying no to him, and I rejected his advances every time."

I play with my napkin, gathering the courage to continue. "After a couple of months of this, he cornered me in the boardroom, and told me he needed me with him on a corporate weekend at the head office in Denver. I knew the agenda, so I knew the meeting did not require my attendance. I told him so. He disagreed and pulled rank." I pause. "He booked us one room, claiming it was an unintentional mistake afterward. I called ahead to verify arrangements and avoided this 'mistake'. He was furious, Lauren. I was wondering if he was ever going to stop. How could I work with this egomaniac?"

"Jesus, Em! Who does that? Shrivel-dick fuckwad! How did you not at least verbally tear him limb from limb? You're not meek, I've heard you eviscerate competitors and lazy staff members. Professional, but brutal, and remorseless," she says, looking proud for a moment. "If I ever meet this asshole..." Fuming, she downs the rest of her pinot grigio.

"Evan, I need a refill. Make it the red one I like." She slides her glass over. Uh oh, red wine only makes her feistier. Based on the look our bartender is giving her, he also knows this.

"Don't give me that look, Ev. We are having a moment. Moments require wine."

Evan frowns at her, pours her wine and says, "I don't have time to drop your drunk ass at home later, I have to pick up Trent. So, this is your last one, Teach."

She rolls her eyes, but agrees. Then turns to me, sipping her wine and waiting until I'm ready.

I heave out a trembling breath. "It gets worse. Lauren, I don't even know how to..." I trail off, dejected. I have the emotional coping skills of a cabbage.

"The week after the Denver trip, I started receiving random anonymous emails. That's when I knew he hadn't let it go." I look down and keep my voice low. "He insinuated that my position was contingent upon my complete 'cooperation' with all upper-level executives. He sent me a time and place to meet him. I threatened to go to HR and the company president if the harassment continued. It was too little too late though. I may have been a vigorous leader and professional, but he could sense my personal weakness."

"It's not weakness to expect professionalism and respect." Her fists are clenched. "Please tell me you went to HR." She looks at me, sees my expression, then asks, "Emma... what else?"

"He attacked me." I gulp my wine and shut my eyes. No

avoiding it now. My therapist would be proud. This was a big step I was taking.

Lauren looks at me, eyes wide, but says nothing, hand fluttering up to cover her mouth.

"I was working late after a long international conference call. He waited until our floor had cleared out and came to my office. I didn't see him come up behind me until it was too late. He grabbed me and shoved me facedown onto the desk." God, reliving it makes me so angry and helpless. I need to join a gym. I was weak, slow… the next guy is going to get his ass handed to him.

"He spoke, but I only remember bits of what he said… I-I panicked." I shake as I recant the worst three minutes of my life. It comes tumbling out of my mouth. I am there again and can feel his breath, hot on my ear as he attempts to assert his authority over me.

"He leaned over me and told me I was not to resist anymore. He expected to be taken care of. No one says no to him. He threatened to fire me, ruin my career, and some other threats." The color rises in my cheeks. I don't make mistakes and I do not submit to chauvinist assholes. "I started hitting him as best I could, but I only got a couple in before he stopped me. Then I heard his, um… his buckle." I stop and look at Lauren. She's shocked, enraged and grabs my hand, but I can't feel my hands, my face. My avoidance has reached a new and physical level: numb.

"I pulled with everything I had and rip a hand away. Grabbed the only thing I could reach, a pen." Pausing, I look at her, chin held high. "You asked if I stabbed him in the eye. No, Lauren. I stabbed him in the leg."

I explain that he'd been arrested and had a slew of charges filed against him from multiple coworkers once the investigation began. He spent time in jail, but I don't know how much. I was working on being content and fulfilled, not dwelling on Dale.

After I answer Lauren's many questions, we drink in silence as she keeps her hand over mine. After a few minutes, she hops off her stool and envelops me in a hug.

"I'm proud of you, Emma-Jean," she smarts.

Lauren has called me this since high school. I looked it up a long time ago, curious as to why she kept calling me that. It's supposed to denote a smart, beautiful, sensitive, and funny girl. I was so shy in school that I'm certain, until Lauren took me under her wing, no one ever even knew my name. Lauren latched on to me, saying she recognized that I was special and everyone else was too stupid to see the gem hiding beneath the sand. Her nickname for me is how she tells me I'm the complete package.

"Look at how far you've come. My gorgeous little pearl has emerged from her shell ready for the world."

"Pearls don't 'emerge' from their shells. They get torn open and ripped out."

"Well, your shell was shit. So, good riddance!"

Then she asks, "Want me to sniff test you now?"

I give a weak smile. Then laughter. It's a crazy laugh, but she still got a laugh out of me and for that, I'm grateful. "Yes, please. Be as descriptive as possible. I need to know if I smell like good-guy repellent."

Jess

It's late afternoon on a weekday and I'm on my way back home from a long run by the river, sweaty but energized. Thinking life is pretty good, I feel my phone vibrating in my pocket.

I see it's Tasha again and let it go to voicemail. She knew where I stood with relationships. Why do some women think they're the exception? They will fix me, make me whole, reinforce my faith in love. Sorry, Tasha, not happening. Maybe someday I can have what she's offering, but not now, and not with her. I listen to the voicemail to make sure she's alright—I'm not a monster—and then call up Taylor so we can grab a drink.

After showering, I meet Taylor at Taps & Tapas and see him looking a bit squirrelly.

"What's going on? Why are you acting weird?" The guy can't sit still and keeps glancing at the bar. I follow his gaze. Oh. Someone has his attention… or a couple of someones. They're hugging and one of them looks familiar.

"Nah, I'm fine." He stops for a moment, slaps my arm. "Stop looking over there! They'll catch us staring or Evan will and he'll rat us out!" He nods toward the young, perpetually grumpy bartender who is doting on the women with a scowl on his face.

I laugh. Taylor is likable, quick to make friends, but doesn't date much. He's a busy guy. Coaching, teaching, and speaking at colleges about his college-prep program. He is a pillar in the community and a role model for those kids. He's not shy or introverted, he's just selective in those he keeps close.

"Sorry." I grin. "So, are you going to explain?"

"You remember Lauren," he whispers. Ah, his English teacher friend who moved here last year. I've seen her around town a few times since I moved back. Taylor introduced us, but I haven't spent much time with her.

"Yeah..."

"She's gotten to me, man." He shakes his head, mumbling, "You ever put yourself out there, thinking there's something between you, only to get shot down?" He lifts his Landry Lightning cap and rakes his hand through his hair. "I don't understand it. So, I'm giving her some space."

"Uh, not my area of expertise." He shrugs, agreeing. "So… are we following her now?"

Taylor doesn't usually have any problem with gaining female attention. I've had dates ask who my Adonis friend is. So, I'm a little thrown by this reaction to his coworker.

I look over and consider inviting the ladies to join us.

"Don't!" he barks at me.

I widen my eyes, feigning innocence. "Fine." I hold my hands up in submission, but sneak a glance at the bar. "Which one is Lauren again?" I tease, pretending I don't remember her.

He frowns at me but answers. "Brown hair, with the smile."

"They both have brown hair."

"No, asshole. They both have dark hair. Lauren has the varying shades of brown, while Emma's is nearly black." He looks at me as if I'm the one being thick.

"Right, okay. So, what are you going to do?"

"Nothing. I took my shot, and she turned me down, hard." He shakes his head as if to clear it. "We probably should have kept to being platonic."

This is another reason I don't do this shit. So much drama.

"So, you stare at her from afar, stalk her, stage these run-ins. Sounds like a plan that may involve law enforcement at some point." I slap his shoulder.

"Don't be a dick." I take a sip of my stout as he takes a long pull of his lager. It's a small enough town that we will probably run into his little obsession again, and then I'll push. For today, we'll drink and have a night out. Although maybe I'll go talk to Lauren's friend. I angle myself toward her and check her out. She has shiny black hair that falls in a straight curtain around her shoulders. A pert nose within a heart-shaped face. Her smooth white skin is so pale, it nearly glows. She's thinner than Lauren, a wispy figure with a straight, harsh posture. She radiates elegance, but not ease or grace. It's an interesting contrast of beauty and discomfort.

"What's up with the friend?" I ask Taylor, noticing Emma's somber expression intensify.

"That's Emma. Lauren told me about how her friend quit her job in Seattle and is looking to start fresh. I heard her planning to meet here for drinks." He stops and looks over at me, caught.

"We *are* stalking then. Good to know." I laugh and finish my drink.

I can tell when the ladies notice us. Lauren spots Taylor,

freezes, then looks away. Emma does little more than give us a shy glance.

There's something there alright. I hope they figure it out, because then maybe Taylor would butt into my personal life less. The guy shows up at all hours. He's probably used to having to socialize Garrett.

Taylor just needs a shove in the right direction. He won't like it, but sometimes we don't like things that are good for us. Like kale. Sometimes we have to eat kale. We know it's good for us, but it can be hard to choke down.

CHAPTER 4

Emma

It's been a month since I moved here and I have nothing but snacks and wine at my house. In the past, I never had time for food, entertaining or cooking. I've always wanted to learn how to pair food and wine, so I've decided to add cooking to my list of 'new life' skills.

However, I can't do that if I can't push the damn cart down the damn aisle so I can purchase my damn food! Why did I have to choose the dilapidated cart? Squeaky wheel, an uneven base, gunk stuck in a rear wheel.

I grunt as I head up another aisle. Pushing this cart is akin to moving a couch, up a set of stairs, by yourself. I plunk canned tomatoes, sauce, and beans into my cart, hoping to make chili for the first time later this week.

The weight of the cans is not helping me heave this evil cart to my next destination: feminine hygiene products. With a menstrual cup dropped into my cart, I make my way to the frozen aisle. It only makes sense to get the frozen food at the end of your shopping trip. See? I am getting so good at this domestic stuff.

A light sheen of sweat covers my neck as I huff my hair off my face and round the corner to the frozen goods.

Searching for frozen peas, I glimpse an olive-skinned, broad-backed, brown-haired delight standing between me and my frozen vegetables. I am no prude. I appreciate the male body, the muscles, the stature of a filled-out man. Not putting myself out there much means that when I do, it leans toward awkward.

I am thankful it's a chilled aisle so I don't have to explain why specific parts of my somewhat visible anatomy have perked up. My nips are embarrassing me—future title of my autobiography.

The nipple enticer bends to grab a bag of corn and I get an eyeful. Must. Drag. Eyes. Away. Instead, my head tilts as I look in surprise at the wonder of his glutes.

He looks back, feeling my gaze. I look away. Good, saved it. That was close.

I sneak another look a moment later. He's watching me and grinning. Crap, dammit! He knows.

The deep shade of ruby my entire body turns isn't helping. I smile, feigning nonchalance, and casually walk over to get my peas.

"I'm just going to sneak by you and grab some penis." Oh no. No, I didn't. Please no. I look at him, eyes wide, praying. His eyes are wide too. Yup. I said it. This is the direct result of not properly socializing as a child.

"PEAS! Grabbing some peas! Oh god..." I cover my face with one hand while I grab the bag with the other. I can hear him laughing as I try to run from the frozen section. But my cart won't move. The freezer aisle has done it in, or it's too embarrassed on my behalf and is stunned into immobility.

I drag it from the front just so I can escape.

Well, that's done now, and there is nothing I can do about it. I will focus on buying my groceries and getting home to watch my first cooking tutorial. If I'm quick, I won't see him at all!

I get in line after what feels like an hour of scraping the linoleum while dragging my cart behind me. Piling my items onto the checkout belt, I hear a voice behind me.

"So, what are you using those peas for?"

Nooooo! Why would he choose this checkout? Let a girl recover from her embarrassment in peace. Are there not social norms dictating the rules for handling these situations?

I look back, straight into sea-green eyes. Dammit! His eyes are as alluring as the rest of him. They sparkle at you, teasing you to look longer, get closer.

His eyes are a human Venus flytrap.

And I recognize him now. He runs the trail behind my house most mornings, always stopping to chat with neighbors, pet a dog, or pick up garbage. He's like a small town 'what do they put in the water?' advertisement. He even sings along to his music sometimes and it's pretty bad, but he couldn't care less. He has swagger and a confidence that I wish was contagious. Or at least easily learned. I stop staring into his eyes, groan in embarrassment, and cover my face again.

"Good Lord..." I mutter, eyes wide, fight-or-flight impulse in full effect. "Did you follow me?" My voice comes out in a squeak, tinged with mortification.

"I asked you a question first," he points out, waiting. Grinning with a crooked, laughing smile.

"Soup," I say. Yes, keep to monotone, one-word responses.

He thinks about that, nods, then says, "Yes."

"Yes, what?"

"Yes, I followed you. It wasn't hard, with that cart of yours screeching throughout the entire store like an alarm." He grins again.

"Guhh," I breathe out an incoherent noise as my brain stutters. My head screams, "Put that grin away, you could poke someone's ovaries out with that thing!"

He bursts out laughing.

I said that out loud too! Am I drunk? They should not allow me to leave the house.

If I had to be honest, I haven't spoken to a man I was super attracted to since college. And that was nearly a decade ago! I don't chat up random strangers, let alone discuss body parts with them!

Biting my lips to keep them closed, I quickly turn around as the cashier finishes putting my groceries through. I toss her my credit card. I don't even know if I have all of my groceries. Complete panic has set in and autopilot is engaged. Breathe. This is a beneficial, risk-free practice of my social skill development. Sweat covers my upper lip. I wipe it off with my palm and then cringe after remembering I've been maneuvering the gross ramshackle of a cart and now probably have cart grease on my face.

I drag my cart behind me out of the grocery store's main doors. I hear, "Wait! Emma!" behind me, and I startle, wondering how the hell Green Eyes knows my name. I pick up the pace.

After throwing my groceries into my vehicle and hightailing it out of there, I look in the rearview mirror and see him pushing his cart through the parking lot while looking around.

Pulling up at home, I start breathing at a regular rate. Heart rate back to normal, I loop the bag handles into my hands, ready for a 'one-trip'. I always try, even if that means popping capillaries in my arms and fingers, half dragging part of my purchases through the doorway or collapsing once I make it into the house.

I hear my neighbor pulling into his driveway, as I continue to pile an obscene number of bags onto my arms. I've never seen him during the day, so I'm quite curious. One handle of a bag tears away, I try to save it, toppling another bag I'm holding and soon half my groceries are tumbling to the driveway, cans smashing into my right foot. I spew a litany of growled curses, hopping in pain. Oh, great. I embarrass myself in front of Green Eyes at the grocery store and now Neighbor Guy gets another show too.

"You okay? Looks like you'll have another use for those peas!"

I freeze. NO. Please, no!

I look up at Green Eyes. Did he follow me? What do I do?

Where is my phone? Do I drop these groceries? Ack! Who cares about the 'one-trip'!! You have a stalker!

I release the grip on my groceries and plunge a hand deep into my handbag, coming out with pepper spray. Holding it out, finger on the trigger, I ask, "Are you following me?!?"

He sees the panic in my eyes and I see concern flash across his. "No. Shit. Sorry, Emma—"

"How do you know my name?" I cut him off, shouting, moving backward.

He scrubs a hand down his face "My friend, Taylor, teaches with your friend, Lauren."

I study him. "Okay… but why are you here?" I ask, pepper spray still held out at the ready.

"First," he says, coming closer, "you should flip the safety cap off the spray nozzle if you ever need to use it." He points at the cap where my finger is resting. I flip the cap up, finger at the ready for real now. "Second, I'm your temporary neighbor. I wasn't following you home, I just live here, too."

Stunned, I drop my sprayer hand while my brain tries to process. "What?!?"

"I said, I'm your neighbor," he repeats, likely thinking I'm simple.

"No, I heard you. It was more of an incredulous 'What?!?'" I glance at his vehicle, recognizing it as the truck I see daily, parked in the driveway. Then I look around at the mess. Groceries everywhere, pepper spray still in my hand, foot swelling. He picks up the undamaged groceries and puts them back into the bags. "You don't have to do that, it's fine."

He looks at me and shrugs. "It's not a problem. Plus, I feel a little responsible."

I tell myself I am unaffected by his charm.

He walks the bags up to my front step, then comes back to check how I'm doing with the rest. Huh. One-trips are much more manageable with a partner. This has to be one of the main reasons people date and get married, right?

"Well, it was nice to finally meet you, Emma." He stares into my eyes with amusement.

"You too, Green Eyes." Stop talking. Just. Stop. I should have pepper-sprayed myself.

"I go by Jess. But 'Green Eyes' is nice too."

I watch Green Eyes—Jess—walk back to his house. Is this really any worse than my fire pit night or the comments I shouted at his lady friend?

Yes. Yes, it is.

Jess

I always liked puzzles as a kid. Emma, while clumsy, odd, and a danger to society, is 'solve the puzzle' interesting. If I'm going to be honest, she's stunning. Subtly stunning. From up close, I noticed that the front of her hair is a bit longer than the back. She is on the skinny side of lean, which is a bit different from my usual type. Her big, honey brown Bambi eyes reel you in even as they try to hide, or worse, dismiss you.

After our grocery store encounter, I started seeing her everywhere and it's awkward, yet amusing. I still catch myself smiling about our frozen aisle interaction. Now, whenever she sees me, she ducks away or says something to herself in a whisper, lifting her head high and turning in the other direction.

Tonight I am planning to head to Taylor's for poker night, but had to stop at Baked Delights to pick up some pastries as requested. Taylor has a huge sweet tooth for someone who still somehow maintains the body type of a professional athlete. I hear the door chime and see Emma heading toward me at the counter. After I give Dani, the owner, Taylor's list of requests, I decide it might be nice to offer to buy Emma's order too. A little 'welcome to the neighborhood, please stop avoiding me awkwardly in public' olive branch.

I turn around to face her. "Hi Emma. Go ahead and order, it's on me today." I turn back to the bakery owner. "Dani, can you put her order on my tab, please?"

Dani nods and looks to Emma, who scrunches her brows at me and says, "Oh. Is this… Are you…"

"Am I what?"

"Is this your method of picking up women? Is this flirting?"

What? "Uh, no."

"I see. Good. Okay, then yes. I'd like a pie, please, Dani. The strawberry rhubarb if you have any left." She turns her gaze back to me. "Thank you, Jess. That was very nice. I can see now why you have so many women friends."

I pay for our baked goods in silence, unsure what to say. She gives me a jerky wave before leaving the bakery with her pie.

Landry is small, so there's really no avoiding each other. Now, though, I look for her, intrigued by her innate ability to take the mundane and normal, and turn it odd and uncomfortable.

She also joined my gym recently, and it's difficult for her to hide there. I decide I'll just talk to her and get us back on track to neighborly head nods and a quick good morning / evening.

I finish on the leg press and spot her coming out of one of the fitness classrooms.

Jogging over, I catch up with her and put my hand on her shoulder. Before I can even greet her, she grabs my hand, cinches it between her raised arm and her neck, then drops me into a shoulder lock. I'm bent over, my arm extended backward and straight-up to the ceiling.

What. The. Fuck.

"Emma!" I give her leg a few quick taps. "Ow! What the fuck?!"

The little she-devil has taken me by surprise.

"Oh! Jess!" She releases me. "I'm so sorry! Are you okay?" Her warm brown eyes look me over with concern. She comes closer to assess me, but thinks better of it and steps back instead.

"Uh… yeah." I rub my shoulder and elbow. "Damn, lady!"

I'm impressed. And a little turned on, but I'll circle back around to that thought later.

"Sorry!" She makes a guttural "ugh," sound. "I'm in the self-defense class. The focus today was rear attacks, so I was still in the zone."

She looks at me and gives me a lopsided attempt at a smile, "I have peas at home if you need them… you know, for your shoulder..." Then shoots me a big, even smile.

"I may just take you up on that, Killer." Her eyes light with concealed laughter. "So, is the playing field level now? You've been avoiding me and I wanted to check in and clear the air."

"Oh… Well, I wouldn't say I was avoiding you." She grimaces as I tip my head in disbelief.

"Okay, yes I was. I just wanted to ensure no further embarrassing encounters occurred while I was getting settled in here. Social ineptitude is a recurring theme for me. Grew up without a mom for most of my childhood. Raised by nannies and home-schooled until high school. My father wasn't around much either."

She's rambling, but then she gulps, eyes wide as if she realized she made a mistake, "That was an overshare. I apologize. I should have just said 'playing field leveled!'."

Then she blurts out, "I'm not crazy!" Then quieter, "That's what crazy people say, isn't it?"

I can only give a noncommittal shrug.

"Okay, sorry again. Ignore me. Have a good day. Put ice on that shoulder." Then she walks off, heading straight to the women's changing room. She glances back, concern filling her eyes. Emma carries a vulnerability about her that makes me feel things. Things I have no business feeling.

Three thoughts take over my mind for the rest of my workout.

First, my neighbor is odd.

Second, she's hot. That little maneuver; defending herself even from a guy like me that's a half foot taller than her… hot!

Third, she intrigues me. Being that I don't tend to form

connections with women that extend beyond the sexual, I should probably stay away from Emma aka Killer. She's trouble. Adorable, weird, hot, interesting trouble.

Emma

When I do something, I put all of my effort into making sure I complete my goal. After undergoing much-needed therapy for the attempted sexual assault, one of my main goals for the last six months was completing a self-defense class, which I was able to continue here. While I can now kick ass, it should not have been my neighbor's ass—or shoulder.

How can I attempt any relationships, romantic or otherwise, if I act moronic every time I talk to a guy? I scare away potential suitors and if that doesn't get them, my big mouth and awkward disposition does.

Although, this implies that Jess is a potential suitor, which I can guarantee he is not. I have seen the ladies he dates. Lauren pointed out a few when we were out one night. I had asked her about Jess's situation, curious as to which one I may have seen in his yard that night I was spying. I mean, researching.

Lauren introduced me to Becca, one of Jess's previous dating companions, when we ran into her at one of the vineyard tasting events the other day. Long, blonde, curly hair, sky-high legs, an ample chest, a quick wit, and a bubbly charm.

It's safe to say, I am not Jess's type.

Observing Jess' dating habits from afar is fine, educational even. Up-front encounters don't seem to end as well.

My therapist suggested I work on my avoidance behaviors and start confronting my fears and triggers. Clearly, some of those avoidance habits are still firmly ingrained based on my reactions to Jess. I need to refocus.

Lauren has been helping and we have our list of growth experiences I will tackle. She's got her work cut out for her, though.

She tried to 'socialize' me in college, and it was only partially successful. I was dragged to parties, introduced to new friends, and even taken on a wildly unsuccessful double date.

Lauren and I sit on my couch, drinking our chardonnay as I tell her about the incident at the gym. She stifles a laugh and then isn't able to hold it in any longer and lets out a stream of giggles and snorts.

"It's not that funny." My face is grim. "I remember a panicked phone call last summer when you went full ninja on a fellow teacher. The one you thought was a school burglar or teacher serial killer. Was that just as funny?"

Her face falls a fraction. "No. But I'm loving this anyway." She sets her shoulders. "What are you going to do, my fellow ninja?"

"Keep things normal, casual. A friendly, neighbor-like wave as we come and go. Oh! I'll probably also continue to assess his dating patterns and habits. Get a glimpse into what men like him look for in women and relationships."

"Uh, yeah, that sounds super normal. Good luck with that." She stands up and tips her head toward the large front-facing window, she grins. "Prepare your neighborly wave, he's heading over here."

She wiggles her eyebrows. Then looks at the panic on my face and goes into problem-solving mode. "I'll get the door. You say as little as possible."

Jess bounds up the steps as Lauren opens the door to greet him. He looks directly at me.

"Hi! Thought I'd take you up on those peas, but I see you have company." He turns to Lauren. "Hey Lauren, nice to see you again."

"Hey, yeah it's been a little while." Lauren turns toward me. "Jess and I met through Taylor when he first moved here," she explains. "Not as entertaining a meeting as yours with Emma."

"Yes, it's never a dull run-in with her." He laughs. She laughs. Everyone is having a great laugh at my expense. Wonderful.

Lauren peers around Jess to a beefy, tall man who is standing at the bottom of my steps.

"Nice you meet you Emma. I'm Taylor, I work with Lauren, and am friends with this guy." He points to Jess. "Lauren." He nods to her and looks away.

Lauren hesitates, then takes off down the steps to chat with him. What?! Thanks a lot, best friend!

I shout to her, but she just mutters something about the school burglar.

Jess focuses back on me. "I came by to let you know about Stella, your other neighbor, who will likely be inviting you to her monthly book club she started up last year. Stella is also a part of a neighborhood watch type of program here called the Landry Life League. It's an odd, but integral part of the town. Stella knows everyone and everything that happens here. Going to book club would be a great way for you to introduce yourself and get to know people. I haven't had a chance to go yet, but I've heard it's fun, sophisticated, and intellectual." He shrugs. "Just a thought. You appear to be the book reading, analytical type." He winks at me playfully.

"Are you going to this next one?"

"No, not this one. I'll have to wait and see when the next one is scheduled." I nod, unsure what else to say.

He dips his head in farewell and starts back down my front step again.

"You know, if you like him, you could always ask him out. Dating, relationships, feelings. Those were three big things you wanted to include in your fresh start."

I consider this for a moment. "I don't think I'm quite ready for that yet, Lauren. I need some practice, observation, and I really need to figure out how to date."

"You can't just watch others date from afar." She shakes her head at me. "That's weird and creepy. How about we go out next weekend? I'm not interested in dating right now, as you know I haven't had the best luck lately. But I could help you either find someone or just get comfortable approaching and talking to guys. Baby steps."

I do need to put myself out there more and I won't know how to do that until I get some experience. Or at least collect some research.

~

"Oh sweetie, glad I caught you!" I look up to see Stella walking down Main Street right for me. She's speed walking again with her visor, her hand raised in a brief wave.

"Hi Stella." See? Normal. Why can't I be normal around Jess?

"What are your plans this Thursday evening?" Her voice holds a level of excitement that makes me nervous.

"Well, I was going to—"

"You're coming over to our place for book club!" she interrupts, clasping her hands as if the matter is closed.

"Oh, Stella, thank you, but I don't think I can make it this week." I prepared for this, thanks to Jess.

"Nonsense! You are coming! I am taking you under my wing, introducing you to the town, helping you 'network'. Knowing faces and names for your financial advisor position at the bank is prudent, don't you think?" Oh, she's good. At my old job, communication was most often via email. Not in Landry.

"I haven't read the book. Or even know which book!"

She hands over the book. Where she had it stashed, I don't have a clue. "*All the Light We Cannot See* by Anthony Doerr. A moving novel about a German boy and a blind French girl in World War II. I can send you a link to the summary if you aren't able to finish it by Thursday. See you then!" She pats my arm and starts speed walking again. "Bring wine! Toodles, gorgeous!"

CHAPTER 5

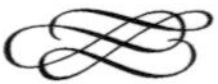

Emma

I gave the novel a quick skim a few days before the book club event. I have never taken part in a book club. Or any club, I guess. What do they discuss? After researching book club topics and major themes from the novel, I had topic notes and discussion questions ready.

I didn't bother asking Lauren to come with me as she has parent-teacher conferences tonight. Slipping out unnoticed may be easier this way.

I grab the book, my notes and discussion points, and head to Stella's.

I hear it before I even leave my front steps. Book club sounds suspiciously like a kegger.

That can't be right. My palms become sweaty.

I walk right into Stella and Greg's since no one can hear the door. It gets much louder as I make my way to the kitchen. I take in the people, music, drinks, and debauchery around me.

This is no book club. This is a rager in disguise.

That sneaky bastard. There's no way he didn't know what book club was.

As soon as I enter the kitchen, I set my bottles of wine on the counter, ready to head straight back out the front door, but get wrapped into a big Stella hug. "Oh, Emma, I'm glad you made it!" She introduces me to her friends, other neighbors, and local business owners. This event must be popular because even town council members are here.

I open my bottle of wine and pour a generous amount into a goblet.

I've discussed the book with only two people the whole evening so far. Most people are gossiping and socializing or talking about the 'Landry League' Jess mentioned. They haven't talked about or even brought the book.

I meet dozens of people, attempting to remember their names, and come up with small talk. Getting the same questions on repeat is tiresome. So far, I have two consultation appointments booked for next week, several coffees with ladies in different committees in town, and a few invitations for far more intimate meetings.

The music cuts out.

"Everyone, attention! Everyone, quiet!" Greg, Stella's husband, tries to round everyone up. "The official lightning round of book club will begin soon! Last names A - L on this side." He points to the side of his yard that is closest to my yard. "And last names M - Z on that side." He points closer to his own porch.

Everyone shuffles around, as do I, but with tremendous caution. I look around at my team and wonder what in holy hell is happening. I lean over to Margerie, a manager at the bank I work at, and ask her for details.

"Oh, it's the best part of book club. You'll see!" She winks at me. I give her wide eyes back. That's super cryptic, Margerie!

"We've all played this game before, so you should all—" Stella elbows him and nods in my direction. "Oh right, sorry, Emma. For those that haven't met Emma, she is a new resident to Landry, our next-door neighbor, and the bank's new financial advisor? Analyst? Sorry, honey, that stuff goes right over my head."

Great, more attention, I smile as my cheeks burn, raise my head, and give a stiff nod to the group.

"Emma, the lightning round has rapid-fire questions about the book." He laughs. "I bet you were wondering when we were going to get around to the book, weren't you?" Everyone laughs.

Yup, got me, Greg! At least it's a team game, so I'll just wait until it ends, then make my excuses and leave.

"We have chosen team captains, then rock/paper/scissors will decide the starting team." He looks over at me, "Emma, you are team captain for your side. It'll be easier to familiarize yourself with the game this way!" So much for just blending. I plaster a fake smile on my face, which he takes for agreement.

"Once we decide the starting team, we will have a series of questions or debates. The judges—Stella and I—will choose the best answers and the losing team must take a concession."

A smattering of chuckles echoes through the crowd. I'm about to ask what a concession is when Greg holds up a couple of bottles of Patrón. "Shot or Strip!"

I don't hear the rest of the instructions. Instead, I look for exits. I try disappearing. There's a whooshing sound in my ears, my heart is hammering, my head is spinning. I am not equipped to deal with this. This is not easing into the pools of social engagements, emotional and personal growth.

No, instead I was tossed in without a life jacket.

Jess

KNOCK KNOCK KNOCK.

I shoot up out of bed.

BANG! BANG! BANG! BANG!

There's someone at the door. Wait, there's someone at the door? At midnight on a Thursday evening? I pad over to the front door, peeking out the side window. I don't see anyone until I look at the porch floor. There's a tiny someone sitting with their back leaned against the door, hand raised, banging again.

I open the door and Emma falls backward, flopping onto my front entryway floor, book in hand. She's wearing a navy tank top, cherry red Bermuda shorts that clearly are not hers, and a skirt over top.

"You lousy, lying asshole!" she slurs from the floor. Trying to get up takes most of her energy and her balance is lacking.

Emma is drunk off her face.

I try to help her stand, but she swats my hands away.

"'Sophisticated.' 'Intellectual'." She sneers at me with a mocking tone. "Liar!" She points an unsteady finger in my face. "J'accuse!"

Book club. I grimace. I didn't know if she'd go, so I talked it up, hoping she would and it would help her socialize with the town a little. They've been curious about her and wondering why she keeps to herself so much.

Did I wonder for a moment how much she would hate it and how it might make us even for our last few encounters? Sure. Did I think it would be funny as shit? Definitely. I'm reconsidering looking at the state of her, though.

I smirk. "You didn't have a good time?"

"Does it look like I had a good time, Jess? Hmmm?" She's fuming.

She's a wreck, but still looks good to me. Long smooth legs, small but perky breasts, hair disheveled, chest heaving, eyes bright with anger. In my head, I laugh. She's an angry drunk tonight, but still very sexy.

This is never a factor with the schemes I engage in with my dad and brother.

"I guess that depends on our definitions of 'fun'."

"Dontchu be cute!" She's still pointing that finger at me like a weapon. "You *knew* what would happen there. I did s'many shots of tequila as I could until I couldn't feel my face. Or stand upright. Then I had to choose between naked or alcohol poisoning. I can't drink like Moe! He has at least a hundred pounds on me. I snuck on other people's clothes, layering up for the next question. I'm just smart like that." She gestures at herself and I take the time to look again.

"My team *sucked*! They only allow team captains to answer a maximum number of questions. I don't think anyone on my team read that damn book. Thank God there's the 'first to yack' rule that ends the game." By this time, she had wandered over to the couch and draped herself over it. "Once I gave Tony the Heimlich, he yacked, and it was game over!" She punctuated this by flopping her head on the couch pillow.

"Emma?" Jesus, I don't even know where to start. "This isn't your house. Need me to help you over to yours?" I go over to check on her. With closed eyes, she reaches out to find my face. What she believes is a soft caress is more of a light face slapping. Her fingers reach for and trace my lips as I call her name again.

She bites her own lip. "Mmm no, I'll stay here. Your couch is comfy. And your beautiful lips are so soft." She keeps touching them and then opens her eyes to look at me as she whispers, "and your eyes are hypnotic. Did you know that about your eyes?"

Her gaze wanders to the rest of me as if she is just now noticing that I am only wearing plaid pajama pants.

"Oh! You even have that 'V' abs thing that leads to your man treasure! Of *course* you do." She flicks a look back to my eyes and laughs at my shocked face. "What do you have in your treasure chest, Jess? Oh! Maybe we should share our treasure chests."

Holy shit. Don't get excited, don't get excited. She doesn't know what she's saying.

"Emma, that sounds pretty fucking fantastic, but I'm sure you'd regret that in the morning."

She is still looking at me, licking her lips as her hand wanders my chest, not touching, but just barely. She looks up at me in question. I suck in a breath and catch her hand in mine, chuckling.

"Emma...."

Her other hand wanders now, picking up where the first stopped.

"May I?"

I nod while entranced. She gets just to the waistband of my plaid sleep pants before I shake myself alert in time to catch that one too.

"Spoilsport!"

Adorable.

I pull myself away and get her a puke bucket, a glass of water, a blanket, and Tylenol for the morning. By the time I return, she's out. I watch her sleep for a moment, then shift her hair out of her eyes, fingers lingering on her cheek. She's filled out more in the last few weeks. She looks great, but I shouldn't be staring at her while she's asleep on the couch.

I head to my room to get a decent sleep before she wakes, and I get to experience the consequences of Emma's actions tonight.

CHAPTER 6

Emma

Someone is sitting on my head, and my stomach is on fire. No, that doesn't make sense. Why do I feel so awful? My tongue could file nails with how rough it feels. I peek an eye open and see an empty room. No one is sitting on me, but I am acutely aware of the fact that I am not home.

What in the hell happened last night?

Patrón. Freaking Patrón and book club and my team of illiterate imbeciles.

It all comes flooding back to me. The details I hoped to forget.

I thought I'd wandered back home last night after being unable to sort out my own clothes from the ones I pilfered at the party. Yes, I stayed. This too was an experience I needed, and I learned more than I anticipated.

I go to the window to get my bearings. Huh, it's my street, that's good. There's the walking path right across from the driveway, the street sign, my rental car, and out front is Jess's truck.

Oh my god. I'm in Jess' house!

No. No, no, no! I came over to yell at him. Groaning and trying to smother my face, hoping it will undo everything I did and said. I had my hands on him. Said 'our treasure chests should meet'.

No, wait, I told him we should share treasure chests. Oh, sweet sugar-tit.

Why didn't my brain kick in and say, 'keep it in your pants, Emma! You know what unwanted sexual advances feel like!'. Am I a sexual harasser? My stomach has another reason to revolt.

I take comfort in remembering that he gave no signs my advances were unwanted. I even asked permission, and he nodded at me. Regardless, I am so ashamed, I just want to go crawl into a hole. Or my own bed.

I need to apologize, no matter how awkward it will be. Old Emma would grab her things and race out of this house, hoping never to see or hear from him again.

New Emma, who is learning, growing, feeling, and working on becoming her best self, she needs to face this situation and smooth things over.

Coffee! I'll make him coffee and breakfast! As an apology. It will help in redeeming myself and keep his mouth occupied so we don't have to talk about what happened.

I look down at what I am wearing, readjust the ill-fitting shorts/skirt combo and notice my thin tank top is covering very little, I use the throw blanket like a shawl and make my way to the kitchen. I grab some eggs and cheese from the fridge hoping I can whip together something resembling omelets.

In a wonderful surprise, the final product looks quite edible. Although, the smell of cooking eggs almost got me. I heaved over the kitchen garbage twice, ate a chunk of bread, drank some coffee and hoped it would pass. How do people drink to excess regularly?

As I am washing up the dishes, my obnoxiously sexy neighbor walks in.

I blush a deep red and greet him, "Good morning!" I temper my smile to convey seriousness. "I am so sorry!"

He looks at me, face scrunched, leaning against the counter.

"For which part?"

"All of it!" I think. "Well, except the part where I called you a lousy, lying asshole… that was justified."

"Fair enough." He looks around me. "What's for breakfast? And what's up with the blanket? Are you cold??"

"Omelets! I've never made them before, so hopefully they're edible." Then I wave a hand over the blanket. "I borrowed this as a shawl to cover my lack of proper attire." I look at it, realizing the blanket has egg goop on the front. "Oh no, I'm so sorry! I'll have it cleaned and bring it back good as new!"

He just stares at me. Maybe he doesn't like eggs?

"You're not going to eat?" I ask, disappointed.

"Oh, don't worry, I'll eat." A smirk takes over his face. "With my beautiful, soft lips…"

My gasp of indignation turns into a sharp glare. How dare he use my own drunken words against me!

I may not have flirting skills, but my blurting skills are strong.

"I… you…" I huff out a breath. "Why? Why would you bring that up?" Astonishment lacing my tone.

He shrugs and chuckles while he chews his omelet.

I lunge for the plate, but he's faster. "That breakfast constituted a silent and binding agreement to not rehash last evening's humiliating events. You have forfeited your omelet, sir!"

I make another grab for the plate. He holds it higher.

I reach again, without success. Sighing, I hold my hands up, feigning defeat.

Jumping as high as I can, I knock off the fork. A second attempt also fails. I land with a growl, not enjoying losing this battle due to genetics. I look up at the breakfast betrayer, his plate now creeping downward as he bends over in laughter at my attempts.

I swipe the plate out of his loosened grip, turn around, and toss the omelet into the sink. "You should have just eaten the damn omelet, Green Eyes."

Then I walk out his front door.

• • •

Jess

"Did you rub one out on this blanket, dude? Fuck!" Taylor heaves the throw blanket across the room.

"It's egg. Emma came over and made omelets. She's a bit of a disaster."

"Wait, did you sleep with her?" Eyes wide, waiting for details, Taylor leans forward. "This better not come back to bite me in the ass, Jess. You getting closer to Emma, puts you closer to Lauren. Don't fuck it up."

"No. I, uh, may have encouraged her to go to Stella's book club, and she got a little wasted."

"Man, that's cruel. That 'book club' is insane. I've attended once, which was one time too many." He looks traumatized. "It ends in nudity. I left before Martin could get both legs out of his pants." He shudders. "You ever been? I'm sure Stella invites you."

I grimace. "Yeah, she says she gets requests for me to go. Which is weird as fuck. But no, I've never gone. I've seen parts of it from my deck, though." I quickly count the months I have left here. "I've only got about six months left in Landry, then I'll head back to San Francisco for a while."

"We'll see. Maybe Garrett and I can convince you to stay. Come on, it's not so bad, is it?" He sets his phone and keys on the coffee table, settling in on the couch.

It wasn't. I actually love the area and the people in this town. I'm just not ready to set down roots again. It builds hope and expectation.

"No, but I'm not looking for forever here. Even if I was, Taylor, you're not my type." He laughs, glancing across the room at the blanket again.

"So, how did her being wasted result in an egg blanket?" Good question.

"She was, uh, upset about my inaccuracies in describing book club." A guilty smile spreads across my face. "Around midnight she came banging on my door, used a bunch of colorful words to describe my character, felt me up, then passed out on the couch."

Taylor perked up at that one particular part I tried to breeze past.

"She must have felt guilty in the morning because she made me an omelet." I shrug.

"What?!?" he shouts.

He sits up straight. "Okay, so she drunkenly felt you up, and you did what?"

"Nothing happened. She was totally wasted. She literally fell into the house when I opened the door." I look at him, my face stern. "Plus, she's my neighbor and a bit odd. I mean, it would be funny as hell if she meant to do half the things she does. She mentioned being homeschooled and you can tell, man."

I don't mention that I found these unintentional blunders amusing. And adorable. Adorable is dangerous. Good sex and no commitments is much safer. I have a feeling Emma wouldn't be the type for that kind of arrangement.

"Okay, good, fine." He nods, thinking. "But again, the egg on the blanket?"

"She had to wear it to make breakfast and made a mess."

"Why did she have to wear it to make breakfast?"

"Because she was only wearing a nearly see-through top and someone else's shorts from the party." I grin.

He smiles at me. "She yelled at you, felt you up, passed out on your couch, and made breakfast for you while only partly dressed?"

"Garrett's couch. She passed out on Garrett's couch. And she was technically fully clothed." I point out.

"Not the point, my man."

"What?" I ask. "It's not a big deal. I have girls over here plenty."

"They don't usually stay, though. You only have sex. Yet you've already had breakfast with Emma." He waggles his brows at me and takes a big swig of his beer.

My phone buzzes with a text. I ignore Taylor and check my phone. It's my mom. She's been in Italy for a couple of weeks now, and I haven't heard much from her.

MOM: Ciao, Jesse!

She always reverts more heavily to intermingled English and Italian after spending time with her family.

MOM: The ladies have been keeping me up to date on Landry on-goings. Mrs. Henderson tells me you have una ragazza a casa.

Shit. Landry Life League is really on their game lately. Great, now Mom thinks I have a girlfriend when I definitely do not. And no wishing on her part is going to make that magically happen.

MOM: I can see you are reading my texts, tesoro.
MOM: I was told she stayed for prima colazione.

She was technically *here* for breakfast but she did not *stay* for breakfast. And how the hell would she know that? I glare at Taylor. He's trying to read the texts over my shoulder.

"Did you do this? Did you sic my mom on me?"

He raises his hands. "Dude, no. I just found out and my phone has been there the whole time." He points to it on the coffee table.

ME: Mamma, how is Italy? You sound well. Did you hear Mrs. Davis caught the kid that was painting those rocket ships on her fence?

They weren't rocket ships and the whole town knows it.

MOM: Si, I am happy for her. She is getting that boy to repaint her fence and her shutters. I almost wish someone would paint

rocket ships on my fence so I could get someone to do all the painting.
ME: No, you don't, Mamma.
MOM: Do not distract me. Who is the girl? Is this the one you will bring to the BBQ? Maybe someone you met around town?
ME: There's no girl. One of my neighbors wandered over here last night, I let her sleep on the couch, she went home in the morning. Sorry to disappoint you.
MOM: Ah. I see. Well, that was kind of you. You deserve to be with a nice woman, that's all I can hope for.
MOM: Tell me about your neighbor. Is she the new girl that's working at the bank? The pretty, shy, quiet one? Margerie says she likes her. Sweet girl, smart, but maybe a little unused to the friendly but nosey type of community Landry is.
ME: That sounds accurate.

The less I say, the better right now.

MOM: I can't wait to meet her. And whatever girl you bring to the BBQ. When I get back, we will be talking about what you are doing with all these women—especially the ones you see out of town. Don't think I don't know about all that. Your father and I want better for you. You lost a part of yourself after that woman. Ashleigh. We are clearing the air. You'll get it off your chest, then put it behind you. No more ridiculousness. Please, cuore mio.

Right. As if just settling down with someone, anyone, will make everything better.

ME: We can talk when you and Dad are back. But I'm doing fine, Mamma. You might not like how I decide to date, but it's my life.
MOM: You are right. I do not like it. You were not this way before. You are not happy, your Mamma knows these things.

Time to try it my way, I think. What is the downside, Jess? You meet a few lovely young women that Mrs. Henderson and I find for you? Make your mamma happy and just open your mind and heart to trying this for me. And for you.
MOM: I will call tomorrow, to check in and so Tia Elena can talk with you. Think about what I said. Miss you lots. XXOO

"How's Mamma Millie?" Taylor asks.

"She's meddling and being fed targeted information from the Landry Life League spies." I toss him my phone and let him read our conversation.

"I mean, she's not wrong here, man," says the traitor.

I leave the room.

"Where ya going, Jess?" He pauses. "Oh, come on, man. It's nice. Your mom loves you and wants you happy. And she's going to find a nice girl for you. Or Mrs. Henderson will." He laughs.

Looks like I'll just have to keep my distance from the pretty girl next door and the rest of the women in and around town. I wouldn't want those Leaguer spies to get any wrong ideas.

~

I've signed the last form for my investment portfolio at the bank, when I see Emma walking toward reception. This is one of only a few banks within thirty minutes of Landry, so I should have known chances were high she'd work here. Keeping my distance lasted less than a week.

She makes a low-pitched growl sound at the printer and starts button mashing. Margerie notices the mounting frustration from her coworker and excuses herself to help.

All I can hear from my position at the reception desk is low murmuring. Then Emma hits the printer. Feisty.

I walk around the desk and approach the two ladies. One wound all the way up, the other wringing her hands in sympathy.

"Ladies, can I help?"

Margerie goes to respond, but Emma holds out a hand. Her back straightens as she gives me her sternest look.

"Are you a qualified technician?"

"Not technically. But I am a software developer and IT specialist. I can probably handle a small printer issue."

Her eyes narrow at my 'small printer issue' comment.

I check the printer settings, then ask to see her computer. We move to her office and I settle myself down at her laptop. Her browser window is open and I'm surprised to see my own Instagram profile staring back at me. I don't even get the opportunity to close the window before she slams the laptop lid shut.

"Damn, you almost got my fingers!" I look at her with dramatized alarm.

"Sorry! I just—let me just… give me one minute with this before you work your magical tech fingers on it!" She swipes the laptop away and starts clicking away.

"Magical fingers, huh?" I grin.

"Tech fingers! Magical *tech* fingers!" she corrects. I wonder how long it's been since she's experienced any downstairs magic. She seems wound up regularly.

After she finishes shutting down her browser tabs, she hands over the laptop. I reconnect her printer, correct a few settings, and within minutes, all is well.

"Okay. All done here. You should be good to print." She heaves a sigh of relief and gives me a grateful smile.

"Thanks, Jess. Really." She twists her lips in contemplation. "Maybe we could start over? Put our awkward run-ins aside and be friends?" she offers.

"I'd like that." I make my way across her office, grab the doorframe and turn to face her. "Oh, and Emma. Since we're friends, let me know if you ever want to learn how to clear your browser history, you know, just in case." I wink at her and hightail it out of the bank.

CHAPTER 7

Emma

I decided that my small-town nervousness and uncertainty need to meld with the fierce, confident, and sharp personality I maintained in the corporate world. I am choosing to let go of the negatives of my past and focus on the future. The self-defense class is helping a lot. As a perk, my ass is more shapely and my arms are strong and looking good in my new sleeveless summer dresses.

Who is this woman who stumbles through regular conversation, can't buy a goddamn bag of peas without humiliating herself? And why is she endlessly intrigued by a certain neighborhood ladies' man?

I'm not sure, but I am fixing it. Am I confident in the ways of relationships? No. Definitely not. Do I understand men? Nope. Do I even understand myself? Not yet, but I will soon. Am I confident about sex? Yes, and no. Sex has never been an issue, but I recognize that the emotional connection is the integral part missing.

It's been well before I was attacked that I've been physical with a man. The vivid, sensual sex dreams I've had the last few weeks have been a surprise.

One recently jolted me from a dead sleep, uncertain what's

sparking them, but hoping it's the changes in my life. Opening myself up to feelings, thoughts, and experiences I previously shoved to the recesses of my mind.

Last night's carnal dream was all subtle touches, playful looks, blazing green eyes, and a kiss that awoke me with a jolt.

I try not to analyze it too deeply and am just glad for the progress. My list of life reparations and goals now includes companionship. And not merely the friendship, community, connecting with other human beings type of companionship. I want to build a life with someone, share and grow with them. The full relationship experience.

However, in past experiences, men aren't able to handle me for very long. Which was how I preferred it, anyway. I had never put myself out there or attempted any attachments. In fact, I did my best to ward them off. Typically, by being cold, dismissive, and aloof.

Most of the men I had intimate relationships with agreed to the sex-only arrangement I insisted upon. However, in the few times men have shown extended interest, it would usually end with, 'I don't think this is going to work out, Emma. We are very different' or 'I'm looking for someone a bit more easygoing' or a mumbled, 'So this is why they call you the Em-bot…'

Last, but not least I've gotten, 'Geez, Emma, do you have any feelings at all?'. Yes, Greg, I do! I've kept all my feelings shoved deep inside for so long I don't know how to use them, so they come out in awkward bursts. At least I don't have a raging case of gingivitis, Greg!!

I think Lauren and I will go out tonight. I need to work on my conversational and flirting skills. It can't go worse than it has with Jess, so my night is looking up.

"ou want to go to a bar? In Santa Rosa?" She smacks a hand on my forehead, pretending to take my temperature.

"Yes, Laur. I need practice. Flirting, dancing, engaging in conversation and social activity." I am firm and she nods.

"Okay. Well, how about we start smaller? Let's go somewhere local, that way we are closer to home in case it's a bust. There's a Teachers & Tequila event organized for tonight, so a few coworkers will be at Taps. Evan has come up with new theme nights and tonight's is Honky Tonk. Should be a hoot!" She cringes. "I'll be the responsible sober driver, while you absorb all the 'social activity' you want!" She's already a flurry of motion, texting, grabbing items from my closet.

"I decide what you wear. And we will go over some bar basics and interacting tips. Okay?" Lauren waits until I agree then adds, "Whatever your first instincts are tonight, ignore them." She smirks and mumbles, "This should be interesting."

Lauren dresses me in a dark cobalt dress. The top shows a plunging cowl neck with thin straps. I move to put on a strapless bra and Lauren apologizes, knowing I won't like what she is about to say, and then informs me that 'this is not a dress you wear a bra with'.

I've never encountered such a dress, but now feel naked as my breasts just do whatever the heck they want. In the dress, out of the dress, it's just semantics. Lauren finishes my 'look' with cowboy boots.

I leave my hair down in a sexy tousled style.

"Good?" I twirl, hoping the makeover is complete, as we've been at it for an hour.

"Perfect!"

Then she frowns and puts a hand on my shoulder. "You hate crowds, talking to strangers, and trying to pick up on social queues. You ready for this?"

I nod, taking a breath, "Yes, understood. I think I need this as a type of immersion therapy. It can build confidence, instill self-assurance, and it may be the best way to get past what that slimy bastard did to me."

Confident, but still nervous, I'm glad I have my best friend with me.

"You'll help me, right? Don't leave me alone, ok?"

"Of course, hon." She adjusts my dress straps once more and hurries me to her SUV.

"Oh, I forgot to ask. Who is coming?"

"Cassie from work, Dani from the bakery, and Sadie who is another teacher friend, but she teaches at the elementary school, and a bunch of other teachers."

"Alright, let's do this. I have talking points in my phone, but do you think I should write them out so it doesn't look like I'm checking social media or something while I'm supposed to be engaging in conversation?"

Lauren tilts her head at me, curses under her breath, then guides me into the passenger seat without answering my question.

Jess

Jesus Christ, that dress.

I have a bad feeling about tonight. I'm not sure if liquor will help or hurt my current situation, but I know I have to stop staring at Emma. I should have positioned myself farther away and not a few barstools down from her, gawking and eavesdropping.

Taylor is doing his 'teacher talk' thing with his coworkers and has barely noticed my shitty conversation skills tonight.

Emma is not the fuck buddies type. I'm fairly confident she's the full-on relationship type. That's not me. Not anymore. I know this, I've come to terms with it and yet, my neighbor still intrigues me too damn much. She's awkward, odd, and in the middle of some kind of life crisis. She is not a casual woman.

Yet, I cannot tear my eyes off of her as she takes part in some kind of social experiment.

She walks up to complete strangers and starts up a conversation. From afar, this seems normal, but for her, there are two notable exceptions.

One, the topics of conversation are eclectic: geothermal heating, something about asset amortization, enology (the science of winemaking, yeah, I learned this from eavesdropping during our 'wild honky-tonk night'), and several one-liners that never land and are mostly just confusing. She may believe pickup lines are to pick up friends or to 'pick up' the conversation. I only wish I didn't find it so fucking adorable.

The second exception: she has to give herself a short pep talk before each conversation and has Lauren hover around waiting to be tagged in for help.

She smiles at herself when she believes the exchange went well. I smile with her, not able to help myself.

Then later, I see her pointing out a guy's uneven sideburns, using her phone to show him the difference. The man just walks away, leaving Emma's face pinched in confusion.

It's the social equivalent of a car wreck.

As entertaining as she's been, I should focus on my own group of friends. I also had hopes of finding an attractive woman to go home with tonight.

I scope out the dance floor, looking for Taylor and a few of his teacher friends while trying to avoid looking directly at Emma and her flailing dance moves. I spot Taylor off to the side watching Lauren, fists clenched, eyes dark. Jealousy. Not a pretty look.

There are a couple of younger guys dancing with the ladies. Or at least I assume they are younger as they are leaner, wiry, but they seem to dance well and the ladies are enjoying that. Taylor loses the war with himself and wanders over to the women.

Emma is taking this outing quite seriously, but from what I've seen so far, she can't two-step to save her life. Still, she seems to thoroughly enjoy it.

I am drinking, taking in the rest of the crowd, when something shimmery blue pops up in my peripheral vision. It's Emma winding her way toward me. Shit.

"Are you going to just stand here by yourself? Come dance with us! Or are you on the prowl, watching for a woman who may appreciate temporarily enjoying your company?" She smirks at me. Upping the sass tonight, I see. I think all the prowling she's been doing has left her feeling more confident.

I roll my eyes at her. She grabs my arm and drags me over to where they are on the dance floor.

The music theme is far outside of my usual taste, but I appreciate it when they play modern country versus the classic honky-tonk style that is currently playing. She dances wildly to a song about tears in beers, enjoying the sense of freedom that dancing encourages. She dances with total abandon. It's ridiculous. And mesmerizing.

The music changes to something by a female country singer, her voice sounding vaguely familiar.

Emma gets closer and laughs at me, "Oh, come on, everyone knows this song! It won't hurt you to dance to it." That's when I realize I'm no longer moving. I was just watching her, unable to do anything more than stare.

I need to get a grip. I give myself a mental shake and start moving again. She comes closer to me, closing her eyes and dances in front of me. "I get why people like to go to bars and dance. It's fun. I don't think I'm very good at it though."

Yearning glitters in her eyes as she watches couples two-stepping with ease.

I hold out a hand, offering to two-step with her. She bites her lip. "I don't know how to two-step."

"Come on, I'll show you." What am I doing? My two-step is only slightly better than hers, if I'm being honest.

She hesitates. "Alright. You'll need to provide dance skill feedback. I'm here to learn."

I pull her in, guiding her hand to my shoulder, then sliding a hand around her waist and pulling her closer. She smooths her hand along my arm, swaying, unsure at first, then gives herself another hushed pep talk. She takes one more scan of the crowd and starts mimicking their moves. I guide her and give her a few tips, whispering the steps to her as we find a rhythm that works.

Knowing she doesn't have much two-step experience and won't know how badly I fumble the moves, I add a few spins and swing moves. Taken by surprise, she throws her head back and laughs, beaming her contagious smile at me.

Emma turns around and wraps my arms around her, mimicking what other couples are doing. Her ass brushes my dick every few seconds and I'm trying not to react. Baseball. Grandma. Head cheese. Nope, I'm out.

She leans the rest of the way back so that her back rests against my chest, holding her up as she sways against me. Fuck. How is it that normal dancing is beyond her capabilities, but for this sexy version of country swing dancing, she's some kind of expert?

She turns again and presses her chest against mine, tilts her head back to look up at me. She squeals, "I totally nailed that spin move thing! Almost as good as Lauren's friend Sadie!"

I bring her closer.

"Better. Although, I'm a little biased since I'm the lucky recipient of your spin move."

She's looking up at me, a blush tinting her cheeks, lips parted, heated eyes. We breathe the same air, faces mere inches apart thanks to her boots.

I can't kiss her.

Wait, why again?

The song ends and I snap out of it, easing her an arm's length away from me. "You picked that up pretty fast, Em." I give her a weird smile. Why is my face doing that? I need to get off the dance floor. "I'm going to go grab a drink." I hitch a thumb toward the bar and take another step away.

"Oh. Ummm..." She thinks as she wipes her forehead, eyes trying to refocus. I wonder if she even knows how hot that dance was. "Okay, well, thank you. I should probably go mingle." She gives me a tight smile and darts away.

As I approach the bar, I see the strawberry blonde in a smoking hot red dress who has been eyeing me for the last half hour. Pegging her for a tourist, I walk over and start chatting with her, buy her a drink, and see if she's what I'm looking for. Isn't this the game we always play? Flirt, assess, check for chemistry.

I can't help my gaze from wandering, looking for a certain raven-haired disaster. She's a couple of tables away talking to Stefan, a math teacher friend of Taylor's. She's showing him something on her phone, raising her voice so he can hear her above the music.

"Well, actually municipal by-laws state that seventy-two hours is the maximum allotted time for parking in that zone. So, I'd have to disagree with you, Stephen. Want me to send you a link to the by-law ordinances? Then you'd also have my number, if you ever needed it. Or wanted it. Or something."

The way she can take flirting to such cringe-worthy levels is impressive.

"It's Stefan, not Stephen."

I wince. She mutters an apology and asks if he still wants the link. Or just her number. My mouth twitches as I appreciate her moxie. I don't think Emma has ever hit on anyone, ever, until tonight. And I can't even be sure that's what she's doing right now.

I hear a scoff behind me and see the redhead I had forgotten about disappear into the crowd.

Emma wanders over to me at the bar.

"How's the mingling going?" I pry.

"Not sure. I think I'm striking out. My conversation topic ideas are a bit of a miss."

She looks so dejected, I say something utterly stupid.

"If it makes you feel any better, they grabbed my attention. Actually, I think you've had my attention most of the night."

"Oh. Really? Have you been watching me?" She leans toward me, flirting. Maybe it's the practice she's had tonight or the fact that some part of me happens to be way into her, but it's working.

"Tried not to, but between that dress and your mind-boggling, pre-planned talking points, I've been in awe."

Compliments with a hint of sarcasm. Not sure if this is the best tactic to use on someone like Emma.

She tilts her head at me. "Are you making fun of me?"

I lean in closer and smooth the crease between her brows. She freezes.

"Not even a little. Don't doubt yourself. Don't strive to impress anyone. Just be you. You're captivating. Let that work to your advantage."

She stares at me, her face softening, her gaze making a slow trek to my mouth.

"Jess, I need a partner for darts," Taylor shouts from a few feet away, startling us both. He's standing there, a smug grin taking over his face.

Lauren pops up out of nowhere, smacking Taylor on the arm and shoving him away from us.

Clueing into what our friends are assuming is happening, I mutter something about seeing her around. She nods, but her gaze remains on my mouth.

Taylor came over on purpose. Starting something with Emma would be pretty stupid for a lot of reasons, so I should walk away.

~

I suck at darts and Taylor knows it, so he shouldn't have been surprised that we lost. Doesn't stop him from grumbling about it and chirping at our opponents for a rematch. Thinking of heading home, I check around for the ladies. Seeing if maybe they need a ride home since we are headed to the same place.

My gaze lands on Lauren, but she is shouting at some guy and trying to manhandle him out of the way. I don't see Emma.

"Taylor!" He's already seen her and is pushing past the dart players. I keep looking for Emma, wondering why she isn't with Lauren.

I catch a glimpse of that blue dress over by the doors as some guy has his arm thrown around her, leading her out. Huh. I'm not sure what I'm more surprised at, that Emma managed to pick someone up so smoothly that they are already headed home together or that she left her best friend behind for a guy.

Nah, she wouldn't do that.

I make it to them just before they reach the doors and hear Emma's raised voice say, "Again, I didn't say you could touch me."

"Babe, you were the one flirting with me. You want my hands on you, so don't be one of those girls." Oh, hell no. He must be new here, because this kind of shit doesn't happen in Landry. Or at least not for long.

I shout in their direction, getting his attention. "You new, asshole? Because I believe she made it clear she didn't want you touching her." I grab his arm and wrench it away from her.

He steps up to me. "Not your concern, back off. We were just talking. Emma here was going to tell me about, uh, her love of gardening. Everything is fine here, so fuck off."

"No, I believe I said I was going to *plant* my foot in your groin if you didn't stop dragging me around. Not exactly gardening and it would likely yield infertile crops."

Huh. She jokes. At a time like this? And about debilitating a man's sperm 'crops'?

He grabs her arm again, and I lunge forward anticipating his dick move, but it's too late.

Killer Emma attacks and it's a glorious sight. She steps forward quickly, stomping on his foot. He shouts in pain, loosening his grip on her arm. With a quick grab of his wrist, she steps toward his opposite side, turns and with a quick hip toss, slams him into the floor. His arm is still up and locked in her grip, one cowboy boot pressed against the back of his shoulder for leverage.

I'm immobile for a moment as I take in what just happened. Then all hell breaks loose.

"You fucking crazy cock tease! Let me go now!" the asshole says as he tries to fight the position. A few of the bar staff are making their way over, including Evan. I'm gonna catch so much shit from him later.

I reach over and angle Emma's grip sharper so the prick can feel that zing of pain that tells him his arm could be easily broken in this position and he should shut his fucking mouth.

After a brief explanation, the staff throws Kurt aka Asshole out on his ass and lets him know he's no longer welcome at Taps & Tapas. Lauren ends up driving Emma home and I head out right after them.

CHAPTER 8

Emma

The car ride home was focused on reviewing the evening's events.

Before we even walk through my door, there are more questions.

"Can I move on to the other part of the evening?" Her eyes are wide and begging me, but unsure how hard to push.

"The dancing? The flirting? I know, I'm a mess."

"Yes, the dancing. But not the carefree crazy flapping you were doing."

"Did I not dance enough?"

"Cut the crap, Emma." She smirks again. "Jess."

That dance was so freaking hot I thought I was having an out-of-body experience. It wasn't even a sexy dance. I mean, the theme was Honky Tonk, so it was mostly country music, but I could feel him. Every part of him and that was enough.

I shiver and can feel my cheeks heating just thinking about it again. At the end, when his ragged breath fluttered across my mouth, I thought I might lose all control of my legs. He smelled amazing, felt amazing, and looked amazing. I can't even come up with adjectives anymore. I'm at a loss.

And I now understand the premise of *Footloose*. Dancing leads to sex. Or, at the very least, sexy thoughts.

It took me a long time to recover after our dance. Once my brain caught up to what he was saying, I snapped out of it. He was trying to escape, politely.

"Not much to tell." I feign indifference. "We danced for one song, then he went to get a drink with the tall redhead." I brush it off, but Lauren knows me well. I'm sure she saw every single thought on my face.

"Oh, really? Because as soon as I mentioned his name, you went somewhere else in your head. You were giving me 'fuck me' eyes, but I assume that look was for Jess?" She gives me her mocking stare, chin perched on her fist.

"Nope. I want you, Lauren. Let's do this."

"Funny. I'm liking this new Emma more and more…"

We are quiet for a while as I reflect on our night.

"What do I do, Lauren?"

She chews her lip, thinking. "I don't think you need to do much of anything. In case you missed the look on his face while you were dancing, he was eye-fucking you the whole time. To give in to a man giving me a look like that…. Wooo!"

Lauren had steered clear of the opposite sex tonight, instead talking to friends and dancing circles around the rest of us.

"Be serious."

"I am. So... what are you going to do? What do you want to do?"

It's a deeper question than she probably intended. I wanted feelings, connections, and to put myself out there because that's how you get what you want. For my career, I held nothing back. I was singularly focused on my objective and systematically achieved exactly what I wanted from that life.

Until I came to the realization that my career, my life, was not at all what I wanted. It took being physically attacked, harassed, and a good amount of self-reflection in therapy to come to this conclusion. Now that I have, why wouldn't I put that same effort and vigor into achieving the vastly different but fulfilled life I crave?

My eyes snap to Lauren's and I give her a lopsided grin.

"What? You're freaking me out. I have never seen that look on your face. What is happening?"

My eyes are in fact wild, but determined. Just wait until she sees what I am going to do. I'm not running away anymore, I'm not pushing my feelings aside. I am going to do what Lauren has been trying to get me to do since our teens. Jess can definitely show me what dating is all about. This is the next logical step in my progression toward change.

Right?

Too late now, my plan is in motion.

I run to the door, hearing, "Shit!" from behind me and some stumbling as she attempts to follow me, but I keep going.

"Stay here. I'll be right back," I shout behind me.

I am off the porch, rushing across my lawn, and realize I forgot to put shoes on. No time to stop, I'll lose my nerve.

I climb up his porch steps and bang on his door.

I don't see any lights and don't hear anyone. I knock louder and peer through the side window.

I see him! He's already shirtless, getting ready for bed. Focus, Emma, eyes up!

He looks confused as he answers the door. "Emma? What's wrong?" He looks around, spotting Lauren on the porch, wide-eyed and clinging to the porch rail, not missing a single second.

"First, I wanted to thank you for stepping in earlier when you thought I might have been in trouble."

"Yeah, of course. That guy was a piece of shit, and you shouldn't have had to deal with that. You had him handled, though." He nods, then his face changes and he moves back abruptly, trying to put distance between us. "Goodnight, Emma."

I place a hand on the doorjamb. "I think our dance should have had a different ending."

"Emma." A warning.

I step closer, now less than a foot away from him, and he is clutching the door, bracing himself. Smart man. Especially since I am trembling with uncertainty and nerves, so he may need to hold us both up in a moment.

I slide up against him and get on my tiptoes, lifting my face to his.

A low, soft, frustrated breath rumbles in his naked chest. I beam up at him, covering my hesitancy, then slowly, so as not to spook him, I inch closer to his mouth and brush my lips across his. His hands move to grip my waist. Mine settle on his bare shoulders, then I feather my fingers along his chest.

"Kiss me," I try to demand, but it comes out as more of a question.

My eyes pop up to his, and that's when I see his resistance snap.

He wraps his arms around me and lifts me to meet his hungry mouth. I drink him in, kissing with everything I have. Only a fool prioritizes breathing over this smooth, magical mouth.

His tongue sweeps across my lower lip, and I open. My mouth is exploring his and I can't get enough. Then it's nipping the corner of his upper lip before I swipe the spot with my tongue. My hands are in his hair, oh that hair. Long enough to have a slight hint of a wave, but shorter on the back and sides. I grip it with one hand while I hold on to his immense bicep for dear life with the other hand.

His hands roam my back and make a slow trek to my ass. At first, he just cops a feel of my newly toned backside, but then he grabs it roughly and pulls me against him, lining up the parts of us that are begging for attention.

I gasp, "Unn mmmm." What word I was going for, I have no idea. My mouth is only good for one task right now.

He eases me down, lips still on mine. He lifts his head, severing our connection.

My body sucks in air now that it doesn't have to extract it from remnants in my body cells. I can see that he is similarly affected and I grin in satisfaction. We stare at each other as our breathing returns to normal.

Then through the heavy breathing and pounding hearts, we hear, "Wow. Hot!" Lauren comments from her spectator spot on my porch as she goes back inside muttering about needing a cold shower.

I laugh, nervously. "So that was…"

My mouth is still refusing the communication aspect of its job.

"Uh, yeah." He is scrubbing his fingers through his hair.

"Okay, then. Good." Good, what? Come on, brain! Mouth! Are there any parts on board unaffected by hormones?

I walk back to my house, but stop and turn to him again.

"I had fun tonight. Even before… this." I gesture between him and me. He stares at me, speechless. My feet continue their journey to my front door. He is still in his doorway, looking at me.

I give a small wave and then shut the door.

"Holy. Shit. Emma."

I collapse against my door and slide all the way to the floor.

"I may have to change my panties. I can only imagine what state yours are in!" She slips to the floor beside me.

"I've never done anything like that."

"Remember earlier when I said not to trust your instincts?" she asks, then flicks her hand. "Instinct privileges reinstated!"

I chuckle as I lean my head on her shoulder.

Jess

"I think our dance should have had a different ending."

It was a mistake giving into her sweet seduction, but damn, that one sentence had my blood pumping. Chances of me being able to turn away something I've been thinking about for a few weeks was slim. Her mouth was so soft, warm and tasted as sweet as fresh honeyed juice.

But she's not like the other women I typically see. She's a good girl who happens to be going through something. She wants a relationship, or will pretend at first, she doesn't, then bam! We end up having the relationship talk. Nope, not happening, I don't do serious and those curious hands and shining doe eyes are whispering 'love me'.

Grabbing my travel mug, I head out the door, locking it as I see Emma's door swing open and someone stumble out. Well, so much for my early morning avoidance idea.

"Hey. You're up early."

Lauren is walking toward me, hair a mess, face pale and free of makeup.

"You too."

And now I wait.

"So, are you getting out of here early to avoid Emma?"

The best friend, mama-bear talk. She's feeling me out and she's not subtle about it.

I try steering the conversation in a safer direction. "Nope, just have some work to do. What are you doing up this early?"

"Nuh-uh. We aren't talking about me, sweet cheeks."

Sweet cheeks, really?

"Look, Emma is awesome, the best really. As her best friend, I think you should know that she's been through some shit, and doesn't handle most people very well. Her dating history is... nearly nonexistent." She gives me the stink eye. "Then there's you with your colorful dating history. Women talk and it's a small town, so while I am pumped Emma is putting herself out there, I worry someone will take advantage or hurt her."

She walks closer, fists on her hips, then smiles at me with crazy eyes. It's fucking terrifying.

"But this is all new to her, so if you fuck this up or ruin her—I will destroy you. I may look like a wholesome, kind, shaper of young minds or whatever, but deep down, I am a savage."

Has Taylor seen this side of Lauren?

She takes a couple of breaths as I quickly send a text to Taylor about Lauren, hoping he can advise me how to make it stop. There's no way in hell I am breaking eye contact and alerting her to the fact that I was texting while she's giving me the gears so it ends up being, 'Laur. Scary. Help.' in three separate texts.

"Emma doesn't have a dad, mom, or siblings around to grill you or give you the 'don't hurt her' speech. But she does have me. And I don't pull any punches." Then she smiles a genuine smile, finally taking pity on me.

"Ummmm, okay." Unsure if it's safe to explain anything to her, I go for simple honesty. "Look, I don't tend to do relationships or commitments. I'm pretty sure Emma knows that. But I will talk to her. She'll decide what she's okay with. No surprises, completely up to her."

"Fair enough." She looks me up and down as my balls try to shrivel into non-existence under her scrutiny. She has a searing gaze and a genuine threat of violence about her.

"Well, I'm off to get coffee and prep for next week's classes." She walks away, but then turns. "Tonight, okay, Jess? She stews when she's worried about something."

I nod and get into my truck. We aren't even dating and I'm already in over my head. Part of me is adamant that I steer clear of this entire situation. The other part, the less reasonable part, wants to see what's between Emma and me.

~

"Dude, Lauren hovers on that hot-crazy line and this morning she was firmly in crazy territory," I tell Taylor over lunch.

"Uh, yeah." He's wearing a happy, lopsided smile that has me rolling my eyes. Jesus, he loves that she's a maniac. "When she cares about someone, she cares hard! I've seen her verbally destroy an eighteen-year-old football player who was being a dick to a freshman. She's a savage and… It. Is. Hot! Well, unless it's directed at you, then it's fucking terrifying. Still hot, though."

"You're just as insane as she is. She grilled and guilt-tripped me just hours after her best friend seduced me. We are not even together, so it's a nonissue."

"Hey, she's just being protective. Emma gave up a top-level, corporate position to move here and rebuild her life after some kind of trauma. Tread lightly."

This is news to me, which is evident by the look on my face.

"How did you find that out?"

"Lauren mentioned it back when we were still... whatever we were. She was really excited about Emma moving out here."

I nod, but I'm lost in thought, trying to figure out how to handle the Emma situation.

"Talk to her, I'm sure she'll tell you when she's ready."

"I will. I don't want to cause her any problems if she's going through something shitty."

I'm starting to wonder about the self-defense classes and pepper spray, hoping her trauma isn't what I think it might be.

She deserves more than what I can give. I've got less than five months left here, and then what? I'll leave and she will be alone again. She doesn't like people, but she seems to like me and that's a lot of pressure.

I won't be the one to let her down. I won't let myself get into that position.

And not just because Lauren will stab me in my sleep, but that's definitely a consideration.

Emma

My hangover has allotted me some extra time in bed this morning to ponder the events of last night.

By the time we got home, I wasn't slobbering drunk, but I was tipsy. Impulse control was out the window and a desire to be 'better, braver Emma' was in full effect. To connect, experience, and try something exciting and new.

I've only had sexual relations with a handful of men, but they were more of a transactional exchange of sexual needs than romantic. We both got what was required and kept our personal lives separate. After talking with Lauren and experiencing some small-town interactions, and the potential for real-life connections, I realize that I am missing out.

My sex life should be personal. Maybe 'should' is the wrong word. I want my sex life to be part of my personal life. I want everything I can get from future relationships.

Accomplishments stem from self-set goals, and now my goals have changed. And change is challenging. I moved, started a new low-stress job, and have been stumbling through finding the life I've always wished for. A real-life where I feel, experience, and integrate with others.

Today is a cooking day and I refuse to postpone it to lie in bed and overanalyze everything. Things like my failed attempts at flirting and socializing last night. Most guys didn't even realize I was trying to get their number until I bluntly asked for it. It's a good thing it was just practice.

My mind skips over to the most prevalent thought kicking around right now: how I kissed Green Eyes last night. What am I going to say? I didn't consider the repercussions, and we didn't make plans that would allow us to discuss what the kiss meant.

I shove those thoughts aside, not because I am avoiding them but because there's not much I can do about them right now. Plus, I'm learning to make lasagna today.

Maybe Jess would like some when it's done? I mean, at the very least, we're friends, right? Neighbors, for sure. A friendly, neighborly lasagna wouldn't be weird.

By the time I roll out of bed, it's almost midday, and I don't even know how long lasagna takes to make. I find a recipe online and make a grocery list. There have been no further embarrassing incidents at the grocery store, thankfully. Probably because I haven't seen Jess there again since our first meeting.

Jess doesn't appear to be the serious, settling down type. Knowing this, I still ran over there. Why? Because Lauren asked me what I wanted.

The answer was that I wanted to experience attraction and simply act on it. I wanted to connect with a man and see where it leads. Maybe Jess wasn't the best choice, but he has the experience of someone who could guide me through the harrowing task of dating.

As I arrive back home, I notice Jess's truck is still not in his driveway. Lauren said that she ran into him when she left early this morning. Maybe he's using my beloved avoidance coping mechanism today, too.

I bring all the groceries in with my usual 'one-trip' strategy, just able to get a couple of fingers free to unlock the door. I kick my foot out behind me and the door slams closed.

My tablet is out and ready to walk me through the best lasagna I have ever tasted, which I hope is true because I spent a small fortune on fresh mozzarella, parmesan cheeses, and organic ground beef. I enjoy a lot of veggies in my lasagna, which is not traditional, but I am throwing caution to the wind! It's not recommended for novices to modify recipes when they haven't even tried the original, but I know what I like.

I made my own noodles because the video I watched was quite insistent that I not use the dried noodles out of the box. It's some kind of Italian sacrilege.

By the time I am wrist-deep in homemade pasta dough, I question the entire process.

It is sticky and bright yellow. Why is it so yellow? Did I get weird eggs? Omega-3, that's what makes the eggs good, right? I feel like I am really screwing this up and my tablet is a mess of flour and goopy egg fingerprints.

I stare at uneven sheets of yellow, tacky noodles that are laying on the island now awaiting sauce I still have to make.

Once I have the sauce bubbling away on the stove, I prepare for the layering. The lasagna's layers turn out stable, and it smells surprisingly decent. Recipes are, at their core, cooking task lists, and I am great at checking off list items!

It's about twenty minutes into the lasagna baking (I know

because I just finished an episode of *Life in Pieces*), when I smell something burning. I look outside first, hoping that's where it's coming from.

But I know where it's coming from.

This is confirmed by a high-pitched beeping blaring from the kitchen.

Racing to the kitchen, the smoke billowing out of the oven is visible the moment I enter the room. Frig, what do I do? I refuse to ruin what's left of my lasagna with fire extinguisher foam.

I'm coughing and staring at the oven when my front door bursts open.

Great, I am experiencing an oven fire and a break-in. I grab a knife from the butcher block and position myself so I can monitor the fire and the entry to the kitchen. Someone comes in, someone much bigger than me, and I take a lunging step forward leading with my knife.

"Jesus, Em, what the fuck?" Oh thank God, it's Jess.

I drop the knife into the sink. "Sorry! There's a fire…"

"Yeah, I can see that. Where's your extinguisher?" Then he mumbles, "I knew I'd need to use one around you one day."

"No! Don't you dare foam my lasagna, it took me all afternoon!" My attachment to this lasagna, combined with the disregard for my house and personal safety, likely doesn't portray someone of sound mind. "Please, can we just see if we can salvage it?"

He grumbles and gets closer to the oven to check it out. "You have a fire death wish, woman!" He peeks inside. "It's that white paper shit that's on fire. It's basically touching the top of the oven."

He grabs my silicone oven mitts and opens the door. Carefully, he grabs the bottom of the dish and pulls it out, still on fire. How embarrassing.

He brings it over to the sink, while some flames extinguish on their own.

"Now what?" Water? Blow on it? I need to review fire safety protocols.

He uses the oven mitts to smother the rest of the flames coming off the parchment paper. I knew I should have trimmed that down, but wasn't sure if the lasagna would expand like muffins do.

I tried muffins last week, and it was another oven disaster with muffin spreading all over the pan. It was like a muffin sheet with twelve divots underneath.

Jess tears away the tall pieces of parchment paper and then puts it back in the oven. "Your lasagna is going to have a hint of smoke flavor. Hope that's what you were going for." He smirks as he washes up in the sink, then opens my kitchen and dining room windows.

"Perfect!" I say with fake enthusiasm.

He stands in my kitchen, looking at me, and I feel the oxygen being sucked out of the room. Can't blame it on the fire anymore, it's all him.

"You all good now?"

I nod, still breathless. He sighs.

"You're going to be a lot of work, aren't you?"

I shrug, unsure.

"Want a drink?" I ask.

He hesitates.

"We should maybe discuss what last night was…"

"Sure," he says after a moment, but it sounds more like, 'hell no'.

"I'll try to make it as painless as possible."

We sit on the porch to get away from the smoke smell. He's looking at me. Now what?

I decide to lay it all out there. I never backed down in my career, why would I shy away from achieving what I want in my personal life?

"Um, so I know you don't do relationships and I'm sure you

have a valid reason. I've never had a relationship, so, no judgment here." I smile awkwardly while his expression is blank.

Moving along. "I am trying to grow and become... whole, better. Just working on myself this year. The list I'm tackling is long and the learning curve steep. That list includes learning to cook and... having a real relationship. Hopefully that goes better than the lasagna." I look at him and he shifts in his chair.

I take a steadying breath. "Look, last night was impulsive of me. Which is very out of character, so I consider that progress." I chuckle and he gives me a small, tight smile.

"You already gave me some great advice at the bar, you seem very capable of reading people, and are able to engage others with ease. In comparison, well, you've seen my skill level. I could use a little help. Last night, I felt something and went for it. But if you're not into commitment or emotional involvement in relationships, maybe you could still help me out a little? Maybe I could just practice with you! You could be my warm-up relationship! Except, not really a relationship. You can teach me, be my dating coach! If you don't mind, I mean. No pressure."

Curiosity transforms his face, but he still hasn't said a word. I wait.

He clears his throat. "What do you mean?"

Well, I've got his attention now at least. I guess that means I have to explain this little idea that's been kicking around in my brain after watching him at the bar and around town. He is so at ease, so charming, it's almost maddening how good he seems to be at dating. I didn't plan to propose this during our post-kiss conversation, but here we are.

"It can mean whatever works for the both of us without it building toward anything serious." That sounds reasonable, but vague, so I give myself a mental pat on the back.

"I leave in less than five months, Emma."

"Okay." I wait for more.

He's staring at the floor with a serious expression moving over his face. "We may actually be able to help each other out with that scenario... I need to think about this." Jess frowns, and then stands up.

I'm not sure what I'd be able to help him with, but I'll sign up for just about anything if he'll help me.

"Okay," I say as he gives me an odd look. I begin to wonder if he thinks I'm just a little bit pathetic.

Jess intrigues me, riles me up, yet soothes me. He could teach me to feel, to live, to love. In a risk-free, informative way. This could be exactly what I need to jump start the most terrifying part of my life transformation.

He goes to leave, sliding by me. Then he steps back into me again and runs his thumb along my jaw, taking my chin between his thumb and fingers. Unanswered questions and untapped passion swirling around us. He releases me and backs away, looking more conflicted than when we started.

CHAPTER 9

Emma

It's been two days and I'm starting to wonder if he isn't interested in helping me. Understandable. Maybe he thinks I'm more work than I'm worth. Maybe he wanted me to be one of his short-term women instead of a dating charity case.

I've seen him a few times and sent him a shy smile and wave. I dropped off a large portion of the lasagna he helped me save. He returned the dish the next day with a 'thanks' Post-it note attached.

In other news, I decided to start running. The people running behind my house typically look happy and fit. I have a bunch of pent-up energy and loads of time, so I figured it was a good idea. Lauren runs whenever she is feeling any kind of strong emotion, and not only does it help her get rid of her 'murder feelings' as she calls them, but she also looks great!

So today, I am going to put on my running shoes, stretch and head out on the trail.

Fifteen minutes later...

Running is hard. My lungs are bleeding! Well, probably not, but it sure feels like it. I work out, it shouldn't be this hard!

I am doing some fierce breathing techniques as I come around a bend in the picturesque five-mile trail that goes by a nature reserve. Once I get to the small shore and picnic area it leads to, I drop on to the green space just outside the tree line. Arms and legs spread eagle, huge breaths shaking my entire body. Nobody can say I half-ass anything!

The sun is glaring down at me as I try to push air into my oxygen-deprived cells. A large shadow falls over me and my immediate thought is 'bear!'. I squeal but cannot move.

I mutter, "Oh, just take me," between gulping breaths.

A deep laugh startles me out of my defeat. I shield my eyes from the morning sun so I can try to see who is standing over me.

"Tempting, Emma."

Jess. I'd recognize that voice anywhere.

"For a 'killer' you run out of steam pretty quickly, huh?"

I make my way into a sitting position and bring my head up to look at him.

"Hey." My voice is breathy and quiet. Nervous.

"Good run?"

"Just started running today. Why do people do this?" I squint up at him, hoping he can enlighten me.

"Runner's high. You get a release of endorphins, better stamina" —he looks around— "and it's beautiful." For someone who isn't planning on sticking around, he seems a little too enchanted with this town. "Gets more beautiful all the time." But now he's looking at me.

I blush, wondering if he's referring to me.

I shield my eyes from the morning sun to get a good look at him and realize he is wearing running shorts, his running shoes (with socks, thankfully) and has earbuds in. That's it. No shirt.

Just his chiseled, glistening chest. Now I'm seeing the benefits of running…

He smirks and I realize I have been quietly ogling him for an uncomfortable amount of time. Holding out a hand, he offers to help me up.

"How much of my run did you witness?"

"Enough." He puts a hand over his face to conceal his expression. "My favorite part was the end where you threw your body at the ground like you were attempting to practice water rescues on land."

"Or!" He smothers a laugh with his hand. "The bee dance. Arms flapping, running in circles and then jogging away like nothing happened." He thinks briefly. "Nope, can't choose. It's a tie."

I glare at him, eyes narrowed, lips pursed.

"Adorable."

I huff at him. "I don't know how to run, okay? I just go full tilt until something gives." I point at him. "And I'm allergic to bees!" Take that!

He squints his bewitching eyes at me. "Really?"

Gasp! He doesn't believe me! How… appropriate.

"No. I'm just a chicken."

He sighs and puts an arm around my shoulders, squeezing my neck between his forearm and bicep in a teasing way as we walk.

"What am I going to do with you?"

"Apparently not much…" I grumble.

"What's that?" He holds a hand to his ear. "Someone getting a little impatient because I'm still thinking about her proposition?"

"No, someone needs a male companion and is hoping running will help burn off the excess pent-up energy since there's not much hope of acquiring dates given my lack of knowledge and general dating deficits, as I'm sure you've witnessed at the bar on more than one occasion!" Not keeping my thoughts or feelings on lockdown anymore has turned me into a blurter. But an honest one, so there's that.

"Well, fuck." I cringe as he looks at me. "I'm in running shorts, Emma, so if you could please stop talking about how wet and horny you are, that would be appreciated."

"I didn't say I was wet and horny! Gross," I whisper-shout.

He laughs and then it's quiet for a long while as we make our way back.

"I want to help you, Emma. I just can't keep you. It wouldn't work out and would complicate things."

I give this consideration before responding. "What if we did a trial run? Literally. You teach me to run. We spend a little time together, get to know each other, and then see if we want to explore the dating coach idea."

"Hmm. Well, one thing you should know about this town, and likely already do, is that gossip—or 'information' as the League likes to call it—travels fast. People will start talking about this—us—even if it's just morning runs together." I shrug, not really caring about that. "This means it will get back to my mom, who will likely blow her top and head straight back from Italy, demanding to meet you. She worries I'll end up alone and unhappy. She doesn't understand or approve of the way I live my life, and explaining the benefits of casual relationships to my mom is not something I plan to ever do. Again."

Wow, he must really never get serious about women if his mom would react so drastically at hearing he has a female companion.

"Even if we told people we were just friends? Running together, getting to know each other," I ask, trying to understand.

"Uh, yeah, that might actually be worse. She's not used to hearing about me spending a lot of time with a woman. Or I should say continued time with the same woman. I don't usually date women here in Landry for this very reason. So having an attractive female friend would set her off for sure."

"Okay, well, if you decide to help me out, beyond this running trial, you can tell your mom whatever you want. Maybe if she suspects you're in a relationship, that would appease her for a while?"

He gives me a curious look, then a slight grin. His eyes take me in, traveling over my chest in my bright coral sports bra and dark gray cropped Lululemon running leggings. I know I look good, even with sweat and grass clinging to me.

"Tomorrow at six a.m. That's when I run during the week. I'll show you some basics and get you into a progressive running routine."

I'm grinning like a goof as we part ways to go into our homes.

I have a running date tomorrow.

~

Jess is a good running coach. He is patient and fun, willing to slow down his workout to accommodate my slower and unpredictable pace. I'm hoping this means he'll also be a good dating coach.

After a few running sessions this week, we've gotten to know each other better. We covered the basics in the first few runs. Favorite shows, comfort foods, pet peeves. He hates gum chewers and we are both on the same season of *Suits* on Netflix.

Today we got into deeper topics. Family, career, bucket lists. When he talked about his family, I was quiet. Not because I felt bad for myself. No, I was taking in the awesome delight that is his amazing family.

With an Italian mom who is the eternal caregiver, an Irish dad, a slew of aunts, uncles, cousins, and other extended family, he has a support system I am envious of. In his immediate family, he has one brother and one sister who both live within an hour of here. It's his older brother, Garrett, he's house-sitting for right now. He will be back from Africa in a little over four months. Jess said this with a warning tone, as though I didn't know he'd be leaving once his brother returned.

He doesn't live here. The 'don't get attached' sign he was waving around was crystal clear.

He's been engaged. The look in Jess's eyes when he told me was dark and intriguing. Nothing indicates hidden fury quite like darkened crazy eyes. I hit a hot topic button and was shut down. Whatever happened with his fiancé, he's not ready to share it.

I change the subject, and explain how Lauren and I became friends and what she was like as a teenager. What I was like. Not much to tell there. I was timid, shy, and awkward. I experienced the world second-hand through Lauren. That's all I was capable of then, but now I want it all.

We finish our runs with stretching. He's keeping me stable as I do a quad stretch. When I drop my hand from his shoulder, he turns to face me.

"Tell me what you mean by 'practicing'? What parts of the 'relationship' would we be practicing?"

"Um, I don't even know where to start. I've never been on an actual date, so that would be kind of nice. What do you talk about? What do you usually do? How do you act? How do I put myself out there? I need a lot of practice and I want to do it with someone I feel comfortable with." I ramble out all the thoughts I've been keeping locked up tight.

He doesn't have time to answer because I keep thinking of more things I've missed out on that I may love. Things that may fulfill me, make me feel cherished, accepted.

"Holding hands just to hold hands, sleeping next to someone, sharing my day or my dreams, dinner parties, a couple's weekend trip, getting to know someone's idiosyncrasies, connecting intimately and intellectually." Finished, I take a breath and then wait.

He blows out a breath and then surprises me by softly chuckling, "So much work, Emma."

"Yes. For the first time, though, I think I'm worth it." I give him a confident look.

"You are, Emma. I just worry I'm not the right guy to help you with this." His eyes flit back and forth between mine. "I can't promise you anything. It would be a friend helping another friend —no attachments. This is strictly knowledge gathering and practice." My smile creeps up my face, slowly, so as not to betray my level of excitement. "We would try regular relationship stuff, but it's not real, and when it's time for me to go, that's it. Temporary arrangement."

"Temporary arrangement," I agree. Then I think about his current lifestyle and I can feel my nose scrunching in distaste.

"What was that?" He circles my face with a finger.

I shake my head, waving the thoughts off.

"Come on, if we are going to do this, no bullshitting."

"What about your usual... conques—"

"Don't say 'conquests'," he interrupts, shaking his head.

I laugh. "Fine. Will I be sharing your time?"

"Oh, so you're a jealous one. Good to know."

"I think it's pertinent to know if I am getting the full experience. I also would prefer not to worry about any women coming after me. Or this town talking about our unusual relationship." I put on my serious face.

"You can have the 'full experience'. If things change, as in you meet someone during this, or I do, and either of us want to change terms, we will discuss it first. And about what you said the other day about telling my mom whatever I want. I was thinking we could actually use the Landry Life League to spread the news to my mom that we are dating, seeing each other regularly. That we are in a relationship..." He's having a physical reaction to that word and it would be funny if it didn't directly involve me.

"I am perfectly fine with that, if you are. Actually, it makes me feel a little better that you are benefiting from this arrangement in some way as well. That way I'm not just dragging you around on fake dates demanding you teach me how to not screw it all up."

Why is he looking at me like he's trying to figure something out?

He leans down, turning me to face him. It's everything I've been craving. His smell, his entire presence so close to mine. His eyes dart to my lips, making them flutter in anticipation. He tilts his head, moving in closer, breathing in deeply as if he's about to delve deep into the ocean and isn't sure when he'll be back up for air. He places a soft, heated kiss to the corner of my mouth. I don't know if he meant to kiss me there or if I turned my head, hoping to catch his lips while he was actually aiming for my cheek. Either way, I'll take what I can get and soak it in.

"Was that my first lesson?" I ask in a daze.

He grins, his eyes lighting up, before walking out the door.

~

Hours later, my mind is still processing as Lauren sits beside me at the bar. She immediately asks for details, so I tell her about the relationship arrangement Jess and I discussed.

"You need to discuss relationship parameter details and clarify what happens at the end of this little arrangement. He's only here until when? October or November? He's here a lot because he grew up around here and has family here, but he doesn't plan to move back here," Lauren clarifies.

I nod.

"Regardless, I think this will be great for you! Get yourself some feels, feel yourself some man. Win-win. Are you ready to turn off your Em-bot and turn on all the feelings?"

"Yes, but it's already a little overwhelming."

"Just have fun, practice dating, test out your emotions on your practice man. But maybe draw a mental line not to cross so you can keep things from getting serious or liking him too much?"

"Well, I mean, I like him. You should in order to date someone, even if it's pretend, right?"

"Yes, Em." Then she uses her mom voice on me. "Just—" She rubs my arm. "Be careful. If it's not real, you need to keep that in mind."

"Sure. Of course." Be careful as in 'go slowly'? Is she worried about what I may inadvertently do to the poor guy, or is she worried about what he'll do to me?

I'm wrapped up in thoughts of this pretend-dating scenario all morning. Then something clicks in place and I realize, this is practice. Experimental dating. This 'who calls who', 'what is he thinking', 'what does it all mean' is a part of what we are doing. All I have to do is ask him!

The whole point is for him to teach me all this stuff.

ME: Who contacts whom after a date? From a guy's perspective.
GREEN EYES: Huh?
ME: What are the appropriate wait times and procedures at this point in the relationship?
GREEN EYES: Oh. Right.
GREEN EYES: No idea.
ME: What do you mean? I need some guidance here. You are the guy and have done this before. When the next guy takes me out, or shows some interest, I need a plan. How do I know he is interested? What's my next step?
GREEN EYES: You have a lot of questions already, Killer.
GREEN EYES: What type of learner are you? Visual? Tactile? *winky face*
ME: I am rolling my eyes at you right now. I don't know how to do the emoji faces, so use your imagination.
GREEN EYES: Oh, I am.
ME: This conversation has been much less informative than I expected. Please get back to me when you have real relationship knowledge to share.
GREEN EYES: Ha. Fine. Serious answer: some people might say wait until the guy contacts you, but I don't think you'd do well with that, and it's an archaic mindset. Be yourself, Emma. If you had a great night with a guy and want to text him, do it. You want to talk to him, call him. If he doesn't like that, he doesn't appreciate what he has and is not the right person. Don't waste your time.

I am blushing and feeling those little nervous, stomach-jolting feelings when I hear someone coming down the hallway toward my office. Hopefully, it's Julio with our printer paper and toner delivery.

Swiveling my chair around, I see... not Julio. Definitely not Julio. Jess.

"What are you doing here?"

"Well, hi to you too."

I blush again. "Sorry. Hi."

I gulp and then choke on my own saliva. What is wrong with me?

He laughs and holds up a bag. "You okay?" I nod. "Burgers for lunch?"

"We're having lunch?" I ask.

"Yup. Try to keep up." He smirks at me and then sets up our lunch. "Remember what I told you about just being yourself. Well, this is me being myself. I wanted to have lunch with you, so I came by. Perfect example of what guys do when they are interested." He winks at me. "Wow, I'm good at this dating coach thing so far."

I smile at him and survey our meals. "I call dibs on the one with guacamole!" I snatch the California burger up and tear a bite out of it.

"Jesus, woman!" He said to be 'me', this is hungry 'me.'

I am attacking my burger with vigor, thinking about what dating Jess entails. Should I worry that him showing me what a boyfriend is like, what it feels like to share meals, thoughts, feelings with him, will exacerbate the butterfly sensations already taking up residence in my abdomen?

Jess clears his throat.

"Sorry?" I ask, confused and embarrassed about zoning out with already swirling worries about our arrangement. Lauren may have been right, and a parameter discussion is necessary.

"What do you want to talk about?"

"Uh… I don't know. What do people talk about on dates? Should I think up topics in advance?"

"No. Just, no. Please don't make a list of talking points. I've seen how that goes down, remember? With Stephen? Or was it Stefan?" He grins at me, waiting again for me to strike up a conversation.

"I don't know. This is all new. I rarely approach anyone to start a conversation. Let alone flirt. I have no idea how to behave around a boyfriend."

"Yeah, sorry. It probably doesn't help that this is not a typical situation either. You and I."

"Yes. And the specifics of our situation are a bit hazy too. I like details, rules, clear boundaries."

"We are friends, helping each other out."

I frown. I guess that answers the lingering questions I've had about the physical part of our relationship.

"I think it's safe to say that we are attracted to each other. However, while you want the full relationship experience, I prefer to keep things casual and that would be hard to do with you, Em. So yes, we'll be friends, help each other out, and leave it at that for now."

"What was the kiss then? How does that affect our future relationship arrangement?"

"That was… unexpected. And I won't lie and say I hadn't thought about kissing you. Or about doing it again. But, to give this practice dating or fake dating thing a shot, we have to put the sexual part aside, alright?"

I nod in agreement. He's right. I asked him to help me learn the ropes of the dating world because he seems well versed, even if a tad dysfunctional. Whatever other feelings we have going on will need to be put on hold.

"Let's acknowledge that this temporary dating arrangement of ours differs greatly from a real relationship. We can talk hypothetical scenarios, practice some basic dating dos and don'ts, and hang out for the next few months.

"There are plenty of guys out there who want the whole committed relationship thing. That's not me. I don't want that anymore." Now he looks very serious. His wall is back up and reinforced.

"Anymore?" You could practically hear the tension cracking. Like fresh ice thrown into a lukewarm glass of water.

"Yeah."

"Oh?" Come on! Give me something. I won't know how to disable the landmines unless I can find them first.

"All done with that Cali Burger?"

"Mhmm, all yours." I offer the rest of my burger as a sacrifice for the information I hope he will relinquish. "You wanted the fully committed relationship thing at one point, though? You mentioned having been engaged. What changed?"

Those sea-green eyes go on flaming lockdown.

"I mean, this could be something for me to learn. Teachable moment?" I've heard Lauren use that term when something goes awry at work.

"So, you're not prying, this is for educational purposes?"

I think about how to spin this. "Can't it be both? This is pertinent information to our arrangement." Professional and firm, I nod at him with an amiable smile.

He rolls his eyes at me. "Uh huh. How exactly?"

"It should be obvious, Green Eyes. First, I should learn from any of your dating mistakes. You've formed this anti-relationship stance based on some sort of negative experience. I would prefer to avoid as many of those as possible." Which is true. I've seen the fallout of many relationships and don't understand how people find themselves in these situations. If I can piece together a few of these reasons, I can avoid the underlying issues causing the implosion of relationships.

"Secondly, it's important to share our relationship background information. What if you are bisexual and don't want only one form of genitalia for an extended, exclusive period?"

He chokes on his burger. Effective, good.

"Or perhaps you were in a relationship with the daughter of a Mafia boss, but he threatened your life if you didn't marry his now tainted baby girl and you ran? That could put me in danger."

He mutters, "Jesus Christ," while shaking his head and taking another bite of his burger.

Fine. I'll keep hunting for landmines. "Maybe you found out your previous lover turned out to be a distant relative? Not being able to be with her in the loving—yet disturbing—way you desire has turned you against women."

Eyes wide, voice strangled, he asks, "Where the hell are you coming up with this insanity?" He looks baffled but slightly amused.

"I watch a lot of TV, remember?" I tap my chin and keep rolling. "See, this is why knowledge is power. I never would've had to jump to conclusions or fill in any history gaps if you did so yourself..." I don't think I look smug, but I feel smug.

"Hey, I'm pretty sure delving into personal and inconsequential details of my ex from years ago is not essential knowledge."

"Okay, so no long-lost cousin that's pining for you?" I pretend to think. "Abusive lover? Cheating ex? You had opposing opinions on procreating?" He just frowns and continues attacking his burger with gusto. "Oh, god. Did she pass away?" I hold my breath, feeling like an asshole.

"No. Stop guessing. You're making this weird."

Pass. My need to solve this mystery trumps his weak request for me to put a stop to my interrogation. Plus, he just admitted this has to do with a specific ex.

"She was married?" No response from him, so I lean in the opposite direction. "She was Catholic and saving herself?" I chuckle at his expression. "She was a criminal?" His eyes shoot up, angry. Kablooey! Landmine located.

Oh. Shit. She was a criminal. Or into some criminal-like activities. Well, Christ on a cracker. That's messed up.

My wide eyes do nothing to hide my surprise. Or my confusion.

"You done now?" He's cleaning up lunch with angry, jerky movements.

"Fuck." Lauren's penchant for cussing has been a bad influence on me. Focus! "I am so sorry. I didn't mean to upset you. I really didn't think… I mean, I had no idea…" I feel apologetic with my entire body, but he won't even look at me.

"You didn't upset me."

Uh, liar. I've noticed he touches a particular spot on his neck, behind his ear, when he feels upset or uncomfortable.

"I just don't want to talk about it. I'd appreciate it if you respected that. Or would you like me to ask you for details about what happened to push you to pack up your life and come here? Why you take self-defense and martial arts classes."

His eyebrows are raised and while I feel the panic building when I think of that night, I get his point. Trauma is trauma. I shouldn't have pushed.

"You're right. I'm sorry. I'm pushy and need to work on understanding boundaries." He nods, looking only slightly appeased by my apology. Lesson learned the hard way today.

He walks over to the door. "I'm going into the city this afternoon, so I better get going."

I reach for him, but he's already halfway out the door before I can say or do anything. "Jess—" I sigh. He's gone.

Really bungled that one.

CHAPTER 10

Jess

"Dude, what are you thinking so hard about?" Taylor asks, loudly.

"Huh?" Shit, he's going to know I wasn't listening.

"I've been telling you about the team—because you asked—and you completely spaced out the moment I started talking. Rude." He props his sweaty gym sock covered feet up onto the coffee table.

I frown at his feet, kick them off, then apologize. "Shit, sorry, just thinking about what I've got going on this week."

"Uh, huh. Well, the team is doing great. We have an away game this week against a tough rural team. That town builds them strong, like beasts. Either that or they bring in ringers from Texas. Those boys are big." He catches my glance. "You coming to our home game next week? If you have time, I wanted someone to talk to the boys about cardio training. Some of them are interested in trying a beginner running program. I know you led a runners group when you spent some time in San Jose last summer, so I was hoping you'd be able to help them out? I need to get these guys in shape for next school year," he asks.

"Yeah, sure. I'll put something together for next Monday's

practice. I've been teaching Emma how to run and she is still in one piece, so I'm sure the boys will be just fine."

It's a near miracle she hasn't injured herself yet. She gets so focused on any one part of what I am trying to teach her, she ignores everything else. Like other people on the trail, dangerous obstacles, and trail directions. I spend most of our runs preventing catastrophes.

"I'd heard you two were spending a lot of time together. Mrs. Davis says she saw you two getting coffee this week. Although, she made it seem much more indecent."

I laugh and make a note to keep an eye out for the town's gossip group.

"So, what's happening there? Because Emma seems great. Not your usual type, though. Odd maybe, but a nice girl, smart, attractive, and funny. Though, I don't think she means to be funny, which is even better."

I cringe and evade. "Small town rumor mill works just as well as I remember."

He nods in agreement.

"So, you going to answer my question?" he asks again.

"What question?"

"About you and Emma. What's happening there?" He nudges me. "Any more half-dressed, middle of the night visits?"

"No, just helping her out. Being a friend. She's had some issues in the past with relationships and asked me to coach her a bit in the relationship department."

"You? You?!" He barks out a laugh. "It'll be the blind leading the blind." He laughs again, rolling over the couch arm, grabbing his stomach. I just wait for his girly giggle-fest to end.

"What kind of dating coach does she want? She saw a few women wanted you, you're not an asshole, and that was enough for her to think you'd be a prime dating coach candidate?" He stops to catch his breath. "When was the last time you were even in a relationship?"

"Whose friend are you?!"

"Oh, come on, man. You know what I'm saying. You're anti-relationship, yet you're offering to help her build that part of her life while she undergoes a lifestyle overhaul?" He tilts his head away from me, probably pondering how I'm going to fuck this up.

"Look. She's a bit awkward and introverted. I mean, she was homeschooled until midway through high school. You've experienced those kinds of kids. Pretty sure she had a really shitty childhood, and that translated into some dysfunctional adult relationships. Or lack thereof. Her dating history was even more detached than mine, but in a different way."

"I figured it was something like that. She has that lost look about her. What's the plan, then? Being her dating coach and taking her on practice dates could still blow up in your face. That's how my kicker, Johnny Deluca, got that scar above his eye last year. Chemistry lab experiment gone wrong. One wrong move and boom! You're in shock, bleeding, and walking around with a scar the rest of your life."

"Damn, Taylor. Reel it in. You're starting to sound like my mom with her worst-case scenario bullshit that always ends in blood, death, and devastation." I shudder.

My mom knows how to get right to the core of any worry you've ever had, flay you wide open, and pry it to the surface. It's terrifying.

"We've discussed some boundaries. Emma just needs help to get out there, setting expectations, and deciding what she wants in a partner."

The thought of her finding someone else to fulfill these relationship goals grates unexpectedly.

"She knows I'd only be helping her out and I'm having her do the same for me. If my mom hears that I'm seeing someone regularly, she'd settle down a little with all the life, love, happiness talks. I'm only here for about four more months, which should be more than enough time to teach her some basics. Then after our arrangement is over, I'll be back in San Francisco and out of my mom's reach with no spy group to feed her info."

"And you'd be okay with that? You're okay to teach her how to build a relationship, a future, with another guy?" He shakes his head, confused. "I thought you liked her."

"I do." I take a breath before continuing. "But Taylor, you know I'm not the right guy to give her more. Women who want more are the ones I do my best to steer clear of." I tip my head down.

"I considered having just a physical relationship with her. But then she started talking about not knowing what she was doing and making herself whole. How do I counter with 'hey, I only want to fuck, that's okay, right?'"

He grimaces like I'm an embarrassment to our gender.

"She wants quality time, thoughtfulness, fulfillment, attachment, and the 'life-altering intermingling of two people's lives.' Direct quote. While she didn't specifically say she wants those things from me, she deserves the chance to find it. So I am going to help her."

He's quiet for a moment, problem-solving this dilemma. That's what he does, he's a fixer. I grab a couple beers from the bar fridge and wait.

"What does your little experiment entail?" Using the term 'experiment' is his sly way of implying this will blow up in my face.

I shake his beer before I hand it to him.

"She wants a safe, risk-free way to learn how to date. I take her out, teach her what to watch out for, what guys typically think or expect, how her behavior is perceived, set some standards. She gets to experience different aspects of dating and decides what she likes and what she doesn't. We set a deadline—when I leave—and we part ways, remaining friends."

"Okay." He nods a few times. "What about sex?"

I omitted that topic on purpose, but that doesn't deter Taylor.

"Giving into our… attraction, may confuse things. I want to

help her, and it'll get my mom off my back too. Win-win. I just don't want her to think it's all real."

"I don't think having a real relationship would be a bad thing. But I understand that's not what you'd want." He hesitates, then asks, "Is this still about Ashleigh?"

I don't answer him. He knows I won't. Emma already poked at that wound today.

"Fine. It's been over six years and you still won't talk about it. There's a variety of scenarios running through my mind. I doubt you could surprise me."

Garrett is the only one who knows the whole story. I only told him so I could tell someone who wouldn't press or dramatize it. Emma now knows bits and pieces, so maybe it's time.

"Ashleigh never wanted to get married. She fucked me over. Or tried to." Taylor pushes up straight on the couch.

"She canceled the wedding, kept the deposits without telling me, and stole money from my business. She never wanted that life with me, she just wanted me to front the money for her ideal lifestyle."

"Oh, shit. What?" Taylor flops back onto the couch, shocked. "Christ. That wasn't one of my made-up scenarios." He thinks, a silence falling around us. "Did you turn her in? Is she in jail right now? Because that was one of my imagined scenarios… her in jail, you taking off periodically for conjugal visits."

"While trying to guess what had turned me off of relationships, you imagined conjugal visits as a part of the story?" I cuff him on the shoulder.

"Where she is now is anyone's guess and I couldn't care less. I had the stolen money transferred back. She tried to play the common-law card, so I let her keep the deposits, no legalities, just get the fuck out. I didn't see who she really was until it was too late, which still bothers me. Did you?"

He grimaces. "Did I think she was a one-of-a-kind girl? Your soul mate? No, definitely not. I should have said something, but you appeared happy enough at the time." He grips my shoulder. "No one could have known."

"Not sure I'd have heard you anyway, man. I was in over my head." I rub a hand on the back of my neck, easing the tension. "If I'm real honest with myself, I think it was our physical relationship that made me believe we had something real. Made me think we were closer than we were." I give a sarcastic bark of laughter. "There was lots of sex clouding my mind."

"Yeah, she kept you distracted, that's for sure. You guys exhibited a disgusting amount of PDA and not the cute kind." I make a face at him.

"It's shitty that it's taken me so long to see the relationship for what it was: all sex and no substance. Hell, I thought I wanted to marry her."

Yet another example of how I let sex muddle things. Add that into the emotion-building context of what I'm helping Emma with, and we could end up starting something that would end in disaster.

"No, your dick wanted to marry her. Let's keep that straight. Maybe stop letting him make any more life decisions."

We are on the same page there.

I shake my head and throw my keys at him. "We're going for drinks. You're driving."

Emma

I felt awful all afternoon. I stayed late trying to get work done, but was too distracted after Jess left. After eating dinner alone in my office, I eventually went home and noticed his truck missing.

Settling into my living room and reading a book with a glass of wine, I get this churning feeling in my stomach. Guilt. Worry. Feelings. I remember why I used to shut them out. Maybe the good ones outweigh the bad on average?

Either way, you can't cherry-pick your feelings.

I fall asleep on the couch, not waking until after midnight. Headlights sweep through my living room, muffled voices following.

Throwing the couch blanket off, I go to the window to see Jess stumbling across the lawn with a blonde woman.

I step out the front door and watch from my porch. She helps him to the door and then turns looking for help. Jess isn't opening his door, just leaning against it. I look at the woman again. That's when I see it's Becca. I've run into her a few times around town, and recall that she was one of the women Lauren pointed out as having casually dated Jess.

She sees me and waves, giving me a sheepish grin. "He's a mess."

"Looks like it." Employing a monotonous voice and no smile. "He has a spare key on a magnet behind the last porch railing on the left."

"Oh yeah! I forgot!" Of course she knows about the spare key. Cool. I shut my eyes and close off the unwelcome feelings bubbling up. Jess is staring at me, I can feel it. I glance at Becca and then nod my head at him.

"Emma," he groans.

"We can talk about the change in our arrangement tomorrow. Goodnight Jess."

The pretty, sweet blonde takes a couple of quick steps toward me. "I wasn't staying! Just dropping off a friend, Emma."

She has nothing to explain to me.

"Jesus. I'm not..." Jess takes a big breath and collapses back against the door, exhausted by his inebriation and this conversation.

"Oh geez, just stop and let me do the explaining," Becca chastens Jess and then turns to me. "My boyfriend and I saw him at the bar and offered to drive him home." She leans toward me and whisper-yells, "Since he's so wasted!"

"Mmm ya, that." The man-child joins the conversation.

What do I even say to that? This is awkward.

"This is awkward." Creepy. Is she a mind-reader?

I laugh and agree with a nod. "Here!" Becca throws me something. It lands halfway between my house and Jess's. In the bushes. "Uh, shit. Sorry. That was his key." She grimaces. Great.

"Okay, I'm going to leave you guys to talk. Or whatever."

Awesome, thanks, Becca.

Jess sits on his front porch, unable or unwilling to stand any longer.

"Nice seeing you, Emma. Good luck!" She runs to the truck. Runs.

My brain is telling me to ignore this and just go to bed. He will find a way into his house or can call Taylor. My heart and newfound objective to make myself whole insists I go over there and help him. Talk to him.

Be stronger. Be better. Deep breath. Walk over and have an uncomfortable, incomprehensible conversation with the guy you are quasi-dating.

"Do you know where your keys are?"

"Evan took them." Smart bartender.

I sit on the ground beside him and wait. I've learned from Lauren that sometimes people just need the opportunity to talk.

"I wasn't going to do anything."

Uh, help! I need someone to decode this for me. "You mean, you didn't mean to get drunk?"

"No. That I planned. Becca. She wasn't here for me. I mean, she was, but wasn't. You know?"

No, I really don't.

"She saw me leaving. Walking. She and Todd dropped me off."

"Okay."

"You believe me?"

"Should I not?"

"No, you should. I wouldn't make a promise and break it. I told you it'd just be me and you until I leave. Even without the sex." He looks at me, swaying slightly. "I meant it."

"Good. I like Becca, but I realized tonight that I'm not a sharer." I smile at him. "Come in and sleep off some of that tequila."

"Did you just invite me into Garrett's house?" He laughs. "I don't have keys... here I thought I was the drunk one."

"I'm inviting you to my house, booze breath!" He's cute when he's hammered.

He smells his own breath and finds nothing wrong, so he leans back against his door and closes his eyes.

"Oh, no you don't! There's no way I'm strong enough to lug you across the yard and up my steps while you are unconscious. Up you get!" I pull him up and help him lumber across our yards.

He wanders over to the couch and drops on it. He takes his shirt off and throws himself across the cushions. I cover him with the blanket, tucking him in.

He looks up at me as his hand reaches up to touch my face. His thumb caresses my lower lip and then pulls it down just a little so my mouth opens. "Your beautiful lips are so soft." He grins at his cleverness.

"Hey! You can't mock me about my last drunken night while you are drunk on my couch, mister!" It's interesting that even when drunk, he remembers what I said.

He full-on belly laughs.

"May I?" He lifts his hands up to my boobs, eyebrows wiggling. "Only fair… you got to cop a feel last time. My turn."

I scoff and then dramatically cover my boobs. "My inebriation was at least partially your fault. My request for permission to caress you was a direct consequence of your bad and unneighborly advice."

He pouts at this and puts his hands back down, eyes closing.

His eyes pop back open. "A kiss then?" He's deliberating going against our discussion of not complicating things with our attraction to each other.

I lean over and give him a quick, chaste kiss on the corner of his mouth. I pull back to look at him. "Mmm still so beautiful. Still so soft." I wink at him, grab him a glass of water and then head off to bed.

Ten minutes later, Jess barges in with the fuzzy sheepskin throw pillow and plush blanket I gave him.

"Our dating arrangement includes sleeping in the same bed when we stay at each other's homes." Then he drops to my bed and tugs the duvet over himself.

Inside, my smile is so big it hurts. Okay, maybe on the outside too. "You just made that up."

"Yup." He throws his pillow across the room and grabs me to tuck against him instead. "Sleep."

And I do, eventually. If this is what it's like to have a partner, a boyfriend in my life, I think this life overhaul was exactly what I needed.

CHAPTER 11

Jess

Waking up to a warm and soft body cuddled against my side is a surprise. Then the night comes storming back into my brain like a painful psychic vision. I pull Emma closer to enjoy this question-free time while I can.

Maybe I can tell her what happened with Ashleigh? Draw that firm line. Explain why I am not interested in a serious, committed relationship, even if she is the closest thing to sway me toward more. I'm not staying in Landry, and I can't do the relationship entanglement again. It's a gut punch when it all goes to hell.

With the pang of loneliness that's been creeping up on me, I might move toward relationships again. Just not the all-encompassing kind Emma craves. More than anything, I don't want Emma getting hurt. So, I'll show her how to date, safely. Maybe even teach her a few things I've learned about spotting the liars, crazies, and dickheads.

While contemplating how to keep her safe from all the assholes, I feel her stirring. She wakes, then snuggles back into my side, a sleepy grin on her face. Breathing in like she's trying to absorb all of my smell.

The little faker is awake.

"Are you pretending to sleep just to get extra cuddle time?" Her eyes pop open and a blush tints her cheeks. "You can just ask. I know I'm an excellent snuggler."

She hides her face in my chest. "How are you feeling?"

"Not bad, just a headache. My stomach is surprisingly fine. I skipped dinner last night, so I could go for a massive breakfast." I tuck a piece of hair behind her ear and watch her squirm, unsure of what to do.

"So… breakfast? I could look something up to make. It may or may not be edible."

"Haven't had many overnight guests, huh? It's just breakfast, Em. What do you normally have?"

"Oh um, a bagel, an apple, or a granola bar if I'm in a rush." She looks frazzled. "I could try making eggs again!" She glares at me. "This time I may even allow you to eat them."

I smirk at her. "Oh, I still ate those eggs. Well, the bits that weren't halfway down the drain."

She beams at me and bounces up off the bed. "Eggs! Coming up!" I watch her pajama short-covered ass skip out of the bedroom.

She comes back in with a shy smile. "I'm going to wash up, if that's okay? Got a bit carried away."

I shake my head and go hunt down my clothes and start some coffee.

Emma pads into the kitchen wearing moccasins and grabs the cup of coffee I hold out for her. She's getting the eggs, cheese, and other fixings out for breakfast. I ask if I can help and she shakes her head as she lines everything up on the counter.

Oh, she's got a process. She thinks I am going to mess up her organized breakfast procedure.

While she turns to grab the frying pan, I move all the ingredients she just set on the counter. Just a few things switch places. She notices immediately and eyes me as I innocently sip my coffee. After fixing it, she goes to grab something else out of a drawer behind her.

I bunch the food together so it's no longer in a straight line, then jump back onto my stool. Just sipping coffee over here.

"Jess!" She has one hand on the counter, the other at her hip, eyeing me like I'm a hoodlum.

"What? Problem?" I try very hard to keep a straight face.

"Are you mocking me?"

"No, of course not. Just a little teasing." I try grabbing her, but she backs up. "You are very organized. It's cute and more than a little OCD." I reach out again and snag her waist.

"You messed with the process, now you chop the onions!" She pushes an onion against my chest. I grab it and agree. She's still giving me the stink eye, but it has a sparkle of delight in it she can't hide.

"Should I be chopping in any specific measured increments? How deep is the compulsion?" A grape tomato pings my cheek. Better than an egg, I guess.

"If you have so much time to talk and tease, you can start explaining what happened yesterday."

I blow out a breath and scratch my head. How much to tell her? "I'm not sure where to start. I have a pretty messed-up dating history. My last serious relationship ended badly, and now trust is an issue for me. I like to keep things casual, simple."

Still mixing the eggs, she's quiet for a minute.

"I guessed most of that, Jess. Can you expand into new information territory?" She's extra sassy this morning. Maybe she's pissed about how I handled things yesterday. "Please?"

"It's complicated. I was engaged to a woman who betrayed me. Sh—" I search for words, not wanting to give too much away. "She wasn't who I thought she was. She stole from me."

More than just money. Ashleigh stole the future I wanted.

"I was stupid, naïve, and led by my dick. She was cunning, fake, and very alluring. When I met her, I was twenty-four, and a burgeoning, talented programmer about to come into decent money. I was a chump."

Emma gives me a strange look.

"Experiences shape us. This one shaped my future goals and dreams."

Then I thought about the rest of my relationships after Ashleigh. All complete failures, some epic disasters.

"Ashleigh was a huge mistake, one I'll never make again. Although, right after the breakup, I hadn't given up on relationships quite yet. I dated, had relationships. One turned out to be a serial cheater who had group orgies. She made me want to scrub every skin cell from my body and burn my sheets. Some were unstable, needy, codependent women. I had to get a restraining order." I threw my hand aside as if I could cast them from my mind and history with one swipe.

"Emma, I have good reason to take a break from the idea of commitment. It's not just Ashleigh. Sure, that's how it started and the women I dated after were, well, they were not ideal girlfriend candidates. Looking back, I realized I found exactly what I was looking for. Relationships just don't work for me, but my casual arrangements do."

Emma's quiet, taking in everything I revealed. She opens her mouth to say something, changes her mind and snaps her delicate mouth shut again.

Opening her mouth again, she pops in a grape tomato, chews it and then says, "Wow."

That's it? Here I am expecting a full inquisition, and she's more stunned than curious.

"That sounds terrible, Jess." She shakes her head, eyes wide. "I know little about dating, but that doesn't sound normal. I hope you've just had rotten luck, because otherwise my dating future is not looking too bright." She chuckles, nerves tainting the sweet sound. "Why did you say yes to this?" She swings a finger back and forth between us. "I know how I come off. Eccentric, stunted, possibly full-on crazy—something you should avoid given your history—and you still offered to help me out with this whole dating thing. Why?"

I keep it simple and say, "I wanted to." I shrug to convey my nonchalance.

Inside, I am compressing the worry and panic. Those fleeing instincts. I could face those later if they are still relevant. We have about four months of this arrangement. We'll be fine so long as she sticks to the temporary, informative nature of this 'relationship'.

"This isn't true dating or a relationship, we agreed on that. We are mutually benefiting from this special little fake relationship. Although, I suggest taking any advice I give with a grain of salt since I attract criminals, the sexually depraved, and obsessive-compulsive people." I give her neat line of vegetables a poke, teasing her.

"Well, at the very least you can help me identify qualities to avoid, right?" She smiled, seeming to take my reminder of our end date well.

"The eggs!" Racing back to the stove, she tries to rescue the browned eggs she just threw on the stove minutes ago. She just adds more cheese and gives them a smirk, like she bested them by ensuring their edibility.

Emma serves me a plate of extra cheesy eggs and sits to eat with me at the island.

She eyes me, contemplating asking me more questions. There must be something about my face or demeanor that is telling her I have reached my detail sharing limit.

"No more questions?"

"No, based on your expression, I don't think I should push anymore right now."

She's staring at my face, taking in every twitch, curve, and furrow of my brow.

"You should keep trying to read people. Their behavior will often tell you more than their words. Although, what the fuck do I really know about it? My fiancé was stealing from me and my company, and I had no fucking clue until it was too late." Her shocked face freezes as she examines my eyes for emotion. She gives me a sad look and I get that feeling of rage and shame again. I push it away. Maybe I can help protect Emma from fuckers like them. Today, I'll show her a few things about recognizing these shady assholes.

"What am I thinking now?" I try to give nothing away as she studies me.

"You're thinking… that you are taking me out to show me how to identify the crazies?" she asks, eyebrows raised in question.

How in the hell did she know?

"How did you know that? That's freaky." Maybe the student is actually the master.

"This morning, just as I woke up, I heard you mumbling about taking me out to 'scout for crazies'. That makes a lot more sense now." She's quiet, but laughing at me on the inside. I could tell.

"Huh. Yeah. That's what we are doing today. Get your people-watching sunglasses, Em. I'll be back in an hour, then we are going into the city."

Emma

It's well past lunch, but the coffee shop is still bustling with customers. It's people-watching overload!

"Okay, who are we watching? What am I looking for?" Excited to get started in my journey trying to understand people and relationships, I am nearly vibrating with energy.

"Hold on there, eager beaver." I frown at him. "Break it down for me. What did we discuss on the ride here?"

"That road lines are not suggestions. You should try to drive in the middle of them," I sass.

"I believe that discussion concluded with you acknowledging that you are an obnoxious 'backseat driver'."

He gives me that 'challenge me, I dare you,' eyebrow lift I would hate if I didn't find it so attractive.

I huff and then start reciting the information he inundated me with on the drive.

"Vagueness, sentence fragments, superlatives, excessive compliments, and repetitive grooming ticks tend to point to some sort of deception." I drone on in exact repetition of our vehicle study session. See? I'm taking this seriously.

"Good. Now, sometimes people can just be stressed or nervous for unrelated reasons. Remember to pay close attention to other details: background story, ability to answer follow-up questions, how they say 'no'."

He is a veritable fountain of knowledge about people, their mannerisms, and body language.

After Ashleigh, he started looking into educating himself about body language and nonverbal communication. This was what helped him detect issues in later relationships.

"I want you to look around the coffee shop right now and pick out a person who looks uncomfortable or stressed."

My gaze wanders around the couple dozen tables in the cafe. Slowing down at a loud group of teenagers. Nope, they are just being teenagers. Next is an elderly lady reading a newspaper. She's frowning, but when she shifts the paper, I see she's doing the crossword.

I glance at the set of tables by the far window. There is a couple there with their coffees abandoned on the table, she is leaning forward, he is leaning back rubbing his neck. He grabs her hand, tilts his head and seems to be talking fast, but hesitating a lot. Her back is straight as she flings a hand out again, speaking slowly for him. The man is looking a little shiny.

"I have found our first victims, Mr. Caldwell." I tip my head toward the arguing couple.

He rolls his eyes at me. "Don't say that out loud."

He knew what I meant. "Whatever. By the window. The arguing couple." My eyes are alight with excitement. "Let's get closer."

I grab both our coffees and start moving to a closer table before he can stop me.

I plunk us down three tables away, right next to the windows so I can still wear my sunglasses without people thinking I'm a weirdo.

He slips in beside me instead of across from me so he can observe too. "What do you see?"

"He's sweating and stuttering at her questions." I pause, listening and watching. She's asking where he was last night. "Oh, I bet it was nowhere good. He looks like a slimy weasel."

Laughter explodes out of his mouth while he tries to stifle it. The man in question glances over at us, probably grateful for a distraction from his current situation. Jess turns to me and slowly strokes my cheek, moving my face away from the couple. He gives me a delicate kiss on the hollow of my cheek, watching my face. He quickly flicks his eyes toward the couple.

I think he wants me to watch them covertly while he cups my face and stares into my eyes. If so, he is going about this the wrong way. His lips are much too close to mine to allow for much cognitive function.

I lean an inch forward and press my lips to his, then glance up at his eyes. They fill with a similar look of mirth I see when he's teasing Taylor, but softer and a hint of hunger in them too. "Emma. Focus, babe."

"I am."

My eyes stay glued to his mouth. We never ascertained the exact physical boundaries of our relationship. We just said no sex, so maybe we can still have some forms of affection practice.

"Over there." He points with his eyes again. Oh, right.

I sigh and turn my gaze toward the couple about to break up.

I watch as the lady stabs her finger into the table in front of her boyfriend, while he rubs his lips, hesitating. "Ooh, that's bad, right? Seems bad." The guy tells her she's beautiful and amazing, and he'd never ruin that.

I scoff. "That sly asshole did not answer her question at all—

oops! She noticed because she batted his hand away to ask him where he was again. That woman knows he's shifty."

I watch as he tries to placate her more and eventually answers her question.

He was at 'Phil's'.

Jess's hand is caressing my arm, making it very difficult to concentrate. "Did you see her face? She knows he's lying." Taking a sip of his coffee, he whispers in my ear, "He is still trying to avoid her questions. Idiot. Women don't let shit like that slide."

The woman pushes her phone at him, explaining that her friend saw him at a nightclub with another woman. He looks down at her phone and must see some pretty damning evidence. He combs his fingers through his hair and scrambles for some excuse.

"Oh shit!"

The woman dumps her iced coffee on his lap and walks out.

I've never felt strongly enough to argue about anything in public like that, let alone toss my drink on someone. I mean, if anyone messed with Lauren or tried to hurt me, sure.

A relationship, though? No way. Would I make a scene with Jess if he lied to me? I don't think I'd have the right to.

I will admit that I've been in this fake relationship for a hot minute and I'm already getting attached. This just means I've opened up a little and am feeling a deeper connection to Jess. Progress.

"I think you liked that a little too much. Come on, weirdo. Let's go for a walk and find some other sketchy behaviors to entertain you." Jess gets up and grabs my hand.

For about an hour, we walk around as Jess points out what some gestures and body language cues can mean. We discuss predatory cues and my self-defense training. We observe and chat with some locals testing if I can detect lies, discomfort, or other emotional indicators.

"So to summarize our dating experiment so far: you have taught me to run-ish, and how to identify red flag behavior, but have yet to give me any actual dating pointers." I tap my chin. "At this rate, I'm going to be in retirement, lounging on a beach in the Cook Islands, completely solo because I only know how to run away, or keep people away with my defunct relationship skills. I hate to point out the obvious, but I am well acquainted with both of those reactionary measures." With my hands on my hips, I look at him expectantly.

"Good. People are crazy. You don't want to keep company with any of the lunatics we witnessed today." He smirks and walks away. Just walks away.

I chase him down the sidewalk to his truck. "Are we leaving? Where are we going?"

"On a date, Ms. Mahoney." He grins his cheeky grin and opens the door for me.

I grin back and walk toward him. Stopping once I get to him, my mind fills with doubt. "With me, right?"

He snorts a rude laugh and picks me up by my waist to help me into his truck. Then he goes around to the driver's side and starts the vehicle.

"You didn't answer me. Did you not learn from that epic fight in the cafe? You could end up with an iced, caffeinated crotch," I sass him to cover my relief that he thinks it's funny that I would think he'd be going on a date with someone other than me.

He puts the truck into gear. "I'll take my chances."

I guess I am going on my first official date.

CHAPTER 12

Emma

My initial excitement is clouded by uncertainty.

Where is he taking me for a date? What will we do? Did I wear the right shoes? Panic! Panic! My brain is screaming at me to prepare for this upcoming event.

"Where are we going?"

"You'll see."

Wrong answer. I put my professional mask on and shoot him a complacent nod. Don't let him see the anxiety.

"It'll be fun, promise. Nothing to worry about," he reassures me.

Uh huh, right.

We are driving through town, past some great restaurants I've heard about, but I find I am not disappointed when we keep driving. He rolls the windows down and picks up speed as we hit the highway. It smells amazing out tonight; like sweet flowers and warm honey floating in the air.

We end up driving to a park just outside of Santa Rosa. I've only known Jess for a few months. Like any woman with self-preservation instincts, I think, 'hmm, what a splendid place to bury a body. My body.'

I shake off the wayward thoughts and look at the man beside me. He looks happy with a hint of mischief twinkling in those green eyes.

Grabbing a bag from the back of his truck, he tells me to hang tight and hops out. He grabs a backpack out of the back, then opens my door, offering his hand to help me.

"Any chance you will tell me what we're doing here?"

"Nope. You'll see."

I grab his hand and hop out. He keeps my hand, shifting them to fit together. It's nice and I mentally check hand-holding off my new life wish list. Sometimes it's the simple things that make the biggest difference.

We get on a trail and start hiking through one of the most serene paths I've ever experienced. The sun is at just the right angle in the sky to sneak through the leaves. Birds and woodland creatures chittering among the fading rays of sun highlighting the redwood's natural beauty. It is otherworldly.

My eyes sweep through the canopy, then around the forest floor. I breathe in the scent of wood, moss, and warm sunlight. Did I know I was an outdoor person? Without the stinging insects chasing me, nature walks are something I could fall in love with.

I feel Jess pulling on my hand, so I look up at him. He's smiling at me.

"Come on, there's more."

We get to a spot that opens out to the lake with the sun beginning its descent in the background. Jess drops the backpack on the ground at the top of a crest that leads to the lake below. He sets up a blanket for me to get cozy, while he pulls things out of the Mary Poppins backpack. A bottle of wine, two glasses, snacks, and a small lunch cooler with a couple pieces of decadent looking chocolate mousse pie that I may consume in its entirety, without utensils.

We have yet to chat much along our walk. It hadn't even occurred to me until now. I think we both needed time to soak in the peace and beauty. It is restoring something in me I never even knew felt depleted.

I take the wine offered, a local pinot noir, light with a hint of sweetness. Sipping, breathing, and engrossed in the view. Not just the lake either. My date looks delectable. Had I ever wanted to breathe in a man before? Or try to be nearer to someone just to feel them?

This is what it feels like to want. I get this itchy, achy feeling in my chest that takes my breath away for a moment as I stare at him, mystified.

He offers me the pie and a fork.

"Go ahead. I know you want to. I'm not a big pie fan, but I saw you and Lauren take down an entire pie at Baked Delights a few weeks ago when Taylor dragged me in for his cinnamon buns." He wafts the aromatic pie under my nose like the pie-lover seducer he is.

I yank the fork out of his grasp and dig into the pie.

"I hope you don't want any." I shovel an enormous piece into my mouth while he tries to go in for a bite. "Uh uh!" I garble through my pie-laden mouth.

I swallow like a lady before I continue speaking. "You may have planned the most magical date I could ever imagine, but mocking my love for pie forfeits your pie-eating rights."

"It does, does it?"

I nod as I lick the creamiest chocolate mousse I have ever tasted in my life.

"Who made this pie? This isn't from Baked Delights, I would have noticed it." I shovel more in my mouth. "It's way too good. There will be some pie porn happening over here soon. Look away! It's about to get kinky."

"My mom made it."

I choke. Actual pie in the back of my throat, I'm frantically attempting to dislodge. He gives me a few hard pats on my back and it loosens.

I'm still coughing while he's laughing. Tears in his eyes, laughing so hard that he's not making any sound.

I catch my breath and then give him a shove so he can laugh at me from a little farther away.

"You let me drool over your mom's pie and say I planned to do indecent things to it. Then she'd ask how you liked it and you'd say, what? That you had your lady friend 'come for pie'?"

I shudder and grimace at the tainted pie I set down. It has betrayed me. Or maybe I betrayed it. I'm not sure, but I feel a tremendous loss.

He's still laughing. "Emma," he starts, taking a breath between bursts of laughter, "I was kidding. Dani from Baked Delights makes them, but it's a limited time flavor she *usually* only offers around holidays. You clearly hadn't had it before, but Taylor is obsessed, so I knew it was a good one and asked her to make one."

"You almost ruined pie for me." I poke his chest. "It would have been a short ruination, followed by an inevitable pie binge, but still."

"I'm just going to eat all the pie now. Please say nothing." I avert my gaze and pick the pie back up.

After a few mouthfuls, I take a peek at Jess again. When my eyes lock with his, he smiles the biggest smile I've ever seen grace his striking face. He takes my hand, still clasping the fork, and kisses it. My brain short-circuits. That aching feeling in my chest is back. Something inside me is vibrating, shifting, creating a turbulent feeling.

This dating thing might just work out. He's unlocking compartments inside of me, causing magnificent chaos within.

~

The drive back to our little town is quiet. Too quiet? Should I be filling this void? What happens at the end of a date? Our arrangement didn't exclude physical affections, but it also didn't assert an immediate course of action. Don't men have expectations of reciprocation in the form of sexual acts? I know I've heard several coworkers discuss this.

Jess seems different, but that only makes it more confusing.

My mind goes about a million miles a second. Questions. Doubt. Uncertainty.

That feeling of inadequacy combined with the certainty that I am ill-equipped to meet another person's expectations and needs overwhelms me. This is where I power off my feelings and stick to perfunctory conversation with simple interactions.

Quiet is good. Quiet prevents blurting and blunt statements. I'll just sit here and wait for him to speak.

He looks over at me, eyes darting up and down my tense body, and raises a brow.

He knows I am freaking out. No, he can't know that. Can he?

"What happens now? Do men expect sex after a successful date? Does the couple discuss the date? You know, break it down into what worked, what didn't? Or would we just do that—me and you—" I motion between the two of us. "Because learning is an integral part of this pseudo-relationship thing? Would you suggest making advanced plans with your date to indicate interest in continued companionship? How do I know if he wants to see me again and is not just being polite?" I take a breath, then cover my mouth, realizing I just let out the crazy I agreed not to spew. I can't help but think I am ruining what was, without a doubt, the most incredible first date a thirty-one-year-old relationship virgin could imagine.

"So, full freak-out then, huh? Here I was wondering what the hell you needed dating help for. Just had to wait you out." He winks at me. Wait, was that a chuckle? Did he just laugh at my freak-out?

"Those are relevant questions, Jess." I feel indignant. "This is why sex-only associations were an appropriate choice for me. I successfully avoided all the feelings, questions, and entanglements."

He shrugs and hums a noncommittal sound.

"That's it? A shrug? Come on dating guru, lay some knowledge on me. Enlighten me!" I'm getting riled up and letting it show. I'm irritated, but proud of myself.

"How did your past 'associations' make you feel?"

"What do you mean? They weren't about feelings other than short-term pleasure. Sometimes, they didn't even provide that, but then I'd just end our meetups. Easy come, easy go. Simple," I explain. No point beating around the bush. I won't gain the knowledge and self-improvement I seek by being evasive or coy.

"Why aren't you still doing that then?" he asks.

"Because I don't want to feel empty anymore." I hadn't meant to say that, but it's the truth.

"Okay."

"Okay? Okay, what?"

"Did you feel empty today?" His face, serious, jerks to me and then back to the highway.

"No…" I think about what I felt today. "No. I felt connected, different. I had fun, Jess." He smiles at me and I keep going, "I felt like I was on the cusp of something I never knew I'd always craved. Something great that's just beyond reach, but if I keep going, keep reaching, I'll get there." Blushing at my admission, I fix my gaze outside my window, watching as other cars blur by. What would it be like to feel this every day?

Too caught up with my own thoughts, I take a while to notice that he hasn't said anything for a while. I turn to look at him. He is chewing on his thumbnail, but seems relaxed otherwise.

He notices me studying him and turns to look at me, smiling. But something is off about it. It's a smile I recognize from observing a few people on our walk earlier. It's not genuine.

"Did I say something that made you uncomfortable?"

"No." He seems to be searching for the right words. "I think it's great that you have not only realized what you want, but are working at getting it. You're strong, smart, and determined. You'll get there, I know it." He pauses, then continues, "Maybe you shouldn't be taking advice from me, though. You're already a step ahead. I have no fucking clue what I want. I'm not reaching for anything, Emma."

He winces a bit, so I prepare myself for what he's about to say.

"I'm good with who I am, the way I am. Casual dating works for me. So, I want you to know that while I'm here for your relationship questions and to be your guinea pig for the next several months, I don't want you reaching for something that's not there. You'll find everything you're looking for, Emma, I don't doubt that one bit. I'm just not the guy you're likely to find it with. I want to prevent any confusion later, as we spend more time together." His regretful gaze zips over to me, assessing the damage his words may have had.

"I appreciate that."

His 'no line-crossing' speech is understandable and, given the situation, appropriate. Yet here I am having mixed feelings about it. I need to start thinking of Jess as an educational practice in emotionally rehabilitating my progress toward a new life. Perhaps cracking open the feelings vault has me feeling new things for him. These are just precursor feelings and attachments, not real, just a product of circumstance. They are mere shadows of feelings, not substantive ones.

He assesses me to see if I'm grasping the guidelines he's setting. Wanting to ease his mind, I expand on my acceptance of his stance on the future of our odd relationship.

"Jess, I get it, honest. I understand that opening myself up can unleash feelings I know little about. I'm grateful for your help, company, and guinea pig status."

He laughs good-naturedly.

"Whoever or whatever you believe yourself to be, just know you are, at the very least, an excellent friend."

His face colors. "Thanks, Emma. Although, I'm not sure if Taylor would agree with you. I raided his fridge this morning after our run and ate the rest of the cinnamon rolls his mom brought over. He may have sent me a text declaring the end of our friendship." We both laugh.

It's quiet again, and that's okay. My questions, which just minutes before, were reeling in my mind, have drifted off. I just appreciate this moment. Even if I allow the shadows to grow unchecked and it amounts to nothing but heartbreak. In this moment, I hold tight to today's unchecked feeling: happiness.

CHAPTER 13

Jess

Emma basks in simple affections and thoughtful attention, and it's addicting.

How have men in her life not extended the courtesy of showing her how special she is? How cherished, beautiful, and appreciated she is?

Even though I haven't participated in much traditional dating for a long time, I still take women out and show them a pleasant, respectful, fun time. I take them out for events, drinks, dinner, the usual. It just isn't a consistent thing. If I need a companion for the day, evening, overnight—I find one that knows and respects the predetermined level of commitment (or lack thereof).

I already want to change the arrangement. That doesn't bode well for me, does it?

I'm not sure if I want more or less from her. Both concepts affect me in a way I hadn't expected.

My attention refocuses on football practice as I shove those thoughts aside.

Taylor is still yelling at his team. I'm watching and trying to assess their general fitness levels while they practice.

"Ben! Come on, you're letting him slip right past! You might as well just throw our QB at him!" he shouts while setting the boys up again and running the drill while he stands right in the mix. After a few more attempts, he calls the end of practice.

"Before you guys hit the showers, we have a special guest here today to talk to us about conditioning and cardiovascular fitness." He motions toward me. "His name is Mr. Caldwell, or whatever the heck he wants you to call him—" He looks at me expectantly.

"Uh, Jess is fine." The 'Mr.' part is a bit formal for me.

"Fine. Jess is a running coach." I hold up a hand to interrupt him. I am not a certified running coach. I have taken some courses as a level one trainer, but that's it. "And will be available to us for the next few months. He has offered to take on anyone who wants to improve their endurance or is just wanting to start a running program."

He holds out a clipboard.

"Anyone interested needs to sign up today. This is a twice per week, volunteer-led running program. Jess will set you up with a tailored running plan as well as organize a full team run once per week." There are some groans. "Hold up now. This is not mandatory, but can take the place of one of your weekly weight room workouts."

The clipboard gets passed around and I see at least a dozen kids have expressed interest.

"Jess, floor's yours."

I spend about ten minutes going through the program plan used for beginners. There are regular runners in the group who want some advice to step up their running. I take questions and arrange a time and location that seems to work for everyone.

I'll take Emma out to check out some trails. If it's Emma-friendly, then it'll work for the boys.

"Coach, you still need these guys for anything?" Taylor shakes his head and waves them off to shower.

Taylor is packing up his stuff when he looks over to the staff parking lot that faces the field. As Lauren is walking to her car, she stops to look over at us, waving. We both wave back, but

Taylor keeps his eyes glued to her as she gets into her car and pulls away.

"That was some serious eye-stalking."

"Just making sure that she left the school safely. The lights in the parking lot aren't the best."

"It's four-thirty, man. The sun hasn't even begun to set yet." I try to keep the laughter out of my voice. I fail.

"Can't be too careful."

He gets an eye roll in response.

"She told me earlier that she was heading to Emma's house after work. They are having a girls' night in."

"And?"

"Should we crash it?"

Oh, I'm understanding now. I'm his in. Emma and I have a thing, not a real thing, but still a connection.

"You are using my association with Emma to get closer to Lauren."

He contemplates this accusation. "Yup." He nods. "I'll meet you at your place in an hour?"

The sneaky bastard walks off, not bothering to wait for my response.

Guess we're heading to Emma's.

~

I knock on Emma's door while trying to ignore the nervous energy radiating from the nervous beast beside me. As much as I give him shit, his behavior is at least distracting me from my own thoughts and nerves. I don't get nervous around women.

I shake it off and ring the bell.

I hear light footsteps heading toward the door.

Maybe I should have texted her a warning.

She opens the door in sleep shorts, a San Jose Sharks tank top and the tallest, fuzziest socks I've ever seen. Her eyes are bright, cheeks rosy, hair in a lopsided bun on the top of her head.

Maybe this was a great idea.

"Jess!" Her voice comes out just a few decibels too loud. "What are you doing here?"

"Just wanted to see you." Part-truths are still true. "We thought maybe you ladies would want some company."

"Oh. That's nice of you." She stands at the doorway. Not inviting us in, but not telling us to leave.

"Everything okay? Can we come in?"

I peer around her to look for Lauren, but can't see anything from my spot at the front door. Taylor does the same, but likely for a different reason.

"Oh! Yes, sorry. We are fine!" She smiles up at me.

"Alright. So, want to invite us in, Killer?"

"Oh! Right." But she still hesitates, then her eyes comically widen. "Let me just… um, one moment, please." Then the door closes.

Okay…

Taylor throws a bewildered look my way. We both stare at the door, then I peek around to the front window.

Before I can say anything, the door is pulled open again.

It's Lauren this time. "Hey guys, come on in!" She ushers us in. "Sorry about that. Slight misunderstanding."

She moves to get around Taylor, but he's not moving. Just stares at her. She has to brush against him to slip by. Well played, Taylor.

"We are having a girls' night in. We are just about to pick a movie, so if you guys want anything to drink, let me know and I'll grab it. I think Emma has a pinot noir and a crisp sauvignon blanc she picked up last weekend." I look around for Emma as Taylor asks for a beer.

"Yes, we have beer, however, it's wine and cheesy rom-com night. The only drink allowed if you are crashing our evening is wine."

He grins. “sauvignon blanc, then. That’s the one that’s most like juice right?”

Lauren fake coughs, “pussy,” while heading to the kitchen, Taylor hot on her heels. I guess Taylor and Lauren are working toward becoming friends again, which is great because things have been a little awkward the last few times we’ve run into her.

“I’ll get you the Moscato this one time, but only because that’s another allowable choice as it’s still technically wine.”

It has not escaped my notice that they have completely ignored my drink needs during whatever this wine foreplay is.

Emma comes into the kitchen, looking a bit skittish.

She hesitates, then turns to me. “Sorry about earlier. I wasn’t sure if Lauren was okay with having men at our ladies’ night. Plus, tonight was a bit of a research night. We were going to watch a bunch of romantic movies and make notes.”

Lauren is shaking her head. “He didn’t need to know that, Em. Remember what we agreed? ‘Ladies night’ was a suitable description to use without divulging any details.”

On the plus side, studying rom-coms isn’t the worst idea. They fill those movies with misleading information and unreasonable expectations, but it’s a good place to start.

We’ve moved to Emma’s living room and I choose the spot right next to where she’s made herself comfortable.

They’ve picked a rom-com with a southern blonde who moves back home and runs into her ex. The treats are being passed around and we all agree Taylor should be the last person in the treat sharing chain. His sugar addiction knows no bounds. Or manners.

While I haven’t ever seen the movie, I’m sure I’m not missing much as I instead watch Emma watch the movie. She is laser-focused on the movie, and I can tell she’s itching to grab a notebook to take notes.

I wrap my arm along the top section of her seat, lean over and whisper, “You know it’s not like that, right? Having those kinds of expectations of your significant other is unrealistic.”

Without tearing her gaze from the TV, she leans over and whispers back, "But what if it could be like that? Even for a few moments here and there. Relationships are a series of choices and expectations. We set expectations based on who we are with. Maybe the magic is in knowing your partner."

Shit, well maybe she doesn't need my help.

Although based on her track record, she could still use some guidance to at least understand where to draw lines and practice how to be comfortable in dating scenarios.

"Maybe." I drop my hand to skim the side of her arm.

She looks over at the hand, then twists her head back to me. I smile, mouthing, "Date stuff."

After a few minutes, she relaxes and settles into me more. I think the movie is distracting her from thinking too much. Her skin is soft and warm, but as I brush my fingertips up and down, little goose bumps erupt over her arm. She leans in more.

"Cold?"

She shakes her head, frowns, and then returns her gaze to the movie.

By the time the movie ends, she is fused to my side, her shoulder resting against my chest, her head leaned against me.

"So, what's the next movie?" I know they had a complete night of movies planned, I'm curious to see what their other options were.

Emma looks nervous, so Lauren answers, "Well, we were starting out with sweet and sappy and then moving on to raunchy. Don't feel obligated to stay if that makes you uncomfortable."

"Why didn't we start with that one?" Taylor teases. "So what porno were you ladies planning to watch? Your porn picks say a lot about you."

"We weren't going to watch porn, you perv!" Lauren smacks him.

"You said 'raunchy movie' and that makes me the perv? I don't think so." He's still wagging a finger in her face, that brave, brave man. Had that been me, I'd be minus one digit by now.

"Hey, children, stop fighting. Uncle Jess doesn't like it." I chastise. "So, what movie is next?"

"Um. Well, I started reading some romance novels. You know, for research." She pauses. "I believe you are correct about some of those stories building a false sense of expectation." She plays with her fingers. "There was a series I started that was made into movies. Want to give those a try?"

"That was a lot of words and no answer, babe." Taylor nods to agree with me.

"*Fifty Shades of Grey*," she answers with more confidence.

She is not ready for *Fifty Shades of Grey*. I've heard of it, but haven't watched it. Several women I've dated have not only mentioned it but wanted to recreate the scenes. It is BDSM with a detached, controlling man who wants a contract arrangement with a quiet, normal girl who craves more from him.

"That might not be the best movie for you, sweets. Unless... are you into BDSM and dominant men?" I ask.

"Oh! Um, no! Well, I mean, I don't think so. Maybe? But, no. No, just regular sex would be great," she rambles. "Multiples would be great, but my experience has been that once the guy finishes, things wrap up pretty quickly. Regardless of whether I've gotten where I needed to."

We've been having this conversation acting as if we don't have two wide-eyed friends attempting not to act uncomfortable.

"Sorry, Taylor. That was personal, pretend you didn't hear that," Emma apologizes.

"Okay then. Um, sorry about your troubles with achieving, uh, what you wanted out of past partners." I cringe.

"Yeah. That's why I thought we'd watch. It would be educational to study more adventurous sex. Even if the relationship between the two lovers is fraught with problems." Her eyes light up. "Oh, but that's excellent information too! Although it begs the question why it seems so many guys don't want to commit to women. We should watch and then Jess, you could give us your opinion as an anti-relationship man."

Sounds terrific. Yes, let's watch people fucking and then talk about my thoughts and feelings as they pertain to the male character and his lifestyle dilemma.

"That's a good idea for a date, just you and me, Em." That sounded creepier than I intended, but if it gets me out of this mess, then so be it.

"You mean a practice date, Jess?" Lauren seems to have some feelings about the arrangement Emma and I have.

"Laur," Emma lectures. "He's helping me and has been great about it. So cut the attitude."

I clear my throat and answer her anyway. "Yes. A practice date. At the very least this will be a lesson in consent, not just sexual kinks."

She hums and walks over to the remote to browse more movie selections.

Emma looks at Lauren, then me. "You might be right. This probably isn't the right forum to glean any information or insight. Plus, I'm pretty sure Lauren didn't want to see it, anyway. She's not one who could relate to a submissive female role."

She laughs as she looks behind her to see Lauren and Taylor fighting over the remote.

"I will not watch *Vampire Diaries*. Get your horrific blood-sucking jollies off on your own time." He's holding the remote above his head.

"It's great and they only suck for pleasure or nourishment. I can almost guarantee you've seen way worse sucking elsewhere." Every few words are punctuated with a jump as she tries to reach the remote.

She stops, realizing she is being watched. "Fine. *Friday Night Lights*. That's my only compromise."

"The movie or TV show?"

"Either, but I'd prefer the TV show."

"Deal." He hands over the remote. She fiddles with the

buttons, right before two dark-haired guys with blood dribbling down their chins fill the screen. Ha. Taylor is going to—

"Hey! No vamps! We had a deal." He gets up and starts moving toward her. "Alright, you asked for it. No take-backs on deals." She tries to flip over the back of the couch, but he catches her by the ankle. She wriggles free, faking a leftward attempt before making an abrupt run at his right side. He immediately stops her.

"Shit, sometimes I forget that you are a football player."

She drops to crawl through his legs. He picks her up by her waist, upside down. She squeals at him to put her down.

"Your friend is full of sass, but also a big goof," I comment to Emma.

"Yup. I love it." She grins at her best friend.

"FINE!" Lauren shouts, throwing the remote in defeat. "You win. Let's watch *Friday Night Lights*. Just put me down!" Taylor easily flips her back around to her feet.

He pinches her chin while looking down at her. "For that little stunt, we watch *Vikings*." He grabs the remote, taking his place back on the reclining chair.

"Hot, bearded, brawny men." She pauses and taps a finger on her chin. "Oooh what a punishment!" Laughing, she heads toward the kitchen.

Next time, I'm coming over solo.

CHAPTER 14

Emma

I'm staring at a container filled with my hard work. She brought my cookies back. There were some that have bites missing from them, as if the person couldn't possibly take even one more bite of the vile treat.

I would have finished the cookie out of politeness. It's what you do.

Lauren came over after work today and brought back the cookies I made for the Landry High staff. "Yeah, babe, those did not go over so well. What the hell did you do to them? Mrs. Randal lost a crown, she'll be out for a half-day tomorrow getting it replaced."

Lauren drops the plate on my counter without care.

"And I have to be honest, the taste is worse than the texture. You'd think with chocolate added, there'd be a redeeming quality to them, but nope."

"I don't understand. I followed a recipe. Maybe I was distracted, but I mean cookies should be easy. It's all white powders with nuts and candy." I grab one and smell it.

"No idea, hon, but I was told to dispose of them." Making shoo motions at the cookies, looking at the garbage.

"Why didn't you just toss them and not tell me. That would have been the polite thing to do."

"That would have taught you nothing. You insisted on an honesty policy, remember? You want to open up, well open wide sweetie, we call this constructive criticism and it can hit you in the feels."

She contemplates, then amends, "Well, maybe the way I delivered the news was more just regular criticism than 'constructive criticism,' but you get what I mean."

Boy, do I ever.

"Okay. No problem, I'll try again. A new recipe this time." One of my goals was to learn how to cook and bake. Stereotypical gender roles may sound archaic, but being able to keep a warm, cozy, clean home filled with homemade food, and lots of love is a dream of mine given my upbringing. Not just because I was denied this growing up, but because it's something I want for my future.

And these goddamn cookies won't stand in the way of my dreams. Maybe I will take a cooking class at Napa Valley College. A couple's cooking class would be an awesome date night for Jess and me.

I haven't seen him the last couple of days because he's been in San Francisco at meetings for his new program? App? Are those similar things? Regardless, he is back tonight and I can ask him for another date night.

Do couples take turns planning outings? Or does it depend on the individuals involved? Maybe some couples don't like going out. I have scant months left with Jess and I plan to use every moment.

I text him to see his ETA and if I could plan the next date.

ME: Hey neighbor! Are you still planning to be home by tonight? Also, I have a date idea I'd like to run by you.
GREEN EYES: Oh, really? You ready for that, Tiger?
ME: Tiger. Yuck. Cross that one off the endearments list.

ME: And no, I have no idea if I am ready or capable of planning a date. But I do have an idea for one that will benefit both of us!
GREEN EYES: Noted. You prefer the nickname sweet cheeks.
GREEN EYES: Okay, hit me with the date idea.
ME: A couple's cooking class.
GREEN EYES: Hmm, that's a great idea. You could, at the very least, use some safety demonstration guidance. The rest is gravy. When? Where?
ME: *Scoff* I have only ever had ONE fire.
ME: And it's at Napa College next weekend.
GREEN EYES: And how many times have you tried to cook? And during those times, how many led to injury, burning, or general mayhem?

Well now, no need to kick the cuisine-challenged puppy while it's down. But he has a point.

ME: I concede.
GREEN EYES: A quick victory feels cheap. You don't want to fight more about it? I like it when you get fired up.
ME: Nope, not now that I know it means something to you.
GREEN EYES: Fine. I'll just do your part in my head. Leave me a voice text with that cute scoffing noise you always make when you disapprove of something. It'll make it more authentic.
ME: You're weird.
ME: So you'll be back today?

I don't use 'home' because he's corrected me a time or two. It's Garrett's home, not his.

I can recognize a fellow detacher of feelings. A bottler. That's not to say he detaches from me, but he keeps within the lines he's drawn for himself. He seems to put a lot into our arrangement. Or perhaps that feeling stems from a lack of experience and an overwhelming joy knowing Jess is spending his time and efforts on me.

GREEN EYES: Yes, I'll be back by dinner. Want to come over for some Chinese? I'll order on my way back.
ME: Ling's??
GREEN EYES: Hell, no. Chiang's. You're about to have your mind blown. Or maybe just your stomach. Depends how hot you like your Chinese food.
GREEN EYES: Come over around 7pm.
ME: Acceptable. See you later.

We've been spending most evenings together, either just talking, drinking on one of our decks, walking or doing something the other person already had planned. Just doing it together instead. Getting to know Jess and establishing what it's like to have companionship, a life partner, has my stomach in knots. Even though that's not what he is, I catch myself feeling it, thinking it. To have someone care for you as much as you care for them. Support, love, thoughtfulness, adventure, friendship.

Connecting to these feelings has been personal, and I've been keeping most of these discoveries to myself. Lauren has been checking in with me regularly, but she has been a little distracted, off. One day soon, I'll tell her of my worries that I'm falling for my dating coach and temporary neighbor. And she can share why she continues to deny her feelings for the giant football coach who makes moon eyes at her.

~

The scent of Chinese food pulls me deeper into Jess's house. His luggage is still at the bottom of the stairs, waiting to be taken up to his room. No one is in here, but I hear some voices from another area of the house. Wanting to make my presence known and to dig into that delicious food, I go find Jess.

"You sure you don't want to come for poker? You could bring Emma if that's what you're worried about. You guys have been spending a lot of time together lately."

Surprised by Taylor's presence, I stop in my tracks, unsure what to do. Was I cutting in on guy time? How important was that to men?

"Your point?"

"Hey, don't get pissed. I like Emma. And it's because I like Emma that I have to ask. Is this getting serious? I thought this was an arrangement in dating practice. She said she needed the help and guidance, sure. That was noble of you, but that's not all I'm seeing."

"It's not like that. We've become good friends. How the hell else am I supposed to help her if I don't act like we're dating?"

"I don't know. I'm just pointing out that fake dating may feel like real dating, which could turn fake feelings into real feelings." Taylor's voice is soft and slow.

"That won't happen. That can't happen. She knows that."

"Okay. Can I just say one more thing?" His tone conveys an indifference in the answer to this question.

"Might as well, but then I'm going over to Emma's for dinner. I'm supposed to be there already."

"It wouldn't be a terrible thing if genuine feelings developed. I know it's not what either of you set out to find. That doesn't mean you should discount it outright, though."

"No," he sighs. "I can't. Emma is great, she—" Another sigh. "I wish it could be different, but this can't turn into more. Emma, while great, is still a mess. She may be miles ahead of the litany of messed-up chicks I've dated, but she's still not on the right side of balanced. Being her real-life attempt at a real relationship where it all counts, it all matters..."

I hear some scuffling.

"It would be another mistake I made. A mistake for both of us."

Oh. Wow.

No, he's right. I'm a mess. I am. I'm working on it though, and Jess is helping. Right? There's a tiny seed of doubt that burrows in, wondering if I'm not good enough for Jess to consider a serious dating prospect.

Did I ever really think our relationship would turn real? Not at first. I accepted what he offered and what I could gain from our arrangement, and that was enough. But now…?

"Alright, man. You'd know better than me what you're capable of, I guess."

I have to do something so it doesn't look as though I was just out here listening.

"Hey, I'll pop in after Em and I have dinner, okay?"

"Sounds good. Whenever, just bring cash."

I tiptoe back to the kitchen, plunk my bag on the island hard enough for them to hear.

"Hello? Jess?" I shout.

"Yeah, one second."

Taylor and Jess walk into the kitchen, looking sheepish.

"Just get here?" Taylor asks, eyes darting between Jess and me.

"Nope."

They both look elsewhere, Jess rubbing that spot behind his ear like he does when he's nervous or upset.

"'Kay, well, I'm out." Taylor walks straight out of the kitchen and we hear the front door shut a few moments later.

"I thought we were meeting at your place."

"No, you said you'd order the food and to come over at seven."

He frowns, then nods.

"So, you've been here a while, then?"

"Yes. I heard you two talking and didn't know what to do, so I made some noise in here to give you a heads-up."

"Always so honest, Emma." He gives me a crooked smile. "I wish you hadn't heard what I said in there. I was trying to get Taylor off my back. He's always wanted me to get a girlfriend. He hates my way of dating."

"Well, it's not a *balanced* way to live for some people."

"Shit." He shoves his fingers through his hair. "I wasn't calling you unbalanced. You're working through some stuff, we all are."

"I get it. You have boundaries set to prevent anything from getting too real." I grab my bag from the counter and offer, "Maybe we should pull back for a while?"

I don't know what to do here and the person I should ask is the one causing my conflicted feelings.

"No, no. Honest, Emma, everything is great. We don't need to pull back. Let's just keep going as things are." His eyes plead with me. "I agreed to help you. I want to. We're friends and I enjoy spending time with you. Boundaries are difficult even when you fake date someone. Another lesson to learn, as I coach you through this, I suppose. We'll be more careful."

"Okay." I don't know what else to say. "Feed me, Coach."

And that's where we leave it for now.

Jess

What Emma heard has been nagging at my conscience. I don't think she's on the wrong side of balanced or that she is a mistake. It was merely an excellent excuse to give Taylor.

Truthfully, I am more worried that if I let myself, I'd screw her up, not the other way around. The need to fix this, making sure she knows that she's worth more than what I can give, makes me antsy.

Emma is lost. Once she finds herself, she won't need me and that's exactly what I want. Most days anyway. Other days it feels pretty nice to just be here with her in her self-discovery mission.

Emma has a date planned for us this weekend. Things have been a little awkward between us after her overhearing Taylor and I. She assures me she isn't harboring any bad feelings and she didn't say she was 'fine', so I believe her. This means that the awkward is coming from me.

CHAPTER 15

Jess

For someone who seemed so stunted and detached, Emma has become very affectionate and comfortable with me. There's no longer a wide berth when we walk together. She is right there, her arm brushing mine. She is not super subtle in showing when she'd like affection.

I have started holding her hand as if we are walking around town or when her hand is dangling near mine. She always gives me this sappy grin that she immediately tries to quash and play it cool.

We've been continuing her movie research by watching romance movies. On repeat. The only upside is that she gets cuddly during the movie and snuggles into me without even noticing. If I point it out, she is quick to correct her position.

We have already watched a whole slew of her chick flicks. *The Notebook, When Harry Met Sally, 500 Days of Summer, 50 First Dates, You've Got Mail, Friends With Benefits*. Some were better than others, both as movies and as learning resources. There were a few uncomfortable moments as she drew comparisons to our current scenario, minus the happily ever after ending.

We still haven't watched *Fifty Shades of Grey,* though.

Hazarding a guess, she's not quite ready to approach the sexual aspect of dating yet. She mentioned that the sex part is not the area she needs the most help. It's easy to have sex. Emma wants to build up the interpersonal connection aspect first. Otherwise, she wouldn't be much better off than she was before.

It's a valid point, but only if she knows what she likes on an intimate level. Confident women open up about their likes and dislikes and thus tend to both have and provide a better experience.

Her thoughts were that she will be more open, physically, if she feels an intimate, nonsexual connection first. Emma admitted she's never had sex with anyone she's had feelings for.

That made my chest hurt. Certain it was a reaction to remembering what it was like to be in a sexual relationship with someone I thought I loved, I brushed it aside. I felt a renewal in desire to help Emma find, hold, and nurture a romantic relationship. Emma doesn't realize how deep she can feel, but I can see it every time I'm with her. She's just so used to suppressing it.

I'm going to turn that suppressor off, starting tonight at dinner. This means getting closer than I've previously allowed myself.

I've been warning myself against this, ensuring I don't get too close. That I don't let it get real.

Hell if it isn't feeling pretty damn real. That's okay. Emma is a beautiful, smart, and fun woman who deserves to be adored. I'm going to set the bar appropriately high and hope to God she doesn't settle for some loser who won't treat her right.

I make my way to her front steps, wondering how she's feeling about our dress-up date. She must have been waiting and saw me coming over because the door opens and Emma comes out in a deep emerald green dress that has a magical float to it as she walks. I freeze halfway up her steps.

Her dress drops off one shoulder, tight across her chest to her waist, then floats to just above her knees. Those tanned legs, toned from our runs, have my mind wandering for a few beats. She looks spectacular.

"Hi." She waves two different ways before seeming to give up and putting her hand away.

I smother a chuckle as I continue to take her in. Long, raven hair gleaming in the evening sun, soft peach lips being nibbled by her perfect teeth, and a sparkle in her eyes that has nothing to do with the light, casting her in an ethereal glow.

Shit, I haven't said anything yet. "Hi."

She smiles and walks down her steps to me. I have an overwhelming sense of disbelief that this woman is giving me the time of day. Is trusting me.

In this moment, it occurs to me that I agreed to a relationship with no sex for another four months. That's going to become a problem soon. Particularly now as I try to stifle my physical reaction to this innocent woman I've committed to helping.

"You ready?"

She nods.

"I'm a little nervous." Then she laughs, uncomfortable. "I know it's just practice, but you look so handsome, and you're taking me out for a fancy dinner and I do not know what to do. Or say. I have a knack for saying things that bring conversations to a halt. You've noticed, right?"

She gestures toward me to answer, but doesn't give me a chance.

"And then there's the rambling." Her fingertips rise and dig into her forehead while she shuts her eyes.

She's freaking out.

I walk up to her, remove the hand that's abusing her forehead, and place a kiss there instead. She locks her arms on top of mine and takes a deep breath.

She gives me a shy smile and whispers, "Thanks."

"Mhmm. Anytime, pretty girl."

"I almost seemed cool for the first half a minute, didn't I?"

"You did better than I did, that's progress."

"What? What did you do wrong?" she asks, that forehead scrunching now.

"You had me stunned. I always make it all the way to the top step to greet a date and compliment her. I froze on the second step and you complimented me first."

She gives me a lopsided grin as I grab her hand and guide her to my truck.

"You look incredible, Emma."

I get another whisper of thanks.

She giggles while I help her into the truck.

I give her a questioning look. "I'm still not used to the whole gentleman routine."

"Hey now, I have opened the door for you plenty. My mom would smack me upside the head if I didn't treat a lady with the utmost respect and consideration. She'd also stop feeding me during visits." She laughs. "So don't you indicate otherwise. You'd be stripping me of favorite son status if she ever found out."

"You're just the favorite because you're the baby."

"Incorrect. I'm not the baby of the family."

"What? I thought Garrett was the oldest."

"He is. I am the middle child." I love only giving her snippets, it brings out her inquisitive side.

"That explains so much about you."

"What are you implying?" I give her a fake stern look.

"Middle child personality. I have been doing some reading about family dynamics and interactions. There are a lot of myths about middle child characteristics like being quiet, even-tempered, lost, and neglected. While a middle child, like yourself," she gestures to me, "may have had less attention as a child, it can bestow some very beneficial traits. For example, middle children are often more independent, trail-blazers, and more adventurous—both sexually and in their life path. They can also have avoidant personalities and have a lower self-esteem because of perceived neglect and/or failure."

Whoa. Maybe she has me more figured out than I'd like to admit.

"Some of that might check out," I confess. "Why are you reading about family dynamics and digging into all of my mommy issues?" I tease.

She lets out a sharp laugh. "You don't have mommy issues." She hesitates. "Commitment and self-worth issues, those we could get into."

"Pfft. Nope. Leave that for the fiftieth date." I chuckle. Then I put on my serious voice as I give her my first dating advice nugget for the night, "I wouldn't be doing my dating coach duty if I didn't point out that guys probably don't want to hash out their deep psychological or family dynamic trauma this soon into the relationship. Unless they are some kind of mental health professional. Even then, that's work talk."

She considers this. "Right. That makes sense. This was just the opportune time to put my newly gained information to use." Her head spins toward me. "So who is the baby of your family? You've only mentioned Garrett."

"My baby sister, Chloe. She lives down in San Jose." I rub my neck. "We don't see her as much as we'd like anymore. I have a place down there she lives in. I'm down there every couple of months and some summers, but otherwise, it's her place."

"She didn't want to move back to this area?"

"She had a falling out with someone here." She frowns a little at me, confused and wanting to ask why, but that's not my story to tell and Emma doesn't push. "You'd like her, she's sweet and upbeat." Emma may not get to meet Chloe, but I think they'd get along great. Chloe cares with her whole heart and would want to take Emma under her wing.

"I'm sure I would. I'd love to meet her someday."

Chloe only comes here if forced or to see Garrett, but maybe someday.

"So what's the plan for tonight?" she asks, clutching her dress and then upon realization, smoothing it back out.

I put my hand on her thigh in comfort. Her warmth and soft skin meet my palm. Her breath catches as her dark amber eyes lift to mine.

"We'll have dinner, you can try the dinner topics I know you have stashed away in that tiny bag, we'll take a walk around the vineyard and be home at a respectable time." Her citrus and linen scent is more noticeable being this close in the vehicle, and it's distracting me.

Tonight there's another scent mixed in that I can't place. It's seductive yet subtle.

She nods at me, and mutters something I can't make out. I can feel her eyes on me the rest of the drive. I roll down my window to get some fresh air. Air that doesn't pull me in like food to a starving man.

I can't allow my physical attraction to Emma to fuck this up. I shift in my seat and hope she doesn't notice the uncomfortable reaction I'm having.

We pull into the vineyard at the restaurant entrance. I help her out of the vehicle and she blushes as my hand skims down to her lower back while I lead her to the dining area.

Testing some boundaries, I slide my hand lower and wrap it partially around her hip. She bites her lip and tilts her head to eye me. Yeah, she feels that too. Touching her is too good.

We are seated under the pergola in a quiet corner, with some fragrant shrubs enclosing our romantic dinner setting. Holding out Emma's chair, she sits while smiling up at me.

I take a seat and gesture toward her. "Commence with the questions, Eager Emma."

"Veto. Eager Emma makes me sound desperate." She rolls her eyes. "Although..."

"None of that. You're not desperate, and that's not how I meant it. Your eagerness for life and learning is endearing," I correct. "There were at least three guys here who checked you out when we walked by. Not that you would want to be with one of those douchebags. The kind of man who would eye another woman instead of giving his undivided attention to the woman he's with, is not the man you're looking for. Agreed?"

"Yes, agreed. But, um, isn't that kind of normal among the male population? They do plenty of looking, even if they are happy with the woman they are with? The grass is always greener, or however the saying goes," she asks.

"There'll always be those men, Emma, but you need to think about what you want and not settle for less. Do you want to be with a man who looks at other women, thinks about other women? Or do you want one that wants only you?"

Imagining if she was mine, if we had what we can't, I begin telling the story of us without obstacles. "A man who wants to wake up only to you. Loves listening to everything your intriguing brain has to share. Gets lost in you, your eyes, your hair, your grace—and your lack of grace. A man happily stomaching your failed cooking attempts with only a small, well-hidden grimace. Someone who would describe their perfect night as drinking a bottle of wine with you on the porch while you read the best parts of your trashy novels aloud. The best part of their life is the part they share with you."

Coming out of the stupor my mind trapped me in, I see Emma staring at me, eyes shining, mouth gaping open.

I clear my throat and feel the heat creep up from my chest.

The server comes by at that exact moment. I always get the one that comes mid-bite to ask how everything is, but this lady's timing is spot on.

The server tells us there's a preset dinner as they have a guest chef tonight. I turn and ask Emma is she's good with that, not sure if she likes the scallop option for the appetizer. She nods.

Once the server leaves, Emma says, "Yes."

"Yes to the scallops?" I ask.

"No." She swallows. "I mean, yes to everything else you said. Yes, I'd want a man just like that. That's exactly what I want." She tilts her head. "Does that even exist? Because outside of those movies we are watching and my novels, I have seen very little evidence of that existing."

"It exists. For some. It's a bit of luck, a lot of effort, and a healthy amount of appreciation. Or so my parents say. They're the lucky ones." I smile thinking of how in love my parents still are. I wanted that at one point. Maybe in trying to achieve the end result, I forgot how important the rest was.

Emma reaches across the table, soft fingers sliding across my hand. "That's amazing that you've had that your entire life. They are very lucky."

I turn my hand over and lock my hand around her tiny fingers.

CHAPTER 16

Jess

We are driving back to town, Emma content, window down, smiling at the blurring sunset scenery. She didn't reference her dinner topic list even once while at the vineyard. The tour of the estate was quiet. We held hands, reminiscing about our youth, and then watched the sunset sitting on the benches overlooking the valley. She didn't ask questions about future dates or men, we just enjoyed each other's company.

I decided that tonight was about showing her what dating should be like. It's the kind of date I would have planned for Ashleigh, but I didn't realize how disengaged she was until I experienced Emma's complete attention.

Ashleigh was the female equivalent of those douches at the restaurant.

I pull into the driveway, eyeing her house and my temporary home, settled next to each other. Emma puts her window up and with a small smile, lets herself out before I even have a chance to open my door. *Probably because you were just sitting here staring at her, idiot.*

I snap into action, jogging around to meet her.

"You don't have to walk me over, it's right there."

"Sure, I do. Don't argue, this is what gentlemen do for their dates. Plus, how are you supposed to get your goodnight kiss if you cut a guy off at the knees before he even hits your walkway?"

"A kiss?" She looks surprised.

Shit, I did word it like I was going to be the 'gentleman' who gave her a goodnight kiss at the door.

I try being as direct as Emma is. "After a few dates, your date will probably expect some kind of sign of affection. Guys aren't into subtle. One of the ways they will base the success of the date and determine if the girl is into him is from her response to physical affection and reciprocation."

Emma has slowed her pace as she listens to me.

"And if she's interested in another date, of course. I don't think you'll have any issues being direct, but you needn't be... affectionate with anyone you're not into just because they took you out on a nice date."

I guide her up the steps, keeping a steadying hand on her back. She puts her keys back in her handbag, then turns to me. One hand hooks around the inside of my forearm and flutters up to my bicep. She leans in, her scent invading my senses, silky black hair slipping across my arm.

She's going to kiss me.

On her tiptoes, she glides ever closer to me, her body pressed against mine. My hands land on her hips and reflexively slip around her.

Her nose lifts to graze mine, her breath soft and sweet on my mouth as I breathe in, frozen, waiting. My mind flashes back to our drunken doorway kiss, and I crave another taste.

Not a sample, not a single sip. I want a thousand sips followed by a deliciously long savor.

Rocked by feeling this woman against me and her unwavering pull, I inch closer, eager, impatient. Her other hand skims up my chest and latches on to my shoulder. My hands flatten against her back, pulling her the rest of the way to press into me.

For a moment, all I can process is the soft swell of her breasts pressed against my chest. Then she shifts her head to the side and brushes her feather-soft lips against my cheek.

What?

Cheek. Kiss.

Damn. My brain and body need a minute to decide who gets control back.

Lowering her arms to my forearms, she locks her elbows and tilts backward.

"I had a great time, Jess. I've never felt so appreciated." She smiles sadly. "Before you, I felt doomed to participate in a series of very awkward dating catastrophes, but now my eyes are open to some wonderful possibilities. Thank you."

She's easy to appreciate and doesn't even see it. Her eyes shine with gratuity and happiness, and I can't help but feel proud that I did that. Just by treating her how she deserves. It reminds me of how I used to be good at this, but my partner didn't appreciate me.

I can't seem to form the words I should say, so I just hold on to her for a little longer. I think about the line I'd hoped for a moment we would cross.

Emma

He's rubbing that spot behind his ear again. Have I said something wrong? He said I should be direct with men, showing them that I am interested. Sweet, coy words are not something I give much thought to, but I need him to know that his efforts and attention have meant so much to me.

His arms are still wrapped around me, so I take that as a good sign. I give his arms a little squeeze. I feel a warm, strong, sinewy man. And he smells even better. If I wasn't one-hundred-percent sure it would be inappropriate, I would climb him like a tree, bury my face in his chest and neck and just live there for a while.

"It's, uh, no big deal. I enjoy spending time with you. It's not exactly a hardship." He's blushing, and it's very sweet.

He rubs my back for a moment, then takes a step back.

"I hope not. I'm charming as hell." Looking back up at him, I ask, "Well, do I get a date performance review?"

Tonight went well, I think. However, Lauren's told me about dates she's had where she thought everything went well, only to have the guy brush her off.

A flicker of surprise crosses his face. Smiling, he steps closer again. "Five stars. You are a great date, Emma Mahoney. You are fun, smart, intriguing, enchanting and irresistible. Do me the honor of going out with me again this weekend?"

His thumb rubs my chin, so close to my lips, I open my mouth just enough to make contact. How much of this is real and how much is this the fake dating scenario we've crafted?

He's going to ruin me for other men. Why does he have to be such a fantastically great fake boyfriend?

After a stilted moment, I clear my head. "Aren't we going to the couple's cooking class this weekend?" I give him a confused look. He smooths my wrinkled nose with a long finger.

"So practical… stay in the moment, Emma. I'm showing you how I would indicate my interest. We just talked about this."

Oh, right. He's playing his part right now. That stings more than it should.

I'm getting a fluttery feeling in my stomach. Could be butterflies, could be nerves. Or the possibility that there may be no turning back from the emotional place I've landed in.

Lauren has been on board with this unusual but progressive developmental opportunity in dating. Yet here she sits calm and intensely focused on me.

"Something's changed." She tilts her head. "What's going on? You and Jess get naked yet?"

"What? No. That's not happening. And it's probably not going to happen, either." I sigh. "Unfortunately."

"Still want to bang him, huh? I mean, you've been drooling over him for a while now, so that checks out. But if nothing has happened, what's changed?"

I sip my (ungodly early) morning coffee, while I sift through my thoughts. Lauren could only meet first thing this morning because she has an out of town, student-led literary workshop starting at eight a.m. Teachers do more than enough during the school year, then spend their summers doing more? Lauren may look and act tough as nails, but she's got the biggest heart of anyone I know.

"Yes, I'm attracted to him. But I don't want to just—" I swallow, not used to using the term as readily as Lauren, "fuck anymore. I'm here to rebuild my life. I've never had a healthy approach to intimacy. After the attack, it forced me to look closer at my behavior."

I glance at her to see her face, soft and attentive.

"I could have slept with Jess. We could have casually dated. I wanted to, oh, did I want to. But I also want something more. So much more, but I didn't know how to get it. I can't do those dating apps, Lauren. I don't have the knowledge of red flags, what to expect, or even what I want. I needed someone to show me, but" —I let out a broken breath— "this was way more than that."

She waits, but then says, "Oh." Eyebrows raised. "Oh!"

"Yeah." My shoulders droop. "I'm conflicted in that I am feeling so many things and it's exciting and exactly what I had hoped. I don't know what's real and what is just Jess putting on a show to help me. I don't know if he's feeling any of the same."

"Are you in love with him?" she asks.

"I don't know. But I am in 'like' with him. Very much in like."

She squeals. "I am so proud of you! This is a tough situation and you are still acknowledging your feelings. Look at you!"

She gives my shoulders a jaunty little shake.

"I'm being serious here, Laur. This could be very bad. He clarified that we can't go anywhere beyond this. That it's not even really dating. At the start, he probably would have been up for a physical-only relationship. And I use that word lightly because it's not a term he is comfortable with. He's not going to be on board with starting something real given his stance on relationships and his impending move."

She thinks this through, scoots her chair back and leans across the table, grabbing my hands.

"You know I am not one to be giving you any kind of 'love' advice. However, you need a little more information before coming to any kind of conclusion. Talk to him about what you're feeling. That's a part of this whole process right?"

I frown at her.

"Maybe this is your heart sensing something that looks damn appealing after so many years of emptiness. You're feeling what you should be while going on great dates. Now you need to figure out if it's the dates and lifelong yearning for intimacy, or the man. Then go from there."

A quiet voice inside me whispers, *'the man.'*

No, she's right, it's too early to tell, but I have to ask anyway.

"What if I realize it's him and he leaves anyway? What would I do? I'm not equipped to cope with that. I don't respond well to rejection or detachment that's not instigated by my own self-preservation skills."

"You would do what the rest of womanhood does when shit like this befalls us: you cry, destroy something—your hair, his stuff, sometimes your self-image—then you heal, and move the hell on. Try to find one that's better than the last. You don't repeat the same mistakes. You stay true to who you are, no matter what."

Sometimes I forget that Lauren has a tarnished love history and subsequent rage inside her. It appears we all have that bit of damage inside of us.

"Emma, if it helps, I think he cares about you. I don't know how it'll play out, but he wouldn't be helping you like this if he didn't have some skin in the game," she offers with a wink.

That's a valid point. He's not getting any significant benefit from this relationship other than my company at the occasional event, and he gets to tell his parents he's dating someone.

So how do I figure out if these feelings stem from my affection-starved heart or the man who is filling it? Maybe I date this amazing man like it's not practice.

CHAPTER 17

Emma

"Uh, babe, you might want to actually watch the pan while you're pouring the alcohol in," Jess warns, snagging the bottle from me and moving us a considerable distance away from the flames.

"I had it! It was supposed to catch fire."

But I take another step back, knowing he probably did just save our lives. I was not watching the pan, instead focusing on the instructor's tips as we flambé.

His eyebrows twitch at me like they do when he finds me amusing. He leans toward me and I lean toward him, wondering why he is getting closer to me, but not wanting to wait another second to find out. He reaches out toward me. Then flips the burner off and sets the flaming pan farther away from us.

"It'll be perfectly crispy."

"That it will be, no doubt." He's laughing, flame reflecting eyes find mine. I give him a little shove.

"You're eating it and you are going to tell me you love it. Never will you have tasted such perfection. Got it?"

I already screwed up various portions of our four-course French cuisine. I'm fairly confident my blood is in the Salade

Niçoise, but hopefully the tomatoes will mask that. Jess agreed not to eat it and then did the rest of the chopping for me.

I made the mistake of opening the oven to check on the soufflé. The chef had specifically warned against this earlier, but I didn't hear him. It was probably while I was bleeding.

Our soufflé didn't make it.

"Well, it may be the only thing left to eat, and I'm starving. Chances are good I'll scarf it down, regardless." I poke him in the abdomen and holy mother of cheese biscuits, those are some solid abs.

"Sorry, my mistake. I meant, I'm sure the Coq Au Vin will be a masterpiece of flaming goodness," he placates, but does so while rubbing my arm.

Forgiven.

"Do you want me to take the pie out?"

"It's a tart," I correct, then whisper, "I know pie, mister, and that is no pie!"

"Uh, same thing. Crust, filling, round." He hitches a shoulder. "Pie."

I gape at him, exaggerating my offended state. "Now you get no tart either!"

"Good, I hate lemon pie." He laughs when I shoot him a disapproving look. "Tart. Although I imagine it will taste exactly like lemon pie."

"That is being overly generous of our baking skills. Our dessert has maybe a fifty percent chance of tasting like a lemon tart."

I don't even remember how many eggs I put in, and I definitely didn't divide them. And did I put lemon zest or lemon juice in there? We are about to find out.

I pull the still gelatinous looking tart out of the oven, then refill his wine and mine. We are going to need it.

Coq Au Vin is ready and smells surprisingly good. The sad soufflé sits deflated but still warm, and we have served the unhygienic blood salad. Most couples have moved to the dining area and are enjoying their hard work.

Jess pulls out my chair then scoots his chair closer to mine, swiveling it so he's right next to me. He clinks forks with me as we prepare to dig in.

I pick the safe bits out of my salad, the ones that didn't get mixed in with my DNA. He starts right in on the Coq Au Vin and appears pleasantly surprised. Eyes wide, staring, I wait for his assessment.

"Crispy." He winks at me. I roll my eyes and cut myself a bite to try.

It's good. More than just edible. I would make this at home and then lick the remnants off my plate. "Oh my god, this is delicious!"

I offer him a high five which he returns enthusiastically, gaining attention from our fellow cooking students.

He scrapes his plate clean while I dig into the soufflé. It's crispy on the edges, but as I break through the concave top, it's gooey in the middle. Oh! It's like cheesy lava cake. I'm on board. I scoop up a liquid part with a bit of crispy edge and am about to stick it in my mouth when an enormous hand slaps it away, spoon clattering to my side plate.

"Hey! You could have just asked for the first bite!" I pout as I try to get the bite back on the spoon.

"That soufflé is undercooked. Chef Gagnier said it should only be slightly runny in the middle."

He lifts my spoon from my fingers, dips it into the soufflé getting the gooey center then tips the spoon as we watch it pour out.

"Oh, no, *ce n'est pas bon*! Do not eat, *amie*," our French instructor calls to us as he walks toward our table. "Soufflé *est difficile*. No worries. Try the tart." He clucks, then is off to check on the other participants.

"So, entrees, you have in the bag. Baking" —he motions

around the table— "of any kind, that's going to be a hard pass from now on."

"You haven't even tried the pie!"

"Ha! You called it a pie!"

He's bouncing his feet up and down doing some kind of awkward and adorable victory dance.

"Dammit. You fluster me, stop being adorable." I give him my pleading eyes. "Will you try it if I call it pie?"

He hums then says, "We try it at the same time."

"Deal!"

We dig in and realize the tart is just as runny as the soufflé.

"Oh, no." My lip gives a slight tremble. "Hot oven plus baked goods should equal cooked treat. How am I so bad at this?"

I frown and put my fork down. Defeated and teary.

He looks over at me, his eyes flicker with an emotion I can't name. Then he trades his fork for a spoon. I'm stunned as he scoops up some tart and shoves the bite into his mouth before I can protest. My hand freezes midair in a delayed attempt to stop him.

He chews once. He gives up on that solitary chew partway through, then I hear a loud swallow.

Smiling, he grabs my hand and gives my fingers a soft kiss before returning our joined hands to the table.

This man is absolutely, positively insane.

Insanely amazing. Insanely wonderful. Insanely hot.

"You ate that lemon goop," I state. "You don't even like lemon pie yet you ate that massacre?" I point at the offensive dessert.

He gives my hand a squeeze, drags his tongue across his teeth and answers, "If it makes you feel better, I don't think there was any lemon in there."

Before I can think about how I messed up the lemon part of the disgusting pie-tart, he gives me that dazzling smile.

I turn to face him, push his plate aside, grab him by the shirt collar, and pull him toward me. Once his face is mere inches from mine, I look into his eyes and pause.

"Emma, what…"

"I owe you dessert."

I press my lips to his and open to devour his lush mouth. A buzz zips through my body as I move my mouth against his. The hand that was gripping mine a moment ago is gliding up my arm. It reaches the back of my neck and eases into my hair, holding me in place. His mouth takes over the kiss and locks my bottom lip between his as he sucks on it like he's trying to get every ounce of my taste off that lip before he moves on.

My tongue slips out to dip into his mouth, smoothing it over the crest of his bottom lip. I'm gripping his jaw and neck now, nearly in his lap.

The moment my tongue breaches his mouth, I can taste the tart.

It's awful. Like a sweet, oily egg.

I lift my mouth from his, blinking a few times to clear the fog, then give a sharp laugh.

He's still looking at my mouth, thumb caressing my neck. I lean into it like a touch-starved, sex-crazed hermit.

"Tasted the pie on me, didn't you?"

One side of his beautiful mouth stretches wide as he tries to hide a grin. I should stop staring at it.

I bite my lip hard, lift my eyes back up to his and nod, trying not to laugh.

"It's so bad."

He throws his head back and a booming laugh comes out, his chest heaving. If people are watching, I can't tell, all I see is him. I made that happen, and it lights a spark inside me, one I want to pour gasoline over.

I'm staring at his green eyes in awe, unable to look away. My hands settle onto his thighs as I retreat. Casual touch is not something I am accustomed to. Yet, it feels very natural with Jess. It's a need, a curiosity that allows my hands to move of their own volition.

"Let's go get you some ice cream."

Before we arrived, I had offered to buy him unlimited ice cream, the only dessert he actually loves, if I mangled the meal —or him.

He smiles at me, then scrunches his brow. "While I'd never turn down some ice cream, I have to ask, do you think you owe me ice cream?"

"Ha! Yes. This was sixty percent disaster, forty percent success. At best!" I gesture to the table. "Most of this was inedible, I nearly seared your skin off, and was constantly in the way. I was not productive and was too much of a bumbling, nervous mess to participate in proper date conversation."

I bring a hand to my face, feeling it warm.

"You were a champ. Basically hero status. Heroes get ice cream."

"You were nervous? Why?" He ignores the rest of my statement.

So many reasons.

"I'm not good at cooking or baking. I don't enjoy being 'not good' at things. To say I was downright dangerous in there would not be an exaggeration. Also, you." I swallow briefly, wanting to gather my thoughts a little more. "You make me a little nervous."

"I do, huh?" He grins at me.

"Well, you are…" My pointed finger moves in a circle to outline his Jess-ness. "Jess. Hot, smooth, sweet, and intriguing. You're Green Eyes and I'm a mess—no, not a mess, a work in progress. We were in that tiny kitchen and your Jess essence takes up so much space. It messed with me."

"It's normal to be nervous on a date. What kind of nervous was it?"

Am I supposed to know this?

I remember him brushing against me as he reached to drop dishes into the sink. That tingle I got as his palm caught my midsection, pulling me away from the knife I dropped. The way his hands gently moved me around the kitchen as he tried to keep tabs on me and contain the chaos. I was so distracted I could barely rinse vegetables, let alone chop or sauté or keep up with his witty banter.

"Good nervous."

His eyes light up, then cool, his face an indifferent mask as he takes my hand. "Let's get out of here. Before Chef notices the pan you scraped or the towel you torched." His pace quickens as he drags me along behind him. I shout a thanks to the chef as we make our quick getaway.

On the drive back from getting ice cream, Jess talks about his running group with Taylor's football players and his upcoming work trip to San Francisco.

He eats his mint chocolate chip and I demolish my apple pie ice cream cone. He rolled his eyes at me when I ordered, but I couldn't care less because inside my mouth was the most amazing explosion of pie and ice cream flavors. We trade cones, but Jess licks mine with hesitation. So, I snatch it back. I peer at him while he continues eating his ice cream.

"I'm going to make you like pie one day."

"Only if it's mixed heavily with ice cream," he challenges.

"It'll be baby steps, don't worry. We can keep the ice cream to pie ratio high and reduce the ice cream until it's mostly pie. Soon, you won't be able to eat ice cream without pie. It's simple cognitive association formation."

"So now I'm your psychology guinea pig? Don't mess with my brain any more than you already are, woman!"

"You don't want to be my guinea pig?" I pout. "Don't be so hasty. You might like my experiments."

He pauses mid-lick, shocked by the implication I made.

"Uh, I'm sure I would. Very much." He takes another lick, swallows. "But that might cause some confusion given our other ongoing experiment."

I find it interesting he thinks of this as an experiment.

He's not wrong. About any of it. It would be confusing. He just doesn't know that I want the confusion. I want to meld it all together and see where this goes. What I want is to ask him to throw this fake dating, love-life coaching agreement out the window and to explore what we could be.

"Fine. I'll just feed you the pie without ice cream, then. No more sweet treat experiments from me, mister."

"The flirting thing you're doing? I like it." He grins at me. I blush at the compliment. Not because I think I've gotten good at flirting. I haven't. I like that he likes it.

Jess pulls into his driveway, putting the truck in park. "Alright, Mahoney, I'm ready to go over the post-date notes. You ready?" His face is still, serious.

What we notably have not yet discussed is the epic, scorching, breath-stealing kiss I initiated. We have to talk about it, though. What it means and how we each felt about it.

The answer, in case he asks, would be, *everything*.

"Yes, Coach Caldwell. Proceed." I sit up a little straighter, waiting to hear what advice he has. This information is now more important than ever because I want to keep Jess. Or have him for real for as long as he'll let me.

We don't always debrief a date. Only if he has something specific to say or something intense happened.

"The cooking class idea was fun, interactive, and a good date idea for a newer relationship. While your overall cooking skills are a work in progress, it didn't negatively affect the date. In fact, it was genuine and damn near mesmerizing watching you cause chaos at every turn. If I didn't know better, I'd have thought you were doing it on purpose."

He shakes his head at me while giving me a cute smile.

"As for date conversation advice, try to direct some personal 'getting to know you' questions his way if you are unsure where to lead the conversation. It's a good time to ask about his family, if he prefers Mexican or Italian food, what his travel bucket list is, that kind of thing. It'll also mean more if you have a few follow-up questions after he answers, or add your own personal anecdotes."

I nod numbly, while thinking how I could take my focus off

him if he was confiding personal information to me. That's why most of our evening ended up such a mess. My focus was solely on him.

He clears his throat and my gaze flies between his eyes and his mouth.

"The kiss was surprising." His voice pitches high for a moment and he does a small throat clearing again, rubbing under his ear. "In a good way. Lots of guys like a woman who makes the first move." He looks everywhere but at me. He's not telling me if he liked it or what he thought of the actual kiss.

"Alright. So, it was okay then? The kiss."

Did he feel the same thing I did during the kiss? I haven't ever kissed anyone like that before. Just to kiss, show my affection and appreciation for the man I'm with.

He grimaces. "Sure, yes, it was a good kiss, Emma. Definitely. You're instinct to take a fun moment and make it more intimate, affectionate. I was... yeah, it worked for you." The word 'good,' feels incredibly inadequate right now...

"It was a pretty great date, Emma." He gives me a light pat on the shoulder. I feel the side of my mouth dip in response. "I think we should probably draw a line here, though. You're new to this and I've seen it happen a lot with other women I've spent time with. When it comes to affection, we should be more careful. I'm not saying there shouldn't be any." He pauses, choosing his words carefully. "But I think it's time we talk about the physical aspects of our arrangement."

I agree and am glad we are going to open up this line of communication.

But he starts again before I can comment. "While some affection is fine, I think it's best if we keep this platonic, so we don't obscure our goals."

I look away, disheartened. I think I nod.

Now I know we felt very different things during that kiss.

He talks again and I force my gaze back to him. "Emma, you're an attractive woman and I enjoy spending time with you. I just don't think it's fair to you to let things get complicated, given the entire reason for our arrangement."

He's talking a lot with his hands, which I stare at as my brain plays catch-up to what my heart already knows he's trying to say.

"Tonight, you were completely immersed in our date and you acted on your feelings. Your instincts are great and I should have stopped you and just told you that. We've talked about cues, scenarios, and timing for displaying affection. You nailed it. Your skills are more than proficient. So, let's keep the physical affection strictly for your future dating companions." He gives me a friendly shoulder bump. "You don't need any practice there, so that's an A-plus in your report card tonight, Mahoney."

I tear my gaze from him, repeating, "Proficient," in a confused whisper.

"Oh, okay. Yeah, good then, I guess. Got it." I look down at my lap, not wanting him to see how devastated I am. "I'll see you tomorrow then."

I decide to stay strong and not feel completely rejected, but I don't have the firmest grip on that yet, so the claws come out a little.

I open the truck door, and without looking at him say, "I can walk myself to the door since we already had a kiss and I wouldn't want to make you uncomfortable not knowing if I'd try for another. Goodnight, Jess."

I slip out of his truck just as I hear him sigh my name.

CHAPTER 18

Jess

Sleep sucked. Guilt does that.

I hated having to do that to Emma last night. It was fucking horrible. What she doesn't realize, and what I won't admit to her, is that the line I told her we can't muddle is for me, not her. Sure, she could acquire complicated feelings if we acted on our physical attraction. But the real problem is that I want to make things physical and I might acquire feelings too.

I need to keep myself planted on my side of the line, or everything will fall apart. She and I, in that kitchen, pressed against her, touching her, while trying to keep her from maiming herself. It was way too tempting.

The allure of Emma is a physical presence in my life, one I don't need to inflate by invading her sweet mouth again or feeling her small hands clutch at me. After getting over the initial shock of her kiss and attempting to keep the lust at a manageable level, my sex-depraved brain was picturing the things I could do to her, with her, given the chance.

That kiss was, by far, the single best kiss I've ever had. And not just because it was spontaneous and sweet. It was because, as hard as I try to avoid it, she means something to me. To have her pour all her affection, hope, desire, and adoration into that kiss. Her feelings were palpable. It felt real because it was, and I couldn't let her do that to herself when I know where that road leads.

I tried to hint at keeping to our arrangement while we were getting ice cream, but then she flirted with me and kept looking at me like she wanted to lick me instead of her dessert. That hopeful, sexy smile of hers does me in every single time.

This was not the smile I got as she left my truck.

Emma has been very accepting of everything so far. She hasn't reacted poorly to any advice I've given, the walls I've put up, or even when she caught me telling Taylor that she was a wreck and I couldn't ever date her for real.

Tonight, though, she fired back at me and I don't blame her one bit.

I stretch on the front lawn for a few minutes before heading over to knock on her door. The door swings open. She's in her running gear, which teases those lustful feelings to no end. Short spandex, a loose, gaping running tank tied in a knot at the side of her waist, showing several inches of her hip and abdomen. And a neon-colored sports bra keeping those perky breasts in check. I study her face, scanning and then zeroing in on her eyes to assess her mood.

"'Morning!"

Chipper this morning. That's… confusing.

"Yeah, good morning! Ready?"

"You bet!"

We always run our first mile on the trail behind our houses. Most days, she's right beside me and we chat, her arm brushing mine, swatting at me as I mock her lethargic nature in the mornings, ponytail whipping me every time I lean down to talk.

I notice right away she's not running beside me today.

It's harder to give gait or breathing pointers if she's keeping pace behind me.

"Is everything okay?" I ask.

I know it's not.

"Yup, fine! Which way are we going today?" she asks, not looking at me.

Ah, shit. This doesn't bode well for me. Although, it's what I deserve.

I slow down to align myself with her pace so I can look at her. "Through town ending at the bakery. My treat. That sound okay?"

Yes, I'm not above bribing her to like me again.

She tips her head, looking right at me. Progress?

"You trying to butter me up, Jess?"

"I just thought you'd like a pastry at the end of our run today."

She keeps a firm ten-foot buffer between us for the rest of the run. Even when we get to the bakery, she skirts around me. As I order her pastries and our coffee, she says only a few words to me. In another attempt at contact, I put my hand on her lower back, leading her out the door. She jumps at my touch.

On the walk back to her house, it's quiet. Whenever we stop for coffee after our runs, we meander back at a slow pace, either holding hands or my arm thrown over her shoulders. Now I'm worried I may have ruined that. I didn't realize how much I touch Emma or just put myself near her until now when she is unreceptive to my nearness.

At first, it was to get her used to casual intimacy between a couple, then occasionally as a show for the League, making sure they had details to feed my mom.

From Emma's perspective, she may have thought the next natural progression was kissing. I should've been clearer about the kinds of touch that were okay and what she should expect in a normal relationship.

I throw an arm over her shoulders without looking over at her. "You still upset with me?"

She opens her mouth, feigning a shocked and confused expression. Then snaps her mouth shut.

"Let me finish my Danish first, then ask."

She takes an enormous bite, then smiles around the crumbs stuck to her lips. I grin and brush at them.

When she's done, I try again. "So, what's the verdict?" I flash my teeth at her in a wild and nervous and hopeful smile.

"You are hard to stay mad at."

"I know, my mom says that too." She rolls her eyes at that and shakes her head. "Can you tell me what part of our conversation last night upset you?"

"It's not being upset that's bothering me. Being upset is good. Well, in my messed-up head, anyway." She chuckles. "I don't know what to do from here. I've never been an affectionate person. When you said we need to keep to friendly affection, I understood your reasoning. You don't want me to confuse any new feelings I am having with actual feelings."

She frowns at herself.

"I'm a hesitant affection-giver and now I'm even more hesitant because I don't know what's okay."

She looks up at me with her doe eyes and now I feel worse. Didn't think that could happen.

"Dammit, I'm sorry, Emma. I didn't quite know what to say to you about the boundaries of our arrangement and I fucked it up."

I reach over for her hand, and after a slight hesitation, she takes it.

"Hand-holding, sitting next to each other, touching in non-erogenous zones, high-fives, hugs, and the affection you'd show a friend like Lauren is good. The touch we need to steer clear of is the sexual kind: kissing, nibbling, licking, groping, fondling, humping, sucking—"

She cuts me off. "Okay, okay! I've got it." She shoves me as her own example. "Is that type, okay?" She smirks at me.

"Also, you know way too many verbs for sexual contact."

"Yes I do, glad we cleared that up."

My cocky smirk appears and results in another shove. Being pushed around never felt so good.

I put my arm back around her and turn more serious. "Affection is important for you, Emma, and I don't want you thinking we can't be affectionate. It just can't be sexual affection."

"All affection feels pretty darn sexual right now," she mumbles under her breath, but I hear her anyway and give her shoulder a squeeze.

Too true, Emma.

Emma

He's plunked me right in the middle of friendship-zone territory as we continue our date coaching activities. It's a punch to the gut, but I don't let him see me flinch. For a moment, I thought something real was forming. Something warm, sparkly, and magical. All we had to do was give it a little nudge and it would ignite.

I hear the slap before it registers in my brain. "Wow, looking hot, hon!"

"Jesus, Lauren. We've talked about the ass slapping."

"Yes, but you love it. Isn't that what we decided?" It's true, I pretend to hate it and she delights in surprising me.

It's July, so Lauren is off for the summer, meaning I've gotten to see her more, but she was visiting her family in Piedmont last weekend. She tends not to stay in touch when she is with them. She likes to keep the nightmare separate from the dream life she has fashioned for herself. Her current lifestyle is both miles apart from her old life and the polar opposite of how she grew up.

Lauren accomplished what I have been floundering at these last few months. And she did it solo.

"I'm proud of you." My voice is full of adoration and respect.

She stops her tirade of indecision about which wine to pair with the appetizer, taken aback.

"Huh? For what?"

"You've built the life you want, free from the tyranny of your family and their influence. You know who you are, what you want, and went after it, undeterred by other people's thoughts. It's your life, and no one decides the story of your life but you."

"Shit." She looks away. When she looks up at me, she's scowling. "You don't compliment me with that mushy, profound, and sob-worthy stuff in public. I can't lose it and smother you with sappy hugs and tears."

Her fake glare narrows.

"That's why you did it here, didn't you? Hmm… clever. Well, guess what, I'm still coming at you."

Then she zips around the table and is gripping me in her firm arms.

I laugh then tap on her shoulder while wheezing, struggling to get a decent breath.

Lauren sits back down and tells me bits and pieces of her trip back home dealing with her family business. She never discusses this unless there's an overlap with her current life or some juicy gossip.

We are halfway through the pecan pie and vanilla bean ice cream before she tells me she saw her ex and her dad during this trip. They both have been putting pressure on her to 'reunite the families'.

"They've been sabotaging all of my relationships post-Andrew, bribing or threatening them, even interfering with several of my teaching positions at schools. That's why I wasn't hired back at the Fine Arts High School in San Francisco. I seriously think they may have hired a private investigator to follow me."

I stare at her in shock. Not knowing what to say or how to help. No wonder she moved away and has been avoiding them for over a year.

"I'm so sorry if I've been a bit off lately. It's just been a lot to handle and I wanted to just enjoy you living here. I wasn't quite ready to admit how fucked up my family is. I mean, you know. You've experienced them at holidays and events, but trust me when I say those people and the ones trying to manipulate me into following their agenda—two very different breeds of the same evil litter."

Her man-hiatus makes so much sense now. And why she's been more downcast than usual.

"That's awful and yet I'm not completely surprised. But Lauren, I don't think just waiting it out will be an effective tactic against your family's brand of scheming. They are…" I search for the right words.

"Heinous and persistent?" Lauren suggests.

I give her a sympathetic nod.

"Forget my absurd family. I've moved away, and I'm going to stay away. Except for my grandpa, of course, because that man gives no shits and loves me to bits. Now, tell me about your week." She bounces in her chair, ready for an update.

Jess and I spent time together this week after the intense, no-kissing conversation. He seemed fine, and I tried to act as normal as possible.

Emma Mahoney, playing the part of an awkward friend harboring feelings of unrequited love. Or at least love adjacent.

I'm not sure if he's noticed, but I've gone back to our playful and innocent touches. During our lunches, we sit on my office sofa, me with my feet up on his legs as I lay down while he gobbles up my lunch leftovers. It feels natural, friendly, but the spark is still there for me and I don't know what to do about it.

"How was the cooking date with Jess? I should have injury-checked you before we sat down."

She laughs while scanning me, even looking under the table at my bare legs.

I roll my eyes, but she just waggles her eyebrows at me knowing I'll spill the details.

She's right. Every sizzling, sensual, and shameful detail is told including my internal reaction to our butterfly-inducing, panty-melting kiss. Lauren has leaned so far over the table, her butt has lifted off her chair, sticking up at any passing patrons.

"Oh my god! That's my girl. Guys love when a girl makes the

first move. Or most do. Ones who aren't Draconian, high-handed assholes." That last comment was pointed. But she doesn't wait for me to question it. "What happened afterward?"

"Nothing. It was a bit anti-climactic. There I was, flutter and fire burning up my insides, and he was cool and detached."

"I bet he's just good at tamping his inner turmoil," she assures. "What about on the way home? At the door."

"We went for ice cream, I flirted, he appeared into it. Until he suggested we keep things more platonic to prevent future confusion given our arrangement." I take a huge gulp of my wine and set it on the table with a loud clunk. "And then later he told me that while my kissing skills were more than proficient—"

"He said what!" I rush to quiet her, but it's too late. "He used the word proficient when describing your kiss? What an asshat. You need to stop getting dating advice from that jackhole right now." She signals our server again, this time ordering red wine.

Shit. She's pissed and looking to let her red rage out.

"He said I didn't need any practice at it and said the kiss was proficient." Thinking back, I try to remember how he explained this, but I was too distraught to remember the exact words he used. "I don't recall the order or specifics, but the takeaway was that he doesn't want our relationship to progress beyond the 'dating coach' and the 'inept and unloved' arrangement we have. He shut me down."

I tell her about the way I left his truck and the following morning's clarification and pastry covered olive branch.

She's speechless for a moment. Which, for her, is impressive and warns of imminent danger.

She picks up her phone and starts typing away. Confused, I lean over and try to peek. I just laid my most embarrassing date story bare on the table for her to assess and comfort me, and she's texting.

It's Taylor. Huh. Oh shit, no, no, no!

"No! Lauren, do not rage at his best friend just because he turned me down and gave me the fake-relationship equivalent of a hand slap. He has every right to do that. I don't want Taylor involved in this. I'm just upset and having a moment. A feelings moment."

"Fine." She huffs and puts the phone down. "But I sent him some nasty emojis. Not knowing what I'm pissed about will drive him crazy, so I'll take pleasure in that." She grabs my hand. "How crushed are we about this?"

"Pretty defeated. Until our run this morning where he explained he still wants to help me and is welcoming of friendly affection. I'm so out of touch, I don't even recognize the difference between innocent touches and sexual attraction."

"There is definite chemistry between you two. His touches are friend-appropriate, but involuntary. He touches you without thought, but they are filled with heat and meaning." She taps her spoon on the table for a few beats. "Did he say he didn't want you?"

I think back, frowning. "No. Just that we shouldn't confuse our circumstances."

She smirks at me. "He wants you."

"I don't know much about men like Jess, but if he wanted me, wouldn't he just take what I'm offering?" Incredulous, it's my voice that rises this time.

"Pfft. Only Jess could answer that. He clearly has some relationship hang-ups."

The conversation Jess and I had when I originally asked him to help me with dating filters back into my mind. He said he only does casual dating—casual sex. "He said as much when I proposed this whole scenario, but I didn't know then what I do now."

"And what's that?"

"That Jess is helping me feel whole again and pretending to date him isn't enough. Everything I want is one door down from me each night, but so far out of reach."

"Look, I don't know what the man is thinking or if this is going to work out the way you want. But I do know that this is a part of real dating. The unknown, the occasional turmoil, the uncertainty of feelings. Just be you. Let him see you and what he could have with you. That way you can't say you didn't try. You want something, go for it. Your life, your dreams, your future. Don't coast through it like you have in your formative years, dead inside and scared of living."

Was I dead inside? I wasn't alive, on fire, heart racing, or nerve-racked, that's for sure. I didn't know any better and lived in complacency. Not anymore.

"Having to convince him to give us a real chance is humiliating, though."

"You're not doing anything other than being real with him. Put yourself out there, continue the 'friendly' touches he deemed appropriate. Don't pull back because of your hurt feelings and self-preservation instincts. He drew the line because it worries him that it's too easy to cross and if he does, you two are real."

"And if that changes nothing? If he doesn't see me or the potential of us?"

Based on our pasts, we have planned futures that greatly differ from each other.

"All it may do is force him to reassess why the hell he thinks commitment and love are incompatible with his future. That part of your relationship is there, now he just has to accept it."

"And if, at the end of this, he still doesn't want a future with me?"

"Then you'll know and you adjust to a different future. One where you are wanted, appreciated, and loved by the person who should value you above all others. Until then, the future you're picturing will just be a little incomplete for a while," she assures me. "It's something many of us are working on, me included."

CHAPTER 19

Jess

Things have returned to normal for Emma and I. We run, we hang out, go out for dinner, watch our favorite shows, and see who can get the other hooked the fastest. The usual. She feels comfortable around me again. We are back to the cuddles she enjoys, holding hands, and easy affection. We even have a dinner date set up with my parents, who are returning from Italy soon.

Word about our relationship and our dates got back to Mom in record time. We set this dinner weeks ago, knowing it was the best way to hold my mom off from showing up unannounced the minute she and Dad returned from Europe. Or even returning early, which Dad specifically called me about with a plan to prevent.

This included sending updates, letting her talk to my 'new girlfriend', and photos of Emma and I—some of which she already had, from who I have no fucking clue, but I'm keeping the drapes closed from now on. Freaking nosey town.

All of the pretend, casualness, closeness, and ease of affection is messing with me.

I now have an inkling of how alcoholics feel when they go to a bar because it's the same way I feel when I spend time with Emma and her soft, chaste touches. The proximity to her scent alone is like a drug, then she'll throw an arm around me or put her feet on my lap, mess with my hair. The bottom of the barrel is calling and I'm counting down the gulps as I journey there.

How I'm spending my afternoon is the greatest challenge of all current temptations. Emma decked out in that crazy hot, tight, stretchy athletic wear women own. And I don't mean possess. I mean, she owns that outfit and every dirty thought it pulls from my mind.

July in this part of California is quite warm as we make our way to the peak of our summer temperatures. We ended up having to change our running time to later in the morning. It's already over seventy degrees, and while we are only stretching, I can feel a trickle of sweat rolling down my temple.

Emma still looks cool in her second-skin running shorts and cropped running top. I can see everything. It's also how I know that she is most definitely not wearing underwear under those shorts.

She then goes to do a quad stretch using me for balance.

"You're hot."

"Thanks." I grin, obnoxiously flexing.

"Ha! I meant, you feel hot. Is this going to be okay? I know you're used to running in the early morning. We can skip it if it's going to be too hot. It's my last chance for a run before I head off for the rest of the weekend."

Emma is traveling to Denver to see her dad this weekend. She doesn't talk much about him and I get the impression they aren't very close. She plans on telling him about moving here and starting fresh.

"I'll be fine. Sweaty, but fine. Be prepared to hose me down before letting me into your house."

She giggles like I'm kidding, but it's the reason I try not to run later in the day.

"If you're sure…" I nod. "You set the pace, I'll try to match.

I'm hoping the heat will slow you down to my more moderate pace."

She gives me an ineffective shove and then takes off.

It's grueling. I'm sweating a concerning amount and when I look over at Emma, she appears fairly slick too. The usual pink that tints her glowing cheeks is now a deep red, sweat moving in rivulets down to her neck and chest.

"Don't look at me, I'm disgusting. Let's finish this last mile and find a pool to fall into." She kicks up her pace.

I whip off my shirt and tuck it into the back of my shorts. Letting the sweat gush unhindered.

We come around a bend, one that Emma loves because it means we have half a mile left and the end is near. I love seeing that big endorphin-high smile she beams at me every time we get to this point in the run.

She turns, her smile getting harder to maintain given the heat. Her eyes meet mine for a fraction of a second before they hit my chest. Those honey brown eyes are searing their way down my chest, lingering on my abs, and then ending their journey along the waistband of my shorts. The side of my mouth may stay permanently hitched up in a cocky smirk.

Her mouth is hanging open as she snaps those eyes back up to mine. Her cheeks are glowing brighter, that red tint traveling down her neck and chest. She's still looking at me and running, not watching the path as it curves. With a mind of its own, my hand reaches out to pull her closer. Not just because that's where I like her, but because she's veering off the path.

Too late, I see her stumble then go down hard just off the path. She gives a squeal and an oomph. I'm there a mere second after she lands, but was helpless to stop it.

I'm in the dirt checking her. She took the brunt of the fall on her right side.

"Shit, you okay, babe? Are you bleeding? Let's look, alright? Tell me if anything hurts."

"Uh, I don't know. I think I'm okay. Just scraped up."

I'm checking her wrist, knee, gently wiping dirt from her with my shirt. She's still breathing hard and says she feels fine. I help her try to stand because with running a knee or ankle injury is common and she may not know until she puts weight on it.

Watching, I notice the moment her left foot contacts the ground. She winces, her body jerking involuntarily. I bend to check her ankle. Shit, it's swollen.

"Ow," she hisses. "That's not good." Her forehead crinkles. "I don't think I can walk on it."

I put my arm under hers and wrap it around her waist, keeping her steady.

"How are we going to get back?"

"Don't worry, Emma. It's fine, I'll see if Taylor can come pick us up from the gas station down the street." I shrug. "Don't worry about that. How's it feeling? It can take time for your body to register the pain. Should we head to the clinic?"

It looks like a regular sprain, but if it's a grade two or three sprain, she may need a cast or crutches to help her walk. I should have been closer, I could have grabbed her before she took a spill off the path.

"No, no. It's okay, I think. If you don't mind lending your arm and going at my awkwardly slow pace, I can limp there." She looks so downtrodden, I can't help but give her a hug. Why did I take off my shirt?

She looks embarrassed, and it's not her fault at all. I am the overconfident, arrogant douche who couldn't keep it in my shirt.

Did it feel good to have her looking at me? Sure, but after the line-crossing discussion, I shouldn't be trying to get her to ogle me.

"All runners fall at some point. I went down on fresh asphalt a few years ago. Hurt like a bitch having to pick all the tar and rocks out of my knees, palms, and forearms." I'm still running my hands over her side, rubbing along her ribs to make sure she didn't bruise them in the fall.

"I'm fine, Jess." She flicks at my hands. "I'm just embarrassed, and a little banged up."

"Don't be. You did nothing wrong, just happens sometimes."

"Um, yes I did. I took my eyes off the path." Sounding more like the Emma I know, I'm relieved. "Speaking of, you should probably put your shirt back on for our slow walk back."

"What?"

"You, and the whole rippling hunk thing. You're a glistening specimen of physical fitness, exuding charm and that unattainable vibe. It's like single woman catnip." She snorts. "You are the physical embodiment of distraction on a primal level."

That's even better than what I thought she was going to say. My muscles twitch in a quick flex, wanting to give her another show. Focus man, she's hurt and we should get her checked out because she hasn't even tried to move yet.

My smile must be a mile wide. "You complimenting me, gimpy?"

I pick her up and cradle her in my arms. She gives a small sound of protest.

"I'll carry you to the gas station, then we will grab some water and call Taylor. No arguments. I don't want you putting any weight on that ankle until we see a doctor."

She raises one tiny finger and lifts it up. Like a naughty child in school hoping that by being cute, she'll get her way.

"Yes, Ms. Mahoney?"

"You didn't put your shirt on. I'd hate for us to find more trouble because you are a distracting menace to society." Her eyes are wide and round, a pout plumping up her bottom lip.

I shake my head at her and she lets out a smattering of giggles. Finding herself hilarious, she keeps it up intermittently for a few more moments.

"I'm sorry if you fell because you couldn't tear your pervy eyes from my sexy bod," I taunt as she smacks my chest with the back of her dainty hand. "Really, though, I am sorry if I caused you to get hurt."

"Worth it."

With that, she wraps her arms tighter around my neck and lays her head on my shoulder.

Emma

My flight for Denver departs in a few hours, but it looks like that's no longer happening. This is unfortunate and a relief at the same time. Telling Father about the last year of my life is going to be a gamble. I know he loves me in his own way, but he isn't exactly a comforting confidant.

Maybe I should email him a summary instead. Efficient, emotionless, yet informative, just as he likes most communication.

No, I can't do that. Calling him would be a suitable alternative, since I am clearly not going to make my flight.

When Jess took me to the doctor, I found out I have a grade two low ankle sprain. There was a heavy dose of guilt on his face during the visit. He has hardly left my side, which has caused more conflicting emotions.

A man tending to me and caring about my well-being, especially this man, has been heartwarming. It makes me wonder if it stems from hidden romantic intent instead of guilt and compassion. I cross my fingers for the former, but my heart is messing with my brain and I can't trust it to make rational decisions.

Outfitted with my new walking boot and pain pills, Jess helps me into my house. He needn't carry me, but I couldn't dissuade him.

I mean, I didn't try hard or anything.

I have no regrets about my ankle dilemma. Jess is here taking care of me and I am soaking up every moment. I only have, at most, a couple weeks of wearing this boot before I return to normal activities.

Whatever the good doctor gave me is much stronger than I'm used to, and I feel great. Which is fortunate because the swelling on my ankle and the abrasions on the left side of my body were starting to grip me five minutes into being carried. I was near tears as we spotted Taylor pulling into the parking lot, letting them loose was unavoidable once we got into his vehicle.

I'm gently laid down on my bed as Jess flits around getting me my Kindle, water, a snack and extra pillows from the closet. He even brings me my fuzzy socks.

"Do you need anything else? What time did you take your pain pills? We should set a timer to know when to take more so you don't fall behind on them."

He rubs that spot behind his ear and keeps looking around.

"I'm fine, Jess. Sit. Relax. Everything is great!" I beam at him and starfish on the bed, patting the space beside me in welcome.

He leans in closer, a curious look on his face. I lean in and try to mimic his expression.

"You're high off the pills, aren't you?"

"I don't know… am I?" I feign a concerned face, but then end up laughing.

"Jesus." His lips twitch just the teeniest bit.

"Come on!" I pat the bed beside me. He gets in gently, as to not jostle me.

I lean over and whisper, "I have a hot guy in my bed. What should I do, Coach?"

He puffs out a laugh, rakes his hand over his face, "You're pretty adorable like this. But in answer to your question, for now, you sleep."

"No, no, no. That doesn't sound like fun. Plus, I have to reschedule my flight for a couple weeks from now. I don't want to be wearing this thing" —I hold up my booted foot— "when I fly."

"Oh, shit. Your flight! You were supposed to go see your dad. Sorry, Emma."

"This is not your fault, silly. I'll pay more attention when we run from now on, promise. Although, maybe if you were shirtless around me more, it wouldn't be as shocking or distracting. Let's pencil that in for future dates: shirt optional."

I grin like I've just come up with the best idea ever. Wow, these pills are awesome.

"I'm ignoring that, but will remind you about it tomorrow, which I'm really going to enjoy." I give him a goofy smile at that.

"Do you need to call him?"

"Yes, but I'll do it when I'm not all doped up. Though, being doped up might make it easier. Or you could tell him for me!"

Great idea. Mental high five!

"Sure, I can tell him you are rescheduling because of your injury. Did you have a particular date in mind? We can always postpone the thing with my parents, if you want to go next weekend. It wouldn't be a problem."

"No! I want to meet your parents. Let me do this for you, it's one of the few things I'm providing in this arrangement. Your parents will love me and I'll go see my father the weekend after or something."

"Okay, do you want me to call him?"

"Sure. Can you just tell him everything, though?"

I sit up on my elbows. "Hit the highlights: for the last handful of years, I've lived a hollow, meaningless life built around a company where I was a relentless, effective, yet resented finance executive. Then my boss sexually harassed and assaulted me. That led to a breakdown, therapy, ass-kicking skills, and a big move to a small-town life filled with meaning, satisfaction, and deep attachments."

I take a deep breath, nod, and hand over my phone.

"Uh, Emma…" He sets the phone down and takes my hand. "I don't know what to say, but if you want to talk about this, I'm here to listen, rage, beat some bastard up, whatever you need. I appreciate that you shared that with me, even if you may not have intended to."

"Dale was in jail, last I checked, so you may have to get in line to beat his ass. You'd have to wait behind Lauren and all the other women since I was not the first or only woman he treated this way."

I shift to face Jess better.

"But thank you for that. I appreciate it, and I'm glad you know now."

"Me, too. Also, I'm good with waiting in line behind Lauren. I wouldn't want to get in her way."

He wraps my less scraped up hand in his.

"I'll just text your dad the basics since I'm guessing he doesn't know about me." He winks at me and I know he's not offended. "Emma?"

I hum in response, dragging my tired eyes to look into his.

"You're so fucking strong. What you're doing here, how you packed up your life and just changed it all. It's incredible. I don't know if what we're doing together is going to help you or not, but I want you to know something important: you're capable of anything. So, this whole relationship thing you want, you were built for this. You deserve it all."

He shatters me with his words and my brain is too slow to respond other than giving a long squeeze of his hand and blinking the tears away.

"Thank you for doing this with me, Jess. You've shown me such possibilities. Why didn't I have you in my life sooner?"

"I've only shown you some basic stuff. Answered questions, helped you practice. Nothing out of the ordinary. The date itself is not as important as the company you keep. Another dating tip from me to you." He taps my nose, then looks away. "You should rest. You only have a couple days of those pain pills, so take advantage of the pain-free bliss while you can, Killer."

He gets up off the bed; I frown and protest, reaching for him. He shushes me and smiles, moving around to the other side of the bed, getting in on my uninjured side. "I'm staying, don't worry. Sleep, babe."

His fingers play with my hair. I fall asleep content, safe, and full of love.

CHAPTER 20

Emma

It's been a week of milking this ankle injury. I think Jess knows I'm fine, but he continues to fuss over me. He's been bringing lunch to the bank every day, saying it's too hard for me to take the stairs up and down to go to lunch.

When I mentioned bringing lunch from home with me, he rolled his eyes and said having food poisoning with a limp was not a goal to reach for.

He spent the first three nights with me post-injury. Deep down, I hoped it was more than guilt inspiring him to stay. He is a good man with so much love in him to give, but he tries so hard to fight it. For someone who seems so well suited for love, roots, and family, he's intent on holding himself back from the greatness that surrounds him.

This isn't something you can tell someone, they have to figure it out themselves. I didn't realize what awaited me until I felt it, experienced it.

Would Jess be willing to take a chance on me?

Jess is still teaching me some things about what to expect of future men I date. He seems to be attacking our dating education with renewed vigor. I go along with it only to find out how to be a better girlfriend and for relationship timeline advice.

At what point do you bring up moving in together, how do you know if moving in is even a good idea? How invested to get before bringing up the possibility of kids. Apparently, this should be an early deciding factor that could bring an immediate end to a relationship.

This led to the marriage talk. Jess was very uncomfortable during this conversation, but said that finding out if marriage is even on the table for the other person is important. He said if my intent is a long-term relationship, aim to discuss anything that's a deal-breaker in the first month or two of dating.

I'm meeting his parents this weekend. I've only chatted briefly with them on the phone a few times, so I am a little nervous. The sweats start up every time I think about what they will think of me, if they'll be like Jess, if they'll approve of our relationship, if they'll know we aren't really dating but that I desperately want to.

While it's not ideal to meet Jess's parents under the guise of a fake relationship, gleaning information from him to prepare for 'meeting the parents' has been informative.

First impressions go fifty-fifty for me, but I feel better knowing Jess will be there and has given me enough tips to rock this gathering. I'm also finally able to actively fulfill my end of our agreement.

Jess has been talking to them about us, as has the town, and they are very excited to meet me. Well, mostly his mom because she's been pestering Jess for years about settling down, finding a wonderful woman, and making a home for her future grandbabies.

We've had to discuss topics to steer clear of, and babies are on that list. Jess says there is a ninety-five percent chance she will bring it up today and to prepare for diversion if he is not around to provide it. Would a proper diversion be to tell her that her son can put a baby in me anytime he pleases?

Okay, maybe I'm not ready to have a baby, with him or anyone else, but the practice that comes with trying would certainly be nice.

The question I have been asking myself lately is: would I have been as attracted to Jess had I met him before undergoing this personal growth? Probably, but the difference is that I would not have pursued it. In actuality, I would have veered as far away as possible. Anything that sparked deep emotion was a no-go zone for me.

Yet here I am on Jess's porch, steps away from meeting his parents.

I knock on his door with my booted foot, holding two bottles of wine and a lemon blueberry Bundt cake that my lovely, but eccentric neighbor made.

Stella is a great baker, and shortly after the book club disaster, she started popping in for visits. Maybe hoping I'd continue attending her club, but I think it was also her own way of including me in the community. When she found out I was learning to bake, she started pity-gifting me her recipes, but I just can't seem to get them right.

My baked goods have the flavor or texture of cardboard with a hint of sweetness that lingers at the back of your throat like a lozenge.

My palms are so sweaty, I almost drop the bottles of wine and have to lift a knee to balance them on. Luckily, I remembered to lift my injured leg.

The door opens with a whoosh.

"What are you doing?" Jess asks as he takes the wine bottles out of my hands.

"Um, trying to get invited in?" I answer, confused.

"No, I mean, why didn't you wait for me to come get you. I could have walked you over and went back for all this stuff. Get in here and get your foot up."

He ushers me in, setting everything on the entryway table, before turning toward me to help me.

"Hi," I say, my nerves clear in my voice.

He smiles, a teasing lift to one side of his smile. "Hi."

He wraps an arm around my waist, helping me into the kitchen. "How's the ankle today?"

"Good. Better every day, I swear. You don't have to worry. I'll be back running with you in no time. I'm sure you miss the challenge of running while trying to keep up with a constant barrage of chatter." My eyes twinkle in jest.

"I think you have it backward there. I find running quite boring without you now. So, yes, we should get you back on your feet again."

"Well, that would require you to allow me on my feet."

He frowns at me and continues his mother-hen routine.

"They're not here yet?"

He shakes his head.

"What time are they arriving?"

"Not for another couple of hours. My mom will make dinner here. She typically goes all out, so the fridge will overflow with leftovers for a while."

He has a smile on his face I haven't seen before. It's the smile of a mama's boy and it's heartwarming.

"I thought we were going out to eat? What is she making? I can look it up so I can be more helpful. What if I ruin dinner, or hurt someone, or—"

Big hands wrap around me, one around the front of my body, trapping my arms, and the other over my mouth.

"Shhh. Breathe. She doesn't like to have help in the kitchen because she's bossy and a control freak. She always shoos me away. The kitchen is her office. We stay on our side of the 'desk' and we never go around to her side. Otherwise, it gets ugly," he reassures me.

I consider this. "Okay. So just pour her wine and keep her involved in the conversation?" I ask. I appreciate having a plan of action.

"Yes, exactly. That'll be perfect." He guides me to a stool at the island, then brings over a chair to prop my ankle on.

"We should open up the red wine to let it breathe before they arrive," I say as I grab the wine and move to get the opener. He stops me and then goes over to the bar area to grab it.

"Any last-minute tips or advice? How will I know if they like me? Do parents typically prefer a quiet, agreeable woman for their son or do I pull out all the stops to make that great first impression?" I quickly amend, "Although, I don't have many 'stops' to pull out since I don't really know how to over-achieve in the parental impressing department."

"Can you juggle? My parents love live entertainment."

I give him my best scowl, which he responds to by tweaking my nose.

"Just be yourself. You're impressive all on your own," he says off-handedly. "Party tricks would help though, so what you got?"

"I can fit seventeen marshmallows in my mouth," I offer.

I can't. I don't think. I've never tried, but have always been curious about it.

His eyes bug out, then he tilts his head and stares at my mouth, trying to determine how the hell I can do that being that people typically describe my stature as dainty or petite.

"Really?" There's a hitch in his voice.

I stifle my laugh, but it bursts from my mouth in a very unladylike raspberry.

"No. I was just messing with you. I've always wondered, though. Probably shouldn't stuff my mouth full of marshmallows the first time meeting someone."

He is shaking his head at me and laughing. "You'd fit right in with my dad if you did."

The doorbell rings, startling both of us. I raise my eyebrows at him in question.

"That's not your folks already, is it?"

Panic, panic, more panic. It's so easy with Jess, but I still struggle with people I don't know. I even flounder at the grocery store when someone in the checkout line attempts to start a conversation with me.

He checks his phone as he gets up from the stool.

"Is it?" I ask again, this time he can hear the panic in my tone.

"I don't know. If so, they're early. Either way, it's fine, Emma. It's just dinner and getting to know two new people." He rubs my arm.

That's when we hear the doorbell again, followed by his name being shouted through the door.

"Yup, that's my dad," he says, walking toward the front door.

"You leave your mamma waiting so long, *Mimmo*?" his mom says with a hint of an accent. Her voice is smooth and warm, and I just know she is going to be a hugger.

I get off my stool and make my way through the living room to greet his parents.

As soon as his parents are in view, I see every trait Jess has as they piece together in my mind. His dad is tall, a little taller than Jess, chestnut brown hair with dark red and light gray streaking through it. It's stunning and there are women who would spend a lot of money to recreate it. His eyes are the same intense green as Jess's. So is his expression as he grins at his wife's antics.

Jess's mom is looking right at me like she's zeroed in on her next target. For such a slight woman, she gives off a formidable vibe. Her dark brown hair, braided meticulously, sweeps over a delicate shoulder. I'm looking at the female version of Jess's facial features. She has glowing olive skin and an energy that permeates the air.

Mr. Caldwell is explaining that spending that much time with her family over in Italy seems to revitalize her Italian roots.

"Her accent always fires up after talking to Tia Elena, so I can only imagine how bad it is after months in Italy. Has she started hitting people yet?" Jess asks his dad.

I'm still slowly making my way over to them, when Jess calls out to me.

"Mom, Dad, this is Emma Mahoney. Try not to scare her off," he warns as he comes over to me to help me the rest of the way. "Emma, these are my parents, Camilla and Rian."

I shake Rian's hand first, muttering a greeting I don't recall. Then I turn to Camilla to offer the same.

I'm ripped away from Jess's side and embraced so tightly it forces a puff of air from my lungs in an, "oof!"

"Mom, too much. She's injured, remember?"

"Oh sorry, *cara*."

She releases me, but keeps her hands on my arms as she takes me in. Her warm eyes assess me with intrigue. "She is so beautiful!" She claps her hands in excitement. "Shy, though?" She flits her eyes to Jess who must agree because then she says, "That's okay, *cara*, we can fix that!"

With that, she rubs my arms the same way Jess often does to comfort me.

Then she grabs a bag from the ground in one hand, and my hand in the other. Slowly, but surely, she leads me to the kitchen while giving the men their tasks.

"Sorry if we surprised you by being early. Rian was just too eager to meet you and insisted we head straight over." She winks, then glances behind me to see her husband's reaction.

"Woman, you run this show. What time I want to leave is irrelevant and we both know it."

He walks past her to put the groceries on the counter and smacks her butt on the way by. Rian is part Irish American, and while Jess may get some of his looks from his mom, it's clear of the rest of his features and disposition come from his dad.

"If we are telling stories, should I share the real one where a certain woman wanted to pack up and leave Italy early just to come home and meet her son's girlfriend?" he prods.

Jess is leaning against the island enjoying the show, then smiles when he sees my face. I must have the silliest of smiles on my face. Being raised by these two loving people must have been magical.

"Emma, do not listen to him. He was very excited to meet you, even if it doesn't seem like it right now." She sniffs at him.

"Let's remember, dear wife, that you damn near pushed me

down the stairs in a rush to get us out of the house. While I am very pleased to meet you, Emma, I am also just glad to be alive." I chuckle at their ridiculousness. I should have known being around Jess's parents would be just as easy as being around him.

"Well, I am glad you made it in one piece today. Here, come sit down next to me in the coddled section." I move a stool closer to me. "Jess won't let me so much as get my own glass of water. If it wasn't so sweet, it would be unreasonable," I say pointedly while glancing over at Jess. "Camilla, if at any point you want to rescue me from Coddle Island over here, please put me to work."

I feel a hint of pride in my socializing skills. Offering to help his mom and attempting to connect with his dad. I mentally pat myself on the back before returning my attention to the lovely people around me.

"You're supposed to stay off your foot and I can make that happen."

"Yes, Emma. You sit and rest. I appreciate the offer, but right now all I am doing is washing and prepping." She pats my hand and goes back to washing.

"What happened, anyway?" Rian asks.

I use all my inner strength to abolish the blush creeping up my neck. I see Jess about to interject, and rush to beat him to it. "Your son stripped in the park and in the mayhem, I tripped and fell down an embankment."

Camilla's wide gaze shoots to her son. For a second, I regret my decision to phrase my accident in this way. My sense of humor is not always well received. It's why I used to restrict myself to only superficial or educational contributions in conversation.

"Jess!" his mom scolds at the same time Jess says, "Emma!"

I bite my lip and shrug a shoulder, like 'what?'.

"You're a little shit," he says, stepping closer and pinching my chin between his thumb and pointer finger, then kissing the top of my head.

"Jess!" his mom reprimands again. "No cursing in my kitchen."

"Well… technically it's Garrett's kitchen," he argues.

He gets a narrow-eyed glare that has me squirming in my seat, and it's not even directed at me.

Rian's shoulders are shaking with laughter as he asks, "Sounds like quite the story. What mess did this guy" —he nudges his son— "get you into that resulted in that leg boot?"

"I want to preface this story by assuring everyone that I did not strip in a park." He puts his hands up.

"Well, you took your shirt off."

"It was hot!" he exclaims, but his eyes are sparkling like he's enjoying the way I am toying with him.

I shrug back at him and mutter, "Semantics," as I take a sip of my wine.

His dad, fully immersed in our storytelling stand-off, leans over the island, his gaze going to Jess to see what he'll come back with.

This family seems to enjoy banter. Probably because it seems to come from a place of love.

"Let's just call it like it is. My body is too irresistible. Emma couldn't peel her eyes off all this" —he gestures emphatically to his upper body— "long enough to watch the trail we were running on." He smirks at me.

A challenge, fine. I may not have the best social skills, but I'm defensive and stubborn.

"Fine, that part may be true." I attempt to hide my grin. "I'd like to see how you'd do in the same situation. Next time we go running, how about I take off my top and see if you keep your eyes on the trail?" I cross my arms under my chest, and as expected his eyes dart right to them. "Why is it acceptable for men, but not for women?"

"You run with your shirt off? Like a douche?" his mom says on a tsk.

I probably shouldn't talk about getting half-naked with Jess being that his mom is in the room.

Wait. Did she just call him a douche?

His big, booming laugh startles me. "I was thinking the exact same thing when I was contemplating taking it off." His arm moves around to land on my back. "But now I thoroughly regret my decision for a few reasons." He turns to me, more serious now. "I still feel bad that you fell, even if it was from the obvious gawking."

"I'm fine. Plus, it was bound to happen."

I turn to Camilla. "Your son has been teaching me to run and has kept me safe for a while now. And I have not made it easy. I'm a walking disaster most days." I blush a little as Jess hums loudly in agreement. "This one was all on me, it's just fun to tease him."

I stare up at Jess and I can't seem to keep the adoration off my face. Jess seems not to notice, thankfully. Camilla, though, she may have noticed. Her smile takes up half her face as she walks around the counter, arms stretched out as she puts a hand on each of our faces and lets out a little squeal.

"Mamma is happy. Let's go sit in the sun and enjoy some wine." She grabs the bottle I brought, mentioning it's one of her favorites.

Yes! Wine bribery idea was a success.

We sip and bond over our love of the red nectar and vineyard tales.

When we eventually go back inside, she accepts my offer to help in the kitchen which surprises me given what Jess said about it being her zone.

"Can you put the potatoes on to boil for the mashed potatoes?"

Seems simple enough.

I put some water and potatoes in the pot and plunk it on the stovetop. She looks in the pot, then at me quizzically.

"Um, red-skin mashed potatoes are a good idea, too." The

slight hesitation in her tone shows that wasn't what she had planned.

"I've never made mashed potatoes before," I admit, wincing.

She smiles warmly. "I see. Well, I still think we make them your way. Give the potatoes a little more texture. I'll show you how we do the potatoes. Simple. We cut up, rinse, cover with fresh water, sprinkle a little salt, lid on, that's it."

I nod, making mental notes, paying close attention.

I cut them up the way she shows me. She teaches me a technique with the knife that makes it nearly impossible to cut myself as I chop.

"Anytime you need cooking advice or have questions, you come to me, okay?"

"I appreciate that. I've been trying to learn, but it hasn't been going very well, unfortunately." My face scrunches as I recall the couple's cooking class. "I even dragged Jess to a couple's cooking class thinking it would be a fun date, and I'd learn a lot." I laugh sardonically. "It was a disaster. Jess was such a trooper and tried everything we made."

"No one in your family cooks?"

"It was just me and my father for most of my childhood. He's not the homemaker type, so I've never learned."

"I'm so sorry, sweetie." She steps over and gives me a firm side hug. It's soft, warm, and filled with tenderness. I blink away the tears invading my eyes at the reminder of what I've missed out on most of my childhood.

Camilla shows me how to sear the roast before she puts it in the oven with some herbs, onion, and garlic. Then explains a few different ways she likes to cook and serve the vegetables.

Jess and his dad filter in and out of the kitchen, starting conversation, and sneaking snacks. He gives the watered-down version of how we met in the grocery store and a vague retelling of how we came to be dating. I don't feel right lying to his parents, but Jess's version is all truth, admittedly with some parts left out.

Putting my game face on, I pick up the mashed potatoes and carry my creation to the table like it's a newborn baby. Ecstatic, I set the potatoes on the table and catch Jess's gaze. That's when I realize that he is the perfectly prepared, creamy mashed potatoes of my life. Everything else is just gravy.

CHAPTER 21

Jess

Emma is carrying those mashed potatoes like they are her most prized possession. It makes me smile.

She's fitting right in with my folks, which makes me both happy and conflicted. I've watched her bond with Mom all afternoon while Dad and I gave them space, entertaining ourselves by catching up on the family in Italy, watching a preseason football game, and messing with Garrett's organization system in his 'study.'

Dad and I are the pranksters. Everyone else is so type A, they almost make it too easy.

He hands me a bottle of wine to serve with dinner. "This one is better. Much better."

I think about that, surprised he wants to talk wine. That's usually Mom's thing. "You like the cabernet?"

"Not the wine. The woman." He gestures to Emma.

"Oh. Uh, yeah." I don't know how to respond to this. He knows I don't talk about my past relationships.

"She seems good for you. Not like that woman you were infatuated with. And engaged to, I guess. Nearly forgot that bit." He brushes that off and continues, "Sometimes when we're young, life teaches us a few lessons the hard way. In your case, success comes in different forms and you don't always get all the good cards dealt to you all at once. You won a big hand in your career, then took a big hit with the woman you chose," he sighs. "We get shown these lessons when we're young because we have time to fix them. I had a couple of those mistakes when I was wet behind the ears, too. Almost would have cost me your mom if I hadn't smartened up and left the past behind me. Only then can you fully appreciate your future."

He claps me on the shoulder.

"And Mamma has taken your girl under her wing, so there's no keeping her away anymore." He's watching them in the kitchen as they are plating all the food for the dining table. "She's quirky, that's for sure. I like quirky. She's real and seems to like you for some reason. Considering you broke her ankle."

I roll my eyes. "First, it's not like I pushed her or anything. Jesus. She fell over in delight after taking in my sweaty shirtless form. Second, she has a sprained ankle."

"That's not the way I'm going to tell it." He shrugs, grinning. "Let's get the wine out there and set the table for the meal our ladies made us."

The roast is just making its way to the table as I finish up with the last place setting. I help Emma to her seat beside me and she is nearly coming out of her chair with poorly contained excitement.

"Hungry?" She gives a noncommittal sound. "It looks great. You learn some cooking tips from my mom?"

"Yes!" she practically shouts. "I can't believe we paid so much for that cooking class. Your mom should open a cooking school. Did you know that there are different potatoes, some good for mashing, some for baking or roasting? Apparently, the wrong kind can turn fluffy mashed potatoes into potato paste. We used two different kinds to make them the perfect combination of fluffy and creamy."

She rattles this all off at a pace I can't keep track of. She's so damn cute.

"You made the fluffy kind, right?"

She picks them up and waves them in front of me. "Fluffy! Clearly fluffy."

We dig into dinner and it's delicious. I look up as my parents are chatting about how Chloe is doing and how she's here for Labor Day long weekend this year.

I notice Emma is listening, but not eating. Then I realize she is watching people eat. Her gaze moves to me, then my plate, back to me. Everyone liking the food is clearly important to her.

I clear my throat. "Wow, Emma, Mom, this meal is amazing. You ladies really outdid yourselves. Emma, these potatoes—best I've ever had. Mamma, why don't you ever do red-skinned mashed potatoes? I think we should do them like this from now on." I wink at Mom so she knows I'm not dissing her cooking. I don't want her to stop feeding me.

"That was all Emma's idea. She is a fast learner. I sent her some of my recipes, and she's going to try making some new things this week," my mom informs me while looking at Emma.

Emma is blushing, but beaming.

"Can't wait." I'd be her guinea pig any day.

Although given how this meal turned out, I think she's on the path to significantly more edible kitchen creations. I think back to the mushy, smoked lasagna she dropped off for me after the fire incident and feel especially grateful for her improvement.

I'm still looking at Emma, and she's finally starting to eat, her eyes huge as she tastes her own mashed potatoes. She closes her eyes and moans as the second bite hits her tongue.

"Millie, if you weren't the mother of my—" She hesitates for less than a second. "Jess's mom, I'd be asking you to adopt me. I mean, I do still have one parent, but maybe we could still make it work. Jess and I would just have to hide our relationship due to the whole adopted sibling dating taboo thing."

I choke on a piece of roast, Emma slaps my back, Dad is practically cackling, mom is grinning. I glare at them.

I'm taking a sip of water to clear my throat from the roast's assault when my mom says, "Well, there is an easier way, *cara*. You could just marry my son, then you would be my daughter. Easy, no?"

I spray water across my corner of the table. The coughing starts again.

The entire group is laughing at me and Emma's trying to wipe up the water in my spray zone. She's silently laughing, shoulders shaking. She has to stop wiping to catch her breath.

Then she leans over the table and high-fives my mom.

What?

My voice is a little raspy from the choking. "What the hell was that?"

"We thought it would be funny to see what you would do if we brought up marriage at dinner. Ever since that ice *principessa* you sent packing, marriage has been such a touchy subject. Well, enough! So, when I grilled your girlfriend about how serious you two are, she shied away."

She looks at my woman—no, Emma. Not my woman.

"I told her I would just ask you at dinner and make you talk about it," Mamma says.

"I thought it would be a better idea to say outrageous things and mess with you instead. Your mom was very receptive to our planned attempt at riling you up." Emma gives me a smug look. "I thought you'd be quiet and give us your serious glare."

She points at my mom, "Millie thought you'd blow your top. Your reaction during past discussions seemed to be in her favor, but I held firm."

She looks back at me as she recaps, "He glared, said nothing, but he did literally blow water all over the table. Draw? We can try again next time."

"You two planned this? To mess with me."

Mamma never played pranks on us. She didn't like to encourage us, as the aftermath was often messy.

They both nodded. I'm impressed and a little touched at the thought of Mamma and Emma teaming up to screw with me.

"Mamma, I didn't think you had it in you. I'm so proud." I make my way over to her side of the table and peck her cheek. She laughs and tells me I better watch out now, she's gone to the dark side. Then I circle back around to my seat and lean over to Emma. "You too, babe. Crazy proud."

Then I kiss her. It's short, soft, and sweet. It's not exactly chaste, though. I linger a few moments longer than is acceptable given our audience. The laughter in her eyes is slowly being replaced by heat, and then a question slides over her face. A good question.

What does this kiss mean? A kiss I made clear was a bad idea.

We didn't discuss PDA before my parents' arrival. I just told her to be herself and we would act like we normally do around each other. Our fake dating scenario has allowed us to become close and comfortable in a lot of ways.

But I made a big deal about her kissing me and drew the lines in thick, black permanent marker, then blew past it without hesitation.

I took part well enough during the rest of dinner, but my mind is on an endless loop of questions. Why I want more of Emma, how much watching her with my family has affected me, how real this all feels, why I should pull back, how much I can't let us go down this road.

But mostly, I thought about how much I want to toss out all the rules and obstacles that are preventing me from having her in my life for real.

Maybe we could do this for real. Temporarily, at least. I can't give her marriage, babies, and a full life with a shiny future of endless possibilities. But I could give her a couple more months until November when Garrett returns. Same timeline, different rules. I get to have her in my life for a little while, in all ways, but then let her go to search for what she deserves after I'm gone.

But what does she get, Jess? my conscience asks.

• • •

Emma

"Call me if those peanut butter surprise cookies give you any trouble, yeah?" Camilla offers. Or, Millie, as she prefers.

"I believe you said they were idiot-proof, so if I have problems, I'd be hesitant to admit it."

I've been a very active participant in tonight's conversations and social interactions. There were intellectual debates, personal questions, some light grilling, and a fair amount of ribbing. I think I more than held up my end of this arrangement and as a bonus, I loved every minute of it. I hope Jess agrees.

Millie chuckles, rubs my arm. "If they taste like cookies, you succeeded."

She gives me a hug, then turns to Jess.

"You take care of her and don't forget to call your mamma more. Not just for food, either." She envelops him in a tight hug and places a firm kiss on his cheek.

Next is Jess's dad, but instead of hugs and kisses, they do a half back-slapping, half fake wrestle. My eyes widen, worried I'll get the same treatment. Do not engage in self-defense tactics.

Casually, Rian comes over and gives me a quick hug while gently cupping the back of my head, before he encourages Millie out the door.

The door closes and Jess and I are alone.

The moment I turn to face him, my eyes zero in on his lips.

No more avoiding. We have some things to talk about.

"So..." He draws out the word.

"So."

He opens his mouth to speak, but I cut him off. "It was a good kiss, Jess. Perfectly proficient. It worked for you."

My tone is mocking as I copy his words to me from when I kissed him. Hands on my hips, walking toward him.

"How was the jump over that line you drew to ward off my inappropriate physical affections?" I cock my eyebrow, pop my hip, channeling my inner Lauren.

He takes one long step toward me, eating up the remaining space between us. He's grinning down at me now, amused by my snark.

His hand comes up to my jaw, the tips of his fingers wrapping around to the back of my neck. Surprise and uncertainty on my face.

"Using my own words against me, huh?"

I nod sharply.

"I guess I deserve that. Did I sound like that much of an asshole that night?"

He grimaces as I mime 'higher,' with my upturned thumb. Chuckling softly, he leans his forehead down to rest against mine

"Spending time with my family makes you sassy. I like it," he says watching the grin spread on my face.

His hands link with mine as he wraps them both around my back.

"Yeah? Well, I think it's mostly your influence that has brought out the fighter in me." Rubbing my nose gently against his, a small tease.

He hums in agreement. "I like you, Emma."

He pulls back just enough to look into my eyes, peeking into the depths of my soul. His head dips quickly to capture my mouth in a kiss that sucks the breath right out of me. I am floating on a cloud of delight as his tongue swipes across the seam of my lips, parting them. He's layering gentle kisses at different angles, working his way to learning each curve of my parted, panting mouth.

I stretch up to chase the soft, slow kisses he's drinking from my lips.

Leaning forward, I suck his bottom lip into my mouth, then slide my tongue quickly into his mouth to stroke his. I need to taste every part of this kiss. I nibble along his upper lip and hear his soft groan.

My hands reach up to clutch his soft, cotton-covered shoulders, leveraging them to press closer, kiss deeper. His hands haven't moved to my body and seem frozen as I continue exploring this incredible side of Jess's physical boundaries line.

I withdraw for a moment, gazing at his mouth. His lust filled gaze meets mine before I dive back in. That seems to have done something, because his hands land harshly on me again.

He grips my waist, crushing my body to his, he holds me tightly against him. Pressing forward, he quickens the kiss, bending me slightly backward. I can feel his need for me, and I have never wanted anything so much in my life.

My core is on fire, throbbing, and empty. Just like my heart once was.

That shakes me out of this make-out stupor a little. Does Jess just want sex? He hasn't been dating anyone else for the last couple of months, so I know exactly how horny he must be. I slow down the kiss, pressing him gently back with the hands that are still gripping his shoulders.

The kiss breaks, and the air crackles between us like mini-explosions.

"What was that? What are we doing?" I ask.

He blows out a puff of air, tucks me back in closer to him.

His hand returns to my face, cradling it as his eyes bore into mine. "No more lessons, Em. You don't really need to know all that crap anyway. You just have to like the guy. A guy who will treat you well, one you can be yourself around."

I lift my hand and point at him, lips pursed, silently asking 'you?'

He gives me a quick smile and nods.

"Would you be up for a new arrangement, Emma?"

"Yes!" I respond, a little too quickly.

He laughs loudly. "Want to know what it is first?"

"Probably a good idea."

He leads me over to the couch, where we sit, and I fidget nervously. If he suggests we become casual fuck buddies, I may have to burn something again.

"There are things I can't offer you, long-term, and I think you know that. It's why you asked me to coach you, pretend with you. Not just be your fun summer fling."

I frown a little, not liking where this is going.

"There's something between us and I'd like to see where it goes. I haven't had a relationship in a few years, but I want to try. This whole arrangement, this dating experiment, has reminded me of the good parts. You've reminded me of the good parts."

Don't get teary!

My smile wobbles a bit as I clarify, "You want to date for real? More than hand-holding and dating tips? Maybe use a few of those very specific sexual verbs from our chat after your bakery bribe?"

He snorts out a laugh and nods.

"We'd be monogamous?"

"Yes, definitely."

"No holding back? Give it a real shot, no more boundaries?" I clarify.

"No more boundaries or friend-zoning. I heard you muttering about that the other day."

My face is hurting from smiling so wide. "Yes."

His face softens as his eyes sweep over my face like he's trying to memorize it.

"The end date still applies, though. I move back to San Francisco at the beginning of November. I don't live here and that's not changing." He takes both of my hands now as if, looking into my eyes, he can see my hopes and dreams for us shatter.

"Oh. Right." I nod absently, breaking eye contact. "With your area of work, you could work from anywhere? You've lived in a lot of cities along the west coast, never really settling anywhere because you don't have to."

"Yes, I don't have to settle anywhere. This town was my home growing up, but I don't really have roots anywhere. No home, just somewhere to live and play. That's the way I like it. Staying here would feel too much like settling down."

I take a moment to think about this. There's not much I can say. But I do have a choice here. It's take it or leave it.

I no longer want to avoid love, happiness, or anything I yearn for.

"Okay. Show me what you've got, Jess. We only have until November, so make it count."

And lying together on his brother's couch, he does.

CHAPTER 22

Emma

This could be a huge mistake. Yet, there's this small, firm voice in my head, growing more vibrant each day, that's wondering if the real mistake would be not taking the chance. What have I got to lose?

Jess. Love. A future filled with both.

But I'd still be losing both if I did nothing. If I ducked my head down, shut down, and walked away, I'd still be alone and empty.

It'll hurt more the deeper you get. The more you feel, the harder you'll break.

My answer to the scared, cynical girl trying to claw her way back to the surface is, 'Okay. Then that's what happens. Until then, go after what you want and hold nothing back.'

That's what I've done. I think Jess expects me to have some reservations or hesitation in our new relationship. Sometimes he just stares at me, and his eyes tell me everything and nothing. Then there's something else there, too. Guilt? Remorse? He taught me to look for the signs, but why would I be seeing that in Jess?

The insecure part of me thinks it's because he is regretting changing the rules, moving forward into a genuine relationship.

I tell that nag to shut it and just be present with him because we have scant weeks together and I won't waste a minute.

Earlier, he came for lunch and asked if I wanted to go to the Main Street art festival. Working nearby, I've already experienced some festival activities, meaning I've been on my feet with the walking boot more than I should be.

I asked if we could just Netflix and chill tonight. His eyes swung back to me and a wolfish smile slid over his face.

Confused, I kissed him goodbye and finished up the rest of my workday.

~

Apparently, 'Netflix and chill' is a euphemism for sexual activity. Jess informs me of this the moment we sit down. It's ridiculous that I have to be so careful about phrasing a relaxing evening of watching *New Girl*.

As a treat for our night in, I made cookies with the recipe Millie gave me. They taste like peanut butter cookies! With a hint of burned caramel inside. Progress! I only had to message her with questions twice.

Jess says they are surprisingly edible and even finishes the whole cookie. I can't tell if he only ate it to appease me or because he likes them, but I don't care one bit.

We barely make it through one full episode before making out like unsupervised teenagers in a bedroom with lockable doors. Or so I imagine.

Jess. Can. Kiss.

I knew this from the night I met his parents, but now he's taking things farther and I feel like a shy, unsure sixteen-year-old again. He's being slow and careful with me, knowing that my history with men wavers between traumatic and indifferent.

I've had a decent amount of sex in my life. Good sex, even. Meaning I've orgasmed, but it has never been a production. Jess produces a masterly crafted seduction that rises and falls at the perfect times.

It's in the way he touches me, not just where. He touches me like he's discovering, learning, so enthralled with piecing me together just to figure out how to make me come apart. I have never in my life climaxed from kisses and heavy petting. I suspect that may change.

It started out as simple kisses, then turned into a hot, frantic embrace.

He's braced partially on top of me as I feel his fingers trail down my arm, to my hip, playing with the strip of skin between my top and my shorts, slipping underneath my tank top. Goose bumps spread like fire as he grazes that spot just under my breast.

I close my eyes, my whole body shuddering in pleasure and need. Jess's hands grip my hips tightly, positioning me where he wants me. My hands can't stop touching him, grasping at him. I strip him of his shirt and take a moment to drink in his chest, his muscles clenched from his panting breath. My fingers are drawn to him like magnets as I graze them over his pecs, against his sensitive nipples. He sucks in a breath through clenched teeth as I play. When I dip my head to lick one, he swears and tips his head back in euphoria.

He looks at me, grabbing my hips once again to change the angle, putting me firmly underneath him so he can relieve the pressure we are both feeling with a few grinding thrusts.

I hook my injured leg over his hip, to keep it out of the way. But also to bring my center that much closer to his. His basketball shorts hide nothing. In fact, one small tug and he'd be set free.

His hands explore my body in soft strokes as he mumbles compliments and nonsensical random words like, 'sweet,' and, 'strong,' and, 'impossible.'

He finds a spot on my neck I didn't know existed as a sex hot-button for me. As he nibbles there, his hand finds my breast, bare under my cotton sleep shirt. Alternating between gentle grazes, firm squeezes and pulls, he leads us into a frenzy.

I bring my hands back to his chest and slide them down to palm him through his shorts. God, he's so hard and I'm finding it hard to think of anything other than getting him inside me. After a few firm strokes, he groans into my mouth as his hips jerk, trying to find a rhythm. Brave in a moment saturated with lust and need, I push him back, pressing his side with my leg, encouraging him onto his side.

I roll us and climb on top of him. He shifts to sit at an incline, hands encasing my hips, bringing me where we both needed me to be. I ride his lap unashamedly, modifying my position until I am sitting astride his rock-hard erection at just the right angle.

He nips at my breasts while guiding my energetic grinding. He tucks his head into my neck, then whispers into my ear, asking what I need because he's nearly there already.

I place his hands on my breasts. The fluttery beginnings of my climax begin as my clit hits the head of his cock over and over through my drenched panties and shorts.

I lean forward, changing my angle to put more pressure directly on my clit. He's gripping my hips, increasing the pace, his biceps bulging and flexing, sounds of restrained pleasure escaping his lips.

Then those green eyes lock with mine, and I feel that building pressure release in waves as I cry out, unable to look away from him for even a second. His eyes, his face, in blissful awe as he holds my gaze.

I lean over, my mouth by his ear as I finish riding out the last of the spasms.

"Holy hell, Jess." I pant.

Suddenly, I'm uncertain if he had the same ending I did. "Do you want my mouth?"

I bite his earlobe and suck it into my mouth. Grinding harder on his lap, he grabs my ass and keeps me still as he strokes himself into my crease. A loud, low groan fills the air as he mutters only my name, his cock twitching against me.

He rests his forehead against my chest. Once we are both breathing evenly again, I run my fingers through his dark strands.

He tips his head to look at me. "Jesus. I haven't come in my shorts since college. Just the mention of your mouth on me pushed me over the edge. You do that on purpose?"

I shake my head with a shy smile. He groans and drops his head against the back of my couch, energy depleted.

That was the best thirty minutes of any sexual endeavor I've ever had. Hell, probably the best thirty minutes of my life thus far.

~

We've blown our relationship wide open. He kisses me goodbye every time we part, touches me often, embraces me with every greeting, and cuddles me at night.

He doesn't usually stay the night even though I regularly ask him to. He is firm on playing the gentleman, admitting he doesn't think he'll be able to keep up the gentleman routine if in my bed, and he doesn't want to rush me. It's new to me and it's been a while for him. Dry humping and make-out sessions are a regular occurrence, but the clock is ticking and while I don't want to rush any of the good parts, I don't want to miss out on any either.

Jess

Football practice is back in session, school starts in only a few weeks. I've been coming out to help run cardio drills and continue the running group for my serious runners who have been keeping up with it over the summer.

"Jess. Man, you going to make them keep running those sprint/strides the rest of practice? Or maybe let them take a quick break so they can walk tomorrow?" Taylor asks, clipboard in hand.

Shit. I blow the whistle and wave them off for a drink.

"Taking out some aggression on my boys, Caldwell?" he questions in his Coach Shaw voice.

"Nah. Just distracted, sorry. They are getting pretty good. Particularly the ones who kept up with summer training." I motion to a few of the kids. "Some are running just under five seconds in the forty-yard dash. We should start working on speed training to get them ready for the possibility of college ball. If we can get them down a few tenths of a second, they'd be in a good position for scouts."

I throw a thumb at one player standing near me, "And Jensen here got jacked this summer." The junior year player grins at me as I slap his bicep.

"Jensen hit the gym almost every day this summer. Sometimes twice a day doing weights and plyometrics," Taylor explains.

"My mom's a dietician, she's been keeping me on track," Jensen adds.

"You should ask her if she wants to come offer the team some dietary advice to go with our weight training and" —he looks at me— "our new speed training program this year."

Should have expected that. By mentioning it, I basically volunteered.

"Shaw, I'm not a practicing running coach. I have my level one certification, but—" Taylor cuts me off with a clipboard to the stomach.

"That's all you need, champ. You are our level one running coach, capable of putting together a speed training program. You're the only one with enough experience in this town. I have buddies back in Texas you can call if you get stuck."

His stance changes to face Sam Jensen again, dismissing me as if we settled the conversation. "Jensen, tell Robertson to gather the defensive line and meet me at our thirty-five-yard line."

"I'm only here until the end of October, champ," I force out through my teeth, wanting to use more colorful language.

He looks back at me, studying me as if I'm one of his players. "Sure, sure. So, what's got you so distracted today?"

"Nothing, just thinking."

"Right. Thinking about a certain woman you spend all your time with?" He waggles his eyebrows and I frown.

"Jealous, Coach? I make time for you. Are you feeling neglected? Flowers are expensive. What if I buy you a beer and you can cry on my shoulder?"

"Jealous you have a woman who acknowledges you and wants to do naked things to you? Yeah. It's the Sahara over here and the only woman with drinkable water keeps knocking it out of my hands every time I try for a sip."

He takes his hat off and scrubs his hands through it before placing it back on his head.

"Jealous because I miss your scrawny ass? Nope. Football season is in full swing. I don't have time for your commitment-phobic trust issues and self-sabotage. But I miss beer, so let's do that this weekend. I just got a pellet grill and have been making amazing ribs, so you just bring the beer and your female friend or whatever you crazy kids are labeling the non-relationship you have going."

"She's away this weekend visiting her dad. And she's my girlfriend."

That word will take some getting used to.

"Right. In front of your parents and the town, if they don't look too closely."

"Nope. Old information. We're dating. For real. Not just to help her with her people skills or act as her friendly neighborhood dating coach or because it appeases my parents." My throat involuntarily convulses as I finish, "A real relationship."

Did the air get thin?

"Coach Shaw, you coming? Coach B wants to run pass-rushing drills before the end of practice," shouts one of his linebackers.

Taylor gives a wave of acknowledgment to his player, his gaze never wavering from mine. "No shit?"

I nod and move toward the offensive players to get them set up with more conditioning drills.

"Oh, no, we are not done here, Running Coach. What the hell do you mean you're now in a real relationship?"

He's got his beefy arm held out, blocking my way back to my group.

"I don't know what other information you're looking for. We're dating. No more pretending or coaching or advice."

I'm trying to take things slow with Emma. Given her history, both in terms of trauma and her past apathetic sexual experiences, I need to make sure she trusts me. I don't want her reverting to her prearranged, scratching-an-itch mentality.

"You're not just" —he looks around for any kids, lowering his voice— "wanting to sleep with her? You're doing the full relationship, too?"

"Yeah, and don't give me any shit about it either," I warn, and then he laughs at me.

"You're already in so much shit, man." He laughs again, bigger, louder, drawing a lot of attention. "So much shit." He walks away. "Glad to have you on the team, Coach."

"Only until November."

His mouth purses as he nods sarcastically at me.

"I'm serious, I'm leaving once Garrett is back. I don't live here. You know this, she knows this, everyone knows, it's a done deal."

He shakes his head, mutters, "We'll see." Jogging over to his defensive line. "Go run your drills, Coach Caldwell."

"Temporary Coach Caldwell!"

~

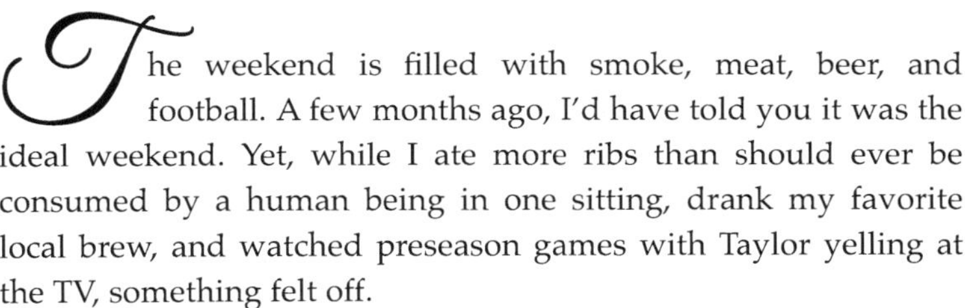

The weekend is filled with smoke, meat, beer, and football. A few months ago, I'd have told you it was the ideal weekend. Yet, while I ate more ribs than should ever be consumed by a human being in one sitting, drank my favorite local brew, and watched preseason games with Taylor yelling at the TV, something felt off.

Unrelated, Emma has been gone all weekend to see her dad.

She chose to take an extra day in Denver after her dad reacted poorly to her life-altering news. I'm not surprised. If my daughter was experiencing harassment on that scale over long periods of time, ending in an assault, I would bust shit up until I got much-needed vengeance.

Although, given that their relationship is a bit tenuous, I worry that Emma may not get the support and response from him she deserves.

This weekend, I snapped at Taylor a few times, to which he laughed and goaded me into admitting I was grumpy because Emma was gone.

I'm surly, lonely, horny, and bored as fuck. What did I do before meeting Emma? Clearly nothing too exciting.

Running? Already ran this weekend, tacked on some extra miles and a cross-country run to mix it up.

I wasn't used to talking while running, but Emma does it, and I didn't realize how much I enjoy that until the quiet seeped in like a dark void during my seemingly endless runs.

Dinner and drinks out? With Taylor being in football-mode, I would have gone solo. The only other people I used to go out with would not be appropriate choices given my newfound boyfriend status and because I never kept those women's company for conversation or friendship.

Netflix? Emma will straight up maim me if I watch any of our shows without her. And she'll know if I watched ahead in *Suits*. She has that woman voodoo magic for knowing all things.

Poker? Nope, that's only every third Thursday.

Reading?

Okay, I'll read and then maybe do some work.

The other things we used to do are not solo activities. Going out for dessert after Emma ruined her latest creation attempt? Great as a couple, but a single man in an ice cream store, licking at a waffle cone while reading a book, screams loner.

Stargazing from the porch with an entire bottle of wine and a blanket, only to end up falling asleep in a patio chair? Maybe hints at a sad, lonely borderline alcoholic.

I cave and text Emma.

ME: What are you doing?
EMMA: Did you mean 'what are you wearing'?
ME: No, but now I'm asking that.
EMMA: Is this the part where we try sexting to bring us closer during our unbearable time apart? Looks like there are still a few things you can teach me about dating. I prefer the hands-on *winky face* learning approach, but am on board for online electives.

Sweet Jesus, Mary, and Joseph. Emma is sexting me. Who fucking knew?!

ME: You and your sexy mouth have thrown me for a loop here, babe. Give me a second for my brain to catch up with my dick.
EMMA: Ha! I'm teasing. I'm in my father's house, right across the hall from his room. I'm not doing THAT here.

Dammit.

EMMA: I'll wait until I get home and see you. During my sexual rediscovery and experimentation, I utilized some amazing devices to help get reacquainted with my urges and self-satisfaction.

Pause. Reread. Yeah, that's what I thought she said.

ME: Masturbating. We are talking about masturbating with kinky toys, and somehow this isn't sexting? You do what you feel is right, and I'll be over here doing what I think feels oh so right.

I see the three dots come and go. I think I've now shocked her. Teasing Emma may be the best part of my day.

EMMA: Ha. You are home alone and can do whatever you want, Green Eyes.

I don't know why, but I love when she calls me that. Maybe because it's what she called me that day in the grocery store and it's stuck with me.

ME: I'm well aware I'm home alone. And I cannot do 'whatever I want'. You'd need to be here for that.

She doesn't respond for a few minutes. Probably unsure what to do with that.

ME: When do you get in tomorrow? I'll pick you up.
EMMA: My flight should be in around 1pm. But Lauren is picking me up to go shopping in the city.
ME: I can take you shopping.
EMMA: Jess, it's fine. Lauren and I want to spend time together before she goes back to work next week.

Did I sound desperate?

Yes. The more time I spend with Emma, the more anxious I get about the date looming over us. I'm doubting my decision to move our relationship forward. I worry that this is going to end badly and the more I worry, the more I try to absorb as much of the good times as possible.

EMMA: It's cute. The whole clingy boyfriend thing is throwing me. I like it. You miss me sooooo much!
ME: Hey, watch it smartass. You're miss-able, take the compliment.
ME: And I'm not cute.

ME: But I do miss you.
Emma: Soooo much!
ME: That's it, I'm watching Suits without you.
EMMA: I miss you, too.
EMMA: And don't you dare.
EMMA: Also, are you available to attend a networking event with me on Thursday? That's what boyfriends do, right?

I cringe. I hate networking events. They're always filled with awkward, pushy people who have very obvious agendas.

ME: Sounds fun! Cocktails?
EMMA: It's going to be awful, but I appreciate the fake enthusiasm. Yes, there will be a cocktail hour before the schmoozing.
ME: How sober do I need to be for this event?
EMMA: Oh, I'm sure you can get a little tipsy. Let loose. I'll get us home.

Sounding better and better.

ME: Deal.

CHAPTER 23

Emma

I may have fibbed. Although, nothing I said was a lie, exactly. The event we are going to can definitely be categorized as networking and there will be alcohol. See? I just left out a few details.

We had dinner with his family again last week. Seeing how fun Jess can be with his dad, hearing his mom talk about their pranks and one-ups, I realized how much I love this dynamic.

I'm at the San Francisco airport walking toward the terminal entrance, when I see Lauren conversing with a dark-haired man. He laughs at something she says, then turns toward me. Jess! What the….

I grin widely at both of them as I approach, and they turn to look for me.

They both come at me for hugs. The moment Lauren realizes Jess is trying to sneak in for the first hug, she elbows him in the stomach, then ducks under his outstretched arms.

"Hi sweets! Ready to shop?" she asks, still pushing Jess out of the way. I giggle and give my best friend one last squeeze before releasing her and nudging her aside.

Jess gets his chance to sneak in, giving Lauren a small hip

bump to clear more room for himself. Then I'm enveloped in his fresh, clean scent. He's clasping me against him, looking down at my face as I smile back up at him.

"We talked about this."

"We did. But I didn't say I wouldn't come, anyway."

He had me there.

"This is very sweet. I didn't think the Jess dating experience could get better, but the real deal is infinitely better."

Then he dips his face toward mine and places a soft kiss on my eager lips. God, I missed him. It wasn't until I didn't see him for four days that I realized how much time we spend together. We haven't been apart for more than a couple of days in months.

I reach up higher and kiss him back, he takes the hint and wraps both arms around my back, bending me backward and pressing more aggressive kisses to my mouth. He takes long pulls from my lips, sucking on my bottom lip before halting his lip attack.

"Hi."

He pulls me upright again while I try to say something resembling, "Hello."

Lauren's waving hands catch my peripheral vision.

"What the hell did I miss? I was only gone a week!"

I blush, regretting not telling her before I saw her today. But I wanted to tell her in person and gush a smidge while we shopped today. She turns her attention to Jess.

"This better be serious, Caldwell, or take the time now to grieve any chance at future offspring." She looks pointedly down.

"Lauren!" I hiss at her.

"It is. We're dating. Emma didn't tell you?" He frowns at me, looking insecure for the first time since I've known him.

"I wanted to tell her in person. We have a whole girly day planned, and this was part of it."

"Dating, as in a committed relationship where you both invest feelings, time, and effort to help the other person achieve their wants and needs? As in, you are no longer ignoring the heaps of sexual tension oozing off you two?" She points a finger back and forth between us. "Like that?"

"Uh… yeah, something like that."

He kisses me again, this time on the cheek.

"I'm going to let you ladies talk and shop and whatever other activities you have for today. I just wanted to see you and welcome you home. You go easy on that ankle, okay?"

I nod with an eye roll.

"I'm off to check on my condo, meet with a few developers, then back to town. I'll see you tonight?" he asks, smiling at me. I kiss him in response.

For a short while, I forgot he lives here. Or has a condo here and plans to return here soon. He sees my playful expression fall and knows why. He tips my chin up with his forefinger and sighs.

"Don't do that, Emma. Let's live in the now, okay?" Kissing me once more, he walks off giving Lauren a wide berth.

I'm staring at his ass when he swings around, walking backward as he asks, "Tonight?" with a boyish grin.

I nod with a crooked smile.

With that, I turn to Lauren and start answering her many questions. She relents and tells me just to start from the beginning.

Jess

Dressed business casual for the networking event, I demolish my mom's special lasagna that I snagged after dropping in for a visit on my way back from the airport the other day. These events tend not to have good food.

I grab my keys from the bowl on the entryway table, lock up, and cut across Emma's yard.

Knocking on Emma's door, she opens it before I get to the second knock, like she was standing there waiting. She looks great. Casual and warmly dressed for a business event, though. Flowing top, linen pants, Keds, a light cardigan, and a scarf made of some kind of flowy fabric that moves with the slightest shift of air. She's going to sweat all night.

"Ready?" Circling my arm around her back as she nods. "Cold?"

"Oh. No, I just wanted to dress-up my comfortable outfit with a stylish scarf."

Makes sense, I think. What do I know?

"I have to take these cookies to Stella's and then we can start our evening."

She holds up a tray of surprisingly edible looking cookies.

"Those look good. Where's mine?"

"Oh, now that I am making good cookies—thanks to your mom—you are vying for a taste?"

"Exactly. Gimme." I reach for the tray.

She ignores me and quickens her pace to Stella's front door.

That's when I hear it.

What the hell is going on? Generally, I try to steer clear of Stella. She is sweet, caring, welcoming, and quite a bit like my mom minus any acceptance or understanding of boundaries.

Emma's dear, sweet neighbor also drinks a fair amount more than Mom and is part of the League, so keeping my distance always seems like the right thing to do.

I'm peering around, attempting to find where the noise is coming from as Emma rings the bell and waits, shifting her weight from foot to foot. She glances back at me, biting her lip, eyes crinkled with mischief. I don't recognize this Emma. What is she up to?

Then it hits me like a ton of bricks as the door swings open, noise erupting from the house. Stella lets out a shrill, tipsy welcome, pulling Emma inside.

She is book clubbing me.

I am frozen at the door, dumbfounded.

A small hand wraps around my wrist and pulls me into the house, my feet moving with the force. Emma is pulling wine, a book, and other items out of her bag.

"Don't you think, Jess?"

Think what? Has Stella been yammering at me this whole time?

"Sorry, Stella, what was that?"

She gives me a friendly pat on the arm.

"I was just asking if you enjoyed the novel choice this month? I'm five years late jumping on the bandwagon, but it's never too late to pick up an excellent book. Don't have to tell you, I'm sure."

She gives a light laugh.

"You haven't been to a single book club, after numerous invitations and requests. Yet here you are for this particular book. Don't blame you, though. It left me on pins and needles needing to read the next one in the series."

I stare at Emma, lips pursed, scrambling to dig deep and come up with a response to shit I have no idea about. I have to regroup here if I'm to survive this.

Her cute little face is analyzing mine. I'm sure her brain is going a mile a minute. Is he mad? What does he think about my little deception? Is he going to retaliate for this?

My answers are: No. Super fucking impressed. Definitely.

"Well, while I found the book interesting, Emma here couldn't get enough. I'm pretty sure she's already purchased the whole series." I'm not sure if she's even read the book. She had mentioned that the book itself made very little difference in participating at this event. What I know is, if Stella loved this book, it's probably something Emma wouldn't like.

Her face turns a victorious shade of pink.

"Have either of you watched the movie? Greg and I haven't yet, we wanted to read the book first." This is a lot of book talk considering I was led to believe that's the way book club operates.

"Oh no, not yet. I think we will finish the whole series first, right Jess?"

I make a noncommittal sound and glance around, waiting for the next wave of whatever this party has in store for me. We are in the Jumanji of social interactions and I am not prepared.

"Well, go on you two and mingle. Our game tonight is going to have a book themed twist." She looks pointedly at Emma. "Make sure you encourage Jess to stay for the game. There will be many disappointed ladies if you let him duck out early."

"What did you do?"

She smiles at me and steps closer.

"We should leave space around us so we can better observe our surroundings. Let's back up against that wall there so no one can sneak up on us." I can hear the hint of panic in my own voice.

"You're being ridiculous," she says, but does as I suggest.

"This is just a fun, sophisticated, and intellectual gathering discussing great novels, remember?"

She twitches her eyebrows at me, a smug look on her face.

"You tricked me."

"Well… did I?" She taps a finger on her dainty chin. "Technically, this could be viewed as a networking event. There are cocktails. You didn't ask for details."

Sneaky woman.

"You willfully volunteered to attend this insanity again just to retaliate?"

"Yes. For purely selfish reasons. Observing your reactions during this fiasco is well worth the price of admission."

She's vibrating with excitement.

I stare at her for a few long moments. She stares right back, trying her best to keep her face blank and serious. After fewer than five seconds, her mouth tips before she schools her expression again.

The women in my family don't get involved in our little pranks and games. They are more sensitive and hold on to shit for longer than the rest of us. Plus, they sometimes cry, which many of us, particularly Garrett, cannot handle. Also, when they feel it's deserved, they can be vicious. We don't mess with them, and they rarely mess with us.

Emma is throwing out the rule book and has already encouraged my mom to pull that little stunt at dinner. I like it, but I won't tell her that. Yet. For now, we get each other through this. I deserve it, but the fact that Emma is here to watch the show leaves me conflicted. Her grand smile and mirth is contagious, but I am going to get my ass handed to me at this party, likely in a few different ways.

After an hour of nauseating talk with many of the town's most irritating and abrasive citizens, we find ourselves in the back yard. I've had only one glass of wine, trying to stay sharp.

Stella is rushing around gathering people as she prepares for the 'game'. Emma correctly predicted that there would be no mention of the book until the game portion of the evening. Well, except for our welcome.

"Okay, okay, everyone gather around. Break yourselves into two groups. Most of you know how this goes." I shift over to the side closest to Emma's yard. There are a few middle-aged women herding me into the back of the group.

Maybe I'm too tall and they don't want me to stand in front of them.

No, Jess, assume nothing. You don't have a clue what fresh hell awaits.

Right. Game face.

Wait, where's Emma? I peer around the hordes of people crammed onto this deck. I see the flutter of Emma's scarf in the breeze. On the other side of the deck. How'd she get so far away?

Then I catch her gaze. Oh shit. This was intentional. What's her endgame?

She smirks at me and gives me one of her usual awkward hand waves and then blows me a kiss. Ah, shit.

"Alright, Greg and I will appoint team captains and then we'll explain the little twist for this month's game. Here's a hint: it's naughty."

Then she winks. Fucking winks. Right at me.

Suppressing a shudder, my eyes dart to Emma who is stifling a laugh with her hand. Then perks up and rushes to the front of her group. Stella and Greg are standing between the two teams.

Emma approaches the couple who are talking to Phil, a local dentist. There's a disagreement, then Stella nods and repeatedly pats Emma's shoulder in delight.

I don't take my eyes off Emma. Bad things are about to happen, I can feel it.

"Listen up! Emma and Tommy are the captains. Please be sure all answers are put through them and a heads-up that they will also choose who acts out the 'concessions' for each round." Concessions? Shit, I need a game rules breakdown. I ask Edward beside me to give me the rundown. At first, he shushes me, waiting for Stella to get to the game twists. He fills me in as the cards are being handed out.

I see now that knowledge of the book will be crucial in getting out of this unscathed. I also understand why Emma ended up half-naked and trashed on my front porch that night some months ago.

I turn to Ed. "What's the book this month?" He rolls his eyes at me while scoffing, muttering how useless I will be. Yeah, I was just thinking the same thing.

Stella starts up again. "I have handed out the special concessions for this month's game. Instead of a shot of Patrón there will be *Fifty Shades of Grey* tasks that are required. If you refuse the task, the whole team does two shots of tequila and the person who refused the original task will get one more opportunity to obey. Otherwise, *punishments* will be doled out."

Holy. Fucking. Shit.

Emma and I had never gotten around to watching the movie. I thought it was because she wasn't okay with it. In reality, she probably wanted to do her research for book club solo, not wanting me to glean any useful information before setting this plan in place. That shifty, devious, brilliant woman. This level of mischief is one that Garrett and Dad rarely put the effort into attempting.

I am inevitably fucked.

The game proceeds, and to be quite honest, I have no clue

what's happening. I've taken a lot of shots, but luckily my punishments have been tame. Probably have Emma to thank for that.

Later, I'm given the task to get on my knees, hands tied behind my back, and take a shot using only my mouth. From Greg's front pants pocket. But I got off easy compared to many others. Emma chose this one for me, likely because she was feeling sorry for my drunk ass. My team sucks. Several of my teammates confessed to watching only the movie and not reading the book.

Currently, Mrs. Williams is whipping Mr. Williams with something called a 'flogger'. He pulled down his pants and by the look of utter horror on Emma's face, he became excited by this new task.

I may never drink tequila again. Which means I may never eat tacos again. How can I do tacos without a salted margarita? Hmm? Or maybe it's the other way around? I need tacos when I eat tequila? Drink tequila? Yes. Eat tacos, drink tequila. That's how it works.

"Where are the tacos?" I shout at no one in particular.

Emma is grinning at me, and her smile is beautiful. She's beautiful and so smart. She thinks there's something wrong with her because she spent so long not understanding how to feel, but I know she can feel just fine. How she could think she's missing anything at all is laughable. She has everything inside her, she just needs to see it, recognize it, like I do.

I'm going to show her. No, I'll tell her.

"Emma! You are whole and you shine so bright. You're perfect and don't let any of these jerkoffs— " I look around and realize this crowd isn't responsible for her personal issues, "—or other jerkoffs, tell you any different."

That came off much less eloquently than I intended.

Her eyes blink at me in confusion. The game has turned to pandemonium as people get sloppier with their answers and their performance of the concession.

Gary is showing Meredith how to box tie one of our teammates while Tommy is being chased by Mr. Abernathy for flogging his wife instead of Greta.

"What?!" Emma is looking at me, shaking her head. This stupid book club novel choice better not have brought up any traumatic memories for her. The role-playing and semi-nudity have certainly tainted my memories. Luckily, the team captains emerge relatively unscathed from this whole ordeal, but I've got to get her out of here. And me. I've got to get me out of here.

But first, I owe her something.

I push through the crowd of horny, obnoxious, pain-loving, sexual deviants waiting at the front of our group to volunteer for concessions. After leaving ample room around the eager participants, I finally reach Emma.

I drop to my knees in front of her, grab her hips to steady her as I press my forehead to her abdomen. I feel her hands on my shoulders before I look up at her.

"Emma, I am so sorry. You have my deepest, most sincere apologies. I was an asshole for intentionally misleading you into believing this was a normal, sophisticated gathering of townspeople. Everyone here is insane. Please take pity on my half-naked self, forgive me, take me home, and never speak of this again."

People around us have stopped observing whatever new task was occupying their attention and are focusing solely on us.

"On one condition."

"Anything." I grip her tightly, desperately.

"I will forever be allowed to talk about tonight. As much as I want." Her face lights up. "And I get to illustrate it with at least one picture I took. But I will allow you to choose the picture."

She took photographic evidence. Garrett and Taylor are going to have a fucking field day with this. I only remember some tasks I completed. Then there's the possibility that she took pictures of my reactions to the more nauseating tasks. *Fifty Shades of Grey*. Nope, fifty shades of puke.

"Whatever you want." I stand wobbling, grab her hand, dragging her behind me as we leave. I fling the pile of Fifty Shades Concession Cards off the table as I walk by.

Emma grabs her tote as we run out of Stella and Greg's house. We get in the front door of her house and I collapse against it. I am drunk, hungry, and may never be able to look dozens of our town's citizens in the eye again.

Then I smell something delicious and spicy. My mouth waters. Opening eyes I didn't realize were closed, I see a plate piled high with tacos, Pico de Gallo, and a chunky guacamole. I think I'm in love.

With tacos. That's what I meant.

She waves the plate in front of me and leads me to the kitchen with it. I don't even remember getting up and walking, I just follow the taco smell.

I'm halfway through my third taco when I glance up at Emma. She's looking at me with fondness and adoration. It feels nice. Being fed, taken care of. It feels nice to have someone adore me.

"How did you know I wanted tacos? I mean, other than me shouting it earlier."

"They use tequila for the book club game. And I know that tequila and tacos are codependent food/drink requirements for you. I had Lauren drop some off earlier."

She combs her fingers through my hair.

"Feel better?"

"Never again. Book club is a hard limit," I state, cringing as I remember the part in the game where everyone had to admit to at least one 'hard limit'. No repeats allowed.

"Agreed. Bed?"

"Yes. I need to sleep and hope my brain does its job and scrubs away the worst parts of the night." I fake a shudder, but I'm only half-joking.

"Stay?"

"Oh, I'm staying. You owe me cuddles after misleading me so deviously. Later, when the night isn't so fresh in my mind, I'll tell you just how amazing your little ploy was."

We prepare for bed, and I am steadier on my feet, the tacos working their magic.

I bring Emma close and drape her over my chest so I can hold her while drifting off. It's quiet and I can feel my body relax. Then she giggles. I look down as those giggles turn into a full belly laugh.

Emma has her phone in hand and is viewing the photos she took tonight. They're not flattering. The derangement depicted in the two photos I glimpsed before she tossed her phone away to keep me from snatching it, foreshadow an embarrassing future family dinner.

She sighs, her laughter winding down. Then whispers, "Best boyfriend ever."

I grin and give her side a playful pinch. She giggles again and settles in for sleep.

So much trouble.

Not Emma, me. I'm in so much fucking trouble.

CHAPTER 24

Emma

One downside of my plan is that the book club was on a Thursday night, so I work this morning. Jess has his arm wrapped around the front of my body as he keeps my back snug against his chest. I slip out from under it and make it into the en suite for a quick shower.

Still tired but feeling refreshed from my shower, I check on Jess before making some coffee.

He's still out cold, cuddling with my pillow, one leg thrown out of the covers. He sleeps like a maniac and is an intense cuddler, even though he denies it.

I lean down, brushing some hair from his face. I'm about to place a kiss on his head when I'm grabbed and tossed beside him.

I am laughing and swatting at him while he tries to pull me in closer.

"Jess, I have to get dressed and off to work. I am not a stuffed bear, here only to serve your cuddle needs."

He plants his body on top of mine, wedging his face into the crook of my neck as he mumbles and grumbles in disagreement.

"Jess… babe, I have to go soon. You sleep in, I'll come home to have lunch with you." I offer.

"You smell good," he says, covering more of me with his body when I didn't think he could get any closer. No complaints here though. If I didn't have a meeting this morning, I'd stay and just lie awake while he held me. It's in these innocent moments, moments he isn't even fully aware of, that the core of me finds purpose.

He relaxes against me, breathing deeply. Good, he's asleep.

I take a few extra moments to enjoy this little bit of intimacy before shimmying out from under him. He moves and I pause, only to shimmy again a moment later when he stops. Then he lifts his body a little off of mine, giving me space to move.

I feel soft lips on my neck, brushing back and forth, then sucking at the skin along my collarbone. He traces it with his tongue before moving up to nibble my earlobe.

He shifts so he is directly over top of me, looking down into my eyes. I have no idea what he's seeing in my eyes, but he suddenly takes my mouth in a fierce kiss, holding it for a long, breath-stealing moment before plundering deeper into my mouth.

I grip his hair and change the angle of our locked lips. Running my hands down his neck, his bare, toned shoulders twitch slightly as I drag my fingers down them.

We haven't gotten to explore each other much after that one Netflix night. That's as far as we've ever gotten and I think only because I instigated it. This feels different, he isn't hesitating or waiting for me to take the lead.

I watch him fumble with the tie on my robe, quickly whipping the flimsy strip of material out of its loops. His hands delve in on either side of the opening, gripping my waist with a quick squeeze at the same time. I try to catch my breath as a hum of appreciation leaves his mouth. The vibrations tickle my lips. Sparks of desire straight through my abdomen, tingling my toes and lighting a fire in my belly.

I lift my hips, hooking a leg over his side, seeking his body and the friction I so desperately need.

The heat of his hands nearly burns as they press farther up.

One wraps around my back, lifting my bare chest up to meet his hot mouth. My skin tingles at the cool air and the possibility of Jess's touch.

Fluttering kisses caress the underside of my breast, his tongue swiping and flicking at my nipple. I cry out, impatient with need as he sucks it into his mouth.

"Jess!"

I quickly shrug out of my robe after he releases my aching breast. He shifts his attention to the other side, not leaving any skin untouched. I wrap my legs around his waist and pull him forward, needing him closer.

With frantic hands, I reach for his boxer briefs, palming his length as he subtly grinds against it.

He moves up the other side of my neck and looks right into my eyes again. I hitch myself closer to him, poking my heels into his butt. I plaster myself against him and move slightly up and down, rubbing against him from chest to groin. He grunts and squeezes his eyes shut for a moment.

"If you keep that up, we may not make it to the extra fun part," he growls at me.

"It all seems like fun to me. Plus, we are fighting the clock here," I say.

"I don't want to rush this, Emma," he says, the fire in his eyes simmering slightly with a hint of worry.

"I want this. Badly," I whisper.

"Are you sure? You feel okay with this? You're ready?" he asks, sweetly, hands holding my face.

The implication of why he is asking, my assault, had not even occurred to me until just now. But the fact that he cared enough to make sure I felt comfortable is pretty incredible.

"Yes. Very." I nod, placing a savoring kiss on his mouth. Against his mouth, I murmur, "That's never been an issue for us. I feel safe. You make me feel safe, Jess."

He comes in slowly for another lingering kiss. While our tongues tangle and taste, his hands move from my face, down my sides until they meet my panties.

He breaks away, hooking his fingers in the top and pulling them gently down my thighs. Once they reach my knees, I detach from him long enough for him to pull back and let them fall down my calves. His fingers linger on my ankles, then his palms swipe up the inside of my legs until they reach mid-thigh.

Finally, his gaze shifts from mine, to look down at what he's uncovered. His face is fierce and hungry.

Screw work, we are staying right here all day.

God, I need him to keep touching me.

He swipes a hand down his face, puffing out some air. "Fuck. Em, I don't even know where to start."

"Anywhere," I plead.

He starts kissing my thighs, then shifts his arms under my legs to clutch my hips. Settling in, he takes a slow swipe up from my center to my clit. My mind explodes as he sucks and licks me.

Eyes rolling in the back of my head, I feel slick sensations, hot need, and a burning awareness that is coursing through my whole body before I begin to shake. My upper body curls up off the mattress as my release tears through me. Surprised, I shout in awe, "Yes, Jess! Oh my—" And then I'm lost for a moment.

A minute later, I finally start to come down, still feeling Jess's mouth on me, lapping at the remnants of my release. My legs are still wrapped around him loosely and I'm panting like an Olympic gymnast.

Looking up, he recognizes that I have come around again. I pull him up to me and kiss the hell out of him. I don't even care that I can taste myself on him, in fact, it's kind of erotic. I'm pushing his underwear off to gain access to his incredibly firm, leaking erection. I give him a few pumps, rubbing the head to smear his precum at the tip down his shaft.

"Condom," he manages to spit out. "I didn't—I don't..."

"Drawer," I say as I twist to reach the bedside drawer. I open the box quickly and pass him one and continue my exploration of his impressive cock. I remove my hands as he rolls down the condom.

I widen my legs, leaving enough space for him to move back onto me. He looks down and mutters, "Fuck," before pulling me toward him.

His sex grazes mine and I hiss in anticipation.

He keeps switching his gaze from my face to my core. He leans over me, interlocking our fingers, moving our joined hands to above my head. His forearm rests beside my shoulder and he positions himself at my entrance.

His other hand grips my hip and he enters me slowly, eyes focusing on mine, making sure I'm still okay. I remove my hand from his shoulder to cup his face, assuring him, kissing him.

It takes him a few more tries to fully seat himself inside me.

He hits that magical spot deep inside of me as he slowly pumps in and out, still gripping my hip. I change the tilt of my hips and grind into his thrusts.

His hand slides to my ass and lifts it and pumps into me harder. Now groaning loudly, he quickens his pace, his eyes jumping to our connected bodies. He releases my hand only to find my clit with his thumb, rubbing it slowly compared to the quick pace he is setting driving into me.

I'm on the edge, my hands grip his biceps, then I move to my elbows to bring myself closer to his face, neck and chest. I nip and lick and kiss. When I flick his nipple, he lets out a little growl as his hips jerk out of rhythm.

He looks down at me as I grin, tongue out to lick him again, when a long, low groan lets loose as even his upper body twitches. I can feel his spasm inside of me as he releases, and it sets off my own powerful orgasm, squeezing him so tight, he starts groaning again, still pumping in jerky motions.

I flop back on the bed, boneless, spent. He follows not a moment later, still inside me. After catching our breath, I wrap my arms around him, lightly feathering my fingers up and down his back.

He starts peppering soft kisses along my collarbones, cheeks, and lips, then just holds me tightly.

Once I finally end up leaving the bed and my house, I arrive at work quite a bit later than anticipated. Normally, this would leave me frazzled and irritated, but for some very explainable reason, I cannot wipe the smile from my face.

CHAPTER 25

Jess

Labor Day weekend is upon us and while my family and their hometown friends plan this event every year, I've only gone twice in the last six years. This Landry-based event is typically an enjoyable event, unless you are single, are only visiting, or don't understand the town. I'm usually two for three, so there is no shortage of questions, helpful advice, and matchmaking.

"Can you reach that butternut squash for me, please?" Emma asks.

I look over at her as she stretches on tiptoes for a squash that's just out of reach. "It is not squash season yet. There will be no squash at this barbecue, babe. We have a couple of weeks of summer still, so let's get some corn on the cob and make a bean salad or something."

She huffs a partially sarcastic laugh. "What are you talking about? Millie gave me a very specific list." They have been in touch planning this family gathering and improving Emma's cooking skills. For now, Emma has taken a break from baking treats and is working on cooking basics.

"If you want to deviate from the list, you must acquire preapproval from this weekend's chefs, Millie and myself. I will defer to Millie, so you call your mom and tell her you are changing the menu." She hands me her phone with a haughty look.

I frown and grab the damned squash, placing it none too gently in the cart.

Emma reads off the rest of the items as I collect them. She pauses and her face flushes.

That's weird.

I go around her, about to grab the frozen peas, when it hits me. This, right here in this exact aisle, was where we first officially met.

I look at her through the freezer door I opened and am taken back to this morning's shower. I saw her through the clear glass of her large walk-in shower. Before she even wet her hair, I was walking in behind her.

I helped her wash her hair and body with some delicious smelling soaps, kissed her soft, clean skin and slid my hard body against her smooth, wet, and delicate figure. She clawed at the glass door, moaning quietly while I slipped into her from behind. I gripped at her hips, pushing in and out effortlessly as her delectable ass slapped against me. This was a new experience for us and I have to say, shower sex with Emma is definitely one of my top five moments.

We'd had the condom talk earlier in the week. Both of us being clean and her with an IUD, we agreed to forgo condoms. We've been going at it daily for the last week without them and holy shit, I forgot how much better it is without them. I'd only had condom-free sex with Ashleigh a few times over the years we were together. It was probably my brain's inner self-preservation system that made me not want to give up using them.

With or without a condom, sex with Emma has been the best of my life.

Movement catches my eye and rips me out of my sexy trance. Emma is waving at me, trying to get my attention, then tilts her head as I focus on her. She closes the freezer door with peas in hand.

Shit, now I'm hard in the grocery aisle, next to the peas where we started.

"Sorry, just thinking about my penis." I cover my mouth, feigning a gasp. "I mean peas!"

My eyes crinkle at her as I hold up the bag of frozen peas.

She snatches the bag from me, laughing. "It wasn't that bad!"

Disagree.

Pushing the cart behind her as she leads the way to the checkout, shooting a couple of cute glares back at me as she walks, I feel an enormous sense of appreciation that Emma had no game and was too socially awkward to approach me then.

I'll always remember this aisle fondly. And Emma, too.

Emma

"So, Emma, may I ask you a question?" Chloe asks me.

She arrived an hour ago and has been watchful, but quiet. Jess has told me how protective Chloe can be with her older brothers, always grilling their lady friends, so I prepared for a deluge of questions.

"Of course." I steel myself for personal questions or a background check request.

"You're in love with my brother?"

The room quiets, my mind swimming with thoughts too loud to process anything else around me.

My mouth gapes as I try to find the right response to this question. Jess prepared me for a lot of scenarios, but not this. I hate lying.

"Yes." I slap a hand over my mouth and close my eyes. "Shit."

My unfiltered honesty has gotten me into trouble with friends and associates in the past.

Chloe sucks her lips between her teeth, contemplating. She

releases a big smile and then leaps over to me, enveloping me in a hug which I return after a confused moment.

She squeals and looks behind me. Oh God, don't let it be Jess!

"Mamma, you were right. Isn't this so great?" I sense Millie behind me as she completes the Emma hug sandwich. "I hadn't planned on coming today, but Mom said I needed to meet you."

"Oh, well, thank you for coming. I was excited to meet you, too. Jess thought we would hit it off. I really only have one girlfriend, Lauren, so I was nervous." I take a breath and laugh. "Sorry, I ramble if I let my thoughts have a clear path to my mouth."

They both chuckle, still hugging me.

Jess walks into the kitchen and stops mid-stride. "What's happening here?"

"Nothing!" I practically shout.

"We were just getting to know your girlfriend and finding out how much—" I grip his sister's hand with a tight squeeze, cutting her off.

"How much I love wine!"

"Okay..." He narrows his gaze at his family. "And this resulted in hugging, how?"

"We got excited about a vineyard tour we planned for later this month."

Well, now that sounds pretty great. Chloe knows how to think on her feet. She saved us from an awkward explanation, and I'm going on a vineyard tour with these two lovely women.

"Don't question our hugs. Now, out! You've got to get the grill going!" Millie orders. Jess leaves, looking a bit puzzled, but his eyes connect with mine before he leaves, making sure all is well. I nod once and send him off with one of my fumbling waves.

Once he's gone, Chloe turns to me, "So, I take it he doesn't know?"

I shake my head, unable to answer with words.

Her forehead wrinkles as she considers this. "He's got a gigantic wall built up, that much I know. The good news is you are at the top. Now you just have to keep from falling off. Be patient, don't be a hero, use the ladder."

"What if there isn't a ladder?"

She looks sad now.

"You may have to fall anyway and hope he catches you. I think he'll catch you, though." She rubs my arm in comfort.

Yeah, or I'll end up with two broken legs and a crushed heart. But I just nod and pick my chin up. This is what I want. The risk is more than worth the potential reward. He's going to have a hard time shaking me off that wall.

Lauren shows up and I drag her over to introduce her to Chloe and Millie. These are my people now.

Taylor, his teacher friend Liam, and a few other friends show up around the same time. I meet everyone and do a decent job of being open, welcoming, and social. I notice a few surprised looks from a few of Jess's friends as he introduced me as his girlfriend.

Stella and Greg even dropped by for a bit. Jess disappeared for most of their short visit. Figures. Stella brought Jess the *Fifty Shades Darker* book so he's ready for the next book club meeting.

Instead of succumbing to the laughter bubbling up, I gave her a huge grin and accepted the book with fervor. No one saw me sneak into Jess's room, tuck that sucker right under his pillow with the handwritten, flirtatious invitation to Stella's event. I imagine the look on his face when he finds this inappropriate invitation in his bed. I giggle in glee, eager for him to discover it.

I leave Jess's room only to come across Lauren and Taylor in the hallway. He has his head tipped down saying something in her ear that I can't make out. Lauren puts a hand on his shoulder and then he puts his hand on her waist, moving even closer.

He looks so intense and Lauren's tongue darts out for a quick swipe of her lower lip. Their body language has me creeping backward, away from the hallway to hide back in Jess's room to give them space.

But Lauren sees me and startles, leaping away from Taylor.

"Emma! There you are! Millie was asking for you. She wants

to show you how to make the garden orzo dish." She grabs my hand and leads me back to the kitchen.

"What was that?"

"Nothing, now shh! Or I'll ask about your feelings for Jess in front of your future in-laws," she threatens.

"Too late. Millie and Chloe already questioned me and I spilled all the beans." Lauren's eyes widen. "And don't say in-laws out loud! That's not something Jess jokes about, given the new seriousness of our relationship."

"What!?" she mouths at me.

"Later."

We get to the kitchen and Millie is tearing apart the pantry, but turns to me when she hears us enter.

"Ah, *cara,* where is the butternut squash?" she asks. I help her look, but can't find it. Suspicious, I walk out to the back yard to find Jess.

I see him over with Taylor, Liam, and a guy whose name I cannot recall. Dammit, I was doing so well!

He looks over at me and smiles. Once I approach, he tucks me against his side, still talking to his friends. I tap his chest, looking up at him. He leans down so I can whisper in his ear. "Where's the squash, Jess?"

He squeezes my side. "Still summer, babe. No squash."

My chin drops, suspicions confirmed. "Jess! Your mom is looking for it as we speak."

He laughs. "She knows how I feel about squash. I'm surprised she put it on the list."

"So, it's not that it's summer specifically, it's that you don't like it?" I ask, confused.

"It's both." He kisses my nose and returns to his conversation with the guys.

I feel totally justified putting that book under his pillow. Now I'll pretend I know nothing about it, make him sweat for a while. I'll bend my honesty policy for this special purpose.

I growl at him quietly and huff away to tell his mom. He chuckles and swats my behind as I stomp away.

It does not surprise his mom at all. Earlier, when I verified that we had purchased a squash, she was shocked. I should have asked Jess what happened to it, but I am in problem-solving mode.

"Chloe, you and Emma go to the store and grab squash and more ice, *per favore*." Most times Millie doesn't have much of an accent, but it comes out clear when she interjects bits of Italian into conversation. I wonder how much Italian Jess knows?

We take my vehicle and head to the store, music blasting. Chloe and I have similar musical tastes, thankfully. Jess's taste in music is horrible.

My heart slams in my chest as I see a large furry creature dart out into the road. I hit the brakes and veer opposite to where the animal is running. We avoid the animal and trees, but we are violently off-roading. After a while, my car jerks to a stop.

"Oh my god, Chloe, are you okay?"

She nods at me, breathing a little quicker than earlier.

"Are you okay?" she asks me, checking me over. Earlier she told me she's an ER nurse, so I'm sure this comes naturally to her.

"Yes. Wow, that was close." I settle the nerves in my hands and attempt getting us out of the ditch.

The steering wheel won't move an inch. Shit. I give it another moment, testing out the steering, but something is very wrong. Chloe is staring at me, a grimace on her face.

I put it in park and we both get out. Getting some distance from it, just in case, I call Jess. He verifies we are both alright, then reveals he's had too much to drink to come get us, so he's going to get Liam to drive him to come get us.

There's a truck pulling up behind us not a few minutes later. I look at the time and realize this couldn't possibly be the guys. I grab the pepper spray from my bag and keep my hand tucked away inside of it, stepping in front of Chloe.

My body and brain are on high alert. I have to remind myself that this is a small town and most people are friendly and helpful. But you can't be too careful.

A man steps out of the truck.

"You ladies in need of some help?" he asks, a concerned look on his face. I recognize him from around town and somewhere else, but I can't place where.

Chloe's hand grabs the back of my arm in a fierce grip before she looks around me at the man. "Ah, fuck," she expels on a breath.

"Chlo?" the man asks, surprise stopping him in his tracks.

"Hades," she returns, her tone full of fire.

Releasing my arm, she steps out from behind me.

The man, whose name I doubt is Hades, sighs.

"Nice to see you too, Chloe."

She scoffs at this.

"What are you doing back in town? Finally visiting the town you are usually so good at avoiding?" he asks.

Oh… there's some history here and it is super uncomfortable.

"There wasn't much here for me. My parents don't even live here anymore."

She taps a finger to her chin haughtily.

"And if I remember correctly, you left this town first."

"I came back," he says, quietly.

Chloe's silent for a minute, then turns and walks away.

He looks back at me. "Did you need help with your vehicle, Emma?" he asks and I am concerned about how he knows my name. Then I remember where I know him from. He's filled in as a volunteer for a few of the self-defense classes I take.

"Hayden, right? Now the Hades thing makes more sense," I say mostly to myself.

He grimaces and I realize I've made it seem like Chloe confided their story to me.

"I have no idea who you two are to each other, but I remember you from classes at the gym."

He nods and gives me a small smile. I wave him over to my

car and he ducks down to take a look under the car just as Liam and Jess pull up. Chloe walks over to talk to them, says a quick greeting, then gets in the SUV. Jess checks me over and I explain what happened before leaving them to it and checking on Chloe.

Getting in the vehicle, I place a hand on Chloe's shoulder. "You okay?" I ask.

"No," she says, and I panic, not knowing what to do. I wish Lauren were here, she's great at this stuff. "This is why I don't come here. I heard he moved away, but I knew he still visits his family." She puts her head on my shoulder and I reach around to give her a side hug. "Stupid," she mutters to herself.

There's a tap at her window that startles us both. I look over and it's Hayden. Chloe is quickly wiping her face as I give her a second to compose herself before I roll down the window for her.

He looks at her momentarily, then drops his gaze before turning it to me. His expression is a bit tortured and I feel for these two who obviously have some unresolved issues.

Will this be Jess and me in a couple of months?

"Your car is fucked," Hayden says bluntly. "It's going to need some major suspension, bearings, power steering, and possible axle repairs. It's not drivable, I've called a tow truck driver friend of mine. He'll pick it up tomorrow, so for now, make sure you grab what you need out of it."

I see Jess and Liam already packing up some of my things.

"I'll leave you to it." He nods toward me. "Chloe."

He puts a hand on the window frame, waiting for her to look at him. She doesn't. After a few moments, Hayden walks away. The moment he does, she lifts her gaze and watches him go. He turns and glances back, catching her staring. He smiles softly, then keeps walking.

When the guys get back in the SUV, Jess turns to Chloe.

"That was Hayden, wasn't it?"

She nods.

"I thought he didn't live here anymore. You okay?"

She shrugs and looks out the window to where Hayden is driving away.

We forgo picking up the extra ice and the squash, choosing instead to head straight back to the party.

When we arrive back at the house, Chloe disappears into the back yard. He frowns and looks at me.

"Anything I should know?" he asks.

"No, not really. Just the accident and then a tense Hayden-Chloe reunion. Put us into a bit of a funk," I explain, trying to remain vague for Chloe's sake. "But at least I have you and all your family and our friends to help turn things around."

"Yeah, plus the obvious perk." He waits, drawing out the drama. "No squash. The universe intervened on my behalf." He mouths a thank you toward the heavens and I smack his stomach.

CHAPTER 26

Emma

"Do you want an assortment of pies, hon, or specific flavors?" Dani asks me as I gaze at the glass case containing the pies and cakes.

"An assortment, but could you please add a few extra cream pies?" I'm currently in the bakery ordering treats for the party. I keep referring to it as 'the party' but in actuality, it is Garrett's welcome home/Jess's goodbye party. Not only is that a mouthful, but it's also distressing.

The nagging voice in my mind opens those old wounds.

People leave, so why do you think Jess won't? Your mom didn't stay, your father was barely in your life, your first boyfriend is at thirty-two years old. No one but Lauren has ever wanted a long-term relationship with you. That's why we don't attach ourselves to anyone. It's futile.

Maybe so, but growing means change. I keep telling myself this, but it's been getting more difficult the more I realize how much I love Jess. It's crazy scary. How does one person give me more feelings than I've felt my whole life? He has me picturing quiet evenings years from now, our oldest child running trails in the neighborhood with him, while I'm pregnant with my feet up on the porch waiting for them to come back. There are trips to the beach, baking together but letting him do the real work. Him having to teach me how to work our smart home devices. And an early retirement in St. Helena with his folks.

But Jess might as well walk around with a shirt that says 'Don't Fall In Love With Me'. Well, too late, so now I have to pull up my big girl panties and take a risk. I have to tell him how I feel. Soon. If he won't stay, maybe he'll want to do long-distance or something. Either way, we should talk about what happens when Garrett comes back.

This phase of our relationship may be coming to an end soon, but Jess is still trying to check off as many experiences as possible on my dating/new life checklist. He already completed many items during his date coaching, but one I was very much looking forward to even before we started sleeping together, was the couple's weekend away.

If I hadn't been in a post-sex haze and ecstatic that dinner surprisingly turned out, I might have tried to push the envelope and pick a date after Garrett returns. That likely would have opened up a serious discussion about our dwindling remnants of time together.

The land of ignorance is where I can remain close to Jess and pretend for longer, which is why I've been putting off this conversation.

Jess

One of the last major dating experiences to check off Emma's list is a weekend away. I want to give her this, but more so, I want to have one last Emma-immersed weekend. Before I leave. And I am leaving.

That reality was made clear shortly after the long weekend when I got a call from my brother, checking in like he usually does.

TWO WEEKS AGO…

"Hey Jess. How's hometown life treating you? Break anything in my house yet?"

"I think you mean, 'thank you, Jess, for taking such great care of my house and doing me this gigantic, imposing favor.'"

"Right. Thanks. Now, what's new there? I've been getting texts and emails from Mom and Chloe, and they have one very obvious theme."

He waits, expecting me to guess.

"The above ground pool I put in your yard?"

I know what those ladies had been saying, but want to mess with him first.

"What?! You know I hate pools. They're so much work, a drowning hazard, and take up a ton of space. I wanted to put a few holes back there for golf practice. Bro, overstepping. Get rid of it." It's amusing how much he hates pools being born and raised in California.

"I'm fucking with you. Of course I didn't put a pool in your yard." I laugh.

There's a pause. "You're an asshole. I was sweating."

I just laugh harder.

"How is it over there?" I attempt to distract.

"It's a different life here. I'm glad I could help, and I learned a lot, but I'm ready to come home. I'm planning my trip back, so once I book my flight, I'll let you know and give you an ETA."

"Sounds good. I'll be taking some stuff back to my condo in a few weeks so I don't have too much to move as the date gets closer."

"Well, I heard you might be sticking around for a while…"

"What have the ladies been telling you exactly?"

"Oh, nothing too crazy. Just that you have found an amazing woman you're likely to marry and have little Caldwells with. They made it clear that they love her and Mom mentioned something about adoption, which I assume is an inside joke I wasn't privy to. It's been hard keeping up." He clears his throat. "Seriously though, you have a girlfriend, Mr. Anti-Relationship?"

I don't even know where to start. Does Mom actually think we will get married?

They want me to settle down, start dating. I did that, and to be fair, it was much more pleasant than I expected. Emma actually made me start wanting more. Made me even think about brushing off the lingering resentment I've been carrying around for the last six years.

Not telling my family that Emma and I won't be pursuing a relationship after I move back home was apparently a huge oversight. I thought they'd just be happy that I was dating, that I was trying. I didn't think about Mom and Chloe getting attached to Emma.

"We are just dating. I don't know where this marriage idea has come from, probably wishful thinking on Mom's part. I'll have to talk with her. Emma and I are ending things when I move back to San Francisco. We said we'd give this a go until I'm no longer living here. Mom and Chloe like her, and that's great, but Emma wants the whole loving couple, marriage, kids, the forever kind of future."

"Ah. Ashleigh strikes again."

"No. It's more than that. I've done serious, I've done relationships, and casual dating. I gave up on the commitment, happily ever after thing a long time ago. I'm happy with the way my life is."

"You're happy with the way your life is now with Emma, or before you started a relationship with her?"

"I made an exception for Emma, for reasons that are none of your business. And yeah, it was unexpectedly good."

I won't divulge Emma's secrets, but I also don't want to have to justify myself to a brother who usually stays so far out of conflict, you'd think he was magic the way he disappears at tense times.

"Alright, fair enough. But please talk to Mom and Chloe and

clear this shit up because my responses to them so far have not gone over well."

"Yeah. Will do," I grit out. "See you next month, Gar. Stay safe."

PRESENT...

Needless to say, the last couple of weeks have been a difficult balance of not getting too serious and appreciating our time together. I'm not sure when I'll talk to Chloe and Mom, but it needs to be soon. During our planned weekend away, I'll be talking to Emma about transitioning back to friends when we get back.

That conversation will suck, but won't be unexpected. I can tell Emma wants to talk about us. I've caught her mid-sentence making plans for us for Thanksgiving or Christmas and then she'll stop and abruptly change the subject, still seemingly as happy as ever.

And she has been happy. We've been happy. She's unlike any girl I've ever dated. She is genuine in every way. Caring, funny, and her presence alone can change my entire day.

I grin as I see her dragging her packed bag over to my house. Our weekend away to Fort Bragg sprung up fast. I'd been spending most nights at her place, but when I told her I had to pack, she offered to stay here instead.

I wonder if maybe it would be smart to begin pulling back. Definitely after we get back and we have our talk. I'm sure she'll agree and want to create some separation when we return. For now, though, I'll gladly sleep with my arms wrapped around Emma's sweet body another night.

The next morning, we are having coffee on Garrett's enormous deck while I tell her how I tried to convince him I installed a pool. She laughs and taps her chin, telling me she is officially considering putting a pool in her yard and asking

Garrett for help with it often. I smirk at her. God, I love this wo—

Nope. I have to get my head straight. We are practically living together and it's messing with my mind.

I open the door, step out, and grab her bag.

"This it? Or is there another bag?"

"That's it. Don't stereotype, I'm not like other women."

I agree and contemplate that unintentionally meaningful statement as I load up our things.

After some music scuffles, we take turns picking the music. It becomes a competition to see what songs we each love that we know will drive the other person crazy. I have what Emma refers to as 'super annoying, seizure-inducing' electronic music on my playlist, but Emma has '90s boy bands, so it's an even match.

The first thing I planned was to take Emma to Noyo Harbor. There you can fish along the pier which she'll like better than fly-fishing or getting out in a boat. She loves learning new things and checking off new experiences. I just love watching her when it happens.

I decide to take her to Noyo Harbor first because she wants to fish. She heard my dad and I talking about our yearly trip and was 'curious what the big deal with fishing is'.

"What if we catch something?"

"Then we get to keep it, bring it back to our rental, and have a great meal this afternoon. I have a cooler we can put the fish in."

Her eyes widen in excitement, then go straight to panic. "I don't know how to prepare or cook fish."

"We'll figure it out. But the winner of the first catch doesn't have to gut the fish. So, I'll just direct you." I grin smugly at her.

Her mouth gapes at me. "You are so convinced you'll be the hooker of the first fish?"

"You mean when I catch or land the first fish?" I laugh hard. "Hooker…" I sigh through my laugh.

"You know what I meant, Neighbor Guy." Her hands are on her hips now and her head tilts, but not playfully.

"I prefer 'Green Eyes'."

"Green Eyes is reserved for when you are being sweet. Neighbor Guy is for when you're being obnoxious."

"I see." I grin. "And yes, I knew what you meant. I just think it'll be me who wins the first fish challenge." This was a game the Caldwell men played well. The person who gets a fish last—or no fish—is responsible for preparing the rest of the fish caught that day.

~

Emma catches the first fish.

I'm about to slice into her catch, with her shaking with glee beside me. She had me take dozens of pictures of her holding her fish. She asked me to document the entire event, even her putting it in the cooler.

The moment she had a tug on her line, I took out my phone and recorded her reeling it in. It's a lot of incoherent garbling with sporadic squealing and my calm instructions, which she mostly ignored. Still pulled it off, though, and I'm proud of my amateur angler.

The sweet, confident smile pasted on Emma's face the rest of the afternoon was contagious.

Emma and I head to the Botanical Garden for an evening walk. She barely speaks, just clutches my hand. I gather her in my arms as we take in the lights and beauty. She looks up at me, her eyes shining with sadness. Then she pulls me along the path and heads straight out to my truck. When we get back to the rental, she's still oddly quiet, pensive.

Before I begin to worry, she kisses me, pulls back, smiles and starts unbuttoning my shirt. Yeah, I'm game. This might be one of our last weekends together. Maybe that's what she was sad about earlier.

We are only wearing underwear by the time we cross the bedroom threshold. I force out a breath of impatience. I plan to toss her onto the bed and bury myself inside her, when she stops me and steps closer, moving only her fingertips over my chest, then my arms. She's kissing me, unhurriedly.

We get to the bed after a little more exploration, soft touches, and careful caresses.

She straddles me and between kisses, her hands cupping my face, she says, "I'm falling in love with you, Jess."

I freeze, muscles locked, hands still gripping her ass.

She keeps kissing down my jaw, ear, neck.

A long time passes before I force out an inadequate, "Emma, I…" Fuck. What do I even say?

I can't tell her what she deserves to hear. I care for this beautiful woman, but I can't give her the life she wants. Why hadn't I considered this outcome before now?

"You're it for me. You're everything, Green Eyes."

Her words are like a slap to the face. A blast to a past I've been trying to forget. Every old wound opens, memories of a selfish, cold, and callous woman flood in, unwanted. Ashleigh said the same to me all the time. That I was everything to her. I realized too late that she was just manipulating me.

To Emma, I don't know what I am. The novelty of a semi-normal relationship after years of detachment is likely coloring her true feelings.

Emma moves to the other side of my neck.

"I thought I'd never get to experience this, let alone feel this way. I thought myself unlovable. It was easier to avoid it, pretend it didn't affect me. But it left a deep, aching hole inside. You helped me heal, feel whole again."

She kisses me again, my body still immobile, my mind racing.

"It wasn't the advice or date coaching. It was you."

She is caressing my face, then she slides her hands through my hair, looking at me with such adoration.

Shit. She's so fucking incredible. Sweet, so goddamn sweet.

I snap myself out of my surprised stupor enough to kiss her back, to hold her close.

I can't give her this. Can't give her much at all because I'm a defeated man.

I had moved past it, changed how I do relationships. It was working for me. Mostly. Well, working well enough anyway.

Yet, if I had it in me to love someone again, create the life I once wanted, it would be with Emma.

I kiss her cheeks, eyelids, nose, neck. Taking in her sweetness, memorizing her taste and feel.

"Make love to me, Jess," she requests on a hushed murmur.

Her eyes are closed now, reveling in my gentle touches. I rest my forehead against hers, take a breath, then flip us over so I am hovering over top of her.

I can give her that, even if I can't give her anything else.

CHAPTER 27

Emma

Lauren is having coffee at her desk, eyes closed, enjoying the early morning peace before chaos ensues and the kids arrive at school. I stopped in for a quick chat before heading to work, but Lauren hasn't picked up on my state of panic yet.

"I told him."

"Told who what?" She swivels in her chair to face me. "Oh. Ohhh! Wow. Okay." She puts down her coffee. "Well, tell me more, everything, now."

I laugh lightly. This is why I needed to talk to her.

"We had an awesome weekend. I caught a fish. A fish! My first time. It was so exciting and Jess was impressed, I could tell." I smile, remembering our fishing afternoon.

Lauren snaps her fingers at me, pulling me from my mental reminiscing. "Focus, girl."

"It was a romantic day. But the longer I spent with him, the more I felt, the sadder I got." She nods, understanding. "I dragged him back to the rental and told him I was falling in love with him and that he's helped heal me. Awakened me. I don't quite remember what I said. I was nervous."

"Wow. Ahhh!" She squeals in a hushed tone as she hugs me. "Okay, and then what?" She motions with her hand to continue.

"I think he was surprised." I chuckle. "He couldn't seem to push a single thought from his mind. He said nothing other than my name. But he kissed me gently, sweetly, and held me tighter. Then I asked him to make love to me and he did."

"Making love, huh? Adorable. Hopefully super sexy. And maybe a little messy? Hmm? Tell me more. Let me live sex-cariously through you."

I frown at her. "We had a moment, and it felt important. It changes things. I mean, things were moving in that direction anyway, but this pushes it firmly over the line."

She's nodding. Lips pursed.

"So, do we feel good about this?"

"I don't know. Yes? No? I feel both good and not good at the same time." I sigh.

"I figured this would be a big deal and he would be taken aback. It wasn't part of the deal. He told me what he could and couldn't offer me. I agreed. Then changed everything with one sentence. He never said anything back, never even spoke after my confession."

I look to Lauren for advice.

"I don't know him that well, babe. You do. Do you think he's capable of love or long-term commitment?"

"Yes, I definitely do," I state. "He cares for me, Lauren. I feel it in everything he does, the way he is with me, in the mundane, the intimate, and even in our disagreements."

My next thought wipes the lovesick smile off my face. "I just don't know if he'll choose me."

"You laid it all out there, right? So, let him sit with it for a bit. When is he scheduled to leave?"

"In a few weeks." I feel a burning in my chest.

"Has he mentioned staying? Or have you asked him about it?"

I shake my head. "I was going to ask him to stay last weekend, but everything kind of got away from me after I declared my feelings. There's no logical reason to go our separate ways anymore."

I need to stop skirting the issue and tell him what I want.

My phone buzzes. Hoping it's Jess, I snatch it from my bag.

It's Chloe. Slightly disappointing, but still a pleasant surprise.

"Jess?" Lauren asks.

"No, it's Chloe."

Lauren perks up, leaning closer to find out why Chloe is texting me so early.

CHLOE: Hey Emma.

CHLOE: So, Jess talked to Mom and me the other day. I have to admit, I was pretty disappointed. I thought maybe we'd get to keep you. I won't be back to Landry for a while, but I hope we can still stay in touch after you and Jess go your separate ways.

CHLOE: Anyway, message me if you're ever in San Jose. I'll be the best tour guide you've ever had!

I'm too shocked to respond. Jess doesn't want to discuss our relationship, but has told other people it's over before telling me? Our original agreement seems so inadequate now.

We agreed it would end when his brother came back, but now that seems like a moot point. We've moved beyond that, no matter what invisible line he wanted to keep in place to prevent us from crossing over into serious.

Why does it have to end when we both care for each other? Why can't we continue to be together? We've both been putting off this conversation. Me, because I hoped he'd say something, do something to show me he still wants this. And because I was scared he'd turn me down and still walk away.

Our original expiration date shouldn't matter anymore. He can technically work from anywhere, live anywhere, so why does he have to move back?

He doesn't... unless he just doesn't want to stay. Unless he doesn't love me.

Crushing reality hits me in the chest. He doesn't have to leave, so if he chooses to, that's why.

I try to slow my breathing as my thoughts fly in every direction trying to find some memory, some evidence of his feelings for me.

"What? Emma! What's wrong?"

I hand over my phone. The burning in my chest now a deadly blaze.

"Em, does this mean what I think it does? Didn't you say you haven't talked about this yet?"

"Yeah. He must have told his family that our relationship was short-term and that after he moves, we are over." I slump, winded without ever having left my chair.

"He told his family before he told me. We haven't talked about what was going to happen at all. I mean, I guess that was the deal —we're over when Garrett comes back. I just thought maybe… God. I thought… and he didn't even talk to me."

I sniffle and put a hand to my chest to smother the rising heat.

"Maybe he told them before your weekend away. Don't jump to any conclusions, hon." She is rubbing my back in the way Lauren always does to comfort me.

The doorknob jingles, then the door flies open.

Taylor waltzes in, assesses the room and stops mid-stride.

"Uh, what's going on here? Emma, you okay? What the hell did Caldwell do?" he accuses. Accurately.

"Mind your business, Coach," Lauren hisses at him. "And why are you barging into my classroom?"

"I, uh, didn't think you'd be in yet."

"Not an answer, Shaw."

"I needed more dry erase markers and thought you might have some." He shrugs with ease.

"No. You know I have a stash of colorful markers and you want to pilfer them for your locker room whiteboard." She points at the door. "You may grab some basic black ones from the office like the rest of the staff. My awesome colored markers are not up for grabs."

"Just, like, a red one?" She glares at him in response. "Orange? Come on, you don't even like the color orange!"

How does he know she doesn't like the color orange?

"I better get going, Laur. I'll call you later if I have any updates."

A smile is plastered to my face as I walk past Taylor.

"Hey, wait up." He follows me out after pleading one last time for Lauren's coveted markers. "I don't know what Jess did, but he's a good guy. Just messed up and stubborn. He cares about you. Be patient with him."

I nod and then head to work. Hoping the distraction will provide some clarity.

~

Turns out, it didn't. All I can do now is talk to Jess and see where he's at.

I need a plan, some talking points before I approach Jess. For months, I've been keeping silent about my thoughts of what our relationship could be. Those thoughts grew louder, bolder, I know I have to voice them before I run out of time.

I'll head over there after work today and tell him exactly what I want. I want him to stay, to give us a real shot. I want the full relationship I know he's capable of. I've seen it because this hasn't been pretend for a long time.

If he didn't love me, he'd have told me, right?

If he says he can't stay in Landry because of his condo or wanting to be in San Francisco, being closer for work, then we consider that. Maybe a long-distance relationship? I'm going to have to look up what that entails so I'm prepared. I'll text Lauren and Sadie. Maybe even Dani as she sees and hears a lot at the bakery.

I haven't heard from Jess yet today, but I'll text and see if he can come over. I don't want to continue on the path to our end, which means Jess and I have to stop avoiding that discussion.

~

We were both out the last couple of nights and haven't been able to meet up. This is hanging over my head like a thunderous cloud ready to unleash.

Jess has also been suspiciously absent. Even given our busy schedules, he used to still pop in when he could. He's texted me a bit, but won't commit to plans to see each other and talk as I have requested. I think he's pulling away.

Tonight, I'm finding out. No more excuses, no more pushing it back.

Jess

There's a knock on the door and I'm pretty sure I know who it is.

Emma wants to talk and I'm positive it's about our relationship and its impending end. I've been avoiding her and the conversation we need to have. I think she might ask me to stay and I can't stay. Fuck... I mean I can. I could. I'm not really needed in San Francisco frequently enough to have to live there permanently. That's the beauty of my career, I can live wherever and work from home.

I've been ignoring this issue for weeks. Hell, probably months. The moment we made things real between us, I knew we'd eventually get to this moment, this conversation. Then and now, I knew my answer would be the same. I don't think I can give her what she wants or deserves.

So, I can't stay. Or won't. Shouldn't?

Take your pick.

Bottom line—I'm going back to San Francisco and my regular life of casual dating and occasional hookups. You know, once I feel like dating again. I think I'll need some time after this to get my head straight.

Now it's time to tell Emma that our arrangement deadline remains. That I will not be staying. I walk my chickenshit ass over to the door.

I open it, but only enough for her to see me.

"Oh, hey," I say casually.

"Hi."

She tries to peek around me into the house, curious why I'm shielding her view.

"Busy?"

"Uh, no. It's fine, just some work." My hand scratches at my neck.

"Have some time for a chat?" she asks, her eyes filled with concern and nervousness.

"Sure." I step out, closing the door behind me with a soft click, and point to the chairs on the front porch. She frowns, but moves to sit.

"Are you—" she starts, but shakes her head and starts over. "Is everything okay?"

I nod. "What did you want to talk about? I planned to stop by your place a bit later if I got my work done, we can always talk then."

"I'd like to get this out of the way, if that's okay? Then later you can help me with a new blueberry muffin recipe I was going to try. Now that I've churned out some decent dinners, I decided I'm ready to try baking again." She grins with determination and I manage a laugh despite the situation.

"Is that what you want to ask me about? Being your guinea pig tonight?" I know it's not, but it's worth a shot.

"No. I think we both know that if you feel badly enough about my disgraceful efforts in the kitchen, you'll eat it out of pity, anyway."

She presents me with her most innocent sad expression.

Yeah, I would.

"What I want to talk to you about—ask you about—is us." She studies my eyes, my face.

"Okay." I nod, looking down.

"I need to know if there's a chance you'll stick around after Garrett returns. I'd like that. If you stayed, I mean. I want you to stay and explore this relationship with me. I know at first you were just helping me, coaching me. But it turned real and I don't see why there has to be an end."

Emma is all about logic, reasoning, and explanation, but I don't have any of that for her. Our relationship is real, too real, and I am struggling with how to handle that and handle this conversation.

She waits for me to respond, but I can't find the words. Her face pulls in tighter, concern deepening her furrowed brows.

"Or if you can't stay, I have an alternative arrangement option. I asked a few people about relationships with obstacles such as ours. Our situation isn't standard, and I realize we agreed beforehand on a set timeline. However, given the change in circumstances, and what with certain feelings having developed—"

"Emma," I interrupt. Because I don't want her to do this. I don't want to tell her no.

"Yes?" she asks, but when I remain quiet, she starts over. "If you don't plan to stick around, I want to ask about a long-distance relationship, instead." She stops to gauge my reaction. "Things are working well between us, right? Long-distance relationships appear to help reduce expectation and are beneficial to those that are wary of commitment."

She's hitting me with the facts, but I know she hasn't considered what long-distance would really be like. She hasn't pieced together yet that it doesn't mesh with what she's told me she's been wanting from the beginning. She wants an emotional connection, intimacy, and a relationship where two people build toward the same future.

I lean forward, but otherwise my body is still, careful, calm. Everything I don't feel inside. I lift my gaze to her sparkling, whiskey-colored eyes and open my mouth to speak, but she rushes to finish her planned speech.

"We could see each other when you're in town, and I'd make my way to you, too. This doesn't have to be our last couple of weeks. We don't have to say goodbye."

She chokes slightly on that last word, and I have to bite the inside of my cheek.

I gather my words, a plan, anything. But I don't know what to tell her, how to make her see. She's doubting herself right now, I can see it in the hunch of her shoulders, the frown between her eyebrows, the slight downturn of her cute mouth.

Needing to make her understand that this isn't what she wants, I'm not what she needs. I have to shut this down.

"I have questions about this long-distance thing."

She startles at my voice, but nods emphatically.

"You'd be okay with being my 'while in town booty call'?"

I keep my face blank, my tone sharp, serious. I'm going to hate myself a little after this.

"Well, I definitely wouldn't call myself that." Her lip snarls a bit.

"And other than occasional hookups, you'd be accepting of a low contact relationship?"

"What do you mean?"

"We won't be living in the same city, Emma, and my trips here will be irregular. That would place it firmly in the 'casual relationship' category, which rarely involves any deep, meaningful conversation or expectations. For that kind of long-distance to work, we'd have to dial back our contact."

She looks crestfallen, shocked. I did that. Shit.

"Oh. Uh, right. I guess if that's how you'd want it to be, we'd need to discuss that."

She's trying to be accommodating and I hate it. She is not being true to herself and we talked about that a lot during our practice dates.

I can feel my jaw ticking.

"That's what you'd want? Really? Don't you want a full, monogamous relationship? A life partner, someone you can build that future you want with?"

"We wouldn't be monogamous?"

"That's not what I—" I stop mid-sentence, groaning a bit from seeing the hurt in her eyes. "You want a monogamous relationship and a future. I could only give you maybe one of those. When you find your future boyfriend or husband, being tied to me in whatever this would be, it wouldn't be fair to you or him. You wouldn't be giving yourself the chance to find who you need."

Just saying it out loud sparks a deep sorrow in me I wasn't prepared for. Though, I don't think I was prepared for any of this. I wasn't prepared for Emma.

"I think I misunderstood what a long-distance relationship entails."

I wince. "No." I pull at my hair, frustrated and feeling like an ass. "You didn't, but that's the way it would need to be for us."

She studies me, trying to extract every emotion, thought, or hint at what I'm thinking.

"Did you already decide that we're over, Jess? Before we even had the chance to talk about it?"

She's sitting up straighter, finally understanding what I'm saying.

"Your sister told me you've informed them about the upcoming end of our relationship."

"I talked to her, yes. Right before we headed to Fort Bragg."

She waits to see if I'll answer her first question, but I don't.

"Emma, we knew this time was coming, and it's a tough situation to be in. For both of us. Why don't you think about what long-distance would mean, what you really want, and just leave it at that for now?" I'm a weak, pathetic asshole that I can't just tell her that she's right, I did already decide we were over.

I knew she'd want to talk about continuing our relationship, especially after her confession last weekend. But I can't do long-distance with her because it wouldn't be enough and it wouldn't be fair to her. And I can't stay because it would be too much.

She nods. "Okay. Yes, you've given me lots to consider." She pauses. "Here I thought I was prepared for this conversation."

She stands, walks to the stairs, then turning around she asks, "Are you still coming over?"

I want to so fucking bad.

She looks up at me with hope and want in her eyes, and it crushes me. I struggle for words, but she steps in to let me off the hook.

"It's okay, I can drop off the muffins I promised you tomorrow morning so you can enjoy them for breakfast. Start your day off with a little risk." She pauses. "Maybe if I could bake more edible treats, you'd change your tune and throw yourself at my feet, begging me to even consider a long-distance relationship."

She gives a little laugh. "Kidding. Goodnight, Green Eyes."

I watch her jog away and it hurts more with each step she takes.

My feet are moving before I can talk myself out of it. My hand wraps around her arm, spinning her around. My mouth devours hers before she can even look at me. I wrap my arms around her and hold her tightly. I kiss her hard at first, desperately.

Then I slow down, soaking her in, coaxing her lips apart. I kiss her with regret, reverence, and want. My hands find her hair, trail down her neck, smooth shoulders, her back, drawing her as close as I can. I meld us together as one before I break the kiss and stagger back.

She inhales deeply, her eyes swimming with hope, happiness. She grabs my hand and tugs on it, leading me to her house. I redirect my hand to her face, give her a short, lingering kiss before slipping away and walking back to Garrett's house. Alone.

CHAPTER 28

Emma

What is he doing up so damn early? I can hear doors opening and closing. It's still dark outside and Jess never goes for a run this early. Maybe he had a hard time sleeping last night, too.

Slipping on the sandals he leaves by my front door, I head out to surprise him. I think about how my hair is a soft, messy pile on the top of my head, my face is devoid of makeup, and I am wearing my usual sleepwear comprising a big, long T-shirt. I don't care, he's seen me look worse and I'm just excited to start my day with a Jess fix after last night's talk.

I approach him, his back to me, and place a hand on his shoulder. "Guess I am not the only crazy one who had a hard time sleeping last night." I laugh as he jumps, startled.

The laugh dies in my throat as I take in his truck bed filled with moving boxes and two duffel bags. My body burns with shock, the unwanted sensation moving from my stomach and radiating everywhere.

He looks at me with those green eyes that sucked me in over six months ago. Regret and guilt shining through them.

No. He couldn't be leaving right now. Could he?

"What's going on?" I don't manage to keep the panic out of

my voice. My eyes dart from him to the contents of his truck and back.

"Emma…"

He's running his fingers through his hair and is rubbing that damn spot on his neck. I didn't think I'd need to identify Jess's shifty body language, but here we are. I'm suddenly and ironically grateful for his lessons.

"Are you—" I clear my throat and look at his truck, the house, anywhere but him.

"Were you going to tell me before you left?"

Utter silence reigned for at least a half dozen heartbeats. Heartbeats are how I'm trying to keep time as my mind reels.

"No." He turns to make his way to the driver's side door.

The air whooshes out of my lungs. That's it? Just 'no'? What the hell!

"No?!" I shout louder than I intended. My eyes snap back to him, but now he's not looking at me. "Look at me!"

He does, with a sigh and a blank face that breaks me.

"So, I was just going to come by your place this morning with the blueberry muffins I baked for you and you'd be gone?!" I laugh a dark laugh. "You couldn't just take your mild food poisoning like a man, no, you had to sneak off in the middle of the night?"

I know this isn't about baking, but it hurts too much to do anything other than distract my brain from what's really happening. My heart has been put out of commission, so my brain is going to have to shake it the hell off and step up.

He grips the door handle of his truck, mutters something I can't hear.

"This, Emma. This is why I thought it would be best not to say goodbye. I knew you'd be upset. I knew it would get messy."

"Oh, no. No! If you'd had some goddamn decency, and we talked about when you were leaving, I wouldn't have been mad. Devastated you were leaving early? Yes. Heartbroken? Yes. Crushed, actually, because for some unthinkable reason I developed serious feelings. Big feelings." I whisper to myself, "Why in the hell did I do that?"

I raise my voice again. "I told you I was falling in love with you and you were going to leave me behind without a backward glance." I smack my head, incredulous. "That's my life, though, right? People I care about don't stay."

I never got to say goodbye to my mom, my nannies moved on with little fanfare, my father wasn't even home when I moved to college. So, if this is goodbye, a little prep time would have been nice.

He says nothing, jaw tense, teeth clenched. I search his eyes, face, body, for some indication of what he is thinking or feeling. Nothing other than anger, it seems. A metallic taste infiltrates my mouth as I realize I've been gnawing on my lip to keep myself from another emotional outburst.

I let the dam break again, just a little.

"You know what, maybe you were right!"

His gleaming emerald eyes lock on mine again for a moment at this revelation.

"This is for the best. Just continue with your sneaking off in the middle of the night. Go on, pretend I never came out here. I'll still show up at your door with my muffins and pretend to be surprised you left without a word. That you were going to consider humoring me with the offer of a long-distance relationship. Don't worry, you'll get all the tears and rage you hoped for, but won't be here to take any kind of responsibility for my despair."

I go to stomp away and then realize I am wearing his sandals. I rip off the offensive footwear and fling them into the bed of his truck.

"Oh! Don't want to forget those. It was probably too risky to ask for them yesterday. I might have been suspicious. Yeah, that was smart," I mutter numbly.

I can't even be angry anymore. My feelings have tucked tail

and run back into the dark cave of my once bleak heart, regretting the salvation it thought to have found in him.

I turn and continue marching back to my house when something cuts into my now bare foot. I fall, hard. Looking at the bottom of my foot, I see it's bleeding steadily and has a black piece of sharp plastic protruding out of it. Shit, why couldn't I just make a clean getaway?

"Fuck," I mutter. Jess swears and starts coming over to see if I am okay. "Stop!"

He hesitates but keeps coming.

"No, Jess. Just go!"

He stops, hands clenched into fists. "You're hurt." He puffs out an angry breath. "Just let me help you, Emma. Are you bleeding?"

He starts toward me again, eyes softening.

I shake my head and hold up a hand. "It's just a cut. Seriously, just go. You are hurting me so much more than this stupid gash. Go. I'll be fine."

I jump up and hobble into my house, dripping blood all over. The front door shuts with a loud, resolute click. My back hits the door and I sag against it, waiting to hear his truck leave.

His voice breaks through the silence. "It was an arrangement, Emma. We agreed…" He pauses. "You—" A sigh. "You knew we had an expiration date. It was best to end it before it became too… serious."

Now it sounds like he's right outside my door.

Oh? Sneaking off in the middle of the night was part of our agreement? He has over thirty guests coming on the weekend to say goodbye to him and welcome his brother home.

The panic crawls up my throat, an unwelcome bile-like substance. I have to tell everyone he ditched before his own surprise goodbye party. I'll need to cancel the bartenders and mobile bar, the virtual reality games that were going to be set up, the food. Crap, I'm listing in my head instead of focusing on what is happening right now. Typical. Creating busy work for myself while I tuck the uncomfortable stuff away.

Peeking out of the front window, I see Jess still standing there, his body tense, his gaze focused on the keys gripped in his hand. Like they can tell him how to fix this horrible conversation.

I sigh and look around my living room since I can't walk to my room without him seeing me. His sweater is laying across the back of my couch, his charging cable is on the end table, the book he lent me on the coffee table. Not even thinking, I race to grab the items, take a deep breath, and throw the door open.

"Sure, Jess." I breathe again, trying to cool the fire in my chest, and channel Em-bot. "You're right. I shouldn't have become so attached. That went against the intended arrangement."

I swallow the tears and bury them deep where they now live again.

"You held up your end. Too well, it seems. I shouldn't have asked you to stay, but I didn't want to regret never asking, never trying or reaching for what I want."

I take a deep breath, shove my heartbreak down into a dark hole and say, "Good luck wherever you end up. I hope you find a home someday, Jess."

His abandoned items hover between us. I've been wearing that sweater most evenings when we cuddled on the couch or went for walks. Or whenever I missed him. That sweater made me feel safe, cared for, happy, free, and wanted.

Fine. Maybe it wasn't the sweater. It was the man. The man I mistakenly considered mine. At the back of my mind, I was hoping he would stay. For me. For us.

He doesn't move to take his things and refuses to look at me. I don't think I could take looking him in the eyes right now, anyway.

"I knew after our weekend away, we wouldn't be able to end this as friends. In not continuing our relationship, not staying, I would hurt you. I never wanted to hurt you, Em."

I say nothing.

Yes, it would likely be hard to be friends with someone you knew was in love with you.

He releases a drawn-out breath, then turns and gets into his truck. I hear it all, but I don't watch. I stand, frozen, numb. His truck races off down the road. I stand outside trying to breathe, trying not to feel because it hurts.

When people you love leave you, when they don't choose you, it can ruin you.

I close my eyes tightly, but can't stop the hurt from resurfacing. So, I let it wash over me. I thought he cared about me, that we had something beyond the arrangement of our unconventional start. It was real, wasn't it?

Mentally slapping myself, I put up a giant impenetrable wall to block out everything I am feeling before I fall apart. There's no time this morning. All those feelings will have to wait until I return. I'll hold up the pieces of that wall until I get home later.

The sun is rising by the time my mind allows my surroundings to trickle back in. How long have I been standing here? Looking down, I realize I am still bleeding. Not from the wound that hurts the most; the one that will leave the biggest scar. No, only the one from my foot.

Jess

My grip tightens on the steering wheel as the mental image of Emma realizing that I was leaving early without saying goodbye flashes across my vision.

Fuck. Fuck. Fuck.

She looked like I had sucker-punched her. Her sparkling eyes round with shock, pain. Even behind the fury, that's all I could see.

I know she doesn't want long-distance. She deserves more. She also deserves a goodbye, an explanation, closure. I just don't have one. Not one that would stand up against her soft looks, kind eyes, and sweet mouth.

I'd like to say it's better this way, but there was nothing better about the way I decided to leave. I panicked. I'm leaving because

I'm too scared to stay, and Garrett returning is a convenient excuse.

I shake my head in disgust at myself.

I planned to send her a text explaining why it was better for me to just leave and not have a whole thing with goodbyes. We both knew what this could and couldn't be.

Or maybe we'd gotten too deep and I was just telling myself that. Maybe I'm the one who didn't really see our relationship for what it was.

She'll get over this. This is just her first taste of feeling something other than indifference in a long time. At the very least this is a convenient excuse I tell myself to prevent feeling like a bastard for hurting her.

Better for her to be angry than for us to have the 'I can't really be with you' talk. I don't want to turn her down again. I can't. She's amazing. She's imperfectly perfect. She'll find someone. That guy will probably be able to give her everything. Yes, some other asshole will get to be with her the way she deserves. Except, unlike me, he probably won't be an asshole.

After Ashleigh, I went looking for all the wrong kinds of relationships. Telling myself I would leave the door open to finding love again. But when you're looking in all the wrong places, it's hard to find anything of worth. Instead, I found trouble. The crazy kind.

Emma found me and before I could figure out exactly what my relationship with her was, I slammed the door shut. I'm not ready to be what she needs. It wasn't supposed to happen with her. We had rules; it wasn't supposed to get this deep.

At first, I thought I was safe with Emma. She was a repressed, awkward, floundering waif of a girl who wanted dating tips, a friend and guide while she bravely upended her sense of self.

And we were friends. More than friends. She awed me, entertained me, fed (and attempted to poison) me, amused me, and showered me in all of her newfound affections. She taught me more than I taught her.

Watching her discover her fire, the center of who she was, and hold it tight while she tackled the next experience made me proud. It also made me face some of my own repressed feelings.

It might have felt real.

Maybe I got confused along the way, too.

Maybe she left her door open, too. She was waiting for someone, and I opened her door, but then walked away.

Maybe one day we can go back to being friends. My mind chimes in, 'friends where one friend is in love with the other?'

Maybe I'm unsure which of us would be the friend in love.

She once said that no matter what happened between us, at the very least, I was a good friend. Could I be friends with Emma while she moves forward with her life, and I return to my normal life?

Ha. No. With her being in my life, even as a friend, I'd be reminded of that hollowness in my chest as I continue on the path my life was heading down for the past half-decade.

Emma forced me to confront some things I hadn't been ready for. But she thinks I need to find a home and I don't. I don't need much in life, I live a pretty simple one. My home is wherever I kick up my feet, right? I can make a home anywhere.

Right?

Fuck.

CHAPTER 29

Jess

I've been on the road for about an hour now and have still thought about nothing other than Emma. I grab some breakfast at a diner before heading back on the road to San Francisco.

Once I get to my condo, air it out and move my limited things back in, I finally settle on a stool in the kitchen. Checking my phone with much trepidation, I notice a text from Garrett, but thankfully nothing from Emma. I wasn't sure what to expect once she'd had time to let our confrontation fester.

GARRETT: Hey man, I made it back already. House looks good, thanks. You really didn't have to clear out early, though. Maybe you could come back for a bit?

Just as I am about to type out a 'nope, bad idea' text, he sends me another text.

GARRETT: You know, and change back my desktop theme, you asshole.
GARRETT: How the fuck did you get everything to have some

kind of dick drawing background? Even my fucking laptop, man. I have to take that to work.

I laugh for the first time today.

ME: You'll just have to come see me in San Francisco, I guess.
GARRETT: Not funny, bro. I hate pranks. And technology. You have combined them in a really hateful way.
ME: Just messing around, man. I made all the settings temporary. They'll go back to normal in a couple of days.
ME: How were your travels back home? Get settled back in?
GARRETT: I slept most of the way, so it was fine. Being a doctor allows you access to the good sleep meds that knock you right out for those sixteen-hour flights.
GARRETT: Settled in fine. Have to go into the clinic later and start getting reacquainted and caught up there.
GARRETT: Oh, hey, is there a reason you put blueberry muffins on the front step? What's in them? What did you do to them? How did you have time to do all this crap?

Shit. Well, that's a kick to the stomach.

Emma really dropped the muffins off. I let her make them for me, even knowing I wouldn't be there. The moment I closed the door after kissing her goodbye, I knew I needed to leave soon. Before she could talk me into staying. Before I could convince myself I should stay.

ME: No. They are from Emma. She made them for me. Eat them.
ME: She's practicing baking, so you're taking a bit of a risk… but she loves it. Baking, I mean. And tell her they're good. Even if they're not. They'll likely be awful, but just eat them.
Garrett: Uh, okay. Sounds horrible. Can I just pretend I ate them? I did not escape malaria just to come home and get poisoned.

GARRETT: Wait, why did she make them if you were leaving early today?

Ah shit. I forgot to tell Garrett that I wasn't saying goodbye to Emma.

I also wanted to avoid the superiority complex lecture I'd get where he calls me a dick.

ME: Uh, so given the nature of our relationship, I decided a clean break was best. She asked me to stay.
ME: I couldn't stay. So, I didn't tell her I was leaving early.

I see the three dots come and go as he decides what to write, and then it stops.

Good. He'll process for a while and I can avoid it for longer. Works for everyone.

My phone rings. It's Taylor. What are the chances that's a coincidence and he's just calling to check-in?

I answer, and it starts.

"For real? You already left?" he shouts. "You didn't say goodbye to any of us? And apparently Emma doesn't know you left either? Man… that's fucked up. Is Garrett supposed to tell her when she eventually goes over there looking for you, because that is going to go really fucking badly. Garrett cannot handle that shit."

He sounds even angrier than I thought he would be.

I take a breath and try to explain. "No, she knows. She was up early and found me packing my truck."

"Dude. That's—you're—" He blows out a breath. "How'd that go?" I can practically see the sarcastic, angry smirk on his face.

"Bad. Terrible." I see her face again and scrub my eyes, wiping the awful image away.

"You're an asshole."

"Yeah." He's not telling me anything I don't already know.

"And fucked up. Jess, you've got to deal with your girl hang-ups. Ashleigh betrayed you, she hurt you, but don't let some crazy felon ruin your whole fucking life," he says like it's so easy to change the course of your life, to drop the ugly habits, to believe in something again. "Emma is great and you—" I can hear a little growl like he's about to throw something but is restraining himself. "You should have handled this really, really differently."

He stops, thinking.

"Dammit, and what are we supposed to do about the awesome party next weekend? I was really looking forward to that," he says.

That catches me off guard. What party? And why is he thinking of throwing a party right at this moment?

"What? Are you planning a party?" I ask.

There's a pause. A long pause.

"Shit," he says. "Oh, man... uh. Nope. No party." Backpedaling, but it's too late now.

"What. Party. Taylor." I really hope it's not what I think it is.

"You know what, actually, you deserve to know. I hope it makes you feel like an even bigger asshole."

He finally tells me, "Emma planned a party for you and your brother. She booked a band, ordered food, including a bunch of pies she insisted on—even though I tried to tell her you and Garrett don't like pie—booked a virtual reality company to come set up a gaming competition in your yard, some kegs, and a bunch of other shit too..." While he pauses, I drop my head back and let the guilt wash over me.

I listen as he continues. I deserve every bad feeling this is causing, so I take it all in.

"Your parents are coming, she talked to them and then your mom wanted to get involved, so they've been chatting a bit. As a heads-up, they really like her, so you'll have that hole to dig yourself out of too. Emma had to skirt your mom several times when she received invites to dinner and future family events, shopping. Dude, your mom was full-on courting your girlfriend."

Fuck.

"You there, man?" he probes.

I have no idea how long he's been waiting for me to respond. What can I even say to that?

"Yeah," I snap. "Just have the party for Garrett or something. Make sure everyone knows I won't be there."

He's quiet for a while.

"You're fucking up. Big time." He doesn't sound angry anymore. Resigned. He doesn't realize that I already know I've fucked up.

He continues to school me. "For what it's worth, I'm not sure Emma would even know how to betray you. Look man, you've had a rough go with relationships and women have been shitty in pretty much all of your experiences. But, when you find the one that makes having to go through all that shit worth it, you don't betray her."

I let that little nugget settle into my brain. Into my heart.

I did. She gave me everything, fell all the way into me, trusted me, loved me, and I betrayed her.

"Look, man, I better let Lauren know to go check on Emma." He sounds distracted now. "Lauren says Emma's in love with you. That quirky, beautiful, closed-off woman let herself love you. Kind of good news/bad news scenario there, huh? You said she wanted to get in touch with her feelings and see what real relationships were like. She can check that shit off her list. Mission accomplished for you. You taught her relationships equal betrayal and heartbreak."

"Hey, lay off, man. This was always the way it was going to end. She knew this going in. That was the deal." He's probably right, but he's pissing me right off. He's supposed to be my friend.

"Sure, man. Fine. I hear you," he relents. "So, I know this was all part of the deal and everything, but how are you doing? You guys were at least friends, right? With the way you left things, I imagine that means you aren't anymore?"

"I don't know." I consider, then say, "Yeah, we were friends. She's—" I grind my molars. "Shit." He's right, I really fucked this up. "We were good friends." Were. Past tense hurts more than I thought it would.

"Well, that'll make things nice and awkward for the rest of us with her living next door to Garrett and being best friends with Lauren. We will see her pretty regularly. You going to be okay with that?"

"Yeah. Do what you want to do. I don't live there anymore, so I'm sure it'll be fine."

It's not fine.

"Plus, you don't know if she'll want to hang out with you anymore. I mean, she may have just put up with you because you're friends with me…"

My half-assed attempt at a joke falls flat.

"Uh, huh. I'm actually more worried she may not want to see any of us again. But that's not something you need to concern yourself with, man. You don't live here anymore, right? So we'll figure it out."

"One sec," he says. "Lauren says she's on her way over to check on Emma. Oh, and that she will rip your balls from your body the next time she sees you. Apparently, you are," he pauses and clears his throat, "direct quote, 'not a real man, so you won't be needing them'."

He lets out a big huff of a laugh followed by a choking sound.

She's right and wrong. I'm a man, he's just buried deeply under some intense bullshit that negates everything that makes me a worthy one.

I can sit here and tell myself I like the single life, I'm not meant for actual relationships, but I'm not good enough for Emma. I don't know what the fuck I'm doing, and somehow, she unknowingly asked me of all people to help her.

"Yup, that sounds about right." I play it off like all is well.

"Want me to update you on how she's doing?" he asks. He already knows my answer though, I can hear it in his voice. He is testing me and I am about to fail, just like he knows I will.

"Nah, man. I don't think that's a good idea."

I wince. God, I'm the king of assholes. Truth is, a part of me wants to get into my truck and drive straight back to her. To take it back. To beg and grovel.

"Cold, man, so cold," he comments. "You just don't want to know exactly how much you wrecked her."

True, but I say nothing back. I know what he's thinking of me right now, it's the same thing I'm thinking of myself. I'm a coward.

I sigh and then tell him I have to finish settling into my place. What else am I going to say? Can't fucking defend myself, so I'll leave it.

Emma

I answer the door that Lauren has been incessantly pounding on for the last ten minutes. I open it and then turn right back around and head to my room. She says nothing, just follows.

I get in under my bedcovers and scooch over when I feel her getting in behind me. She just holds me, but I can feel her shaking with feeling. Likely rage.

"Want to talk about it?" she asks.

I don't reply. I just hold tighter to her arm wrapped around me.

She waits nearly a whole minute before she starts up anyway, "He's an asshole, babe." She squeezes me back. "Don't worry, I'm going to see him eventually and there will be some painful consequences."

Some deep, nearly snuffed out part of me almost laughs. "No, Lauren. Just leave it. I should have known what this was. I just wasn't prepared. I fucked it up. I was naïve. Stupid," I whisper, "so stupid."

"No, sweetie. Not stupid. You've changed so much. You feel, you connect. Sometimes it ends really, really badly. This is a part of growing emotionally. It's just the really shitty part." She gets up on an elbow and looks down at me as I look up at her.

The numbness subsides. The warm, wonderful feelings I'd been absorbing and cherishing over the past months suddenly turn to tingling, sharp pains. I feel something inside me break. All I do is try to breathe for a long while. My face, pillow, blanket, wet with my tears. I don't cry. Not since I was seven, when my mom left, when everyone I knew either physically or emotionally left me. Em-bot never cried. Nothing got to me. You can't get to what's not there. Now, however, that once hollow space contains memories, aspirations, affections, and treasured moments.

Lauren stays the night. It's dark, and the moon is high when I finally speak.

"He took it all away..."

"What did he take away?"

"My heart. My soul. The best parts of who I could have been. Who we could have been together. He took our future. And what he didn't take, he left in pieces," I whisper.

Maybe if I say it quietly, it won't be true.

"Oh... oh god, Em." She hugs me tightly. "I know. Fuck, do I ever know," she whispers back.

"You, Em, are going to be okay. One day. Not today. Fuck today! But we will get through this." She looks down at me, a flicker of something worrisome in her eyes. "Don't shut down, though, okay? I've loved seeing you be whole, open, daring. It's pretty fucking awesome, babe. Feel this, but don't let it own you," she begs.

I wipe my eyes again and let myself go numb again, anyway. Just for a short while. Just to fall asleep. I can finish breaking while I sleep, then wake up and rebuild.

CHAPTER 30

TWO MONTHS LATER

Emma

I'm less of a mess. Honest. Looking back at the last couple of months makes me cringe though. The first couple of days, after I allowed the emotions in, I'd return home from work and not even make it to the door of my house. I'd completely lose it in the car sitting in my driveway. Every day for more days than I'd care to admit, I'd sit in the driveway and silently but violently crying, hunched over my steering wheel while looking at the house next door.

Garrett caught me the second day. Not so much 'caught' as locked eyes with me, gave me a sad pity-filled grimace, and then beelined straight for his vehicle.

I couldn't even help it. Every time I got home, I'd think about what Jess and I would normally do. I'd spend my drive thinking of what I could make for dinner for us, what movie on Netflix would drive him nuts to watch with me, going for a run with him but pretending to fall behind every so often just so I could watch him like the pervert I found out I was, going to a football practice just to jeer at him and get him to do that growling thing he does when he's pissed and then laughing about it all the way home.

I miss those stupid things. Those are what I'll focus on.

Focusing on the big things is too much right now. Like what it feels like to wake up with him cuddled next to me in bed. Or how it feels to have all of his attention and know he wouldn't want to be anywhere else. How lucky I felt to have him in my life. What we could have been, the future we would have had.

We accidentally built something monumental together, and it no longer has a place in the world.

I've finally started leaving the house for things other than errands, groceries, or work. Today, I'm meeting Lauren at the wine bar on Main Street that we love.

Waiting for her, I fiddle with my dress. Lauren requested I wear something much more presentable than she's seen lately. I tried to tell her, my house—my dress code.

I caved and am wearing a simple fall dress with some leggings and boots for comfort. I even swiped on some mascara, but that was all she was getting. I wouldn't be surprised if she held me down, wiped off my ChapStick, and added lipstick just to prove a point.

As much as I complain, she's been a godsend. There with me whether or not I was good company, listening to my muddled thoughts as they exploded from me on the bad days, and now, successfully reintroducing me to society.

The one point I won't budge on is her insistence about dating again. She has been adamant that this experience has been educational and that I need to use that knowledge and momentum to get out there and try again. She is hoping that my love for Jess was about the novelty of deeper feelings for a new love interest rather than being about Jess, the man.

We have agreed to disagree about this. I wish Lauren would trust that I know my heart, my feelings, but I understand why she doesn't.

Where is she? Usually when we go out, she beats me to a table. My phone buzzes.

LAUR: Don't be mad at me.

ME: What? Why? Lauren…
LAUR: So, remember when I asked you about setting up an online dating app profile? And you shot me down with more profanity than I'm used to from you? Well, I kind of did it for you. Now, let me explain before you flip out.

WHAT!?! Oh, she better get here soon, I need to yell at her in person. Well, not yell, but harshly chastise.

ME: WHAT?! Where are you?
LAUR: You deserve everything you want, Emma. You shouldn't have to take whatever shit a man gives you. YOU decide whether what he gives is enough and if not, adios! Take charge of your dating life again. Right now, it hurts, but don't give up. Try this out.
ME: I don't want to date right now. You of all people should understand that.
LAUR: I do. And I don't. This was a bad breakup where you had feelings for a guy and he decided he couldn't do long-term. It is fucking enraging and depressing, but it also means he wasn't the one for you. Fuck him. Idiot. Dating, building relationships, opening yourself up to love and self-fulfillment goals—you were doing it all. Don't give up. Try this.

Sigh. I begin my 'she means well mantra' I've gotten accustomed to the last few weeks.

ME: Lauren, I love you. I am immensely grateful to have you in my corner. But I can't.
ME: It would feel dishonest. I would mislead these men and my heart would feel like a cheater.
LAUR: I'm sorry.
LAUR: In a couple of ways, but currently, because I may have already set you up with a date that should arrive momentarily. He already knows what you're wearing, so he'll approach you.

His name is Sean, he's a mechanic who lives about thirty minutes away, but is moving here in a few weeks.

He knows what I'm wearing? I didn't even know what I was going to wear until about fifteen minutes ago.

LAUR: Just try? You hate him, the date, or anything—you leave.

Is she here? I look around the place, in case she stalked this orchestrated date attack.

I see the peek of her brown hair tucked under a hat, trying to be discreet. I spin on my barstool, about to hop off when a tall, dark-haired man stands in my way.

"Emma?" He's holding out a hand in greeting.

I take it absently, shaking hands while trying to see past his shoulders for Lauren.

"Um, yes. Sorry, do you mind if we relocate?"

His hand still in mine, I drag him over to Lauren's table. She's ducking under her obnoxiously obvious ball cap, trying to hide.

"Sean, right?"

I take a seat beside my traitor best friend, motioning for him to sit across from us.

He sits, looking very confused.

"I'm sorry to have to tell you this, but my friend here figured it was time for me to date again after a bad breakup a couple of months ago. So, she set this all up today." I fold my hands on the tabletop, waiting for him or Lauren to say something.

"Uh, yeah, I kind of knew some of that. Lauren was straight with me about setting us up. I figured it was worth it to at least meet you." He grins at me, cutely. "Your friend really talked you up."

Now I'm blushing and speechless. I look over at Lauren. She's looking back at me with a hint of a smile on her lips, her eyes widened at me, waiting for me to say something.

"Oh. Okay. Sorry, I just wanted everyone to be on the same

page. Crystal clear about what this is and what it is not. Again, Sean, I'm sorry. I am not ready to date yet. I feel bad that we've wasted your time."

He shrugs. "It's no big deal. I mean, I'm moving here in a few weeks, so at least now I'll have two familiar faces to smile and wave at. Maybe even talk to? What about being friends, Emma? I'd love to find someone, find that relationship that would make me also want to forgo dating ever again. Think you ladies can help a guy find a smart, sweet woman? Ideally one who enjoys playing and watching sports and isn't unavailable."

I hold up my hands, shaking my head. "Then you definitely don't want me. Sports are not my thing. To watch? Sure, sometimes. To play? No."

Then I tilt my head in consideration, switching my gaze to Lauren.

"But Lauren here played slow-pitch throughout high school."

Maybe this will work out just fine. Sean is a decent-looking guy. Dark, messy hair, a scruffy look I know she likes, and those shining green eyes. It was the first thing I noticed about him.

"What? Oh, yes, I played. I was talking to some teacher friends about how great a beer league would be. If we figure it out this season, you should join! As for dating, sorry champ, but I'm not in the market for a boyfriend either."

She winces, finally realizing we're definitely wasting this guy's time.

"Damn. At least get to know me a little before you crush my hopes and dreams," he teases. "For real though, having three sisters, I am pretty used to hanging out with the gals. Tell me about the town. What should I know? Who should I know?"

He leans back, cool as can be, as our server comes and takes our order.

I order their signature blackberry chocolate cream pie, but memories have me setting it aside after only a few bites. Lauren asks if I'm feeling okay.

I focus on our new friend as we talk about the town, the

townspeople, and what to do around here. We warn him about the Landry Life League, tell him our favorite restaurants and the places to get good coffee.

He's not a runner, but plans on using the trails I tell him about to do some biking. He asks about the gym and we tell him about the new yoga studio that's opening. He remembers some of the people, businesses, and events the town holds from his visits when he was younger. Some of his family lived out here for a long time, but only a few are still residents.

Intrigued by his quest to find a woman in Landry before actually residing here, I end up asking him why he agreed to meeting me in the first place. Especially knowing I might react negatively to the idea of a surprise date.

He tells us he's a people person and wants to make friends here either way. He's always been social and wants to set up a social circle in his new town.

He was so at ease the whole evening, never dodging personal questions, interested in our lives. Relatable, likable, handsome, and charming. He'd be a great boyfriend. For someone else. Calling him a friend sounds just right.

~

"No, the onion rings give me wicked gas. Pick a different appetizer, Teach," Sean overshares, and if it wasn't so endearing, it would be obnoxious.

"Fine. We can get the potato skins. Again. But I want an order of deep-fried pickles, too," Lauren demands. She loves all the bad foods and makes them seem so damn appealing.

We've been meeting up at the wine bar several times a week for the last month or so. I have nothing else on my calendar other than a best friend who loves wine and a new friend who loves both food and chit chat. The last few weeks have been… tolerable.

"How'd the date go last night? Is she a redhead everywhere?" Lauren questions while sipping her wine daintily.

Sean chokes mildly on his cocktail.

"Geez. Uh, believe it or not, I rarely go to pound town on a first date."

I smirk at his immaturity.

"I'm a gentleman. I mean, I wouldn't mind unwrapping and taste testing the merchandise first." He stops to consider for a moment. "Alright, fair question. However, in this case, I did not sample the goods other than a chaste goodnight kiss on the cheek. She wasn't for me." He shrugs.

Christ on a cracker. The things these two discuss in very public settings are alarming. I've learned a lot in the last few outings.

"I've got another date lined up for tomorrow evening. She's blonde, but seems sweet and like she'd be a decent conversationalist, you know, do more than just giggle and flirt, maybe even be well-read. And not just the filthy sections of whatever women's magazines you ladies are into. Don't bother trying to convince me there aren't sexy parts in those. Tamara made it very clear last night that her latest sex tip came from some magazine and it's a guaranteed good time." He shudders. "She was aggressive. Which can be pretty fucking fantastic, but not if the sex kitten trait is all she's got going for her."

"What's up with ditching all the dates? You just keep going until you find one good enough to keep around for a while and the rest you go through like tissues? One-time use. Is that how dating works for guys?"

Okay, so I am a little jaded right now and have reverted back a little to expecting the worst out of the male population.

"Ouch." He clutches his chest. "I thought we were friends, Emma." His jade green eyes soften as he teases me. I avoid looking at them. They remind me too much of Jess.

"Sorry. I just don't understand men. It seems there are many ways to approach dating and I'm not sure I've seen a healthy attempt, maybe ever." I lay a light hand quickly on his, giving him a short but regret-filled pat. "You are just being discerning. That's good. Admirable."

"It's fine. I know it seems like a lot. I really do just want to find a good girl. And apparently you two have very few single friends. Not helpful, ladies." He shakes his head at us.

"I mean, I can think of one teacher friend who would be perfect for you. If only she'd leave her asshat of a boyfriend. He is the worst. Controlling, interrupts her all the time, acts like a sleazeball but then berates her if she comments on it. I can't even go out with the two of them anymore, only Sadie. Him and I fight every time we try to spend any time together. He's a giant bag of dicks," Lauren states.

"Well, whether you think Sadie is the gal for me or not, she should get away from that douche."

"Agreed. I'll work on it."

"Until then ladies, I need to find an appropriate date for a family event I've got coming up. Any chance my two best gal pals would help this handsome guy out?"

"What kind of date and what kind of event?"

"Originally I was hoping to find a nice girl to bring to my family Christmas party. My sisters usually have dates, and my mom heavily hinted that I should also bring someone. My dad's only contribution to the conversation was to comment on my inability to grow up and my lack of any potential for a bright or successful future. Apparently, he's hoping a good woman will fix that. He's a gem."

"Jesus. What a dick," Lauren bursts out a little too loudly.

Family dysfunction. It's not just the wine talking, but I think Sean and I could become great friends. Not friends like Jess and I were, because I don't feel any flutters or 'stare at his butt' instincts.

"Lauren will go with you!" I practically shout, throwing my hands in the air with glee.

"Em, maybe read the room, babe." She sighs though, looking sympathetically at Sean. "Would I have to pretend to be your girlfriend or date? Because we recently learned how fucked up that can get."

She blatantly points at me while poorly trying to hide it behind her other hand.

"No, no, just as a friend. Honestly, I'd usually say 'fuck it' and go solo intentionally, but Dad is always better behaved when I bring a companion as a buffer. Plus, it also provides me with a convenient excuse to leave early, if necessary."

I cringe, picturing a super awkward gathering.

"My family is pretty damn awesome, with the exception of my dad, I promise. All I was hoping for is a woman wanting to spend an evening with me, eating amazing food, drinking excellent beer—or wine, since I've noticed that's something you're into. See? Observant. I'm a damn good catch."

He laughs lightly, refilling Lauren's glass.

She hums at him, considering. "That sounds intriguingly awkward. And lucky for you, my friend, I was raised for that schmoozing, small talk, dinner party shit!"

She taps her wine glass against his. "When?" she asks.

"This weekend…" I glance over to Lauren, the planner, and laugh as her eyes take on a hint of a glare.

Way to bury the lead, Sean. That's only two days away!

"Two days from now?"

"Yeah. And it's in St. Helena, but I'd have you back home at a reasonable time."

"No can do, champ. I am helping with the Academic Trivia Club Tournament this weekend, since one supervisor dropped out last minute." She mutters a word that sounds an awful lot like 'Taylor.' "Exciting it may not be, but I promised to help the kids."

Lauren leans back, but looks pointedly at me.

"What about Emma?" I should have seen this coming. I volunteered her, but that was for everyone's mutual benefit. I think Lauren needs a kick-start to dating, too. I want her to be as happy as I know is possible. I'm pretty sure she already set her heart on someone, but she won't admit it.

"Emma! So, are you free? I think it would be good for you." Lauren draws my attention to our conversation again. She leans in and whispers, "Can't be too bad if most of Sean's family is like him, right?"

I purse my lips. "Right. Um, yes. I have absolutely nothing on my social calendar. But I really want to be clear that this is not a date. Just a friend helping a friend."

This sounds much too familiar. I shake my head to clear those ugly thoughts and allow my brain to go through the self-preservation details.

"And I will drive myself, because let's be real, I just met you a few weeks ago. But also so I can then bail if it's awful."

He chokes on a laugh, then tempers it. "Absolutely, that's smart. Can't be too careful nowadays."

I nod and he gives me the details about his family, the location, and what to expect.

Later, in bed, contemplating the weekend and meeting more new people, I realize something. I am not an overly social person and I leave inconsistent first impressions. Sean may regret this.

It'll be good for me. I'll just keep telling myself that.

CHAPTER 31

Jess

I miss her. Not in a normal, haven't seen her in a while kind of way. I miss her in a how can I keep this shit up without her way. It's been a rough couple of months, just waiting to get over what we had, let alone come to terms with what I did to her, to us.

I've been coming into town once a week to continue helping Taylor with the team. I created a speed program for the boys and go in weekly to readjust and analyze the players' training.

And every week I torture myself trying to catch a glimpse of Emma. I succeed more often than not, but make sure she never sees me.

I've been secretly stalking Emma for the last couple of months, asking myself, 'Is she okay? What if she's already dating someone else?' Then obsessing about how I would feel about the answer. Either she was devastated or had moved on. Both made me feel like garbage. I'd felt enraged and protective in a way I had no right to be.

When I'm not busy torturing myself by watching her leave the grocery store, or running in town, I dream of her. I dream of the good times, the possibilities of our future together, and then I also have some less happy dreams. The ones where every time I get close to happiness and permanency with the one woman I'd want it with, my subconscious fucks it up.

In one dream, Ashleigh shows up out of nowhere and is best friends with Emma. Or they became best friends? I don't know; I was freaking out.

In another, Emma falls for another man, and runs off with him the day of our wedding. At first, the man looked like my brother, Garrett, then morphs into my cousin, then some nameless man I don't know, but looks familiar.

In my most recent and horrifying of dreams, Emma and I are in her house, happily cooking dinner together.

It's our anniversary. We celebrate based on our first date—the picnic in the park—even though it wasn't supposed to be a real date. Emma tells me that's when our love story began. I lean over and whisper in her ear how much I love her and how glad I am that she gave me a chance at this life. Emma smiles sweetly at me. The smile she uses when she's full of emotion, but is grappling with how to verbalize it. She picks up a fork and feeds me a piece of pie (which by this point in the dream timeline, I have learned to love), and places a hand on my face.

"I loved you, too." The past tense throws me for a moment. Suddenly, I feel uneasy. My heart is racing, the rhythm irregular. I'm lightheaded as Emma and the kitchen become fuzzy. My body won't respond to my commands. "I'm sorry," she says. "But you betrayed me first." I drop to the floor. Emma walks over my prone body and out the front door.

I awoke breathing hard, sweat saturating my sheets. My body was still feeling the phantom sensations of partial paralysis and the cardiac event. The dream was confusing and revealing. Yet, I know Emma would never behave like that. I imparted that evilness to her. She is not vindictive or homicidal. This was my subconscious torturing me, telling me she'll never forgive me. That I deserve to be poisoned by her for real.

My subconscious is a dick.

~

I'm parked in Garrett's driveway, having pulled in slowly, eyes fixed on the house next door. I haven't seen Garrett since I left, knowing I wasn't ready to come back here. Watching Emma from afar has been torture enough, but seeing where we started would be like picking at a scab. The porch where we first kissed, the couch blanket I had to dry clean after Emma's surprise breakfast, the fire pit where I couldn't keep my eyes off her at my family BBQ, her yard just in view of Garrett's back deck when I first experienced her fondness for fire. The front yard where I broke her heart. Both our hearts.

I got her a Christmas gift. Something I saw when I was shopping for Mom caught my eye, and I was buying it before I even realized what I was doing. I was grinning in the parking lot about the purchase until I remembered. Emma and I won't be doing Christmas together.

It's an apron that reads 'Whatever Happens - We're Eating It!'.

It's fucking perfect, and I laughed when I saw it. I'm going to give it to her, anyway.

Disappointment settles in at the 'we' implication, because I'm sure one day soon she'll have a 'we' to share her cooking creations with.

Fuck if that doesn't burn.

I take another moment to watch for movement in Emma's house. She's likely still at work, but I want to be sure.

Finally, I get out of my truck and make my way to Garrett's front door. I use my key almost on instinct before I catch myself and knock.

Taylor answers. "It was unlocked, man. Why didn't you just come in?"

I shrug, not wanting to admit that I felt awkward.

"Well, get in quick before Emma sees you, asshole."

My gaze shoots to her house.

"She's not home. I was only testing you, seeing how squirrelly you're feeling," he says as I follow him out to the back deck where I can see Garrett has already started some renovations.

He hands me a beer. "She and Lauren are out with some new guy in town they've befriended through some online dating app."

I stumble, hard. Fall off the deck, beer spilling everywhere as my hands windmill, trying unsuccessfully to prevent the fall.

"Boom," Taylor roars. "That was the sound of your relationship experiment exploding."

He holds out a hand to help me up. "So fucking predictable. Your reaction was even better than I expected."

I scowl at him. "Explain."

I cross my arms, preparing for whatever he's about to tell me.

"Not much to tell. Lauren created a dating profile for Emma and set her up with this guy. Emma thought she was meeting her bestie, turned out she was being set up. They all hang out a couple times a week, at least from what I can tell."

"How the hell do you know all of this?" I ask.

"Some I heard from Lauren, some from the League."

"So, she is dating, or she's not?" The question slips out before I can reel it back in.

He shrugs, hands up. Sure, now he clams up.

"Why didn't you say anything before now?"

"I was waiting until you removed your head from your ass so you could hear me when I tell you how badly you fucked up. I went over to check on her after Garrett saw her crying in her car. Dude, she loved you and it was fucking painful to watch her question herself.

"Now, you can either pull the fire alarm and run from the explosive mess you made or you can grab the fire extinguisher, put out the flames and clean it the fuck up. Because that nearly picture-perfect future, the one containing your dreams and happiness—that shit doesn't just happen to people. You work for it. Are you really going to let one fucking mistake dictate your happiness? You going to let it run you out of your own goddamn life?"

Am I? Is that what I've been doing?

Yeah. That's exactly what I've been doing.

There's tension in the air as I take in the shocking 'buck up' speech from one of my best friends.

"Hey bro!" I get a rough clap on the back before an arm lands on my shoulders in a side hug. Or Garrett's version of one.

He must be excited to see me if I'm getting this much attention from him. I look him over, noticing that he seems more relaxed, scruffier, less… Garrett.

I blow out a breath. "Hey. You seem good, Gar. What's new?" I mindlessly ask, trying to stop thinking about Emma and her mysterious dating life. Or if there's any way in hell I can fix this.

"All is well. Didn't realize how much I'd miss this place. How's San Fran?"

"It's fine. Same as usual."

Taylor coughs out what sounds suspiciously like, 'liar' and shakes his head at me.

"I miss something here?" Garrett asks, mystified.

Yeah, he missed a whole hell of a lot. Not tonight, with Taylor calling me out, but in the last year, yeah, he did. If Garrett hadn't left, I'd never have gotten to know Emma the way I had. She might have even asked him for help like she did me.

My brain runs through the scenario where our life paths never really cross, never tangle.

The memory reel pauses on our cooking lesson when I first knew I'd do just about anything to make her smile.

Then the weekend we spent together, the feelings she admitted, making love to her and meaning it for the first time in my life.

It jumps to her asking me to stay, but only her voice because I couldn't look her in the eyes as she asked.

Then it freezes on the look of devastation and shock when she caught me bailing.

Shit. What the fuck did I do? This wasn't the best thing for anyone. We had so much together. We really did have everything, and I threw it away because I couldn't get over my fear, my resentment. She deserves every single fucking thing she wants, and I'm going to give it to her.

I'm going to fix this. No more broody, self-deprecating, closed-off bullshit. Emma is my future, I love her, and that is the scariest concept I've let myself admit in a long time. How the fuck could I have let a few bad, fucked-up relationships mess with the best thing that has happened to me in a long, long while. I'm lucky Emma even considered me a suitable option.

I'm a fucking moron.

This, here, now? This is me being a schmuck. Everything before now was just the path to get to her. She never should have listened to a word I said about relationships, since I clearly couldn't seem to keep the best one I've ever had from imploding.

"I'm fixing this. I was barely holding on to my shit-poor excuses for staying away from her, anyway," I assert.

"I like that fire, Caldwell! Now go get her!" Taylor shouts and slaps my ass.

I grin at him, feeling a tingle of relief and elation. First, though, I need to tell my family about what really happened with Ashleigh. I need to put that crap behind me and start making a plan to get Emma back in my life.

CHAPTER 32

Emma

We pull up to a nicely treed yard, Christmas icicle lights twinkling softly, a family of reindeer decorating the driveway side of the yard. I decided to let Sean drive us, that way he had a more believable excuse to leave if necessary and so I could drink a couple glasses of wine during the party.

Sean turns to me and smiles a reassuring smile like he knows I'm nervous. Instead, I give him a lopsided smile that holds no confidence, "Let's go do this. Also, you owe me. Big." He chuckles and goes around to open my door.

I made trifle, brought gifts for the Christmas gift exchange, and of course some wine. The trifle is remarkably edible. I made two just to ensure its acceptability. I found this dessert to be right up my alley. The only thing you can screw up is the cake. Which I kept as simple as possible. Then added some bakery-bought white chocolate brownies for added assurance of its deliciousness.

"Okay, so my sisters, Anna, Noa, and Katie, my parents, Alaina and Ethan, will all be here at some point. My aunt and uncle are the hosts, I'll introduce you to them first. Oh, and several of my cousins will be here, too. Some of them are local, the rest are from Napa or San Fran. One of my cousins just got back from Africa. He's a doctor, I think you'll like him, he's also very anti-technology."

My feet slow down while my brain churns at a maddening pace.

Sean stops at the bottom of the steps, looking back, his forehead wrinkling while probably wondering what I'm doing.

No. It's a coincidence, that's all. Deep breath, feet moving at a normal pace again.

"Is that too heavy? Put it down, I'll come back for it," he offers, but I don't respond, because just then I look through the front window and see Garrett.

No, no, no, no. Please, no. Somewhere in the back of my mind, I'm making a mental note to do thorough background checks on everyone from now on.

I pump the brakes hard, dropping the gift bag I was holding.

Sean knocks on the door, Garrett moves to come open it.

Dumbstruck, I blurt, "Your family is Garrett? I-I mean, your family is Garrett's family? The Caldwells?" Incredulity clear in my voice.

"Yeah. You know them? That's awesome! See, it won't be as awkward and nerve-racking as I know you were thinking." He hops off the steps and retrieves the gift I dropped. He waves at Garrett and starts back up the steps again.

"Ha! There's no way in hell I'm going in there!" Sean is a good ten feet ahead of me now, not realizing I didn't follow him. He looks back, obviously not hearing what I said because he waves me over.

"Sean, wait, stop!"

Garrett opens the door, giving Sean an affectionate pat on the shoulder, then moves to help carry our stuff. He peers around Sean, asking where his mysterious lady friend is. Sean told his family weeks ago that he would bring someone. He promised that he kept things very vague, but I worry they might think we are more than friends.

Garrett spots me and falters.

My hand is over my face, attempting to hide my embarrassment and panic. I shake my head at him, mouth gaping, unsure what to even say.

"Emma?"

I check for an escape, contemplate walking straight back to Sean's car. How big of a deal would it be to ask whoever just pulled in behind him to kindly let us out?

Oh, it's Chloe who just arrived. Fantastic.

"Sean, we have to talk."

I tug him off to the side area of the front porch, holding up a finger to Garrett indicating he needs to wait while I sort shit out.

"That guy I was seeing where things ended badly… it was Jess. Your cousin, Jess." I look at him like he's capable of fixing this.

"Oh. Well, shit." He laughs good-naturedly. "Okay, you know what, I'm pretty sure Jess isn't even in town for this. Jess doesn't have girlfriends, so I'm sure Aunt and Uncle don't even know about any of this, right?"

He sounds so logical, but I am still in a full panic. He sees this and rubs my arms up and down, soothingly.

"They know about me. I've spent time with them. They are going to think—I don't even know what they'll think. God, what will they say? They probably think we ended things amicably, and it's going to be obvious it wasn't amicable. And now I'm with their nephew at a family event?"

My palms are sweating, my breath hacking through my chest in quick bursts, blood pounding in my ears.

"It'll be fine, Emma. They already know we're here. Let's just eat, talk, no pressure. If you want to leave, we leave."

I think about this. We are already here; Garrett and Chloe have both seen me. I can suck it up. Jess is not here. Garrett is the only person here who has seen the aftermath of our relationship implosion. If Millie, Rian, and Chloe are here, that'll be fine, too. We get along and they think Jess and I mutually went our separate ways. I will worry about all the other ramifications later.

Chloe comes over with her arms full of Christmas gifts and food. She squeals in excitement to see me, tells me to find her inside, gives Garrett a quick peck on the cheek as she passes him and then it's just Sean, Garrett, and I.

"Okay… fine. Let's do this super awkward Christmas party."

Sean laughs, but then his expression changes.

"Hug me." I give him an odd look, but relent.

He brings me in for a tight hug, hands spread over my lower back, his hands drifting a little lower than they should. With a sparkle in his eyes, he winks at me and I scowl at him, pulling out of his sudden embrace. I am about to chastise him, maybe even knock him upside the head, when I hear someone come up behind him.

"Sorry, sweets, I was wrong. Had to go a little off-script."

What was he wrong about?

"Oy! Sean, stop pawing your 'lady friend' and come introduce her to the better men in the family," says a voice I haven't heard in months.

Shit. Can I hide? My body stiffens and my grip tightens on the forearms I was attempting to remove from my backside.

I look up at Sean, eyes wide in panic, gasp and then whisper-yell, "You liar!" pushing off his hard chest. "You fix this. I'll wait in the car, tell everyone you'll be back later, you just have to drive me home. Now!" I demand and start to walk away, but Sean grabs me by the arm, keeping me close to him.

"Em, come on, please." He leans down and whispers, "Let him think you've moved on. Don't let him see this affect you. Don't run away and let him off the hook. You've got this, I've got you, it'll be fine. Plus, I doubt Chloe is going to let us leave."

I hesitate. Maybe I can do this. I'm not ready for this, but maybe it will help me get over this whole mess.

I laugh angrily at him, "I'm going inside and drinking the wine we brought. Keep him away from me."

I grab both bottles from the bag he's holding, swing around without looking at Jess, and head straight for Garrett.

"Don't." Is the only thing I say as I walk past the only man I've ever loved.

"Emma? What the..." He sounds confused. That makes two of us.

"Sean, what the fuck?" I hear him bellow.

I can still hear bits and pieces of the conversation I abandoned, but I block it out. This shit here is fight or flight. I choose drink, then flight. I probably should have just said no and headed straight to the car. Well, too late now.

I snag Garrett by the shirt as I pass him and drag him with me. "Garrett, this is going to be awful, meaning I plan to drink a fair amount of this wine."

I hold up the two bottles, handing him one. "Pour yourself some too, you'll need it."

Garrett and I haven't become super close since he came back to Landry, but he has seen me cry, mowed my lawn, accepted my baked treats, and will now be a friend to weather this Christmas disaster with.

"Want me to get you a straw?"

"Don't be cute, Garrett. I just found out I've been suckered into a holiday dinner with my cold-hearted ex, aka your brother, and am about to see his entire family. A family that I came to care for, became friends with, and who helped with my cooking disasters."

My head reels when I wonder what Millie is going to think.

"Help me, or I will drag you into all the drama. Then I will cry on you, Garrett. Is that what you want?"

I have crazy eyes, yes. That's because I am feeling completely insane right now.

Sean walks over to my side, and I smile as if nothing has happened. "Let's go meet your family, yeah? Mhmm, here we go." I flick his hand off me, annoyed, and lead him farther into the kitchen, spotting about a dozen people.

Garrett approaches, hands me my cup full of wine, nods, and moves to the space beside me. I have two buffers locked and loaded. I can do this. I can socialize with the parents of the man I love, escorted by his cousin.

Nope. No, I cannot. Can I change my mind and choose flight now?

Jess

I can't decide whether to be ecstatic that Emma is here or outraged that she appears to be with my own fucking cousin.

Emma walks past me with a firm, "Don't," before I can even greet her or tell her how gorgeous she looks. She's in a red sweater dress and short black boots. Red has always looked fantastic on her. I snap out of my Emma stupor and turn to my cousin.

"Sean, what the fuck?" My voice louder than intended. Calming my anger and shutting down the assumptions my mind is making.

"No idea what you're talking about. I brought my lady friend to a Christmas party." He tries to shoulder past me.

I slam a hand across the doorway.

He looks over and smirks at me. "Problem?"

"How do you know Emma?" I clench my teeth, my rage palpable.

"How do *you* know Emma?" he challenges.

"Fucking hell, Sean. Just answer the question."

"Why do you care? Tell me that and I might answer your question."

Some family and friends I've got.

"Emma is my, well I guess she's technically my ex. But I plan on changing that, so stay the fuck away from her."

"Yeah, heard about that. You left her heartbroken. You don't think she's moved on? You really think she's sitting home alone pining away for you?" He laughs.

"Yeah, I fucked up, big time. I'm trying to fix it, man. I have a plan. She's it for me. I don't want to go head-to-head with you. You won't win."

"Huh. Good. Taylor will be pleased. That guy may be a jacked, ex-pro baller turned Coach, but he is just as meddlesome as the top gossiping biddies in that quirky little town." He places a hand on my still extended arm.

What? Taylor? How does he know about this? Did these bastards set me up?

"Now, I've gotta make this at least a little rough for you. I think we can agree that you deserve it. Now, let me by so I can get back to my date."

I glare at him.

"I don't have a clue what is happening, but let me be clear—you don't touch her. You respect her, treat her well. You are going to stay sober and drive her home later. Again, without touching her. I realize that when Uncle Ethan is in town for Christmas, it can be unbearable, but you are doing this for Emma, got it?"

He nods at me with a grin. "Yup, got it, cuz. This is going to be fun."

Then he ducks under my arm and I let him.

I scrub my face in exasperation and then walk back into my family Christmas party, eyes continually seeking Emma.

CHAPTER 33

Jess

Sean perches his arm on the back of her chair. He sees me glaring at him and the fucker winks at me and lifts his hand slightly as if saying, 'look Ma, not touching'.

I grab my drink and head over to her. She's engaged in conversation with Chloe.

"Did you end up taking that yoga class your neighbor was telling you about?" Chloe asks her.

I interject, "Stella?"

Emma startles hard, her wine sloshing out of her glass, onto her appetizer plate and hands.

She mutters a curse. I grab a napkin and hand it to her, but she stands suddenly.

"I'll just go clean up a bit." She takes off toward the bathroom.

Chloe flicks my arm. "You scared her off! I was just about to ease into grilling her. Did she come with you? Because it seems like she wants nothing to do with you." Sean chuckles, but I can hear him refilling her wine glass.

I'm still watching the hall so I can see when she comes back.

"You guys talking about Yoga Tree? Stella invited me to that yoga group, but was oddly specific about the rules and dress code." Garrett joins our conversation, his timing terrible as usual.

"Dude, don't do it." I shake my head, never taking my eyes off the hallway.

"Jess!" Chloe tucks a finger under my chin and turns it toward her. "You owe me details about what happened between you two. This doesn't feel like the mutually pre-planned parting of ways you described."

"He ditched her in the middle of the night shortly after she asked him if they could continue their relationship because she loves him," Garrett supplies, seemingly indifferent to the shit storm he just stirred up.

"What!?" Chloe shouts. There's more laughter. Probably Sean. "How could you do that? Everyone knew she was in love with you. No wonder she never responded when I texted her about you two splitting up. Oh my god, why would she come here? How has she not dunked your head into the punch bowl yet? Did she know you were going to be here?"

I shake my head. So many questions.

"I brought her." Chloe gapes at Sean, then her mouth moves to start another line of questions.

Sean cuts her off. "I met Emma coincidentally, and we became friends. She's quirky and beautiful. Great combo. Not a hardship to spend time with her and her bestie." He goes to take a drink of Emma's wine, catches my glare and sets it back down. "Ran into Taylor who saw me out with the ladies, put two and two together, and here we are."

"You brought her here on purpose?" Chloe asks. "Your story tells me almost nothing, Sean." She blows out an exasperated breath. "Did you even give her a heads-up that her ex and his whole family would be here?" She smacks him upside the head, just like Mamma would.

"Hey! Chlo, there's a plan in play here. This way we get them in the same room and this asshole can fix it." He slaps me on the back. "Which you are oh-for-two so far. Pull up your big boy briefs and get to it!"

Chloe glares at both of us. She points at me. "This is a major —" She stops, looks around, then whispers, "Fuckup! How are you fixing this?"

I wince, about to tell her about my plan. I told Mom some of it, but knew Chloe sometimes still messages Emma and my sister can't keep a secret.

She continues, not waiting for me to respond. "That Ashleigh shit you shared with us is behind you for good?"

"Yes. I'm willing to do whatever it takes to be the man she deserves. That includes not letting the past fuck up my future."

"Language!" Mom's voice sounds like it's coming from clear across the room.

How does she do that? I look for her. She's talking to Emma. Shit.

Mom hugs Emma and then excitedly brings her over to us.

"Jess! You didn't tell me you were bringing Emma! What a wonderful surprise! You work fast. You said you had a plan to get her back, but we weren't sure if she'd give you the time of day."

She gives Emma a side hug, rubbing her arm like her most prized possession she is showing off to the family.

"This is a Christmas miracle. My boy manning up and finding a lovely woman to walk through life with."

I face-palm and groan. Emma turns beet red and is chanting something behind the hands covering her mouth. I look around for help, but every single one of those bastards are intentionally avoiding eye contact with me.

"Mom, uh, actually Emma is here with Sean."

Emma's head is bent completely to the floor, she's twisting her hair furiously, full of nerves. This is a big ask for someone who can feel awkward in regular social scenarios. No one would handle something like this well.

I stand, inching a little closer to her. "As for the rest, yes, I was hoping to talk with Emma. Tell her how much I messed up and how much I've missed her. How we belong together and I'm going to do whatever it takes to prove that to her." She still won't look at me, but her hand is still now, floating midair. "I just haven't talked to her yet. She hasn't been home much, thanks to this guy." I point to my cousin and he twitches his eyebrows at me in teasing solidarity.

"Jesse Michael Caldwell!" Not shocked for long, Mamma's tone turns to rage and she pulls out my full name. "This is not how you get your woman back. In front of your family? You have embarrassed her! Men!"

She hugs Emma again, then whispers something in her ear. Emma's eyes widen, then she covers a chuckle. It's there and gone in a moment. Emma nods at my mom, who nods back, sends back a glare, crooks a finger at Sean to come closer.

Sean gives Emma a reassuring arm squeeze as he passes. He steps up next to Mom, shoulders tense, expecting the worst. She smacks him, as predicted.

"You don't date the woman your cousin is in love with. Gesú Christo, Sean." She pulls him into the den.

Emma continues standing in the same spot Mamma left her in. I take a step toward her, but Chloe rams a straight arm into my stomach, blocking me.

"Well, this is a special kind of awkward. Fortunately, all of us here know how big an idiot my brother is, so while he figures out how to do better, Emma, come sit and drink with me. Away from the idiot-squad." Chloe gets up and moves to the other side of the table, far away from us.

Sean comes back a few minutes later, strides up to the girl's side of the table and quickly walks away after a short, but sharp tongue lashing from my sister, who is usually sweet as pie.

My brother and I drink quietly, eavesdropping on the women's conversation.

"So, you tried the yoga class, then?" Chloe asks.

Emma hesitates. "No." Then gives a little chuckle.

"Why not?" Garrett shouts from across the table. "Stella said it was hot yoga with an instructor who has ten years of experience."

The women are looking at us, offended that we already intruded in their conversation.

Too bad for them Garrett doesn't care about that kind of social etiquette. Which turns out to be lucky for us because if I know those ladies, they won't hold it against Garrett, but they would Sean or I.

Sean comes back to the table, but sits in the middle, closest to Emma.

"Hot yoga? Never done it. You try it, Garrett?" he asks.

Chloe clears her throat pointedly at him.

"What? I'm not talking to you, I was talking to Garrett."

"Yes, hot yoga is great. I find it helps with some skin conditions too. Humidity can do a lot of good."

"Then why not try this new place. I'll come with and give it a shot," Sean offers.

"No!"

"No!"

Emma and I shout at the same time. Our eyes connect for the first time all night. I smile softly at her, forgetting for a moment what I was protesting a moment ago. She swings her head back to Chloe.

"Why not?" Garrett asks.

"Man, Stella is nice, sure, but she's a complete nut. I went to one—ONE—of her book club events and next thing I know there's a paperback of the next book in the series tucked under my pillow with a handwritten invitation. Under my fucking pillow!" I shudder and cross my arms over my chest.

Someone snorts. I glance back at the girls, but they aren't even looking at us, engaged in their own conversation now that the guys are distracted.

"What? Does she have a key to my house? How concerned should I be?"

"It was during the Labor Day barbecue, I think. She and Greg stopped by. But she must have made her way to the bedroom. And the book was from that *Fifty Shades of Grey* series. That half-naked, inhibition-free, sex-scented party masquerading as a book club was one of the weirder things I've ever done."

I look at Emma and she is full-on laughing, trying to smother it with her hand. Her laughter fills me with hope.

"It was also one of the best," I admit.

She sobers, but keeps her eyes on mine, then the rest of my face, taking me in.

"I have something to confess." Emma finally addresses me, surprising everyone at the table. "I, uh, may have been the one to put that book under your pillow and let you believe it was Stella…"

She bites her lip, so adorably that my brain misses the important part of her confession.

Once it clues in, I'm momentarily floored.

"May have?"

She shrugs.

"No explanation?"

Everyone at the table is fully focused on the two of us.

"Explanations don't really seem like your thing, Jess."

I smile like she just kissed me, not ripped me apart. At least she's engaging with me now.

"Fair enough." I think about what she did and my smile widens. "So, you let me think some crazy neighbor put a dirty book in my bed and then said nothing?"

I stare, daring her to meet my eyes again. She does, her chin held high in defiance.

"I avoided her at the store, leaving without my items if I saw her. I drove down the street before pulling into Garrett's just to make sure she wasn't outside on the days I knew she would usually be home. We started running in the opposite direction for our morning runs just to make sure she didn't see me. I stopped going out on the back deck, Emma. I was traumatized."

She erupts into laughter, holding her belly. Sean laughs, then Chloe. Even Garrett is grinning.

"Oh my god, that's amazing!" Chloe says through a fit of laughter.

Sean is gasping for air and leaning over me.

"Hey jerk off, yuk it up all you want, but I was this close" —I press my thumb and forefinger together until they are nearly touching— "to filing a restraining order."

"Wouldn't be the first time, probably won't be the last. Maybe next time it'll be Greta from the bookstore? I think she has a thing for you and they could consider her walker a deadly weapon," Garrett comments.

I shake my head at him.

Emma is wiping tears from her face. "Better than I imagined," she pushes out between giggles.

The laughter dies down a little, but I'm still staring at Emma.

"I fucking missed you so much."

My heart is ready to bleed all over the table for her. I don't even care that my family is here to witness this.

"Jess…" She looks away from me, playing with her fingers.

"The rest of the Wentholts are here now! Let's eat, everyone! Grab a plate, wine, and somewhere to sit," my mom instructs. "Emma, *cara*, you sit with me, okay?"

Emma nods. "I'd love that." Chloe stands and they go off with Mom.

My own mom is cock-blocking me. Bold move. And works directly against what I'm trying to do here.

The rest of the evening passes in relative ease. I don't get to spend much time with Emma, but she is making friends with the rest of my family. Even my younger cousins who arrived with their dates, seemed to carve out time to get to know her.

We do our gift exchange, Emma winning fuzzy socks, a bookstore gift card, and a lot of chocolate. She seems pleased, but I frown. I could keep her feet warm and her mind entertained. That's my job.

However, right now she is back to not looking at me, so the chance of her letting me big spoon her anytime soon is slim. I've got to keep things realistic here and focus on the goal.

As guests start leaving my parents' house, Mom approaches me. I'm watching as Emma leaves. Mom gives me a disapproving look.

"I know, I'm working on it. I'll fix it."

She makes a disgruntled sound.

"I'm going to marry that girl. Let's hope she forgives me soon, or it's going to be a long time before you get grandkids."

She grumbles at me as we watch Emma leave with Sean. I turn away, not wanting to watch her leaving with another man, even if it is my cousin, who is only her friend.

Mom grabs my arm, turns me around. "Oh no, you watch as your woman leaves with your cousin. Maybe you won't make this *stupido* mistake again?"

"Yes, Mamma."

As I watch her leave, I'm glad I did because I see her look back before she gets in Sean's car. She finds me in the window, startles when she realizes I'm watching her. It may have been a quick glance, but it was there. Hope gains some traction again.

Emma

Sean and I are walking down the sidewalk away from the Caldwell residence. He's driving us home, which is good since Garrett kept my wine glass topped up most of the night. I've decided he's a good neighbor.

Sean grabs my bag and the dish I brought, helping me load it into his car. I look at him, tilt my head and stare at him until he squirms uncomfortably. He lifts his hands in a defensive posture, probably hoping I'll take it easy on him.

"You tricked me, didn't you? You knew who Jess was to me," I accuse.

"Maybe a little. But it wasn't my idea. Well, not entirely. Our friendship was a complete coincidence. The rest was all Taylor."

"What!?"

That brat.

"Don't be too mad. I was just the messenger. And fall guy, apparently." He scoffs. "Aunt Millie and I even had an uncomfortable conversation where she warned me away from you. She was worried I wanted to bone her future daughter-in-law."

"Millie did not use the word bone! Or daughter-in-law!" I argue.

"Fine, no, she did not say 'bone'. But she said 'daughter-in-law'."

He smirks at me and I can't tell if he's serious.

I stab a finger at him. "You owe me even bigger now. That was... awful. That" —I point back at the house— "was a train wreck!"

"No, only the part between you and Jess was... uncomfortable. For everyone." He winces. "The rest was great. My sisters like you, my aunt and uncle think you are highly amusing, and my parents." He pauses. "Well, they were absorbed in their own drama, so they likely didn't notice anyone else was there."

I go around, getting into his vehicle, wanting to leave immediately. I look back up to the house, my gaze catching on the front window next to the Christmas tree. There's Jess, catching me looking for him.

God, he looks so good. I quickly avert my gaze and get in the vehicle.

On the drive home, I call Lauren, not caring if Sean hears our conversation.

She picks up without a greeting, "How did it go?"

I sigh and recount the night for her, hoping she'll see what a bad idea this was and how hurt I am by both seeing Jess and being duped.

"Taylor planned this whole thing? That little meddler. I wonder if he's joined the Landry Life League yet, he'd be a solid recruit." She snorts derisively. "Wait. Jess was already planning to get you back? Emma-Jean, that's great, right? I don't get it. Why are you upset?"

Huh. Good question. Why am I upset?

Oh, right. He left me like I was nothing.

Seeing him again brought back a lot of emotions. Anguish, love, melancholy, but also anger, which was something I had been working to keep at bay. Instead of laying into him, like my brain and heart were both encouraging, I stayed quiet, even after the shock wore off.

The only moment I let my true feelings show was when my book prank finally paid off. I had forgotten all about it. I felt somewhat vindicated in that moment, but it wasn't enough.

Jess hurt me so deeply and I still loved him so much.

He said he missed me. That he wanted to get me back.

The cynic in me is wondering what kind of offer he'll bring to the table next. Maybe he'll offer long-distance, so we can hook up while he is in town. Or maybe lengthen the terms of our previous arrangement. I'll be his perpetual girlfriend he takes places, cares about, but still keeps at arm's length.

The rage is back and I'm not sure I want to lock it up anymore. Acknowledge the feeling, absorb it. Bad feelings aren't bad. Avoidance is only a short-term gain.

Seems like a good enough reason to unleash my feelings on Jess. If I see him again, I won't stifle my feelings about his betrayal.

I wrap up my call with Lauren, unable to properly summarize all of my feelings, and not wanting Sean to overhear them. We agree to meet tomorrow so I can give her the details and she can be my sounding board.

I'm still steaming as Sean pulls into my driveway. I grunt goodbye to Sean and slam the door after he tries to make plans for later in the week.

My phone buzzes as I walk up my steps.

GREEN-EYED MONSTER I didn't get to say it at my parents' house, but Merry Christmas, Emma.
GREEN-EYED MONSTER: I wish we were spending Christmas together. I'll be in touch soon. I have a lot I want to say to you, so much to make up for. Until then, I left you a little something on your step earlier today. Please open it. Goodnight, Em.

Cautious, suspicious, but mostly curious, I scan the porch.

There sits a Christmas present wrapped in reindeer paper. I pick it up and bring it inside, slowly. It's probably not going to explode, so I can just chill out.

I will not open it. I shouldn't. If I do, it'll defuse my rage a little and I want full rage power for when we are face-to-face again.

I leave it on the living room coffee table and go get ready for bed.

Buzz. It's him again.

GREEN-EYED MONSTER: Did you open it yet? I know you're home. Garrett says your front lights just went out.
GREEN-EYED MONSTER: Please open it, babe.

I'm about to type back 'don't call me babe!' But then stop. I don't respond to heart terrorists.

It's already after midnight, and I am exhausted. Today was mentally and emotionally draining. I finish getting ready for bed, turn off the rest of the lights, and get in bed.

ONE HOUR LATER…

I whip off the sheets and race to the coffee table, sitting next to it as I rip the paper off without hesitation.

Once I'm in the box, I feel fabric and pull it out. It's dark and I can't see a thing. I turn on the lamp.

It's an apron with some cutesy writing on it. I read it, 'Whatever Happens - We're Eating It!'. I smile before catching myself. I see a piece of paper on the floor that must have been from the box.

Picking it up, I scan it. My eyes water as I bite back a sob.

Always, Emma.
'We' means you and me.
I'll eat anything, do anything, if we can be 'we' again.
Merry Christmas, beautiful.
Jess

An involuntary smile breaks through the tears.

Dammit. I knew I shouldn't have opened it.

CHAPTER 34

Jess

I dash toward the field on a mission.

"Coach!" I shout at Taylor while he organizes some of his players. His head jerks around to me. Once he sees me, he rightly turns and moves farther away.

Yeah, he knows why I'm here and it's not to run a speed training session.

I'll admit, my first encounter with Emma did not go as planned. Since I blame my asshole friends and family for fucking that up for me, I will take most of my anger out on the creator of this weekend's disaster. You know, since Karma isn't currently available for me to berate.

I didn't think winning Emma back would be easy, but I really didn't think my own family and friends would become obstacles. Well, maybe Lauren, but that's because she's a protective beast with Emma.

"Shaw. Now." I look over at the offensive line and point at the kid closest to me. "Jensen, go tell Coach Shaw I need him."

Sam Jensen nods at me and hustles off.

Coach blows his whistle, announces the end of practice, and

makes his way over to me. Once he's close, I turn around and walk over to the locker room entrance.

"You're pissed, I get it." I glare. "Think about this though, would she have spoken to you in any other circumstance? Your pussy bullshit was tiresome. For all of us. You were barely speaking to most of us, even your own damn family. Mopey, dopey, broody bullshit for nearly two months. I saw a solution, made a game plan. Whether or not you want to admit it—it worked."

"Oh, I'm the pussy? You've been gone over the same woman for what? Years now? And you haven't done a damn thing about it. You really want to start this shit?" I ask, suddenly defensive and reaching the bottom of the barrel for ammo against him.

I would have done fine with no help. Probably.

"The woman I want doesn't want me, isn't interested. So, let's not go there, because our situations aren't the same," he argues. "You had a woman who loved you, yet you high-kneed it out of here like a chickenshit. While I'm glad you got your shit together and found your balls—which Lauren will probably be irreparably damaging soon—you both needed a little nudge. Sean bringing Emma to your family Christmas party worked out pretty great, I think."

"Did you hear about the party? Not only did she barely speak to me, but you put her in a very uncomfortable situation. My mom thought she'd come with me and threw me and my 'get her back' plan under the bus."

He laughs like that's the best thing he's heard all day. "Wow, who knew she had it in her."

"What are you talking about?"

"Millie was fucking with you. I called her and told her about our plan so she knew there might be a little drama at her Christmas event. I'm a gentleman. More or less. I wouldn't throw a grenade at Millie's holiday party without giving her the heads-up. Plus, I needed her to run some interference if Sean pushed the 'bring Emma as a date' card too hard. I didn't want you to beat his ass."

I'm stunned into silence.

"Also, that Stella prank of hers was fucking epic. Garrett says he likes your girl a lot. Except when she cries."

I massage my temples and rake my fingers through my hair, to calm my rising irritation.

"You've got an in now. Your mom let her know the family loves her and forced you to tell her you want her back. Emma needs to let things sink in. This gave her a bit of a surprise, but now she'll know what to expect from you. I'm sure she'll be skeptical. You have some work cut out for you. The way you were pre-Emma doesn't exactly inspire a lot of faith and assurance."

He pats me on the back with two hard thumps and walks away. Just leaves me standing there.

Me giving him shit didn't even go my way.

I think it's time I throw my plan out.

Emma

There is a large hardcover binder on my front step when I return home from work. I park in the driveway instead of pulling into the garage. Looking around in case the person who delivered it is still around, I see no one, thankfully.

I pick it up and read the inserted cover, 'Emma's Recipe Book'.

I look around again, in case someone is lurking, watching my reaction, which is awe and appreciation.

Inside are beautiful pages with detailed recipe descriptions and even some pictures. Each recipe has special notes in the margins. They read like the little tidbits of advice Millie would tell me as we cooked together. It even has common sense grocery lists (no grams, ounces, or cups of ingredients, instead she included exactly what to buy at the store).

I scan the recipes and realize they are Millie's. This was so nice of her. I didn't know what to say to her after Jess and I ended, so we hadn't been in contact. So many times, I wanted to call and ask her questions, or just talk, but felt I couldn't.

The sleeve in the binder's cover has a folded page with my name on it.

It's in Jess's writing.

Emma,

Mamma helped me put this together for you, so most of the credit goes to her. I only formatted it and added the shopping lists because I know how much you hate the conversions of measurements and debating how much to buy.

You're probably thinking it's low of me to enlist my mom's help to convince you to give me another shot, but like I said the other night, I'll do anything. I don't want to be without you. I want to build this recipe book with you, eat with you, bake with you, drink with you, mess it all up with you, order pizza with you. Anything with you.

She also offered to come by and do some lessons for us. Well, for you. While I would love to be there, the offer stands regardless of whether you forgive me.

I'll be back in town tomorrow. See you then.

Yours,

Jess

So. Many. Questions.

Was he in town all weekend and delivered this while I was at work today? Did he come merely to drop this off for me? Why would Millie want to teach me to cook if I wasn't with her son?

Jess always treated me well and, according to Lauren, spent a lot of time with me for what was supposed to be primarily a fake dating relationship, then a temporary real one. He was never this vocal about his wants, the future or his feelings.

No.

I need to remember that he left me with no proper explanation, like I didn't matter. Like I was some chick he was fucking occasionally. He left me right after I told him I was falling in love with him.

But dammit, I love this book and what it represents. But that doesn't wash the rest away. He can't buy me with sentimental gifts and thoughtfulness. I mean, he can because it's not ineffective. But there are some things we need to discuss, and I don't know if I can trust him again. How do we get around that? I am a wary puppy who has been hit on the nose one too many times in my life.

Buzz.

GREEN-EYED MONSTER: I left something by your front door.
GREEN-EYED MONSTER: I didn't wrap it in hopes you'd be curious enough to look through it before you realized who it was from.
GREEN-EYED MONSTER: Can we talk this week?
GREEN-EYED MONSTER: Please? I need you.
GREEN-EYED MONSTER: I mean, to talk to you. I need to talk to you.
GREEN-EYED MONSTER: Shit.

I stare at the screen, not wanting to respond yet. But also wanting to make him sweat a little.

GREEN-EYED MONSTER: I miss you.
GREEN-EYED MONSTER: I miss that you normally would have teased me for that slip. I miss waking up with you. Exploring new things with you. Running with you! Fuck, I miss running with you. And those shorts. But mostly just you. Dating you, both fake and real, was the happiest time of my life.
GREEN-EYED MONSTER: Tomorrow? Can I come by when you're home? Or meet you somewhere?

Do I want to hear him out? Yes, I want an explanation. At least for closure, if nothing else.

Do I want to take him back? Yes, and no.

Do I trust my heart with him again? I don't know. Not right now, that's for sure.

Do I still love him? Yes.

I haven't been dating because my heart feels like it's cheating. I don't want anyone else, I still belong to Jess even if he didn't belong to me. He's the chink in my armor. The roadblock to the rest of my life. The crucial piece missing in the future I've dreamed about. Which is quite the gut punch because I may never have him in the way I crave.

ME: Tomorrow. 7pm. Bring Thai food.

GREEN-EYED MONSTER: YES! Absolutely. Anything you want. I will see you tomorrow, beautiful.

ME: To talk. Don't get ahead of yourself. For now, I want answers.

GREEN-EYED MONSTER: Of course. Love you.

GREEN-EYED MONSTER: Shit. Pretend I didn't say that for the first time in a text message.

CHAPTER 35

Emma

I've been home for hours. Just waiting for Jess to come over. I might as well have not gone to work because it is all I thought about. I've made scenario mockups with mind mapping and charts. Before I knew it, lunchtime!

Lauren is off for Christmas break, so she stopped in and we went over some key topics to discuss. Big topics to hit right off the bat. Just before she left, she clarified that I should not, under any circumstances, be intimate with him. No matter what we decide, give myself time to clear my head and process what we discussed.

Seems both logical and reasonable.

Jess and I are not together. There will be no 'friends with benefits', or long-distance as previously offered. I've realized I am an all-or-nothing woman. Why would I settle for less?

Lauren and I outlined a list of goals for the conversation.

Goal one: get an explanation.

Goal two: unleash the anger and pain I've been pushing down.

Goal three: make my expectations and wants clear.

Goal four: discuss broken trust issue.

I still have fifteen minutes before he gets here. I am already sweating, shaking and reorganizing the fridge in impatient anticipation of his arrival.

I hear the doorbell.

He's early? Oh god.

The bell dings again. How long have I been standing here trying to breathe?

I slowly make my way to the door.

He's grinning at me through the front window, then moves to the door again.

Opening it, I take a deep breath. "Hi."

"Hi, Emma." He holds up the bags of food and some wine. "May I come in?"

I nod and move aside for him to enter. I move to the kitchen, taking a quick glance behind me to see if he's following. We say nothing as we unpack the food on plates. I notice there's also a bag from Baked Delights. I peek inside and sniff. Cherry Danishes and a pecan pie. I bite down the squeal of excitement as my stomach rumbles loudly.

Apparently, I don't hide my squeal well enough because Jess chuckles at me.

"You brought me treats too?" I ask.

"Of course. I didn't dare show up here without them. You are always much happier after pastries. Franny made the Danishes today, so you'll probably want to—" I bring my gaze back to him and he full out laughs.

I already had one of them in my mouth. "It's so good!" I mumble around my bite. The treat will probably get me all sugar-happy, which will negate the stern and serious conversation we need to have.

I put the pastry down, brush my hands off, pull up a stool, and motion for him to join me at the island.

He walks around the counter with his plate, sets it down, but instead of sitting, he comes right up to me. His hand slowly comes up to my face as I sit, frozen. Slowly, he brushes his thumb over my lips and I feel the flakes of sugar fall. He leans down, our foreheads touching, noses grazing. He breathes in deeply, keeping us in this position, his eyes closed. Those gorgeous green eyes that have been haunting my dreams, open and gaze directly into mine.

My hand has lifted to his chest on its own. I close my eyes for a moment and breathe him in too. Opening them again, I lean back, gently pressing against his chest. He takes the hint and backs off.

One of us has to start this conversation, and I think it might need to be me. We're both pushing food around on our plates, barely eating. I need to rip the Band-Aid off.

"You left me," I state. He puts his fork down and brings his eyes to mine. They look sad, full of regret. "You hurt me. In ways I don't think you understand."

"I know, Emma. I'm an idiot. And sorry, so sorry. I've been letting the past dictate my life for a while now. Protecting myself. But I hurt us both. I'm sorry I couldn't figure my shit out before I met you, so I could have been ready for you, deserving of you."

I frown, what were my goals again? Oh, right. "Why, Jess? What were you thinking?"

"When I left?" he clarifies and I nod. "That I couldn't say goodbye to you. I didn't have a good reason to leave, but I didn't feel I could stay. You deserved more. Someone to give you a future. The best future. Everything you wanted."

He places a hand on my knee.

"When you said you were falling in love with me, I panicked. I could ignore my own feelings and deal with the consequences, but I knew we had reached a place of no return when you voiced yours. Since I felt I couldn't give you what you wanted, I had to let you go so you could find it with someone else. That killed me, it did."

He looks at me again, gauging my reaction.

"When Garrett confirmed he'd be coming home early, I figured it was best if I took off early, too. I was going to send you an email or text, something. I knew we likely wouldn't be able to be friends afterward. You don't just stop being in love with someone and resume a normal friendship. I was a coward and talked myself into leaving early in the morning before you woke up."

We're both quiet for a while.

If I don't tell him exactly how I felt, what he did, I will carry it with me.

"I was devastated, Jess. Some of the most important people in my life have left me without a backward glance. You added yourself to that list and it crushed me. Crushed the part of myself I've spent nearly two years rebuilding. I felt whole for the first time since I was a child. I finally felt like me, quirks, scars, baggage and all! It was the new me that got crushed and it cut so much deeper because she feels everything. Then I remembered why I closed myself off before: vulnerability. Caring makes you vulnerable. I told you I was falling in love with you and you cut and run."

I wipe the tears from my eyes, but they keep falling undeterred by my efforts.

"You hit on a trigger I should have expected, prepared for. Yet, I hadn't."

I'm trying to keep my voice from wavering with the power of my tears on the threshold of sobbing.

Jess mutters a curse, then moves toward me and envelops me in a tight hug.

"God, I'm so sorry, Em. I never thought—I didn't understand what memories that might bring back for you."

I nod into his chest because that's all I can do.

"I was so sad at first. Unwanted. Unloved. Tempted to shut it all off again. My old ways were rising to the surface. Bad feelings are bad, useless, unnecessary. Lauren helped, though. I moved on to guilt and self-doubt pretty quickly. Men really know how to tear a girl's self-confidence apart, huh?" I don't wait for him to answer. "Now I just feel sad again. I miss you and don't know what to do with that."

"You were never unwanted, Emma. Or unloved. I'm sorry I made you doubt how amazing you are, how worthy you are.

Never let anyone make you feel that way, definitely not me. If I do, you tell me to pack my shit and leave."

"You already packed your shit and left."

He drops his head. "Ouch. I deserved that."

"You did." I answer, my cheek still resting against his chest. I change the subject back on track. "So, why did you think you couldn't be who I wanted for my future?"

"Because I stopped planning for a future with anyone. I didn't want anything permanent because I had lost faith in that. Ashleigh stole so much more than my money and my time. She stole my future. I pictured a happy future with a wife and children, in San Jose or maybe Seattle. I had it all figured out, but I forgot the most important part. That future wasn't specifically with Ashleigh, but she was there and I put her in it. She wasn't the integral part, and she should have been. Looking back, that was probably because I didn't really see her as my future. She used to tell me I was 'everything' but only when she was trying to butter me up or placate me."

He ducks his head to look at me. Shit. I told him that too. But I meant it.

"Oh."

"Yeah, so when you said it, talking about falling for me, I was right back in the home I shared with her. Right back to the anger, pain, and regret. I never saw Ashleigh again. But when I started dating again, I still saw her face and felt her betrayal each time I imagined moving forward with another woman. In denial, I figured I could still find someone, the right someone, get my life back on track. But I was too messed up and only attracted the crazy, the deeply disturbed, or women just as damaged as me. I told you about some of those relationships. The stalkers, the unexpected fetishes, the violent ones. That's what Garrett was alluding to with the restraining order comment. Oh, and I had one fake a pregnancy once she caught on to my financial status."

That's rough. Trying to lighten the air after both of our

emotional confessions, I tease, "Daddy and sugar daddy?" biting my lip. "Was that also one of the kinks? She would call you Da—"

"No. Uh uh. Not going there. Gross," he says while covering my mouth.

I chuckle into his hand.

"I'm revealing my inner trauma here and you're making fun of me?" He holds me tighter. "There she is."

He kisses the top of my head, then rests his chin on my head.

"Sorry. Kind of. It sounds like you had a shitty run of awful relationships. I can understand why you stopped, took a break."

"Yeah, from then on, there were no more attempts at relationships. It took me a long time to even look at a woman without contempt or suspicion. I found casual dating and hookups to be the easiest. I stuck with women, who, as long as you are up front with them, were on board for those kinds of relationships."

She's listening, open to what I have to say.

"After I met you, I realized those types of relationships, those women, are inadequate placeholders for the real thing. I craved everything you offered. Couldn't keep myself away from you. A man who wants 'casual' won't fake date you and take you out to coach you on how to be in a relationship. It was a horrible idea whether my goal was a one-night stand or, hell, even a platonic friendship. Something inside me needed to be close to you, and I couldn't treat you like the other women I had been dating. You were special, different, exceptional. You thought being exclusive during our agreement was going to be a deal-breaker for me, but I didn't want to be around anyone else except you. Being intimate with someone else wasn't even on my radar."

I get it. The need for uncomplicated sex. I did the same, just a bit differently with a similar intent. Looking back, it was hollowing for me, but I think it was for Jess, too. And maybe you don't realize it until you find the person who makes you feel more. Everything.

"I feel the same. It's why I asked for more. I didn't want us to end and knew the only way I could get what I wanted was to ask you for it."

"I couldn't give it to you at the time, Em. I needed to figure some stuff out first. I wasn't sure if I could ever be what you needed."

"You're here now, though. So, what does that mean?" I ask and hold my breath in anticipation.

He tilts my head up to look at him. "I love you, Emma."

I suck in a breath and hold his gaze.

He continues, "I don't want to be without you. I don't want to let my life pass by without you. What I was doing before you, that was only half-living. I was letting Ashleigh and my past keep me from the future I always wanted. I finally found the right person and I couldn't let my bruised ego keep me from you any longer."

"I'm part of a future you want?" I ask in a whisper.

"Emma. You *are* the future I want."

He loves me.

He skims his fingers up my arms, along my neck and into my hair, holding my head tilted up toward his. Bringing his face closer, his lips hovering less than an inch from mine. His eyes are searching mine, desperate, waiting.

I bring my lips up to brush against his, grabbing on to his neck to keep from toppling over in my fervor to get closer.

His response is immediate. I let him into my mouth, breathing him in, capturing his lips with mine, never wanting to let go. He groans into my mouth and lifts me to straddle his lap.

Yes! God, I missed him. His scent, his broad shoulders, his taste, how I feel against him.

No! Focus. Goals! Emma!

I break the kiss, with a loud smacking sound and a whimper. I stay in his lap, though, because I deserve a little of this goodness.

"Wait," I say while clearing my head.

"Sorry," he responds, serious. "Got ahead of myself. You warned me not to do that."

"I need to know what this is. What we are doing. What exactly are you here for? If it's just this." I point to his lap and mine. "That's not—"

He puts up a hand. "It's not, I promise."

"Should we go over ground rules or, um, parameters, or something? No. Expectations! That's what I wanted to talk about."

"Okay, yes, let's do that," he says, watching my mouth, tightening his grip on my hips as I squirm slightly in his lap.

Every thought drops out of my head as I feel his erection pressing against me.

"Maybe we think about what we want or need from this, us. Then we can talk again? On the weekend? You've traveled a lot this week." I offer.

"If you need time to think about what you want, I understand. But I don't need time. I know what I want." He gives me a lingering kiss on my forehead. "I am finding it very hard." He clears his throat as my body jerks slightly to the word 'hard.' "To focus with you wriggling on my lap, though. I have been craving you for months, so I don't think a conversation in this position is going to be productive."

I bite down a smile and nod in agreement. "True. And it's getting late, you should probably be heading back soon. When can you come down next?" I ask.

"Tomorrow morning. We'll go for our run first?" he says without hesitation.

"Jess, you will not drive there and back just to run with me." I narrow my gaze, "And you're not staying the night here. We aren't even together—"

He interrupts, "Yet." I roll my eyes. "I wouldn't ask to stay here. I'm staying with Garrett."

"What? Just to go running with me? We can meet after work, or this weekend, Jess."

"No. I'm not leaving again. I'm staying with Garrett temporarily until I find a place of my own. Here. With you." He lays that out so casually, it doesn't register for a few seconds.

"What?"

"Yeah, I think I'll rent something near here until I can convince you we should move in together." I can't tell if he's teasing. "Do you love this place? I think it's great, but we can live wherever you want. You can think about that. However long you need. We can buy a different place together, live here, whichever. You're my home, Emma. You told me you hope I'd find a home someday, but I already had. It's you." He picks me up and sets my boneless body back on the stool as he stands. He runs his fingertips down my face once more, before leaning down to my ear.

"Goodnight, neighbor." He kisses the edge of my jaw, lingers a moment as my eyes shoot back and forth between his, trying to determine if he's being serious.

He grabs his jacket and walks to the door. I follow, dazed. He leaves and walks across the yard to Garrett's house, waving with a silly grin on his face before ducking inside.

CHAPTER 36

Jess

Every single day. I will prove to her that I deserve her every single day.

"I hate that you are a morning person. Who the hell wakes up this early to go running?" Garrett sips his coffee, irked.

"We don't usually run this early, but I am a little worried Emma will leave early without me." I look out the window to stare at her house. "She told me some stuff last night and I understand how much I fucked up. I'm not sure if my plan to be around her all the time is enough."

"Well, her being mad at you and telling you to fuck off will be infinitely better than her sobbing in her car for days on end." He comes to stand next to me at the window. "For me, anyway."

"You're a jackass." I shove him away from the window. "And next time you see a woman crying in her car, go over and do something about it. Who knew a six-foot-two, nearly two-hundred-pound man could be so afraid of a woman's tears?"

"I'm not afraid. You know that. I'm uncomfortable. Being useful in those situations is unlikely, and I don't see the point in intruding on their privacy."

I see movement in her house, so I grab my running jacket and sneakers and head to the porch. Not ten minutes later, Emma emerges from her house. It's thirty minutes earlier than we used to run.

"'Morning, sunshine!"

She jumps, sneakers not even tied yet, bends down and mutters a greeting.

"You're heading out a little early."

"So are you," she throws back at me.

"I got up early, just in case someone tried to sneak out without their running partner."

She hums and narrows her gaze on me.

"I still have thinking to do, Jess. Running alone seems like a good idea for me right now."

"Because you need to think, not talk, not be distracted?"

"Yes, exactly." She breathes out a relieved breath.

I knew she'd be tougher this morning. She had all night for self-doubt, worry and distrust in me to grow and eat away at any progress we made last night. Emma is a worrier who now listens to her feelings and follows them. This works for and against me.

"Okay, got it. I'll run several paces back. Won't say a word, won't get in your space." She stops stretching and turns toward me. "Don't feel like you have to cut your stretching short. I'm in no rush this morning."

"You're going to run behind me?"

"Yup. You shouldn't be running by yourself so early in the morning, anyway. Some wildlife is pretty active at this time. Plus, the weirdos waiting in the bushes. Likely just League informants waiting to take photos and send them to my mom, but still. I'm happy to provide some safety for your run." I grin at her.

She opens her mouth to argue. Then shuts it and rips off her running pants. My favorite shorts. She's wearing those tiny, black booty shaping shorts.

It's much too cool this morning to be wearing those shorts. She is doing this on purpose and I can tell because she's smirking at me.

She takes off and I go after her. I'll always go after her.

We cool down walking through town, but she doesn't allow me to approach. A few times when I got too close, mesmerized by her firm, bouncing ass, she shouted for me to keep a few more paces back.

As we approach Main Street, I figure we will walk back together. "Nope." She gestures behind her.

I go back to my spot. I'm quite literally stalking her now. If I wasn't doing it the past couple of months every time I was in town, this falls deeply into that category now.

I pop into the bakery quickly and grab her a cinnamon sugar croissant and coffee and jog to catch up with her. Less than a block away from her house, I reach her. She sees me in her peripheral and points behind her again. I hold out the coffee and croissant so she can see it better.

She comes to a sudden stop, turns to me, and snags my morning offering.

"Acceptable reason to breach the running boundary."

She has already started walking again.

I'll buy her all the caffeine and sweets she could ever want if she lets me breach her boundaries.

That sounded dirtier than intended.

~

The next few days go like that first morning.

She opened up during our talk, but then clammed right back up again. I need to give her time, prove myself.

It's the last workday of the week and I am running behind her, approaching the center of town. I am thinking about what treat to get her today, when she stops and turns toward me.

She looks less closed down today, less aloof. I just can't tell if that's good or bad yet.

"How long are you staying? How long are you going to follow

me on my runs, bring me lunch at work, and sit on the back deck just to watch me in the evening?"

I sigh, grateful for a simple question.

"Always." Then I amend that. "Well, until you decide if you forgive me or not, then I'll either up my game or move in with you. I'm sure Garrett has already petitioned you for the latter."

I give her my most charming smile, then it drops a little as I take in her unchanged expression.

"He has." She tilts her head at me. "That's a pretty good answer. But what if I'm not ready yet? What if it takes a long time for me to get over all of this?" she asks.

"That's okay. I'm comfortable just sticking around until you're ready. I'm here, I'm home, Emma. And I won't stop trying to be the man you want, the one you deserve. Let me know if or when you're ready to let me back in. Until then, I still get to see you every day, sometimes even talk to you. That's already better than the last couple of months."

She sighs. "I'm scared of getting hurt even worse if I give you my trust again."

"Let me prove it to you. I don't care how long it takes. You have me, Emma, all of me. I want a future with you."

I step closer and she lets me.

"You've made me hope and dream for something I never thought I'd have again. You're the one that makes the dream come true. Ask anything of me, tell me what you need, let me love you."

Her eyes are shining, dark and contemplative. I wait.

She turns around and starts back into a jog.

"Croissant."

I almost stumble as I follow her.

"What?"

"This morning, from the bakery. A croissant, please," she calls over her shoulder.

I smile, racing into the bakery. I get her two croissants, one with cheese. She's letting me do something, I am not fucking this up.

Plus, watching her lick the flaky crumbs off her fingers will keep me going for a long while.

Emma

No matter how much I keep him at arm's length, deep down, I know I still love him. I want nothing more than for us to be together.

Now I know why people end up heartbroken. Hearts are stupid. They have the capacity for so much goodness and caring, but are also self-destructive, blind, and naïve.

I need time for my brain to process what I would need to trust again. To love with my whole heart. That's the future I want, and Jess needs to be ready to deliver.

I'm just about at work, deciding to walk today since I've inhaled pastries every day this week. Stella steps out of the new Yoga Tree Studio with Sadie. She gives me a wave when she sees me and I just can't help myself, I walk over. I am getting into the small-town dynamics.

"Hi Stella, Sadie," I greet them.

"Hi, love. How are you doing this morning? I heard Jess has been around town more these last few weeks and was just about to come check on you next. Is he giving you a hard time?" Stella gives me a sympathetic pout.

"I'm fine. Thank you for thinking of me."

"Of course, honey." She gestures to the building. "Have you tried the new yoga studio, yet? Sadie instructs one of the Power Flow classes a couple evenings a week. You should try it. And get your neighbor to come. So far registration is low and we don't have any men signed up. There's even a couple's yoga class! Although, I suppose with your situation, it might be awkward to bring Garrett to couple's yoga," she rambles on.

"I'll spread the word. Maybe you could get the high school classes for some afternoon ones."

They are excited by this idea and I walk the rest of the way to work with a plan in mind.

Jess

She is testing me and I am more than okay with that.

I do, however, feel sorry for these kids she's roped into attempting hot yoga for part of their gym credits. Since the only times that lined up for Landry High students to come to the Yoga Tree Studio coincided with no availability of instructors, I was given the job.

I've taken one yoga class. One.

The instructors left me and the gym teacher a yoga lesson plan, the equipment, and a poorly concealed chuckle of 'good luck'.

Did I do a good job? No.

Did Sadie and Emma use pictures of me on social media to promote the studio? Yes.

Did I embarrass myself? You bet I did.

Did it make Emma smile? … It did.

Worth it.

Even if half of Taylor's offensive line showed up the other day to record my lesson and then greeted me on the field in Warrior Two pose the next day.

Little shits.

Three weeks later…

Emma

The hot yoga is doing pretty amazing things to his already pretty amazing runner's body. I'm hanging on by a thread, but I don't want to take the next step based on my horny, hot-for-Jess feelings.

He took the yoga and surprise spectators well. After several weeks of running, yoga, lunch pop-ins, and longing-filled good-nights on the deck, I invited him for dinner. He was sweet, caring, but never crossed a line. His questions, while never verbalized, hung between us. Forgive me? Trust me? Will you let me be the man in your life? Perhaps that was my subconscious telling me to give the man my decision, the answer my heart already knew weeks ago.

More than anything, I wanted this. My belief in him, in his ability to be in a relationship, to treat me well and build a future with me; it grew, flourished. Was I scared still? Yes, but I think the big things in life can be scary. It means you feel it, you acknowledge that it touches your soul.

Jess packed up his past and rid himself of the baggage and pain it brought. This included his condos and rootless existence. He sold his condos and not just the one in San Francisco, but also one in Los Angeles I knew nothing about. His sister lives in the one in San Jose and he didn't think it would be right to give her the boot. Assuring me that if she ever moves out of there, he'll list it.

I told him he didn't need to do any of that. He said he was doing it for him, for us, because he wants to build everything with me. There's no need to wonder anymore. He's not giving anything up, he's trading up.

I'm on my deck, he's on Garrett's. Usually, before I go inside, I smile at him and tell him something I miss about being with him. It started as a question he asked me. He wanted to know if I ever thought about being back together. He didn't intend to push me. He said he wanted to know what parts of our relationship I liked best, what I miss so that if I ever let him back in, he can make it happen again.

Tonight, I get up, holding my glass of wine, smile at him, and go back inside the house without saying a word. I don't need to tonight, because soon I won't have to miss anything. I close the patio door, hearing Jess's concerned, "Emma?"

I get to the front door, swing it open, and make my way to Garrett's yard. Let's hope he's still on the deck and didn't go inside. I'm through the gate when I hear a grunt.

There's Jess, climbing the fence.

"What are you doing?"

He drops like a rock. "You didn't say goodnight or tell me something you miss."

He looks at me, hurt, confused.

"I know, I don't want to miss anything about you anymore." I reach out and link my hand with his. I lead him through the yard and walk us over to my house.

"Emma? What's happening here? I need to know."

"You still want to be with me, Jess? Build something together?"

"Yes, Emma. Hell, yes."

"Me too. I want you here, with me, in our home."

We barely make it through the front door before he grabs me, picks me up, kisses the grin right off my face, and carries me to my room. Our room.

EPILOGUE

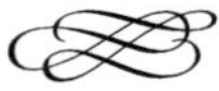

THREE MONTHS LATER...

Jess

If you build it, they will come.

Now, I'm not a huge *Field of Dreams* fan or anything. But I do like the saying. It's applicable in so many ways. In our small town, it works for restaurants, playgrounds, lemonade stands, drive-in movie theaters, and even hot yoga.

In my case, if I build a wedding, I'm hoping Emma will come.

We've already built the relationship, the part crucial for the marriage.

Naturally, we follow that up with a small vineyard wedding, right?

I slip Emma's dark, silky hair away from her face, tracing the edge of her ear as she sleeps. Leaning over, I whisper, "Good morning, sweet cheeks." My morning wood rubbing against those very cheeks.

A muffled, "'Mornin'," is the only response I get. Other than a swat to the hand that is tickling her ear and neck.

I try again. "Wake up, Emma."

"No, it's sleep-in day, mister. Shhh. Sleepy time. You kept me up most of the night, so you better get control of the large thing poking my ass."

Romantic.

"One quick question?"

I get a 'mmphf'. Which I think is an agreeable grunt.

"Marry me?"

I felt so confident the last couple weeks. Not so much in this particular moment.

She jerks up out of bed, almost knocking my teeth out in the process.

"What?!" She's rubbing her face, trying to wake up. "Did you just… what did you just say?"

I grin. She's adorable. "Marry me, Emma. Why are we waiting for a future that could begin now? I don't want to wait, Emma. Marry me." I hold up the velvet box, hoping she likes it. I make a mental note to thank Lauren again for helping me pick it out and keeping this a secret. Surprise covers Emma's face.

She gapes at me. Then tears up and drops her face into her hands.

"I told you to stop poking my ass, and you were trying to propose?" She groans.

"Yup. It was a beautiful moment. Wouldn't take it back even if I could."

She laughs, takes the ring box, and giggles.

"Need to see it first, huh?"

"Oh my god, no! I don't know what to do with my hands. Jess, we talked about just taking things day by day. No rushing, just living together and seeing if we don't feel homicidal after six months, a year. Not a few months!"

"You've mildly poisoned me with the chicken cordon bleu, I've ruined some of your favorite clothing by attempting to wash them. We know the stakes, and I accept them." I shrug and bring her closer, wrapping my arms around her.

She snuggles in deeper.

"Got an answer for me, Killer?"

She nods into my chest, sniffling.

'Is that a 'yes, I have an answer' or 'yes, I'll marry you, Jess, my dream man, lover extraordinaire, tech guru, yoga master'?"

She's shaking with laughter as she looks up at me, humor and love in her eyes.

"The last one, but with modifications."

"Oh, really?" I grin, relieved and excited. "What modifications?"

"Well, you're not really that good at yoga. And you're not my 'dream man'."

Well, shit. "Ow! Direct hit!"

"'Dream man' implies you're not real. You're my forever man, my other half."

"Nice save."

"That sounded bad, didn't it? I'm screwing this up." She hides back into my chest.

I bark out a laugh and kiss the top of her head. "Just say the words, babe."

She stirs in my arms, sits up, holding my face in her hands, leading me to sit in front of her.

"Jesse Michael Caldwell, you've shown me what it means to love, healed the parts of me I thought died a long time ago. I love you. So much." She kisses me. "Yes, Jess, I will absolutely marry you."

I'm on her in a second, raining down kisses while she squeals in glee. I feel around the bed for the ring. She gasps as I slide the sparkling emerald cut engagement ring onto her finger.

She runs her hands up my arms, circling them around my neck.

"You can poke me now." Jesus, this woman.

"Yes, ma'am." I grin and slide my hips between her widened legs.

We spend the morning in bed, touching, kissing, and imagining all the incredible moments yet to come.

Our experiment may have failed, but the aftermath was worth sticking around for.

THE END

ACKNOWLEDGMENTS

When I first started writing, I assumed I'd write a swoon-filled love novel, get it edited, slap it on Amazon, and move along to the next book.

I look back at that younger, naïve version of myself and think, "Oh, honey…"

Needless to say, there are so many people who helped me through this process and deserve many, many thanks.

I'll start with the one who had to put up with me up close and personal: my husband. He is my beta reader, my sounding board, and my pillar of support. You rock, babe.

My mom is always the first to read all of my books. She is who I get my book thirst from. Your insight, eagle eye, and investment in my characters is cherished.

My beta reader team: Sara, Danae, Katie, Winnie, and my sister, Amanda. Your attention to detail and inspiring suggestions helped shape this book from hot mess to hotness. So… please don't leave me! I need you gals.

My brother-in-law made the beautiful cover for this book, and will be making the covers for the rest of the series. That is, if I haven't annoyed him and/or scared him away by then. I'm sorry, and thank you!

THANK YOU READERS!

A huge thank you to all of my readers. I've been alone in my mind's story-world of Landry and am so grateful to have such wonderful company now.

Your feedback and interest in my love stories is invaluable and kind of addicting. So please, keep reading, messaging, following, and reviewing!

ABOUT THE AUTHOR

Amy Alves lives in Alberta, Canada with her husband and two crazy cute kids. She is a romance-obsessed reader, a lover of wine and fuzzy socks, and a loather of laundry. For over a decade, she was a high school science teacher, but now substitute teaches in between writing novels and being a mom.

Stay Updated

Need the next story in the Landry Love Series? Follow for pre-release events and release date info.

Newsletter sign up (www.amyalvesbooks.com/links)
Goodreads (goodreads.com/amyalvesauthor)
Website & Blog (www.amyalvesbooks.com)
Instagram (instagram.com/amyalves.author)
Facebook Page (facebook.com/amyalvesauthor)

You won't want to miss Lauren & Taylor's epic love story.

ALSO BY AMY ALVES

RECENT AND UPCOMING BOOKS

THE LANDRY LOVE SERIES

The Experiment

The Denial Game - Spring 2021

The Forever Plan - Early Summer 2021

DON'T FORGET AMY'S NEWSLETTER!

If you want to be the first to get a **sneak peak** at the next book in the series, **bonus scenes, extended epilogues**—Sign up for the Newsletter.

Manufactured by Amazon.ca
Bolton, ON